ROMMEL'S GOLD

ROMMEL'S GOLD

MAGGIE DAVIS

J. B. Lippincott Company
Philadelphia & New York

ROMMEL, General Erwin A., Afrika Korps
ROMEL (Arabic, دمل), sand

ROMMEL'S GOLD

1

Trust your boat
to the winds but never
trust your heart to a woman;
a wave is surer than
a woman's faithfulness.

—Pentadius

The trouble with the month of May, George Russell told himself, was that it was just too damned hot to walk anywhere in Tunis and enjoy it; the spring was going to be something of a record breaker, and everywhere you went the talk was of nothing but the weather and how hot it was, and how hot it continued to be day after day without a break, even during the nights (when, if anything, it was worse), and how the early heat boded ill for the rest of the summer.

Even before he got to the intersection of the Rue Bouzaine and the Boulevard of the President, Russell was obliged to stop and wipe off his sunglasses, where the sweat had dripped onto them from the free-flowing stream of his forehead, and stand for a second under the futile gray shade of a plane tree. Ordinarily the walk from the Foundation offices in the Rue Mohammed Cinq down the Boulevard was not too bad; in fact it was a pleasant stroll, just as Tunis was a fairly pleasant place. The city was modern and well-kept, much like the French town of Toulon which it was said to resemble, except of course for the palm trees, the presence of the Medina rising like a ziggurat of white blocks on the hill behind the new city, and the Arabs.

9

When it was hot like this in May, the old hands said, there was bound to be one hell of a drought later on, worse than the usual summer droughts, which were bad enough.

Russell lit a cigarette and threw the match into the street and walked on. The taste of cigarette smoke was hot and unpleasant, but after all even the air burned as he drew it in along with the smoke. There was no sun, now, only a glare of white sky which shriveled the eyes and shot sparks off the glass store fronts and the windshields of parked cars and the aluminum strips which adorned the façade of the British Bank of the Middle East. Not a drop of moisture, not a breath of wind. The Boulevard of the President was deserted; even the buses seemed to have quit. On the corner of the Avenue de Carthage, the Café de Paris had only a handful of sunburned German tourists in walking shorts at the tables under the green awning, looking out unhappily upon a street in which there was nothing but George Russell himself slouching past. Their eyes followed him, but he did not even lift his head to look.

He was busy thinking lustfully of a shower, and then bed.

He wouldn't even bother, he told himself, to light the *chauffage*. To hell with hot water; he'd take it just as it came out of the pipes, tepid, cold, or whatever, and then not towel off but lie down on the bed wet and naked and gradually soak off to sleep. He might even throw a pan of water over the sheets, something he usually reserved for the bad days of July and August.

He was, he thought morosely, fed up with Tunis anyway, and all the endless talk of the weather. When you came right down to it, Tunis in the heat was worse in some ways than the southern desert. At least down in the Sahara you braced yourself against the furnace of the sun and the feel of your own flesh frying in it by learning the trick of pulling into yourself, of living completely inside of yourself and staying there. In the desert you even cleaned your head out as a matter of survival and thought very slow, uncomplicated thoughts, Bedouin fashion. Like water, motion, distance, the condition of the animals, the pace, destination. Whereas in Tunis you chased like hell through the streets, your brain was always busy, and you tried to work and live as though the heat didn't matter. Which was stupid and killing.

The fruit-drink stand in the center of the Boulevard was tightly shuttered, which was something of a small surprise. Usually there had to be some oasis down that way, if only for the cab drivers who had their stands around the median park. It was strange, all that silence in a city full of living people; the whole of Tunis made for its bed when the heat was like this, just rolled over on its Arab ass and went to sleep and to hell with commerce and all the things which occupied insane foreigners. The city slept on until four or five o'clock, or until it felt obliged to get out of bed and take down the shutters and make some money by working well into the night. In the Arab quarter the small shops were open to midnight and past.

The Foundation office operated on a different schedule, like the embassies. The Foundation opened at seven in the morning, when the local population was just getting out of bed, and closed at two in the afternoon, leaving the staff the rest of the burning day to enjoy. Shoving the working day up into the early hours of the morning was supposed to be a better system than the long *sieste* and then returning to work again.

And Russell supposed it was, for those like Sir Charles Benedict and the ambassadors, who could hop into their cars and make for air-conditioned houses, up by the Tunis Hilton, or their villas at the beach.

At the end of the Boulevard of the President the modern city came to an abrupt stop at the old French cathedral and a pretentious junior-sized edition of the Arc de Triomphe and the bus turn-arounds. Beyond the arch, the old city of the Medina opened up its maw of alleys. The modern city was flat, built mostly on fill dumped into the harbor by the French, but the Medina climbed a natural cliff with twisting mole burrows of streets, alleys laced over with rush matting through which the sun fell in intermittent streaks, the whole of it close, crowded, and solid like a giant wasps' nest, as comfy and insular as the Arab mind. In the lower parts of the Medina the shops which catered to the tourists were still open, displaying piles of heelless Arab shoes in atomic colors, machine-made *keshtas*, and leather pillows. But now there were no tourists, and the shop owners were asleep on piles of merchandise in the back.

Russell's own flat was midway up the hill in one of the dead-end streets of the *souks attarine*, the section of the perfume makers. But there was damned little perfume being made, since most of the distillers had moved into the new city. As he turned into his cul-de-sac, the nasal, breaking wail of three or four radio singers on as many stations poured out from behind the shut wooden doors and the grille windows above them and seeped under the closed steel blinds of the corner café, along with the peculiarly gassy smell of steaming couscous.

Sweet home, Russell thought. And praise be to Allah, the One God, for the miracle of electronic music.

The thought of the shower grew pressing, like a terrible thirst. He found a sudden burst of energy to run up two flights of dark stairs and bang open the doors to his rooms.

The damned day was his. He was finally alone.

Not quite.

"Goddammit," he said.

Jamila was there, pacing up and down in orange stretch slacks and a white nylon blouse, smoking a cigarette. She turned to him eagerly, defensively.

"Who gave you entrance to my house?" he said in Arabic, not trying to keep the irritation out of his voice. "Who opened the door for you?"

"The concierge," she said in French.

So they were going to play that, he told himself wearily. Her French was a hell of a lot better than his, and annoyingly rapid and slangy. He had a lot of trouble following it. She knew he didn't want her there, so she was going to horse around in the thickets of *la langue* while she tried to keep the upper hand.

"There is no concierge here. Only the woman downstairs who lets the rooms."

"Well, she let me in, then." She gave a Gallic shrug. "Does it make the difference? I am here. Do you not want me here? I wanted to make the pleasant surprise."

Like hell she did.

"Attend me, Jamila," he said again in Arabic, trying to hold on to his patience. "I want thee gone. Quickly. I need my bath and then my sleep. It is the hour for it, and I am tired."

"You can just say beat it," she told him, inserting the Tunisian word, *barra*. "You don't have to say all that. It's really very ridiculous; you talk very old-fashioned."

"I know what I am saying, and I am trying to be polite. Now, leave my house. But delight me with your presence," he added quickly, "another time."

"Oh, shit on you!" she cried in French. Her voice lifted a little, taking on the strident Arab ring. She followed him across the room. "You think you are so clever, but you really are very absurd. You don't talk Tunisian very well; you talk like you are reciting from the Qur'an, like the old ones at a marriage bargaining, or the old ladies in the Melassine. People laugh at you, they really do."

He was in the bathroom, trying the taps to make sure there was water.

"I am going to take my bath," he told her over the first few explosive bursts of the plumbing. He came to the bathroom door and stood there, unbuttoning his shirt.

"I am not going to leave," she said sullenly. "I have seen you undressed before." But she followed him with her eyes as he rummaged around in the cabinet to find a new bar of soap and came back to get a clean towel. "Why did you not call me at work? I waited for you to call me. My God, I wait all the time and make a lot of mistakes in my typing, thinking that you are going to call me. And your Conroy, always comes by and says"—here her voice dropped to an imitation of the assistant American Consul—" 'Miss Zahra, there are too many mistakes in your typing. Can't you do better than this?' Which means that he is going to complain to Baxter"—she pronounced it Bex-tair, gutturally— "about me. You are the fault of it. You know that? You are the fault of it." But she came into the bathroom with him, as he showered, and tried to shout over the noise of the water. When he came out she said nervously, "How do you like my pants? Do you like the color? It is very chic, this color. And chic to wear them tight, the stretch nylon."

He took one brief look and then said, "Does it make you ashamed?"

"What do you mean, does it make me ashamed?" she screamed. As he had known he would, he had hit a nerve. "Do you think I am some country woman, not able to wear slacks because it shows my body?"

"You forget, I have seen them before. They are very nice." Still dripping, he went to the kitchen and poured himself a Scotch. There was no ice in the refrigerator, and it gave off a dank, buttery smell. The electricity was off again.

Jamila had taken up her showy pacing around the room, darting him little provocative looks.

"What is the matter with you?" she complained. "Why are you being so cold to me now? You are treating me like an Arab man, you know that? Do you think it is very clever to treat me this way, like something you can throw away when you do not want it? I think you are becoming Arab all over, Rosul, and not only with the talk. Yes, look at you. You talk the Tunisian very well—I did not mean what I said before—even better than you talk the classical. Does that make you feel very good? But the talk is making you turn into some sort of a camel! You talk to me just like some goat dung of a farmer!" She stopped dramatically, her breasts heaving in synthetic distress, hands clasped to the front of the nylon shirt.

The slacks and blouse, Russell thought critically, were really not very becoming. Jamila's style was too exotic for Western casual clothes. She wore them uneasily, like a desert *bedu* stuffed into a business suit, and only her fine figure saved her. But she had a hell of a body, unusually slim and long-waisted for an Arab girl, and her face was sharp and delicate like a desert woman's except for the thin slash of her prominent mouth. In fact, with her slenderness and her magnificent eyes and wild bush of wavy hair she looked very much like a Bedouin girl. Once he had made the mistake of comparing her to the good-looking Bedouin, and she had shot into one of her instant rages. She was Arab, all Arab, she had screamed. Pure-blooded, high-born like the best of them.

Like most of the things she said, it was a lot of crap. Damned few Tunisians had the pure Arab strain. She was a mixture like the rest of the population along the coast of North Africa: a little Turkish and Berber and Spanish and maybe a little Sicilian from across the straits and, yes, enough Arab. And maybe some Bedouin, too. The *bedu* had no class, like gypsies, but the women were supposed to be particularly passionate, and the Arab men sampled them plenty when they got the chance.

And God knows what else, he thought. Half of Europe and the Middle East had raped and screwed across the country for centuries.

"I have been busy; I have been working," he told her, sipping his drink.

"They tell me," she said, eyes narrowing, "that you are going to be with these American girls all the time, like the Peace Corps."

So she had heard that, too. "You have spoken truly."

The high formality sent her off into another burst of idiomatic French which he did not even try to follow. She wandered around the room distractedly, picking up loose objects and putting them down, her fingers quivering as though she would like to go all the way and pick them up and throw them. She was working herself up into a freewheeling rage.

"And of course you are going to sleep with them! This is what always happens with you. And they are very cold in bed, you know that! This is what everyone says—yes, it is true—that American women are very bad in bed. They say it everywhere, not only here. Even the Italians say it. And the French say it, too!"

"Oh, shut up, Jamila," he said. He used a very nice, coarse street Arabic, and to his surprise she laughed. Her whole face changed, eyes crinkling in delight. Like the eyes one saw in the streets above a *haik*.

"Why are you naked?" she said, in an entirely different, curious tone of voice. "You like to stand before me naked, do you not?" she purred. "Well, I tell you now, it does not impress me." She turned away and looked at him out of the corners of her eyes.

He had to laugh. Yes, very funny. If only she weren't so god-damned tiresome; that was the hell of it. It was always the same with these Arab girls only one step away from their girlhood imprisonment; the underlying hysteria was still there. A couple of years in the city only managed to put a cheap veneer over it, that was all. They were still not able to understand enough, didn't have enough education, not enough damned character to rescue them from being an unholy nuisance when they thought you were cooling off. Jamila would not let herself believe that he had been working damned hard, that he had been tied up with the interminable business of trying to arrange for the Youth Commitment Group to come in, and that now he was tired and wanted to sleep.

They could make your life hell. They made life hell in their own houses with their own men, and for the same reason.

He remembered that when he had first seen Jamila he had been impressed with her because she had looked so delightfully French, so very pretty and charmingly continental behind her desk in the consular office. In fact, he had taken her for a Parisienne because of her accent—which was perfect—her clothes, and the open assurance of her manner. A very damned good imitation of the French girl. But she was all Arab, as he had come to find out, down to the last angry, anxious, pleading pressure of her demands. When she started up her voice altered, turning shrill and slightly hoarse like something out of the secluded back rooms of a village dar.

Now she roamed around in the small space of his rather bare sitting room, shooting him burning looks that were supposed to make much of the fact that he had not bothered to cover himself with a towel.

But on the other hand, he told himself, sometimes she was worth the damned tiresome fuss she always caused. As he poured himself another drink he observed that, although the orange pants certainly didn't suit her, they did cling tightly to her legs and rippled across her backside seductively when she walked. And her breasts strained against the buttons of the nylon shirt.

Damn, she ruined whatever margin there was by swinging her ass atrociously. That was part of it. And the shirt was about two sizes too small. He could never get her to understand that a tailored shirt was not supposed to be as revealing as a cocktail dress.

Still, what the hell, he supposed he couldn't carp. Peeled of her brassiere her breasts were high and round with enormous nipples tapering to long points, very savage-looking. They didn't even flatten out much when he rolled her over on her back. And if she was a little high-assed, the length and shape of her slender legs made up for it.

"If this is what you have come for," he said suddenly, in the same street Arabic, "to offer yourself to me, then take off your clothes." He made a lazy, circling motion with his hand. "And do it quickly. Maybe when I see you, Jamila, I will forget how tired I am and want you."

That was blunt enough. It cut right into her long tirade, and she stopped and looked startled. But he knew that she had heard and understood him perfectly and had caught the use of the dialect and his offhand manner. Her mouth dropped open a little, and then she recovered herself.

"You are a beast to talk to me this way," she said in French.

He shrugged. "Do what I want or get out. Else I might throw you out in the streets."

Frankly, he didn't give a damn. He was not only tired but he had had enough of her scenes and had decided to take the offensive. He doubted that she would leave, but at least he had shaken her up a bit. He had struck the tone she would respond to, just about the level of a good workingman-shopkeeper of the smaller villes.

It was interesting to see her bite her lips, baffled, and try to pick up her harangue where she had left off. But she couldn't. It was obvious she believed him capable of throwing her out bodily if he had to, and that amused him. But it was more than that. In some way he had hit the right note, speaking to her in a way that she apparently knew all too well.

"You are unkind," she blurted suddenly, switching over to Arabic. "So unkind, unkind!"

He said nothing and she hesitated, giving him confused, outraged looks. But he was playing along with it. Dammit, she would just have to make up her mind. She had barged in on him; now it was a question of what it was worth to her.

"You are very cruel," she whispered finally. But she lowered her head and began to unbutton the nylon shirt.

Well, well. He drank his Scotch slowly and watched her, leaning against the doorjamb of the kitchen while she stood in the middle of the sitting room and slowly took off her blouse and then the slacks, keeping her eyes down and her face averted. There was none of the "Parisienne" Jamila in it at all. Even her expression changed, no provocativeness or fake French *vivace* but growing heavy, veiled, and submissive. Turning into an Arab right before his eyes. She dropped the brassiere on the couch and then slid out of the nylon underwear, finally kicking off her high-heeled shoes. When it was through she even put her hands over her breasts and stood, waiting for him to say something.

Like most Arab girls she still used a depilatory. There was no pubic hair. That made it complete.

Well, he thought, I'll be damned; she did it.

He didn't know why there was any surprise, for after all it was what she had learned first and best, that peremptory tone of command. Her father was a potter in Nabeul who had allowed her to go through the government high school there instead of marrying her off, and after the *lycée* she had taken advantage of her chance for freedom and had moved in quickly with relatives in Tunis to find a job. And with a job she had bought herself good clothes and had taken up with a crowd of young French boys who had taught her a lot. But without all that, if she had stayed at home, she would have bared herself like this for some lord and master of an Arab husband back in Nabeul. Standing as she was standing now, waiting for him to look her over and maybe order her to bed during the long hot-weather lunch hour.

He was responding to it; he couldn't help it. Russell put down his drink on the kitchen sink and went to her and guided her to the bedroom, and the bed.

But it had been a long time since he had been out to the villes and the desert; he had almost forgotten how it was. All the old sensations crowded in on him suddenly, the thick, lemony-sweet smell of cheap perfume, the rustle of bare feet, the memory of kohl-smeared eyes. And the whispers.

Tell me, sidi, how do you wish to be pleased? Tell me and I will do it.

A long time ago. The first woman he had had in North Africa had been a Bedouin girl in the Tell, given by a male relative in an excess of hospitality, and he had been so new and raw then he hadn't known how to go about the business of refusing. Scared out of his wits, in fact.

She had come to him in a darkened tent, trembling, very fine-boned and thin, the kind the *bedu* likened in their poems to the deer of the desert. But her fingers and mouth had gone all over him like mice, driving him crazy. He had had women before, some of them prostitutes, back in the States, but nothing like that. It had been quite an initiation into the outer reaches of sex. You were supposed to lose yourself entirely and rage like the lion that has come upon the roe. Exact Bedouin description.

He still remembered it very well.

Russell pulled Jamila down on the bed, and the quivering heat of her embrace was like that at first: the same submissive obedience, the same understanding that he was to take her for his own pleasure and with little regard for her flesh. He fell into the mood roughly and she began to whimper. That was part of it, too.

"Oh, sidi," she moaned, "spare me!" But her fingernails clawed his arms. "Ah, you will kill me; it is too much!"

The room began to lose focus. It was like being drunk, and her pained voluptuousness goaded him. But at the same time it was somewhat more than he wanted to handle. In spite of the oppressive heat she had plenty of energy, and it was all he could do to keep her in the bed; she must have enjoyed herself at least twice and in between times she climbed all over him in spite of her cries, thrashing over him, urging him to more and more. Finally he lost his temper and slapped her around rather firmly, and that was even better. She began to weep, smothering him with kisses.

"I love your body," she sobbed. "It is so beautiful. So beautiful an American body, and yet so passionate."

He had had enough, and he wanted her to leave him alone. When he was finished the last time he dragged himself into the other room and fell on the couch, damned near strangling with the effort to catch his breath. She followed after him, her naked skin shining with sweat, and tried to crawl in beside him, but he pushed her away, not gently.

"For God's sake, knock it off!"

She understood enough English for that and went sulkily back to the bedroom. She flopped on the bed, and every once in a while he could hear her sigh, loudly and unhappily.

He lay on his stomach, feeling the sweat run off his body as heavily as the water in the shower had run off it before, listening somewhat dimly to the radio singers echoing beyond the drawn blinds, in the Street of the Perfumers.

"Now, my love," the electric voice in the flat below sang throbbingly, "Open thy gates to me and do not keep me here beside thy house in the chill night."

The heat was too much; the damned house and the walls of the Medina closed around him, and his own body turned on him in a rage to get away, to break out of it somehow and return to a place where the air was clear crystal with summer and a cool breeze played over lakes and meadows and trees that were birch and oaks, and one never saw a damned palm tree again.

"Um-mah, um-mah," the radio voice grunted, dropping into the lower registers and insinuating the rapid thrusts of passion. "Um-mah, um-mah, uh, uh, UH." Spelling it out. The voice rose to a frenzy, mixed with drums and clanging *oud*, hit a quarter-tone agonizingly, and then broke. There was a silence. Then a smooth voice said pleasantly in French, "This is Radio Tunis."

He was, Russell decided, coughing a little into the cover of the couch, going to have to do something. Get rid of Jamila, for a start. Permanently.

And then—Great God, he remembered, he had to be up at dawn in the morning to meet the Foundation's Youth Commitment Group coming in on the 6 A.M. TWA flight.

2

And every man,
we have fastened
to him his bird of omen
about his neck.

—*The Qur'an*

At eight the next morning it was still miserably hot, and the air conditioners in the offices of the Foundation had not been on long enough to make any headway against the mugginess which had collected in the rooms.

"Silly business, this," Sir Charles said, taking his place behind his desk. "Playing nursemaid to a lot of grotty kids. After all, we're not the bloody Peace Corps, now, are we?" He took out his handkerchief and wiped his hands before poking about in the papers on his desk.

He didn't expect Russell to answer him. The remark was only the morning's opening verbal shot and was intended to show that he was there and in operating condition in spite of its being Sunday, and that he was fairly ready for what was ahead of them. At least as ready as anyone could be in that abominable weather. Also, it gave him a chance to test his voice and make sure his vocal chords were in working order. Lately he had been dogged by a little huskiness in the morning which he rather associated with the sneaking signs of age. He also gave his face an exploratory grimace. Once behind the desk at the office he liked to check out his usual urbane expression, assume a little ironical quirk at the corner of his mouth ("Let's not take ourselves too seriously, shall we?"), eyes with a modified twinkle,

21

head held slightly to one side. He was paid for his face as much as anything else; it was a damned good British public-school visage— not many of them around any more—and he never underestimated the effectiveness of it, even if it was damned difficult to get cranked up on Sunday mornings. It had taken him two cups of coffee and a double shot of brandy to get the face on at all, and it still lay somewhat unsteadily, covering what might be a blossoming hot-weather headache.

Watch for potholes, he told himself. He was not quite up to shocks.

As for the grotty kids, there was nothing to be done about them. They were there and waiting in the anteroom, established facts.

Why in God's name, he thought fretfully, hadn't New York been content to ladle out money as it had in the past, sticking to the customary archaeological expeditions carried out by nice British and American professors? A very reliable lot, archaeologists; they hardly ever got into any sort of trouble.

Or grants for studies.

Sir Charles was very fond of studies; they were decent, traditional foundation work, gave a good tone and a feeling of accomplishment for everybody, and were always picked up and printed somewhere. All the Tunis office had to do was think of titles now and then to forward to New York. They had done two studies last year, "The Revival of Intellectual Inquiry As It Pertains to Twentieth-century Moslemism," and "Commercial Canning of Fruits As an Alternative to Wine Production," both extremely well received. The New York office hadn't any idea what a problem all those damned grapes were, and the wineries built by the French, when the country was now fanatically Moslem and wine was, of course, prohibited by the Qur'an. The country was floating on a sea of wine which it couldn't sell and which no one could drink. Fascinating subject.

In January of that year Sir Charles had come up with another good one, "A Study of Jewish Efforts to Relocate Ancient Hebrew Villages of North Africa," which he had thought would have a lot of appeal. The Jews were going to have to get their brethren out of North African countries somehow with all this resurgent Moslem and pan-Arabic stuff, and the Arabs were cooperating for a change. Showed a lot of human interest and political byplay on a constructive level (which was unique enough); he had been sure New York would jump at it. One of the workers was even an American Jewish boy, interesting chap.

The damnable thing was that New York had jumped him first, with something called Active Youth Commitment. He found even the sound of it distasteful, but, as he knew, he had had only himself to blame: he had been asleep at the switch on that one. He should have known something would pop with a new incoming Foundation president dredged out of one of the civil rights programs.

Well, they were for it. The Tunis office had no business getting involved in youth group work; they were just not set up for it. Not with just the three of them—one had to have a whole damned national government and its resources to pull these things off at all, like the Peace Corps. You didn't find the Ford Foundation mucking about with kids. One had to have a Ph.D. over there even to put stamps on letters.

He was glad he would not have to fool with the Youth Group personally. He had dumped it all on Russell's shoulders. Damned shame, too; his Field Director was too good a man in his present job, took on a lot of work without complaint, and was very talented. One didn't often find Americans with much knack for work abroad; they were usually uninformed (or worse, misinformed) and yet supremely confident of their powers. Americans who could read and speak Arabic as well as the local Tunisian dialect were scarce as hen's teeth. What was even more important, Russell seemed to like his job, he had a positive flair for it, got along well with the primitive Bedouin as well as the locals of the little villes and the assorted zealots, opportunists, grafters, and just plain idiots of Tunis' Government Hill.

Russell turned from the window and settled himself into the chair by the desk. "They ought not to give a whole lot of trouble," he said. "We've cut them as close as we can. They won't take half the chances the Peace Corps takes. The boy goes up to Tabarka to help with the fishing coop there, and he's got a couple of Peace Corps Volunteers in Bizerte to keep an eye on him. The girls get teaching English as a second language in the high schools, which is pretty safe. Puts them in the larger towns, anyway."

"My dear Russell," Sir Charles said. "Any time one is shoved into the youth business, one has a tiger by the tail. God bless children, I'm all for them you know, but I've no confidence at all that they can salvage the world through good works or inspire love in the contrary Arab breast. I've raised two myself and it was hell. One can never tell what young people are going to get into these days; they have a lot of strange ideas." He wanted to get the thing over and done with. "Shall we go out now and make my little speech of welcome?"

"You'd better make a check first," Russell reminded him. "Get the names right."

Sir Charles put on his glasses. The boy's folder was on top. WENDELL FALCK, age twenty-three, St. Louis, Missouri. Sir Charles cast a quick eye over it. Grammar school, high school, Eagle Scout, college transcripts. He supposed it was all right.

GENEVRA COFFIN. Well, this seemed rather nice: Boston girl, Radcliffe graduate, specializing in Behavioral Psychology.

It was, he told himself, quite peculiar the things children chose to specialize in these days: behavioral psychology, creative writing, hotel management. The same thing, too, in the Peace Corps: a surfeit of English majors and social scientists over there, when what was needed was stout agricultural-school graduates.

Miss Coffin's father was a lawyer in Boston, her mother a teacher. She had worked two summers in the Head Start program, respectable work for a Radcliffe girl.

SHARON HOYT. High school—Sir Charles frowned. The reports were so damned thorough. Miss Hoyt's father was an executive with Westinghouse Corporation; the family had made a remarkable number of jumps from city to city during his career. Typical mobile businessman's family. Under high school extracurricular activities was something listed as "twirler with the pep squad."

"My God, Russell, what is this?" He held the page up for him to see.

"Cheerleader. Girls who jump around at American football games."

"Damned little of that sort of thing here," Sir Charles muttered.

Miss Hoyt had gone to the University of Ohio and then to NYU, and had also taken psychology as a major. He skipped through the rest briefly. VISTA volunteer, eight months in Harlem.

Fairly well qualified.

JUDITH HOGGENBERGER.

He didn't have to go through hers too. He made a note of the names.

"I'm sure we'll make out all right," Sir Charles said, half to himself.

After all, Russell was the one needing shoring up. What a damned awkward time to start anything like this. Outside of Tunis, these days, one rather walked on eggs. Yes, of course the Peace Corps carried on, but frankly Sir Charles was tired of hearing about the Peace Corps. The last crisis had shaken them up a bit over there; in fact it had been a nasty shock all around for the Americans. The beloved Ambassador seeing his car set afire in the parking lot of the American Embassy, anti-American rioting in the streets of friendly Tunis. American wives and children cut off in the suburb of Carthage —it had all rather opened their eyes. Not so many remarks about the awful British Empire after that. They had got a taste of what it was like to be hated. The PC director had very quietly closed down some of the more remote stations in the south, and recently, Sir Charles had heard, the office over there had been working on a stand-by evacuation plan to get their brood back to Tunis in the event of another blowout.

"Ah, one more thing, George." Sir Charles took out a small piece of paper on which he had made some notes. "Let me see if I can remember all this. Make a note, will you, like a good fellow? The PC coordinator—I can't remember his name—tells me we should arrange to pick up parcels from the *douane* in Tunis and carry them out ourselves in the jeep. Can't leave a thing to the local post offices; they're still stealing like mad. Also, a jeep trip once a week or so helps keep an eye on things. When you go out to the stations, you might look into bringing the girls some little personal articles which they won't be able to get outside of Tunis. With any regularity, that is." Sir Charles prepared Russell with his slight, ironical smile ("We won't take ourselves too seriously, will we?"). "Nothing much. Deodorants, hair spray, sanitary napkins. I believe the girls will call for Modess or Kotex, but you might check the European brands."

His Field Director said nothing.

"Get Miss Guffin to place the orders. Then all you have to do is carry the things out in the jeep. Nothing more simple than that, is there? For God's sake," Sir Charles said, "let's go out now and get this speech of welcome over with."

Miss Guffin had supplied the Youth Group with Coca-Colas while they waited, and as Sir Charles came into the anteroom they were sitting with their luggage piled around them, sucking on the bottles.

"Ah, you look very American," he said. "Nothing like a Coca-Cola, is there?" A good paternal beamishness seemed in order. He was damned if he knew anything else to do.

The lone boy stood up. He was tall and rather handsome in a sulky, unformed way, dressed in dirty tight white pants and even dirtier tennis shoes. In fact, Sir Charles thought, they all looked dreadfully grubby. The trip from New York was damned tiring. TWA put down in Madrid for what seemed like an eternity after the ocean flight. When one got to Tunis one felt as though one had made the trip by rowboat. He supposed they had had breakfast. Surely Miss Guffin or Russell would have seen to it at the airport.

There were supposed to be three girls, he knew, but he could only find two. While he was looking for the missing girl the boy shifted his position, and he saw that she had been sitting directly behind the boy, her knees propped up on a suitcase. The third girl was quite dark. She was, in fact, a Negress.

Sir Charles kept his smile, but he had had enough experience in this sort of thing not to go on, not to start shaking hands all around and making small talk before he had got his thoughts in order.

There was no reason why New York couldn't have informed them that one of the kids was a Negro. And, he told himself with a positive surge of temper, there was that damned American perversity about vital information, which shifted with every fashion when they came upon what was supposed to be a sensitive area. Used to be that way with Jews. He could almost hear New York explaining that putting "Negro" anywhere in one of their damn plastic folders was as horrible as mentioning one's religious affiliation.

Why the devil hadn't Russell said something? Every once in a while he was quite provoked with the man. It was as though Russell enjoyed catching him off guard.

Well, he had.

The other two girls were comparatively unalarming. The tall, leggy girl had long red-blonde hair and very short skirts, and the small dark girl had hardly any hair at all, cropped short like a concentration camp inmate's. From one extreme to the other. The whole group seemed preposterously young. They were in their early twenties, he supposed, but they appeared, to anyone seeing them for the first time, a uniform sixteen.

He supposed he could grasp New York's reasons for sending a Negro girl to North Africa, but did New York understand that only a handful of Arabs in Tunis government circles would appreciate the gesture? What a pain in the neck! Most Arabs were terribly color-conscious.

As he remembered it, she was the VISTA worker from Harlem.

"This must be Miss Hoyt," he said, extending his hand.

"'No, I'm Genevra Coffin, Sir Charles." The accent was unmistakable. Boston and Radcliffe, father a lawyer.

Good lord, what a *gaffe!* He felt a sudden pain behind his eyes—the hot-weather headache, coming to full flower.

"Will you shut those blinds for me, Miss Guffin?" he broke off to ask. His secretary went to the window and clattered down the Venetian blinds.

That was better. At least some of the bright white light was out of his eyes. Now if they could just shut off the roar of the damnable American air conditioner, he might have half a chance.

The Negro girl was quite charming, he decided. He shook her hand again, warmly. Dark enough to be unmistakably Negro, yet delicately boned, with expressive eyes and mouth. A classic mulatto type, soft wavy hair, slim and tall. A wonder she hadn't thought of the stage. Sir Charles was a great admirer of—he searched for the name—Lena Horne, yes, that was it. One of the world's most beautiful women, and the epitome of sex.

"Ah, then, perhaps you'd better introduce yourselves." He shook hands all around as they told him their names. The girl with the long blonde hair was Miss Hoyt. At least Miss Hoyt was around somewhere. And the one with the prison haircut was Judith Hoggenberger.

"And this young man is Wendell Falck. Couldn't miss that, could I?"

They laughed, but without enthusiasm. He had made a mistake in singling out the Negro girl first, and they knew it. He really wasn't coming off at all well.

"The Foundation," he began, "wished me to extend you a hearty welcome, of course, and wants me to assure you that everything has been done to make your stay and your work as pleasant and successful as possible." Sir Charles heard his own voice droning away and was not pleased with it. He was wandering. Even Russell was looking terribly bored.

"—can't help but like it here. Tunis has one of the largest American colonies in North Africa, lots of people working here, you know. American aid to Tunisia keeps the place going in one way of speaking." Their faces showed they had been told all this in New York. "And the largest Peace Corps contingent in Africa. So you'll find many friends here, embassy staffs, consular people, the USAID people, agricultural assistants, Ford Foundation, and, of course, all the young people of the Peace Corps." It was a dreadful speech. He had even said something about establishing lifetime friendships, and then had to put in a bit about the Arabs and the coming opportunity to know them firsthand. Lovable, friendly people, the Tunisians. He saw Russell staring at him.

But after regarding him in dead silence for a moment, they broke into a little ring of applause. Miss Guffin stood by the window and smiled. At least she seemed genuinely cheerful, he noticed sourly.

He shook hands once more, all around.

"So forward, onward," he heard himself saying, "and Godspeed." Under his breath he said to Cynthia Guffin, "Why is it so damned hot in here with all that racket?" casting an eye toward the infernal air-conditioning machine.

"It's not working properly," she whispered back, and reached out to throw the switch and cut it off.

They had decided to put the Youth Group in the old Tunisia Palace Hotel rather than the Tunis Hilton. "There's nothing for them to do or see up there; it's too American," Cynthia Guffin had said. "The whole staff speaks English and they serve hot dogs and things like that, and it's rather like being in Miami or anywhere else one finds a Hilton. We'll put them up where they can at least use their French and hear a little Arabic. The old Tunisia Palace will do nicely."

To Russell's surprise it did do nicely. The Tunisia Palace was in the middle of the city, a block from the main Boulevard of the President and, as far as life went in Tunis, in the thick of things. They were lucky enough to get out of the cabs at an hour when there were still some people in the streets, and the girls were fascinated with an Arab in a flowing gandourah carrying a briefcase, and a couple of women wrapped in white rayon haiks and wearing high-heeled Paris shoes. Nothing helps like a little local color, he told himself. They perked up at once and the boy said something about an old Humphrey Bogart movie, and the dark girl asked if the furnishings of the old hotel were what you might call typically Tunisian.

Russell was damned if he knew. He wasn't familiar with the old Humphrey Bogart movies, and as far as the style of the Tunisia Palace was concerned, "high class French–North African saloon" was the only description he could think of. The downstairs was a jungle of brass bric-a-brac, deep Arab rugs, deer heads, imitation Versailles furniture, and oriental wood grilles partitioning off every nook and cranny so that he always had a hell of a time finding his way to the bar. Every once in a while you found some old dodderer in a parlor wearing an old-fashioned fez or tarboosh, which he supposed would make the place look very authentic. But upstairs the Tunisia Palace was just like any other hotel in the city, which meant the usual trouble with the keys and getting the porter to follow directions about the luggage. The blonde girl and the Negro girl were going to share the double room, the other girl was next door, and the boy on the floor above. Cynthia Guffin had taken pains to see that the boy was put on another floor; it had never seemed to occur to her that, if he wanted to, all Wendell had to do was take the elevator down to the floor below to molest the females.

So much for propriety. Russell doubted the elevator would get much use. As a group they didn't seem particularly friendly, even to each other. He couldn't quite figure them out.

Lunch had been ordered in the larger room, and Russell rang down for a bottle of Scotch and some soda to see him through. He poured a drink while Cynthia Guffin bustled about, getting the group settled and advising them to take their Entero-Vioforms and get some sleep.

"If you do go out, there's a map of Tunis in your kits. Don't forget it," Miss Guffin said. "But do try to stick to the main streets, won't you? George and I will give you a thorough tour of Tunis next week. Everything you want to see."

"Where's the Casbah?" somebody asked.

"That's George's department," Cynthia Guffin said with a small sigh. She went over to the dresser and picked up her drink.

Why did they always want to know about the Casbah? Russell thought irritably.

"The Medina," he said. "No Casbah, which means fort, anyway. The Medina is mostly shops around a slum. If you want to take a look at it on your own, the only thing to remember is, once you're inside it takes you a hell of a long time to find your way out. Lots of dead ends. How's your French?"

They looked at each other.

"I had a summer in Paris," Genevra Coffin said.

"And we all had an intensive in New York, at Berlitz."

"Fine. You'll have another intensive here, too, the next few weeks, sort of pound it in. And an intensive in Tunisian Arabic. Nobody speaks Arabic?"

Nobody spoke Arabic.

"Don't count too much on French. A lot of Tunisians don't speak it. In the city, yes, but even then a lot of them don't. So you have all sorts of problems. As for the Medina, it goes round and around a hill and comes out on top by the old palace and the mosque at the Place du Gouvernement. That's about it. Nothing important, as I said, mainly small shops and the houses of the poor. Yeah, I know" —as they all seemed to want to speak at once—"not like the movies. No flute players or snake charmers or anything, just poor Arabs and pickpockets. Damned good pickpockets, too—they can get all your money out of your wallet, and your cards sorted out, and they even know the feel of American Express checks and leave them alone. Just Tunisian dinars is all they want. And you might get a pass thrown at you in the crowds. Watch the Tunis boys; they sort of grab and hang on. And you won't get any help from bystanders. They think it's funny."

"Oh, wow." a girl's voice said, unimpressed.

"Take Miss Guffin's advice. Take your pills; get some sleep. And if you go out, stay downtown where the tourists go. It's not San Francisco, it's not New York, it's not Greenwich Village, it's not Paris. Don't make the mistake of trying to get to know the natives by having friendly conversations. You've been told you'll run into some anti-American feeling, and you will."

"I thought we were here to have friendly conversations," the small girl said.

"You will. Just wait until next week; you'll have all you can take care of."

They were through with their lunch, he saw, and he wanted to get out.

"Say good-by," he told Cynthia Guffin under his breath, "and let's go."

"Have your naps," she told them as she picked up her sunglasses and her hat. "And then take your walks if you want to. Just be discreet, won't you? And we'll see you in the morning. Eight o'clock sharp in the lobby. George will pick you up."

Going down in the elevator Russell said, "What the hell was the matter with Charlie this morning?"

"The matter?" she said brightly. "I didn't see anything the matter."

Damn them, he thought, they would always cover up for each other; they were still locked together like Siamese twins after fifteen years. He had wanted her to say something about the Negro girl, he was interested to see what her reactions would be, but as usual she was going to check it out with Charlie first and then take the official stand.

"He was off his stride," he went on. "Something bothering him. The welcoming speech was certainly a bust. I've heard him do better when he was half crocked and really sliding. I couldn't tell what he was talking about and neither could the kids."

"Oh, don't call them that," she said. "I'm afraid it's a bad habit we've all fallen into lately, even Sir Charles. It's time to use some other term. They're perfectly grown up, you know. They're all over twenty-one."

"Well, hell, they look like a bunch of kids. And act it, too."

"But all young people do that now; it's the style. Underneath they're quite mature. It's a mistake for us to think of them as anything else. After all," she added briskly, "we'll just have to do our best, won't we?"

They came out of the lobby into the Rue de Carthage and the all-enveloping light and white heat.

"Oh, dear, we're in for another hot one," Miss Guffin said. She put on her sunglasses. "Can I drop you off? You're sure?"

He shook his head, no, as he knew it was out of her way.

She had turned him off the subject very nicely, he thought, watching her stride off to find her car. Nice little gray British mouse with a backbone of iron; he had never made the mistake of underestimating her. Damned if he hadn't come to believe all the stories that circulated in Tunis, that she was in love with the old bird and always had been, through the first wife and now the second.

What did somebody like Cynthia Guffin do, anyway, with an all-time marathon hopeless love affair with old Charmin' Charlie? The lazy old bastard.

Go to tea in Carthage on a Sunday afternoon, he told himself. With the other gray mice from the embassies.

Yes, but even with all that damned British fortitude, how could she be content with that sort of life? Didn't she ever dream of herself in old Charlie's arms, getting screwed?

No, he supposed, not even he could picture that.

In the garden of Nancy Butler's villa in Carthage they always took their tea in the same spot on Sunday afternoons. They went down to the metal umbrella table under the tamarisk tree on the last terrace, where the view was truly one of the best on that side of the hill, overlooking the old Carthaginian port which had been recently cleaned out so that it resembled nothing so much as a small ornamental pond with a green island in the middle, the blue, brilliant sheet of the Mediterranean beyond, and on the far horizon the mountains of Cap Bon. The terrace was usually the perfect spot to catch a breeze, but this Sunday the air was completely still and the water mirror-smooth, reflecting the light into their sunglassed faces. Cecile was quite uncomfortable, as she was heavy and had the sort of very white skin which was sensitive to even reflected sun, but she would never suggest they move up to the house where it might be cooler. The garden table, the terrace, the tamarisk tree was the spot where they always met, and they never changed their long-established habits.

Nevertheless, it was beastly hot.

"No wind at all today," Cynthia Guffin observed. "Too bad for the sailors."

"Yes, isn't it? Dead calm. I hope nobody's foolish enough to take a boat out and wait for a breeze. I don't think we'll get anything at all."

"I saw the Baxters coming in from Tunis with their boat trailer and the children," Cecile said. "Now that they are here I suppose they won't have anywhere to go. They'll have to sit in a café."

"Oh, surely they wouldn't be that stupid. They can take the children down to the beach."

"But it's really too hot for that, isn't it? I should think they'd get very burned."

Nancy Butler put down her cigarette and held her hand inquiringly over the teapot, "More, anyone?'"

They murmured no. It was really too hot to drink tea, but the form of their Sunday afternoons had been set for years and they prided themselves that they did not use up their time as so many women of their age did, fussing about what spot of the garden would be nicest, or whether they would drink tea or whiskey, or what they would wear. They drank tea, and that was that. They wore Sunday dresses and they came to the same place, and what they did was their own business. Cecile Lambert was the administrative assistant to the French Consul, Nancy Butler was the American Ambassador's secretary, and Cynthia Guffin was—of course— Charlie Benedict's right arm. In odd moments they sometimes referred to themselves as the "old hands," and there was very little they didn't know or could not find out if they put their minds to it.

"I like the Baxters," Nancy said. "They try very hard. Very family-group minded, keeping the children with them like that all the time. I understand they play tennis, too. Very good tennis; at least I hear they don't argue about it."

"Like those dreadful USAID bridge games," Cecile murmured.

"Oh, that's because USAID is so ingrown. Scared to death to get out and meet anybody else."

"How's he doing?" Cynthia Guffin wanted to know.

"Who, Baxter? Oh, very well, I should imagine. At least according to his latest evaluation report. Although he does get a bit thin at times with those nasty girls over there. I can't say I blame him. Why do they always get the very worst of the Tunisian pool in the consular offices? Those girls can't even answer the telephone properly."

"They're down on the bottom of preferences, that's why. No priority. They don't know it, but they are."

"Well, for God's sake let's hope they don't find out. Whoever set it up initially must have had it in for the consulate."

"They're not going to stay," Cecile said. "She's pregnant."

"My word, that *is* new! Bet he doesn't even know about it. Where did you hear that?"

"She goes to Docteur Beaussier. And I understand this time she wants to go home."

"Well, she had a bad time with the last one. And the Pavillion has a rotten nursery. Remember when all the babies had gastro-enteritis?"

"Oh, come now, that was years ago!"

"What a shame, really," Cynthia Guffin said. "They're such nice people to have here. One would think she'd stick it out."

"The nice people never stay."

"Well, *he* can't go, at least not for a while. He won't be released right away. But if we do get another consul, perhaps he'll new-broom the place. It won't affect," Nancy Butler said, "George Russell's little business, will it?"

"Which one?"

"My God, yes, she talks too much!" Cecile Lambert said, switching to French. "She is even telling everyone what they do in bed. So typical, no?"

"Yes, but have you seen her? She's a pretty fiery piece. Trust El Rosul. George got his sheepstealing in before the others even knew she was there. Tell me," Nancy asked, "what do they *do* in bed? Anything interesting?"

"Oh, *nothing!*" Cecile said. "What would they do? They lose their heads, these girls, that is all. It is only because George does not look like it, you know? So intriguing, like the surprise in the box, he is. They become obsessed with him."

"I'm quite fond of George," Cynthia Guffin said, "and he never allows these things to grow into messes. You must admit he's never had any sort of trouble. Besides, he will be quite busy now. He has the Youth Group."

"Yes, tell us. How do they look?"

"Oh, they look quite typical; she has already told me," Cecile said. "That is really not the important news."

"They're supposed to be quite intelligent. All honor students. But I do wonder if they have any idea of the situations they may come across. Living among the Arabs is difficult for most Westerners. And our friends across the border aren't making things easier."

"And what else?" Nancy wanted to know.

"Are you really interested?" Cynthia Guffin looked up from her tea. "Quite tricky, I'd say. One never knows with young people, does one? All rather attractive, and the boy is far too handsome."

"Too bad old Bey isn't around."

"What a shocking thing to say! I'm sure we'll have trouble enough."

"The important news," Cecile said, "is that the General is back."

"What, old von Lehzen?" Nancy exclaimed. "He can't come back—his residency isn't renewed. Besides, I thought the government had confiscated his place down in Nefta."

"How little you know of the General! He is coming back, and he has his residency. And an Irish passport!"

"Irish? That's a good one. I can't see the General as an Irishman. What sort of string pulling went on there, I wonder?"

"A lot of Germans have flocked to Ireland," Cynthia Guffin offered. "They've bought up a lot of land—sharing the family funds again. Been quite a row about it; some Irish don't take to the idea. Perhaps the General has become an Irish citizen."

"But it is interesting, is it not? The last time the General was so without money he had to sell his automobile to raise the fare back."

"No, it was worse than that. He had some woman in tow—"

"She is still here."

"Is she really? That was quite a concession for him, to play the gigolo at his age. Not to mention the Prussian name and pride."

"I can't stand the *boche*, I detest them," Cecile murmured. "All of them, including the abominable tourists!"

"But you know the General—and how charming he can be when he wants to."

"Of course, that is what makes him so filthy! But he is opening the house down in the Nefta oasis and it starts all over again, you see? We—it came in last week," she said hastily.

The French Consulate, as they all very well knew, was one of the main funnels for French intelligence.

"Then the old crowd will congregate. They always do. They migrate south like birds when he is there. The old Vichyist, what's-'is-name? De Bonripeau. And Baron Bergson."

"He's the courier; I decided that last time," Cynthia Guffin said. "Who else for a courier but a Swede?"

"And old Moreau from Ez-Zahra."

"He's not a part of it; he can barely totter. He only goes down to Nefta to hem and haw about the old days of Gide and Cocteau and all that nonsense."

"But this I don't understand," Cecile complained. "After all, he was imprisoned by the Nazis."

"The General is no longer a Nazi," Nancy Butler drawled. "No one is any more. We've got them all cleaned out."

They laughed loudly at this.

"No, of course he is not! He is only making the memorial services to Rommel down there in the desert."

"Well, God knows all the Germans have a fascination for the Sahara. Days of glory and all that. Wouldn't be surprised if they raised subscriptions for a shrine."

"Oh, *quelle horreur!*"

"What's really interesting is to watch our side," Nancy said. "I usually think I know all of them—at least the American agents are fairly easy to spot. But there are so many independents hiring out these days you can never be sure. I completely passed up the little USIS man last time. He was very good. I only found out what he was up to when they closed up his office the day after the General left. He was gone like a puff of smoke."

"Who? MacPherson? But it was written all over him," Cynthia Guffin said. "None of the Information Office men have that much energy. He was everywhere, like triplets. I'd see him sitting in the Café de Paris and never be sure when I got home that he wouldn't be standing in my clothes closet."

"Why, Cynthia, what are you hiding in your clothes closet?" Nancy drawled.

"I never even noticed him," Cecile said. "He had a marvelous cover. He was even a little drunk all the time!"

"It will be amusing to watch, though. I suppose everyone will be working on it."

"Good lord, *we* won't!" exclaimed Cynthia. "We never get involved in anything like that."

"I know it is not popular to say it," Cecile put in, "but I do not think the General can find it. That is why he keeps coming back."

"Find what?"

"Rommel's gold. What else are we talking about?"

3

To the Lady Tanit
and the Lord Baal-Ammon.

*—Inscription on a stele
in the ruins of Carthage*

At 2 A.M. Sharon Hoyt woke in the seaside village
of Ez-Zahra and sat upright in bed. She was not fully awake and for
a moment she had her usual trouble remembering where she was,
but her eyes were wide and straining in the smothering heat and
darkness against the strange panic which had dragged her from her
sleep.

Whatever the reason, she could tell that it was definitely not the
usual night alarms which had made the first few weeks of her assignment so regularly sleepless: the persistent yapping of the Bedouin
dogs, which began after midnight off in the hills and which, if it
continued long enough, usually nagged her back to cursing wakefulness, or the shattering cough of a motor scooter taking some Arab
busboy back to town from the hotel across the street, or even the
thumping drums and handclaps and nasal singing of some wedding
party in a house deep in the groves. In those first few seconds she
did not know exactly what it was, only that it was none of these
and that her room was so impenetrably black she couldn't see her
hand before her face, that she was bathed in an unpleasant slime of
sweat and fright and that she had never been so filled with a groggy

feeling that something unknown and terrible was going on in her life.

"Cripes," she whispered into the dark, and her own voice was oddly smothered, as though the words had fallen into thick nothingness and had been blotted up.

It was more than she could stand. Without thinking she scrambled out of bed and started around the room, and as she lurched into something which might have been a chair covered with her clothes and felt the usual clutter on the floor under her bare feet, she clapped her hand across her mouth to keep from shrieking. It was nothing; it was only blackness and terrific heat and a high wind blowing that made the door downstairs in the courtyard slam and bang as though it was going to tear loose from its hinges. But on the other hand, it *was* something—it was a Red Alert, a state of terror as wild and unexpected as the end of the war or an atomic bomb.

What is the matter with me?

It might be a war after all; from what she had heard there was this tremendous hot wind before you felt the blast, and it was true her room had turned into an oven. There was a hot wind, too. It circled in the dark and around the walls like an invisible tornado.

God, I really am going to scream, she thought in amazement; it's completely out of control. I'm going to yell my brains out without really knowing what's going on, because I woke up already flipped out of my mind and it's way ahead of me. I'm going to open my mouth and yell HELP! HELP! as loud as I can make it.

At that second she hit the wardrobe and it jarred her; in the mirror she was a darker blur against darkness, a naked shape peering forward and rubbing her elbow where it had come into contact with the knob, and she recognized herself. But really flipped out. Like Chicken Little.

Well, she thought slowly, she had bought one of those lapel buttons once that said CHICKEN LITTLE WAS RIGHT, and it really wasn't so funny when you thought about it. In the dark.

There wasn't any war, naturally. She was pretty sure of that. And, as she felt herself growing calmer by a fraction, she was glad she hadn't screamed or yelled. It wouldn't have done any good, anyway. She could have turned her lungs inside out and the ben Omrane family on the other side of the house wouldn't have stirred. The newness of her assignment in Ez-Zahra had worn off; after the first flurry of interest the ben Omranes had left her more or less to herself. Even the older girls who were supposed to help her with her French had grown pretty lackadaisical.

Also, she could just imagine if she had started screaming for help what their reaction would have been. Mrs. ben Omrane, waking up and punching Haidi:

Name of Allah, what is that noise I hear?

It is the voice of Mees Aweet. Perhaps she is dreaming.

Well, Allah protect us from such noises. Are the gates locked?

Yes.

Then let us go back to sleep.

You had to give George Russell credit. He said it would take time to get to know the Arabs, and it had. Only he had failed to say that you'd be sorry, too.

In the darkness Sharon moved to the window nearby and put her hand against the shutters. The wind was really blowing; she could feel the hot blast of it pouring through the slats, full of something as dry and silky as talcum powder. And more than that: the whole dark, inside and out, was filled with a turbulence that made her hair stand on end. It was as though the air was going to explode.

She groped her way along the sill and then the flat expanse of the wall until she came to the edge of the bathroom door and flipped the light switch there. It was dead. No lights. She went into the bathroom and felt around until she came in contact with the wash-basin and the faucets. She turned on the taps and washed her hands, but when she wiped them on the towel the cloth was full of the same strange stuff. It was on everything. She felt her face gingerly, and it was on her mouth and chin and even in her hair.

Dust?

She went cautiously back to bed and found a short cotton beach shift on the floor, under a pile of paperback books, and slipped it on. She wasn't exactly a tidy person, but she did try to have some sort of clothes around to grab in a hurry; the ben Omranes, as she had already found out, had a tendency to wander in and out, especially across the connecting "women's roof" of the upper house. It took a moment to locate the flashlight in one of her shoes where she put it for safekeeping, and then she went to the doors which opened out onto the roof and unhooked the latch. She wasn't prepared for the force of the wind which blasted the doors back and nearly knocked her off the step.

Outside the night was rent with sudden shifts of purplish light and boiling shapes of dust clouds. Turned up, the flashlight shot a beam into a sky so close it seemed to hang just above her head. But no rain, just dust. Sand.

The ben Omranes' house was set in fields of orange and lemon trees and groves of olives; in the clear sunlight of day and from the roof she could usually see the village of Ez-Zahra a mile or more down the asphalt highway set in a wide valley which ran between the hills and toward the sea like some rich and motionless river. The fertile plain was filled solidly with dark-green glistening citrus forest. But now, in the night, the trees were all moving. In the intermittent somber light it seemed to Sharon as though the squat mud-brick house was sailing on a sea of thrashing treetops.

From the courtyard a voice yelled up at her. She turned the flashlight down and it passed along the tarmac and caught the figure of M'neera, the youngest ben Omrane girl, pulling a rope with the goat attached to get the animal into the kitchen, and, beside her, Saida, with her arms full of chickens.

It must really be bad, Sharon marveled, if the ben Omranes were putting the animals inside their house. As she bent forward over the roof ledge the wind got under the beach shift and billowed it up behind her, sending sprays of dust up the small of her back. The flashlight showed streamers of dust like smoke billowing from the edges of the yard. And from the back of the house Haidi and Munseff, the oldest boy, appeared, carrying boards and a rake and shovel. A few feet into the orchard they started propping boards under the limbs of a tree bent down with the weight of ripening lemons.

Oh, hell, Sharon thought, watching them. The wind was going to tear up their crop. The trees would break and she supposed they would lose not only the fruit but some of the big limbs. And they had already had so much trouble with the drought; there hadn't been any rain at all since she had arrived. Even over the howl of the wind she could hear the dull, thumping sound of oranges falling out of the trees and hitting the ground.

Munseff came back across the pavement of the courtyard and saw the flashlight and stopped, looking up to the roof with his hand held to his eyes. He had on pants and an old white shirt but he was barefooted, the wind whipping the hair around his head.

"Mees Aweet," he yelled in French, "are you all right?"

She supposed she was all right. The prickles of sand had raised weird goose bumps on her flesh and the strange freaked-out feeling still lingered, but she was all right.

"Nothing is broken, up there?"

She had left the doors to the roof unlatched and they were swinging and banging as though the glass panes would shatter at any moment, but nothing so far.

"What is it?" she yelled down.

"The khamseen." He made a funnel of his hands. "From the desert."

The warm wind sucked under the cotton shift again and the drifting grit was like a scattering of centipedes along her spine. She grabbed at it convulsively with her free hand.

The khamseen. In Tunis it was called by its Italian name, the sirocco. In France it was the mistral. But in the crash course of indoctrination and orientation arranged by the Tunis office for them in May, they had learned that the real name for the storm was the simoom. It came straight out of the Sahara, wild and hair-raising. The wind which blows for three days, never any less. The wind which makes men mad. A low-pressure storm out of the desert with little or no rain but extraordinarily low barometric readings at the center which raises havoc with the nervous system. Like the feeling before a thunderstorm: irritable, off balance, and depressed, only ten times worse. The Bedouin, they had been told, are the only ones who seem to take it in their stride. But once you've seen the migrant tribes drifting down the fields and highways wrapped like mummies in the gloom and clouds of sand, it will give you a jolt. They look just like ghosts, or the walking dead.

"Hey," Sharon shouted, turning the light on the figures struggling to prop up the trees. "Can I help?"

She didn't really expect them to accept her offer. The first few days the ben Omranes had let her feed the chickens, and they had thought it was very funny when she took a basket and helped to pick oranges. But they had made it plain that only a little was enough. Foreigners, she had discovered, were not all that much of a novelty; they had had the French with them for eighty years, and they knew all about it. The town of Ez-Zahra with its beaches and resort hotels saw all it wanted of the Germans and British, too, on holiday.

You have to remember, George Russell had told the Active Youth Commitment Group, that you're going to live in a Moslem society and the people you meet may think you're mildly interesting but not exactly the most fascinating thing that has ever entered their lives. And with good reason. For no matter how much of a shock it may be to you, the Moslems have a tendency to regard all non-Islamic peoples as physically rather dirty. They know that in our own countries we eat pork, the most unclean of all animals in their eyes. Sort of like the way we'd regard people who eat rats and lizards as a steady diet. Our religion doesn't require us to wash our hands before we sit down to a meal, and we wipe our backsides with dry paper instead of rinsing off properly with running water. And we don't seem to mind sleeping with our women, who have a big mat of untidy pubic hair instead of neatly taking it all off with a depilatory as Arab women do.

When Munseff smiled and waved his thanks but no, Sharon went back inside and groped her way to the bathroom once more. She was coated with the silky powder of khamseen, but when she put the flashlight on the washbasin and turned the taps she saw, fascinated, that the sand collected in the edges of the water as fast as it ran into the bowl. And the towels were already covered with it. She was shaking the towel out and making an attempt to brush herself off when there was a banging on the doors to the roof. She picked up the light and went to the bedroom. It was Saida, her face pressed against the glass, the rest of her body swathed in one of her mother's white rayon haiks.

Someone wants you downstairs, Mees Aweet, Saida mouthed, and pointed downward violently.

Sharon took the flashlight and ran down the outside stairs, which were uncovered and open to the storm, and through the small walled courtyard which enclosed her side of the house. Her dining-sitting room was full of wind and dirt, as the door down there had not been closed all night. And as soon as she unbolted the front door it slammed open like an explosion, hitting her full on the arm and shoulder and across the right side of her head. She dropped the flashlight.

In the dark a voice said politely in French, shouting a little over the wind, "I came to see if you were all right."

Cripes! Her arm felt as though it was broken, but she bent to scrabble for the light.

"Have you injured yourself?" the same voice said quickly. It had got the flashlight; now it lifted it and turned the beam full on her. "It is all my fault; I apologize. It is the accursed khamseen."

Beyond the glare of the light on her she could see the uniform of Ez-Zahra Chief of Police.

The Ez-Zahra Chief of Police, as she had already come to learn, was a real gas, but she wasn't so sure she was exactly in the mood to cope with all his heavy French-style come-on. The Chief spoke very rapid-fire French which he assumed she could follow (and which she couldn't), but she gathered that he was very racked up about the door; it was a gauche thing to do to allow it to collide with her in such a manner and he wanted her to know that he had only blundered in his polite concern for her. That is to say, in his obligation to look in on her and see that she was not inconvenienced by one thing and another such as this execrable khamseen which fortunately Tunisia did not often experience, as it was usually found in Algerie and Maroc and other vaguely uncouth areas.

He was so wound up about it all, she saw, that he was not only taking in her injured arm, where some of the skin had been scraped off above the elbow, but also everything in general including her bare legs and the few buttons of the minishift over her chest which were undone and showed a lot of skin.

No, it was too clumsy; he should have held on to the door, he told her.

The Chief's name was Ali ben Ennadji and he was a very suave type, or at least he worked hard at it, coming on like a combination of Jacques Brel, Alain Delon, and everybody else he had probably seen in the *cinéma*. But he was still Arab enough to look somewhat shook as he was obviously discovering that the minishift was pretty thin and that she didn't have anything on under it. Most of the time Sharon had seen him cruising around the village in the police car in heavy dark sunglasses and neat starched uniform, but once or twice she had seen him on the traffic motorcycle really burning up the dust on the back roads for a joy ride. As chiefs of police went, she supposed he was something of a swinger. But he was tough, too. One day she had seen him chewing out one of his *boliss* in front of the *pharmacie* in the village, and he had been pretty *formidable*. He had a great pair of lungs. But then all the Arabs could really yell. They seemed to have a sort of second voice, like opera singers, and once going they could really rip the paint off the walls.

The Chief of Police liked her. She didn't exactly have to be psychic to know that. The first day she had come down to Ez-Zahra with George Russell, the Foundation Field Director had taken her to the village police station to register her as an alien resident and projected teacher for the *lycée* in Nabeul and get her papers stamped. Russell had introduced her to the Chief and had asked him to keep an eye on her and make sure she got help in any way she needed. The two of them had had a long conversation in Arabic in the Chief's office, and afterward the young Chief had elegantly bowed them all the way to the front door of the station. But he hadn't kissed her hand. One did not, as Russell had explained later, kiss the hands of young unmarried women. So it showed how much the Chief was up on all the little finesses.

She didn't doubt that for a moment. The Chief was a great dude type and snowed you with his French, but all the time she had been sitting in the office in a miniskirt with her legs crossed in one of the squatty little police chairs he hadn't missed a thing. But by then she was getting used to it. She had already had a couple of weeks in Tunis where you practically had to beat off the types just walking down the street. Even worse than Italy, Genevra Coffin had observed. But she didn't really mind; it was, as they had said, part of the scene. Besides, with the Chief of Police you could tell he liked coming on very strong. He wasn't bad-looking; in fact he was kind of interesting. One of the dark, smoldering kinds with a wide mouth and a big square jaw and bigger than most, over six feet. A Burt Lancaster type except for the eyes. Strictly Arab eyes.

He had come by the ben Omranes' house a few times after that to see how she was getting along, but they had been pretty slow and sticky visits. In spite of the fact that he had gone out of the way to speak very slow and simple French at first, it had been a drag for both of them; she had gotten tired of making conversation about whether her rooms in the side of the house she rented from the ben Omranes were comfortable, yes? And the family helpful, no? Once he had come all the way down to the beach in front of the Hotel Fourati to see if she was still getting on all right. She had looked up to see who was blocking the sun and there was the Ez-Zahra Chief of Police standing in the soft white sand up to his shoes tops seeing if she was all right. Down to the lining of her bikini. Just standing there doing his duty and sweating in the uniform of the Sûreté Nationale with its red shoulder tabs and braid and brass buttons which made it look as though it had been designed by a freaked-out military Christian Dior, and the big black belt with a shoulder strap which the ben Omrane kids firmly believed he took off to beat the prisoners in the jail.

Sharon really couldn't buy the belt-beating business; the Chief might try to yell his prisoners to death but she didn't think he would hit them. He was too couth for that.

"I am going," he was telling her, "in the automobile which I have outside to inspect the bridge and the hotels and see that all is well." He was trying to make his words slow and distinct again for her benefit. "Then I go"—here he made a gesture of turning a steering wheel of a car—"to the Bedouin camps, to observe them also." He squinted at her in the flashlight beam. "I would be very honored to drive you. That is, if you are not frightened of the khamseen. There is nothing," he added quickly, "to be frightened of. It is very interesting if you have not seen this before."

It took a few seconds for her to realize that he was actually inviting her for a tour in the police car. It seemed like a kooky thing to do, but on the other hand it could be just what he said: if you hadn't seen a storm like that, it was interesting. And, she thought suddenly, why not? It was better than sitting upstairs in her part of the ben Omranes' house without any *electricité*, listening to the wind and the dreary noise of the ben Omranes' oranges hitting the dirt.

But she needed something for her hair, he explained to her, a scarf to protect her head and face from the sand. Sharon ran upstairs and found a bandana and when she came back down he showed her how to pull the front of the scarf over her head like a veil, back and front, and tie it under her chin. But even something as simple as that was pretty spaced out: he was very careful not to touch her with his hands as he pulled the cloth around.

"The khamseen is very bad for the eyes," he explained solemnly.

He was right. When they went outside the full force of the wind hit them and the silk flattened against her face so that he had to lead her the few steps to the car.

"After one or two days," he told her when they had got inside, "the eyes get very bad. Always the sand gets into them and they become *aggravés*, very red. You must put some cloths—*serviettes*, you understand?—up to the windows in your house and wet these cloths with water to keep out the dust. It makes dark, but it is better. The girls of the ben Omranes can show you how."

Yeah, Sharon told herself, she knew how that worked. The girls would be sent up and giggle and goof around and not do it right, and then Munseff would be allowed to come. After he had checked it out with his mother. But first, the girls, for propriety's sake.

The Chief of Police maneuvered the car out of the gates of the ben Omranes' compound, and they crept slowly down the road past the beach and the tourist hotels. Beyond the car windows a brownish fog swirled along in gusts of the wind. At the end of the road and the turnabout where the hotels ended by a salt marsh, the storm had torn several large palm trees out of the ground. The Chief of Police had to back the car up to get around them; once broadside to the wind, the car caught the gale full force and was lifted and bumped up and down. Sharon grabbed the dashboard with both hands, trying not to fall against him as he struggled with the gearshift.

"Wow!" she yelled.

It was, she was just realizing, not safe at all. Another one of those freaky Arab experiments: a tour in the khamseen, whether it could actually be done or not. By the dashboard lights she could see the Chief was somewhat pissed, his mouth turned down unhappily. No Jacques Brel–Alain Delon now; he was even muttering to himself in Arabic. When he finally got the car back on the road she slumped down in the seat.

"Now it is all right," he told her.

They inched back past the ben Omranes' white stucco walls slowly and went on to where the beach road entered the highway. On the right-hand side was old Monsieur Moreau's house, its side entrance with a little iron gate, and beyond that an ornamental pond and a Greek-style temple set in a grove of cypress trees. The villas of Ez-Zahra were more elaborate than those in the villages of the rest of Cap Bon; at one time the place had been famous as a small and very private resort town and had had a sizable expatriate foreign colony. Lots of stories, too. In Tunis people liked to say that the shut-away place on the coast had a long and wicked history.

In the twenties and thirties Ez-Zahra was supposed to have had quite a vogue among the Jet Set of that time, especially the swingers of London, Rome, and Paris. Even the beys of Tunis had joined in, leaving a rather sulphurous trail of gossip behind them.

Sharon had been dying to find out all about the wicked history, but the language barrier had kept her from finding anybody who really knew. The sound of Arabic had been easy at first, compared to French, even with the heavy-breathing vowels in words like *humeh* and *howeh*, where you sort of puffed along. But it grew incredibly complicated and as difficult as French, finally. Like *nam*, which meant yes. Only if you didn't say it right it was a dirty word. What dirty word? Cripes, people only laughed and wouldn't say!

The noncommunication, as they had been warned, gave you a really paranoid feeling after a while. Especially if you had been by yourself for almost three weeks, as she had. Then it really made you want to climb the nearest wall.

"Monsieur Moreau has visitors," the Chief of Police said. The car seemed to be plowing through a solid wall of yellow dust. He turned on the windshield wipers and they swung back and forth twice and then ground to a halt, clogged with microscopic sand. He said something in Arabic under his breath and shut them off.

Sharon had only a brief glimpse of some cars parked in the villa's driveway.

Now that was the place she really wanted to go, she thought. Even in Tunis people knew Moreau's house was like a museum, full of weird art objects, Roman and Greek statues, coins, junk—even a collection of paintings by French artists (some said a Picasso and a Dufy) and a Carthaginian altar stone which was said to be used as a table out in the garden. Next door to Moreau's and hidden from the road by a high wall and from the beach entrance by a thicket of oleanders was the house that everyone gossiped about— the mansion which had once belonged to a Roumanian prince but which was now owned by the government, standing empty and waiting to be sold for a luxury hotel. During World War Two the Germans had occupied it for a while, and then Winston Churchill had stayed there. At the American Embassy cocktail party a cultural attaché had told her, "You must go to see Sebastian's house, if you can get in." André Gide had been there, too, and was supposed to have called it the most beautiful house in the world. One of the clerks from the West German Consulate had said something about a General Rommel having stayed there.

The police car left the paved road and bumped up an incline, plowing in first gear straight through the sand fog. Then it hit an axle-smashing hole and stopped. The car headlights rested on what seemed to be several large stones, and then Sharon saw the stony lumps take shape: there were random pieces of black cloth drawn over them and little stone side walls like corrals running outward. The bumps were actually little stone houses sunk into the dirt.

The Ez-Zahra Chief of Police got out of the car and held the door part way open while he pressed the horn down, hard. The storm blew in, and Sharon grabbed the scarf over her face. There was no answer to the horn blasts at first, and then something crawled out of the ground from the heap of rocks and stood up, leaning forward a little into the wind.

The *bedu* was covered from head to foot in pieces of rags and stuffed in places with what looked like gunny sacks and fragments of bath towels, just like some bundle done up for the garbage. There was no head or face at all, just a mountain of scraps in the headlights of the car. It stopped, gave a loud Arab shout, and the Chief of Police took his hand off the horn and yelled back. They bellowed at each other for a few minutes, angrily, and then the Chief got back into the car, released the brakes, and the car started to roll backwards down the road. If there was a road, Sharon thought. Once or twice he threw the car door open to look back and see where they were going, and each time the khamseen roared through.

The whole thing was completely crazy.

"What was that all about?" Sharon wanted to know.

"Oh," he told her, leaning out the door again, "it is very bad if the sheep get in the orchards. The *bedu* must keep them out. Even in the storm. You understand?"

Frankly, she hadn't seen any sheep. And the Bedouin hadn't looked as though he was worried about any of them wandering away.

They rolled onto the paved road finally, and he stopped the car and switched off the headlights and turned to her.

"So now you have seen the khamseen, yes?" he said softly. He got out a package of Gauloises from the pocket of his uniform jacket and shook one out for her. He had very white teeth, she noticed; even in the dust-fog gloom his teeth flashed whitely in a large French-style smile. Jacques Brel–Alain Delon was back again. "You are quite all right?" he asked her. His hand reached out and touched her arm, brushing fingers lightly over the place where the door had scraped her.

Beautiful, Sharon thought, and smiled back. The Chief of Police was too much, but he would never know it. The whole thing was the usual setup, but he had made it so complicated, driving around in a howling khamseen just to find a place to get started, that she really loved him for it. She stretched her legs out, watching him admire her knees.

"You are not afraid to be with me alone?" he said huskily. Without waiting for an answer, he slid across the seat to her, which was pretty hard to do as the gearshift came up to his shins and he had to strain to reach her. He tried to put one arm across her shoulders.

Sharon kept smiling. In her mind she was already reciting the whole bit to Genevra, including the weird trip up to see the baffled Bedouin with the nonexistent sheep. But not fighting it, she reminded herself. In a way it was inevitable; you had to consider what was happening a valid part of the whole experience. It was, in some respects, the only way you really got to get people to open to you and relate to you as an actual feeling human being. Besides, after all these weeks something was finally taking shape and she was breaking through; it was what you might say the end of all the non-communication for a change. And with the khamseen blowing all around them, a thousand miles from anyplace, how turned on could you get?

He got his knee over the gearshift and half turned to her and took her by the arms and pulled her to him, going pretty fast now, as though he was afraid she was going to push him away or change her mind.

It might have been the storm, but they came together with a distinct shock, and she could feel him shaking. His hand pushed her skirt up and went all around her hips quickly, because he was finding out she really didn't have any clothes on underneath.

On the other hand, Sharon thought objectively, it wasn't such a really great idea in many ways because the front seat of the police Citröen was very cramped and you had to be sort of an acrobat to get something going. He had pushed her into the corner so that her back was against the door, the knobs pressing into her shoulder blades, and he had managed to squirm the beach shift up over her stomach and her chest.

You could certainly say one thing for him, she thought; he was so flipped out over the prospects that he was trying to do everything at once. But she really didn't know him well enough to try to help. He kissed her, but when his mouth touched hers there were layers and layers of dust. They both pulled away at the same time.

"Hey," she said mildly, because her ankle was jammed under the gas pedal and it hurt. But he had wadded the shift up to keep it out of his way and she was looking down at the top of his head, covered with dust. Suddenly he pulled back and turned his head to one side and made a noise—*splut!*—between his teeth.

Dust down there, too.

She couldn't help it; he must have felt her giggling even though she was trying not to make any noise. But her chest was heaving up and down and his nose was right between.

He let go of her at once and slid over to his side of the car, leaving her with the minishift around her neck.

"I want you to come to me," he said, staring through the windshield, "of your own free will."

That was so great, so really beautiful, that it was all Sharon could do to keep from screaming. Her stomach started bouncing up and down with smothered laughter so that she could hardly stand it. It was something, she was positive, that he had seen in the movies, or read in a French book. But she loved him for it. It certainly didn't have anything to do with a mouthful of sand.

But as she wriggled the dress down she really regretted his having been turned off that way. He had come on so strong at first that he had quivered all over, he was really laying it on like someone who was made for it, and she knew that it probably would have been wild all the way in spite of the little front seat and the gearshift between them. He was still looking straight ahead and she could tell that he was very hassled over what had happened and probably his dignity was somewhat bent. His face was stiff with it. She could see the scar very plainly on the right side of his face in the lights. The ben Omrane girls had told her this was where the Chief had had a *bedu* tattoo cut off. It was true, Saida swore: the Chief of the

Ez-Zahra Police was from a wild Bedouin tribe in the southern desert and he tried to hide it behind all his French cool. But that was where the mark of his tribe, the Bedouin tattoo, had been.

Actually, scar or not, Sharon thought, smiling, he was pretty fantastic. He was so far out, with the wild Sûreté uniform with all the red tabs and buttons, and his rivers of French, and the big gold watch and the gold cuff links, that she really felt for him. He wore a large gold ring with a fake diamond or zircon on his left hand. She wished she could take a picture of him and send it to Genevra. She wouldn't believe it, either.

As he started up the car she told herself that she had better think it over. He came on strong, all right; she had felt it and responded to it and she was already aching. But on the other hand, nobody in their right mind really started out with somebody like the Chief of Police anywhere; if the Foundation ever found out about it she supposed they would really flip completely out. It would be as bad as having a thing with the Mayor. Or the snotty *directeur* of the *lycée* in Nabeul. Too close to the local Establishment.

Which was really too bad. Nothing was more perfect than having somebody in contact, to open up the complete cultural spectrum for the most intimate and productive start. And it was a great way to really get into any foreign language.

When they got to the ben Omranes' house he stopped the car outside the gates but didn't get out to open the door for her. Instead, he looked through the windshield and said, "El Rosul is here."

He was absolutely right. The Foundation jeep was inside the gates, parked by her door. The Chief wasn't looking forward to explaining to George Russell about touring the countryside in the khamseen.

"No sweat," she told him. And then, in French, "*J'vais*," because she really understood how he felt about it.

When she opened the front door George Russell was standing in the dining-sitting room drinking a Fanta orange from the refrigerator.

"Where in the hell have you been?" was all he said.

She leaned into the door and finally got it shut against the wind. An old-fashioned kerosene lamp was on the table, probably brought over by the ben Omranes. She turned off the flashlight.

"Haidi said you went off with the police."

"Oh, great. That's a groovy way of putting it." She started to take off the scarf and was amazed to see little showers of dirt falling out of her hair.

"Sorry I'm late," he said.

"Like late for what?"

"I mean, I didn't plan to bust in on you like this, but I hit the khamseen in Grombalia and it's taken me all this time to get here." He looked suddenly at his wrist watch. "Since eleven. Christ! That's two and a half hours to go ten miles. And I can't get any farther; the storm's too much of a mess. I had—I'm on my way," he said, "down to Sousse."

"Well, I don't think you'll make it," Sharon told him.

She went into the kitchen and got another bottle of Fanta out of the refrigerator. When she opened the orange drink she kept her finger over the mouth as she had seen him do, to keep out the dust.

"Tell me something," she said as she came back in. "Like tell me this crap really isn't going to go on for two or three days or whatever it is they say. Cripes, I don't think I can take it." Her voice, even to her own ears, was jumpy and somewhat shrill. She went around to the other side of the table, trailing her fingers in the dust which had already accumulated on its surface. "I want to know how I'm supposed to take a bath without getting dirty before I even shut the water off. Christ, I can't just wallow around like a dustball for three days."

"Hell, Sharon, I can't tell you how to take a bath. You might just have to do that—wallow around until it quits." He smiled slightly. "It's not going to kill you. Besides, it's going to be rough on everybody. This is a bad one. The wind nearly took the top off the jeep coming down."

"Oh, you're a big help." The oil lamp didn't give out enough light, and the yellowish glow hurt her eyes. She rubbed her hands across her arms irritably. "Why don't you tell me some good news for a change? Like, when are you going to get me my job in the *lycée*, anyway? I'm not going to get stuck with one of those non-job summers, you know, like they push off on the Peace Corps kids. The way they told us in New York this was going to be a whole new thing, really well organized and all that jazz. We were really going to do something because we've got more money for it and we're better trained than the PCVs and the Foundation isn't so uptight about rules and regulations. We were going to do something experimental and creative and counteract the effects of our rotten imperialist society abroad and prove that war and racism aren't an expression of American culture. So when am I going to start, huh? So far I've been doing nothing, you know? There's nothing here— I'd rather be out working on the birth control program in the desert villages like the PCVs, anything. No kidding, if I'm going to be covered with dirt and shit like this, I'd like to get some good out of it!"

"Look," he said evenly, "the next time you go out at night will you watch what you wear? I know you understood that running around in shorts is out, but I forgot to tell you that dresses you can see through with—ah—nothing under them is just as bad. That isn't a nightgown by any chance, is it?" he asked her.

"Oh, knock it *off*. Listen, don't get on me now, it isn't the time for it. And don't try to change the subject. Look, I've been on that shitty bus to Nabeul to see Messadi what's-'is-name twice already, and both times you know what he told me? That he was going to have to give me some exams to see if I was really qualified! And he wanted to know if I had my *baccalauréat*, that damned French high school certificate, for Christ's sake! Is he kidding?"

"Now listen, Sharon," Russell said patiently. "I told you not to go up to Nabeul on your own. We have an agreement to place you kids in the schools on a voluntary basis—theirs as well as yours. We pick up the tab for your salaries. And if Messadi wants to give you an examination and look over your qualifications, he has a perfect right to do it. But you're getting in his hair. And that is strictly against Foundation policy."

"Oh, shit, don't start talking like a form letter," she shot at him. "Look, does the Foundation in New York really know what it's like to be out here? Has anybody told them that nobody really *wants* us in Nabeul? That they've got all the languages in the *lycée* like French and classical Arabic that they want? What are we trying to sell them, anyway? You know what the Arabs say about teaching English in their schools? That we're just trying to spread American capitalism, that as soon as we get them to start speaking English we're going to sell them Chevrolets and color televisions and all our great consumer goods and gradually eat them up and make them part of the American industrial empire. That's what they think about us, and baby, I'm beginning to think they're right! Fuck all that propaganda we got in New York. And fuck this place!" she yelled. "You can take it and shove it. No wonder Genevra turned down the assignment here. There's nothing to do; it's just a big copout. This town was supposed to be a setup for Genevra, wasn't it, to keep our token black out of trouble, right? Well, I don't want it either. It's a fake! I've been hanging around here sucking my thumb for three damned weeks—and I can't take it, I've got to do something!"

"I wish you'd shut up," Russell said abruptly. He wiped his hand across his face, smearing dust, and blinked tiredly. "If it gives you any satisfaction, all right, I agree with you. Messadi isn't exactly burning with enthusiasm to get an English teacher. They had a Peace Corps kid in the *lycée* about two years ago who kept things in an uproar. Wanted to reorganize the school along more liberal lines and even went into Tunis to push it with the Minister of Education. It didn't accomplish anything, and it took about three months for Messadi to get the district inspector off his back. But that's not the real trouble. The big problem is that Messadi's got his difficulty with the wali, the governor of Nabeul district. It's a strictly political thing; the two families are long-time enemies. You'll get used to that after you've been here a while. The wali likes to throw his weight around, and he doesn't like school principals in general; he thinks they're a hotbed of subversion. Half the *moutamed* council are the wali's relatives, and that doesn't help at all. Right now the wali's got Messadi on the hook; he won't even approve his faculty for the fall term. The wali keeps Messadi trotting back and forth to the District Office of Education every day just so he can have the fun of seeing him crawl around on his knees. So you're not the only one with problems. Wait until Messadi can make some headway. And for Christ's sake, stay off his back."

"Yeah, that's what you keep saying! But I've been here a month—"

"Three weeks."

"—I've been here a month," she yelled at him, "and all I've accomplished is a big zero! People are getting tired of me, the new has worn off, and they want to know what I'm going to *do!* All this is a big fuck-up."

"Now why don't you relax," he began, "and stop giving yourself a hard time? You're going to have to get to used to all of it. The weather, not having much to do at first, and feeling pretty shut off from everything. It's a matter of adjustment."

"You know," she said bitterly, "you can get more clichés into a sentence than anybody I ever saw except my mother." But the strange fit had exhausted itself and she felt suddenly tired and shaky. "Let's have a cup of coffee. I think I need something."

"Some other time," he told her. "I've got to get back. It's late, and I've arranged to stay over at Moreau's house down the road for the night. He's got other company too; no trouble to put me up."

"Say, why don't you stay here?" Sharon said quickly. She was discovering a wonderful idea. "I really need somebody to talk to, I really do. I'm serious!" He was starting for the door and she put herself in between. "No, wait! You're supposed to listen to our troubles, aren't you? Well, you just said I had a bad case of the jumps. I might be in pretty bad shape. And you don't have to sleep down here," she said, looking around the dining-sitting room. "It's a mess. You can sleep upstairs. There's two beds up there. I won't bother you," she added, "if that's what you're worrying about."

For a moment Russell stopped and looked at her thoughtfully. Then he said, "Now, I hate to bring this up, but that's not exactly what I'm supposed to do and you know it." And then, before she could say anything, "Besides, I've already told Moreau I'd be back, and old Tewfik is waiting up to let me in." As he moved around her he turned and said over his shoulder, "You've got your dress—uh —caught up in the back," and that was all.

4

God has cursed
his unbelievers,
and prepared for them
a blaze.

—*The Qur'an*

Before lunch George Russell helped himself to two double shots of Moreau's excellent Scotch, filling a fairly large glass nearly to the brim. His host waited until he had poured the second one and then came padding over to say, "Ah, George, I see you like it. MacLaren's, a very private stock, unblended, from Aberdeen. You see we can still get some good things, even now, even though it takes a bit more wangling with this atrocious money situation and the incredible red tape at the *douane*. But it's worth it. Tastes good even with a touch of the damned sirocco mixed in, doesn't it?"

Moreau lifted one long sleeve of the white gandourah he wore and threw it over his arm, toga fashion. "But do drink up, dear boy. Have another. You are the one person I would choose to enjoy it." He touched him lightly on the arm before he turned away.

Russell was somewhat embarrassed, as he was sure the old man had intended him to be. He hadn't meant to lap up old Moreau's whiskey like that, but it was damned good and he had had something of a jolt. For one thing, he hadn't expected to find the General in the house. He had thought the old bastard was dead. Nor the Baron. The Baron, Russell gathered, had been a house guest for about a week, and the General had been trapped coming down from Tunis in the storm, on his way to his house in Nefta.

Or so they said. It always made George Russell uneasy to see all of them together like that. God knows what they were up to. He did as Moreau had suggested, and poured himself another drink.

Well, life was full of little surprises. Last night he had thought all he had to deal with here was one kooky kid over at the ben Omranes' house with nothing to keep her busy and maybe friend Ali ben Ennadji sniffing around, and another kid down in Sousse who had called the Foundation office in tears to say that she was just not cut out for working with the Arabs, that the Peace Corps volunteers in Sousse weren't giving her any help, and the Tunisian women in the clinic were hostile. Judy Hoggenberger had worked herself up into such a state that he couldn't make out what she was trying to say through all the crying except that she had definitely decided to go home. Yes, all the way back to the United States, instantly, if not sooner. It had sounded urgent enough to justify his getting a late start out of Tunis in the teeth of a storm which the weather bureau had, as usual, failed to see coming and which now looked big enough to cover half of North Africa.

So there he was.

He took another mouthful of Scotch and wondered what in the hell he was going to do with these kids, anyway. With this god-damned Youth Commitment Group, trouble popped out like cats from under a blanket. The week before the boy, Wendell Falck, had discovered suddenly what a bloody slaughter tuna fishing could be up in Tabarka, and that had been worth a hectic hour or so on the long-distance telephone. It seemed Wendell was in favor of being kind to all living things, had in fact seriously considered becoming a vegetarian at one time, and was now opposed to all forms of killing except in cases of direct hunger. Russell had had to explain to Wendell that there were all sorts of cases of direct hunger in Tabarka; all he had to do was walk through the town and take a good look at the kids in the back streets. And Russell suggested that Wendell stay off the fishing boats for a while and call him back, collect, if he had any more questions.

As for that damned episode last night, Russell thought he had made it pretty clear to Ali ben Ennadji about laying off and getting all the other Ez-Zahra sports to lay off, too, in the name of Allah and the rich American Foundation. Apparently it hadn't done any good. Nothing was stronger than the fine old Arab obsession with a little screwing, especially when the *pièce de résistance* was a long-legged American *tofla*, gold-colored all over and maybe, with a little luck, even down to the pubic fuzz. *Ah, enough to drive a man crazy, El Rosul, to think about that!*

Still, he told himself, looking down into the glass of Scotch where already the fine desert sand was collecting on the surface of the liquor, he had to give Ali credit for trying. Almost a month was a long time to hold back, especially with Sharon Hoyt swatting through the village and one place and another in her little American mini-skirts, mane of hair flapping briskly against her back, forever plugged into the little transistor radio she always carried with her. It was too goddamned much. The nice soft bottom was a prime attraction; Russell bet half the fingers in the village contracted spasmodically when she went by.

Well, he told himself, all God's children got troubles. The tuna fish they are messy and they bleed, and a well-rounded backside with long sun-tanned legs under it was going to get snatched eventually. The first six months were the hardest, the PC director in Tunis had said. After that the kids begin to catch on and maybe they turn out to be worth something. But only maybe. The first six months they come down on their asses hard, and they're bored and scared and disappointed, and the reality never matches up to what they've expected, no matter how much they've been briefed beforehand.

Also, unless he was very much mistaken, Mees Aweet, as they called her, was getting in the mood to meet trouble more than half-way. It had been written all over her last night when he had gone over there. According to the PC director that was one reaction. Judith Hoggenberger's tears were another.

Russell was considering pouring himself another drink, just a short one, when they all came into the salon together, the old man leading Sharon Hoyt, who was wearing what appeared to be a purple nylon underwear slip about four sizes too small for her (but a brassiere this time, thank God, he noted) and a string of cheap bazaar beads, the General after them with a monocle and an English blazer with silk scarf to hide his turkey neck, and someone new, a very pretty Greek or Italian boy with a bland expression and a head of soft bouncy ringlets. And with the boy, the Baron, stooped and bald as a buzzard.

And, Russell saw, with a start of surprise, trailing behind in the long hall which led around the open courtyard of the house, Madame Moreau, in an ancient, dragging, green velvet dress like the Ghost of Christmas Past. He hadn't seen her in years. Usually she kept to her room with whatever it was that occupied her: books, illnesses, mental trouble. He put down his drink. It was going to be quite a day. He never knew whether to speak to Madame Moreau or not. Usually she came by in her peculiar state of sleepwalking, and once or twice he had seen the whole household turn out when she kept right on going for the beach or the highway.

But this was one of Madame's good days. She gave him a wrinkled parchment smile and drifted over to one of the sofas by the fireplace where she sat down, bent her head, and stared fixedly at the pattern of the Aubusson carpet. The others ignored her. They were busy with the Hoyt girl, calling for a glass of sherry for her, then taking her around the salon and the adjoining dining alcove to see all the junk, the pieces of statues, the peacock feathers, the collections of quartz and marble eggs, raw amethysts spread out on tables, the Punic seals, the Fabergé box, and then finally herding her down the long hall for the gallery of framed photographs hanging there.

If you were interested in that sort of thing you could see them all as they had been in the good old days. Moreau, the famous male beauty of the Paris Ritz Bar at about the time he was changing his name from John Morrow, drifter and sometime able-bodied seaman, to Jean Moreau, professional ornament and house guest, subject of a dozen Left Bank paintings, friend of royalty, forever captured in studies by Man Ray, Cocteau, and others, in spangled feathers and a satin jock strap for a *bal masqué* and even a Nijinski costume as the Faun, in Afternoon Of. And Madame Moreau with the Sitwells and the Lawrences, carrying off both D. H. and T. E. in one swoop (although not in the same photograph), wearing velvet robes then, too. Only in the pictures she was like some beautiful embalmed Plantagenet with dead-white skin and the frizzy piles of auburn hair for which she had been famous. Sebastian Ghrika was out there, too. If any ghost lay over them, it was that one.

The Baron and the General were not represented. They had come along after World War Two.

The Hoyt girl came back into the salon on the arms of the old men, her face slightly flushed and sweating, listening to old Moreau's creaky tales with her mouth half opened. Russell could see that she had finally found something to make her happy, something to tell the other kids about.

He had had his doubts about bringing her over to the villa and getting things started with Moreau, but, he had decided, they were bound to meet eventually and if the old bird liked her (which he obviously did) he could certainly keep her busy. In spite of house guests and the parties which filled up the week ends, Moreau was lonely; he couldn't get enough company of this particular kind. He could have Mees Aweet over every day for lunch and dinner for months before he finally ran out of stories to tell. Maybe they would both have fun. There were lots worse things she could do, Russell supposed. Now he watched her as the old man hovered over her. The long straight hair fell down over one cheek and she held it back with one hand as she listened, a particularly innocent gesture that was very becoming and which counteracted the effect, somewhat, of her usual bratty, free, earth-child quality.

Well, you had to admit, Russell told himself, that Mees Aweet certainly did catch the eye. She was bursting out of the purple dress like a sexy teenybopper and the General was helping himself liberally, when he could get a chance and Moreau wasn't in his way, feeling her up and down the arms and around the waist. In a very friendly way, of course. The old Prussian bastard.

They sat down to lunch and Russell tried to maneuver himself between the girl and the General but with no luck. The storm outside rattled the shutters and sifted under the terrace door like fumes of yellow smoke. The windows in the dining room and the salon were shrouded with old sheets wet down with orange water so that the house was not only dim but smelled like the village citrus packing plant. The girl was enjoying every bit of it: the Arab-style house with its open courtyards, the European knickknackery, Moreau in his bare henna-stained feet and gandourah, Madame in her medieval getup, the two old birds cracking their bones as they lowered themselves into their chairs, the massive Georgian silver candelabra assisted by a naked electric light bulb on a fraying wire overhead, and the Greek-Italian beauty picking his nose delicately behind the cover of his napkin. Every once in a while the khamseen crashed and batted about in the garden and blew something over on the terrace but they paid no attention, only lifting their voices a little to keep the conversation flowing. Madame sat at the foot of the table, but she did not eat. She only looked interestedly at the food put in front of her and stared at it until the others had finished and the boys came to take it away. In spite of the shuttered doors and shrouded windows, the sand seeped insidiously into the water glasses and the wine and showed up like salt on the excellent fish and the main course of lamb ragout. Russell ate his way determinedly, sand and all. Moreau's kitchen was famous, better than any cuisine to be found in Tunis, and he was not going to let it go to waste.

There were seven at table, including the Greek-Italian boy who smiled at everything because he couldn't understand the conversation, and they made enough of a crowd to require all the help in the house with the exception of Moreau's cook. There was Ahmed, the major-domo, old Tewfik, the handyman-gardener and drunk, and the boy, Salem.

Nice boy, Salem, Russell thought, helping himself to more of the lamb. About sixteen or seventeen, as he remembered, and almost as good-looking as the Italian-Greek, but sullen-faced and pissed-off as hell. Something going on. And Salem was making it plain, too. Or at least as much as he could while Ahmed was around.

Russell watched the boy take the platter of lamb back to the kitchen, wondering what was up. Moreau usually didn't make any mistakes. In the past three years or so there had only been two that Russell could recall. The first one, definitely for girls, was engaged to his everlasting cousin before he came to the house. And then there was a smart kid from the *lycée* who didn't complain; he just asked for a hell of a lot more money.

Ahmed, the major-domo, was standing behind Moreau, keeping his eye on everything. Dirty old bastard, Ahmed. He would never write his memoirs—if there was one thing the local people were good at, it was keeping their mouths shut—but, boy, what a book that would make!

"But you are German," the General was saying to the girl. He put down his fork and allowed himself to more-or-less playfully stroke her long hair and then pat her back gently. "So beautifully German."

"American, Heinz," Moreau shouted from the head of the table. "One of our sweet little college girls, the rebel generation. Naughty and irreverent, of course. You'd be amazed at what our youth thinks of us."

"No, I am right," the General insisted. "There is German blood there. The face, do you not see it?" Very playfully he put his finger under the girl's chin and turned it so that they could all see her profile. "A pure German strain. Regard the jaw and the mouth."

They all looked, even Ahmed, and Salem, who was passing the bread.

Now the old boys were having their bit of fun, and Russell could see that Sharon Hoyt was well aware of it. At least she didn't blush or giggle. She had a mouthful of food and she kept right on chewing, looking very calm.

"Why don't you ask her?" Moreau said.

"You are German, yes?" The General said, touching her cheek fondly. "Let me guess—your mother, she was of a German family!"

"Irish," the girl said, swallowing. She broke off a piece of bread and put that into her mouth deliberately. "Irish on both sides."

The General took his hand away quickly.

"What is the matter?" the Greek-Italian asked in French.

"A marvelous people," the Baron put in quickly. "A very marvelous people, the Irish. So poetic and aristocratic. They raise very good horses. And there is a lot of Scandinavian blood in Ireland. From the Vikings."

"Oh, piss on the Vikings, Arne!" Moreau hooted. "American, American, I told you so!"

The General looked extremely annoyed. His neck had turned red. "What does it matter?" he said. "American, then. It is a good time, now, to be an American. The Americans have inherited the earth. What a so-marvelous opportunity, my dear," he went on to the girl, buttering some bread and inspecting it for sand, "for you, an American, to be here at the zenith, one might say, of your country's power. For it is your country, you know, which sustains Tunisia. With the largest foreign aid grant in the world, is it not?" He looked at Moreau, who shrugged. "Yes, well, I am sure of this. Too bad little Tunisia is so poor. Like Israel, it is not such a good investment, because it has no oil. Tunisia has only some oranges and some potash mines and the tourists, and of course the U.S. Foreign Aid, but it is a very nice little country, it is typically one that America would choose for her friend in the Arab world—a very Western-looking little country with a very fine, Western-looking President. And it makes a nice balance, does it not—a little Jewish country which America supports, and a little liberal Arab country!"

"I think," the Baron said, "the whole personality of the President has had a great deal to do with American help."

"Also," the General continued, "one must admit that Tunisia is a little country which has not had the bloodshed and the political unpleasantnesses of the rest of the Maghreb and it does not align itself too much with the Algerians and President Nasser and all those unpleasant people. So with one hand America can feel free to give to their Arab experiment as well as their Jewish one. It gives to Tunisia the foreign aid and the Peace Corps and the USAID program and the new Tunis airport, and America is happy in spite of the so-regrettable incidents when the United States Information Library and the Embassy have been attacked and burned. But then these things always happen in the Arab world. What the United States gets in return is the very admirable, very literary, printed speeches of the dear President."

"He makes very good speeches," the Baron said. "For an Arab leader the President is very enlightened. If you read his speeches you will see how lucid and straightforward they are. This is, for example, what he says: 'We have chosen the way of discipline because it's the way of reason.' That is very admirable. Nasser does not talk like that."

"There's not an ounce of originality in anything the old man says," Moreau snapped. "The French beat it all into his head. He's a product of French training, French thought, French attitudes—he even married a French wife."

"He divorced her and married an Arab wife," the Baron put in.

"Well, one can hardly be president of an Arab country these days with a French wife, you know."

"That is only good politics," the General agreed.

"Don't fall for that bullshit about reconciling Islamic philosophy with Western thought," Moreau said. "Islamic thought doesn't go with jet engines. Just as French wives don't go with Arab presidencies."

"No, no," the Baron protested, "the President has good stature in the world as a statesman."

"Crap. What you ought to know, my dear," Moreau said to the girl, "is that without American money the Tunisians wouldn't love us any more than they loved the French. And they'll turn on us, too, when they get a chance. And they'll kick us out, too. They had the French absolutely taken in with their promises to leave them alone after independence, and what did they do? They kicked them out in the nastiest ways they could think of. They came to the *colons'* houses in the middle of the night, routed them out of bed, and told them to pick up what they could carry and beat it."

The Baron wagged his head. "Yes, that was very cruel, but it was not as bad as—"

"A whole bunch of wog police," Moreau went on, "right behind them."

"It was better than Algeria," the Baron put in. "You must give the Tunisians credit, they were peaceful. They handled it much better than in Algeria."

"Next time," the General said suddenly, "they will come in trucks with machine guns. The Liberation Front liberating everyone. You will see."

"The government says they gave everybody plenty of time to clear out," the girl said.

"Oh, no," the Baron assured her. "I had many dear French friends, and it was not like that at all. Many times there was no warning; the police came and they were told to go away. Yes, sometimes in the middle of the night, which was quite unnecessary. And it was sad for the *colons*—their children had been born here, they had built the farms, the railroads, everything. The beautiful properties here on Cap Bon were all confiscated and then abandoned, that was the stupid thing. The fine pedigreed cows were not milked for days sometimes. The Arab do not care for animals; they are very bad that way. The machinery was left to rust in the fields. Shocking, shocking."

"The Americans bought them new machinery," the General put in.

"It is very sad, this business of liberation," the Baron told the girl. "There is always chaos. And the new peoples, they have not been trained for anything; they cannot do skilled jobs overnight. The country suffers greatly. Here, the Tunisians did not even know how to operate the banks. It was very bad because for a while there was no money."

"They are still learning," the General growled.

"Oh, for God's sake," Moreau told them. "Why don't you explain the Qur'an forbids it. Their religion got in the way, that's all. No Arab is supposed to have anything to do with lending money at interest."

"But overnight all the banks had Tunisian staffs. It was very interesting."

"Interesting my foot," Moreau said crossly. "It was a shambles. We damned near ran out of cash. We borrowed nickels and dimes from each other until the miserable Consul got off his ass in Tunis and finally did something about getting some dollars in." Moreau signaled to Ahmed to clear the table, and the plates were taken away. "Well, that's all water under the dam, now. The *colons* are gone and the American government supplies the money, so the Tunisians have nothing to worry about. My dear," he said, leaning to the girl, "think how lucky we are to be fashionable now and the source of all virtue. That means money. Americans aren't popular, mind you—we can't be, not with that damned Israel thing going off every few months. But we're definitely fashionable."

The girl had been eating steadily, drinking wine and hardly looking up. But now she lifted her head and looked down the table to Russell, and he was caught off guard.

What was he supposed to say?

Russell could tell her that the old boys were putting their case, telling the truth in their own way as they saw it right enough. True, the Arabs had stomped all over the French when they put them out after liberation, but then the French hadn't exactly worked to make themselves beloved during their eighty years of occupation, either. And right, the country had been a mess at first under the new Arab government. Political and economic know-how wasn't something you picked up overnight. But the old President *had* saved them. If he was, as Moreau had pointed out, not an Arab but a product of Western culture and French training, that probably wasn't so goddamned important as the fact that he had made his little country work. Not perfectly, but a hell of a lot better than most Arab nations.

It was true there weren't many foreigners left, but the Tunisians hadn't been as rough on the *colons* as the Algerians and the Moroccans. There were few Italians, few Greeks, few anything left any more. It was the Tunisians' country now.

Yes, Russell told himself, but what in the hell did that prove? He knew the kids had gotten a very gung-ho build-up on the country's struggles during indoctrination, and it was all right; you had to go through that to understand what was going on. What you learned slowly, afterward, was that things changed, but then on the other hand they didn't change. A corrupt middle class had started sucking graft around the corners just as the French had done, only now they were Tunisians. And some things, like the poor, didn't change at all.

Ahmed was standing behind Moreau in his shirt sleeves, his arms folded on his chest. Old Tewfik stumbled past to the kitchen for another nip of *boukhar* and the dessert, if he could find it. You could hardly call them the hope of a nation Russell thought; they had their price written right across their foreheads. And Salem, his lower lip stuck out, jaws clenched in a state of unrelenting rage.

And a lot of things don't change at all. Sixteen or seventeen or whatever it was, and a cousin or nephew of Ahmed's, stuck now because he couldn't quit, because his mother had lost her husband when a dead tree limb had fallen on him in the lemon groves, and had six of Salem's brothers and sisters to support, mainly on what Salem earned in the house and what he could steal without getting caught.

And it's not true, Russell thought, what they say: that most Arab boys that age are that way, and it doesn't matter. It matters like hell to some of them. When the Baron is down, or the faggot cousin of the President, they pass the kid around like a bowlful of oranges.

"—but Sebastian was an artist," the Baron was saying. "One of the great artists of the century. When the house is opened once more the whole world will recognize his genius. It will be in all the tourist books, and the world will come to marvel."

"Sebastian was an old shit, wasn't he, dear?" Moreau shouted to his wife at the far end of the table. She did not look up; she was studying a piece of apple torte as though she expected it to hiss at her. "Cecily always detested him. Once, we were at a party over there and Sebastian was drunk and he came over and insisted on dancing with Cecily, who was dancing with—what was his name? One of the Sutherlands, anyway, who absolutely refused to hand her over—and Sebastian fell into one of his famous tantrums and knocked poor

Sutherland down and—are you listening?—kicked him in the stomach! Cecily was furious. She went positively *regal*. She said, 'I shall
never come to this house again.' And she didn't. She never put her
foot in the place again. Did you, my dear?" he shouted.

They all smiled, and the Baron poured himself more wine.

"I think," said the voice of Miss Sharon Hoyt, "that was a pretty
shitty thing to do."

There was a pause, a rather prolonged silence, and then the old
man turned to her.

"Yes," she said, "and I wouldn't have said all that stuff about
never coming back again or putting my foot in the house. I would
have kicked him in the balls. He deserved it."

Russell coughed quickly, covering a sudden surge of laughter. He
didn't know what in the hell had gotten into Mees Aweet, but she
had certainly cut through the luncheon chitchat like an ax. For
once, no one had a goddamned thing to say. The Italian-Greek
beauty had dropped his fork on the floor, and Salem came to retrieve
it and give him another one.

"Tell me, what is this work you do here in Ez-Zahra, my dear?"
the General said finally. He put his hand on her knee and patted
it. "You must tell me exactly what it is you plan to do here."

"Like the Peace Corps," Miss Hoyt said. "I guess everybody here's
heard of the Peace Corps. Well, the original idea was that since the
Peace Corps is getting so cut back lately, what with the change of
administration and all and getting their budget lopped off, that some
of the private foundations could take over the work. You don't hear
much about it, but the Peace Corps has really sort of been plowed
under. They don't get book allowances any more, they don't get
clothing allowances, all that sort of thing. And the government
brainwashes everybody; they try to get the straightest types they can
find and drop all the others. So the Foundation was supposed to set
up their own thing, sort of like the Peace Corps but better financed
and leaving the politics out of it."

"Actually, that's not the official—" Russell began, but no one
heard him because Miss Hoyt went straight on.

"Of course it doesn't work; it's just as screwed up as the Peace
Corps things, only maybe more so. They didn't have a job for me
when I got here, and I won't have one all summer, and it looks like
I probably won't have one for fall."

The General and the Baron immediately wished to know what Miss Hoyt was supposed to do in the job, and she launched into a recital with full details.

Russell leaned back in his chair and took a deep breath. Damn. Once started, Mees Aweet was a regular little verbal popgun. And more went on in that head than you gave her credit for, as he was finding out. She had come down hard on old Moreau with a perfectly innocent look that had fooled him there, for a second, and now she was starting in on the Foundation, complaining to high heaven about not having anything to do, and in detail. And she had lots of ideas as to just what she could be doing. Youth discussion groups. Nursery school—Russell winced: the Foundation had no plans whatsoever for getting into the nursery school business; that was under the jurisdiction of the Ministry of Health, and they had had enough trouble over there as it was. Organizing a community center. Adult classes in English that could meet at night in the primary school. Setting up a public library.

"Most of the Foundation Youth Commitment Group," Russell cut in loudly, "have kind of a high level of enthusiasm for getting started—"

"I think"—Moreau pounced—"Miss Hoyt should have something to do. She's perfectly right. There's no need to sit here all summer waiting for school to open; that's a waste of her time and talents. And we didn't bring her all the way over here from America for that, did we? We need to get her a nice group of youngsters to work with. That shouldn't be too hard to do."

Before Russell could stop him, Moreau had reached up and crooked a finger for Ahmed.

"Now, Ahmed," the old man said rapidly in French, "we must get a small group of youths for the young American lady here. She wishes to meet with some young people to have conversations so that they can learn more about how people live in America and so forth. You know how it is done. It should be very interesting, and after all it is only a matter of courtesy since she has come so far and wishes to devote her time to this. You must see that they are clean and come from good families and are very attentive."

It was pretty damned highhanded, and Russell wasn't happy. Whatever happened, he wanted to keep Ahmed's relatives out of it. He knew all too well how these things worked. It was the old game of accommodation for the *patron* all over again: you need it, and Ahmed gets it for you, complete with percentage. Satisfaction guaranteed.

"The American Foundation has no money," Russell said directly to Ahmed in Arabic, "to pay for any arrangements. I regret it, but it is so."

"Don't talk about *flouss* in front of me, George," Moreau snapped. "You know I can't abide Arabic in the house. If you start it, they'll all start jabbering like monkeys. And there's no money involved. It's a matter of doing something for this nice child, here. And Ahmed has been told to arrange for a group of presentable young people." He turned to the girl. "You would like that, wouldn't you, my dear?"

"Well, actually I would like—" she began, but Russell cut her off.

"We have to go," he said loudly. "Great luncheon, but I have a trip ahead of me."

"My dear George," the Baron exclaimed. "Surely you are not thinking of making a trip down to Sousse in the storm?"

"Well, it's cleared up some since last night."

He wanted to get Mees Aweet back to the ben Omranes' house before she could get into any more trouble. And he had decided to try for Sousse. It was a crazy idea, but he was fed up with hanging around Ez-Zahra, and the thought of Judy Hoggenberger had nagged him on and off since morning. God knows what was going on down there.

But before they could leave, Moreau insisted that they go into the salon and have a brandy.

"I have to have a little talk with you about keeping your mouth shut," Russell said to Sharon Hoyt under his breath.

"I didn't say anything," she told him, with another innocent look.

"Listen, just don't play games. You don't know the games they play around here; you haven't seen the rules yet."

"Oh, I know those old games," she said airily. She watched Moreau and the Greek-Italian strolling around the salon with their drinks in hand. "They must have been a gas twenty years ago, this crowd."

"Now look, don't let all that wine you guzzled at lunch go to your head. What you're seeing today is a bunch of antiques. Things just aren't like this any more except for a few pockets here and in Tunis. These old birds are still set up for the days when Ez-Zahra had a curé and a Catholic church in the village and all the villas were owned by foreigners and you could go down to town and get a good Breton meal in the *Restaurant de la Poste*, which was run by a great French chef." The boy, Salem, came with the brandy decanter and filled Russell's glass, and she held hers out, too. "And the old Turkish fort in the center of town had a troop of the French Foreign Legion, and you woke up every morning to the bugles blowing down there, and then they ran the French flag up on top. You don't know what a difference that flag meant. And outside of town, just for good measure, there was a barracks of Senegalese like black cats. That's what the Arabs called them—*chats noirs*—and they really hated them. It was a society in which all the mailmen were French, and there was a Greek dressmaker and an Italian girl who made hats, and all the cabbies were ex-stevedores from Marseilles. So don't believe a goddamned thing Moreau tells you, and for God's sake don't adopt any of their attitudes. Things don't work that way any more."

"Did they all get chased out the way they said?"

"You bet your sweet life they did. There was even a pork butcher in town; they damned near ran him out on a rail. It was simple: the Arabs just wanted their country back. Before, it was all French. Except when you had to have somebody to shovel the dirt or pick the oranges or clean out the cesspools; then there were Arabs. The big mistake of the *colons* was that they tried to live as though the Arabs really weren't there."

"Did they run off the man next door, too? You know, Sebastian, the one they were talking about?"

The General had come up behind Russell. "Ah, Sebastian, yes. You must see the house, my dear, if it can be arranged. The house is a mad dream, but then Sebastian was mad."

"Sebastian was *not* mad," Moreau shouted from the other end of the room. "He knew damned well what he was doing; he was only spending Essie's money like water, that was all. Fortunately the old fart had taste. Except toward the last, of course, when he was living in one room with all those nasty little boys. They used to pee in the courtyard fountain instead of using the john. Made the whole house stink."

"I thought," Miss Hoyt said, "it was a beautiful house. I thought all sorts of important people stayed there like the German General what's-'is-name."

"The German General *Rommel*," the General said, "who was to be Field Marshal Erwin Rommel. But you are right; it was a magnificent house or General Rommel would not have stayed there. But he stayed only a short time. It was during the retreat. A magnificent campaign. You have studied it in school, of course?"

"Well," Miss Hoyt said, holding out her glass for more brandy as Salem passed by, "we didn't go into North African history like campaigns very thoroughly. You see we went more into emerging nations after—"

"Not to study the military history? How can this be allowed?" The General turned to Russell indignantly. "But this is incredible. Everyone knows the story of Field Marshal Rommel; he is a giant in military history. What other history is there? You must know," he said to Sharon Hoyt, "what a man he was, how he was always in the desert with his men, always in the front, even though it affected his health. You would not know about desert sores, my little lady, but I can tell you his skin was covered with them. He suffered very much. And so, for a few days he would come to Ez-Zahra to Sebastian's house and rest and bathe in the sea. Then he would go back again."

"My God, she's not interested in Rommel, Heinz!" old Moreau cried. "The Afrika Korps and all that business is *merde, merde* to these children. They detest wars. Besides, they weren't even born then!"

"I was born in 1945," Sharon Hoyt volunteered.

"But you have a book about Rommel," the General said. "You must let her have your book, because it would be very interesting to her. Even if it is a bad book, she is a very intelligent girl and she will not pay any attention to any lies in it. She will read between the lines. Will you not, my dear?"

"Christ, you can hardly call Young's book propaganda. Damned paean of British praise. That is the only thing the English get excited about—writing up old military heroes. Especially their enemies."

"You will read of the foremost General Erwin Rommel," the General was insisting. "You will perhaps take the trouble to find out that this Germany young people of your age condemn now also produced some great men. Not all bad men, not all Nazis. You will see. It is something all intelligent persons of America should know about."

The General wanted the book to be fetched at once, but no one could find it. It was somewhere in the library, Moreau told them. He would send it over to the ben Omrane house if Miss Hoyt really wanted to read about dull things like wars.

"Oh, I really want it," Sharon said. "Does it say anything about Sebastian's house when General Rommel was there?"

"You see," the General said triumphantly. "I told you she would want it. The young people, they are more interested in these things than we think. You must read the book, my dear," he urged her as they walked toward the door, "and then sometime soon you must come down to my house in the desert in Nefta where I can show you also many interesting sights. I am something of an archaeologist; that is my hobby there. You must ask Mr. George Russell to let you come and be my guest and we will talk about many things. I will tell you many interesting things about Germany that you young people have not been told."

"She'll think about it, General," Russell told him. He had Sharon Hoyt by the arm and was steering her firmly ahead. "She certainly will think about it, and thank you."

When they got outside the khamseen was lowering twilight, and they bent double against the wind to get to the jeep.

"Now," he said as he started up the motor, "don't accept any invitations to go down to the General's house in Nefta. You can go over to Moreau's house and visit all you want, I guess that's harmless enough, but don't wander off with either the Baron or Heinz von Lehzen."

"What's the matter with you?" she said, sticking out her lower lip. "It says right there in the contract that we get two weeks' vacation, and it doesn't say what we have to do with it."

"You're not eligible for a vacation for six months, so don't get in a sweat about it. And you keep yelling you want to work—I think we can scrape up something for you to do right away. Even if I have to make a job for you myself. I'll go up to see Messadi just as soon as I get back from Sousse."

"I think I'd sort of like this youth discussion group thing Mr. Moreau suggested."

Russell put the brights on. Getting to Sousse was going to be pure hell. The storm had shut down in a brown fog.

"Now you just goddamn look," he told her. He was busy; he didn't have time to argue. "I don't want you down in Nefta and neither does Cynthia Guffin and neither does Charles Benedict and neither does the New York office. That makes it unanimous. You don't know a goddamned thing about anything yet; you're in a totally strange country here where the best thing for you to do right now is sit still and keep your ears open and your big mouth shut. Which is something you certainly didn't do this afternoon."

As they pulled up outside the ben Omranes' house, she said, "You really like to screw the lid down, don't you? I really thought you were different, George Russell. I knew you were uptight, but I didn't know you were all that uptight."

"Now listen—" he began, but she was already out of the jeep and had slammed the door.

5

O believers,
take not Jews and
Christians as friends,
for they are friends
of each other.

—*The Qur'an*

At three o'clock when George Russell set his
course southward, along the Sousse-Sfax highway, the road was
deserted except for a few heavy trucks barreling up from the desert
with their full brights on, and an occasional clump of muffled
Bedouin searching along the shoulders of the highway for their
sheep. But no one else, except for himself, was crazy or desperate
enough to head straight into the teeth of the khamseen. At the
windswept junction of Enfidaville he pulled off the road to take the
jeep top down before the wind tore it off for him, and while he was
struggling to fold the top and get it stashed in the back seat he saw
a light in a shop across the highway and went to bang on the door
until the owner came to let him in long enough to buy a woolen
keshta to wrap around his head and face. Russell got his sunglasses
out of the glove compartment, although the light was barely enough
to see by as it was, and masked like a Tuareg, with the *keshta* covering everything but his eyes, he made it from Enfidaville through the
long monotonous stretches of salt marsh and gray olive groves that
marked the beginning of what was called the Sahel. Or literally, in
Arabic, the Shore.

In this olive country with its sameness of landscape, the sea on

74

one side and the companion waves of undulating hills of olive trees on the other, Russell was always reminded of his own native stretches of Kansas and Nebraska. There was the same pervading rural quiet— the omnipresent desert breathing just beyond the edge of forest— the same sense of silent people shut away, the same vast and lonely sky. The sky of North Africa was remarkably like the sky of the American plains: an inescapable presence, an awning of driving heat or numbing cold, but always there.

After an hour or so in the open jeep Russell was suffering the tortures of the damned. By the time he reached the city limits of Sousse he was in bad shape and knew it. The khamseen had driven under the sunglasses in spite of his efforts to keep the *keshta* pulled up to his nose, and the sand was lodged in the mucous membranes of his eyelids. But he kept going; he was, he told himself, almost there. No need to give up in the last haul. After a few misses he found the street where the Hoggenberger girl had been lodged in a tidy flat over the Sousse Monoprix, the French version of the five-and-ten, and groped his way painfully up the stairs to the third floor.

Miss Hoggenberger gave a breathless squeak as she let him in, obviously not recognizing who it was. Russell didn't have time to explain. He maneuvered laboriously across a rug, around a low table, unwinding the *keshta* as he went, and got into the kitchen finally, where he turned on the taps in the sink and scooped water up and washed out his eyes for about twenty minutes. He took his careful time, for he knew what trouble the microscopic grains of sand could cause if they worked their way into the surface of the eyeball. He would be lucky enough as it was if he didn't pick up an infection. Half of Tunisia would have septic running eyes by morning. That was the way it usually went after two days of storm.

When Russell finally got his eyes cleared out enough to see, Miss Hoggenberger greeted him with a sullen, "I didn't mean for you to come all the way in this *mess*, for goodness' sake."

She was a dumpy little girl with close-cropped hair, a red nose from weeping, and a definite air of hostile suffering.

"Are you O.K.?" Russell wanted to know. He sat down on the sofa covered with a Bedouin blanket and souvenir bazaar pillows and held his hand over his eyes gingerly to keep the light out of them for a while. "You—ah—sounded pretty upset there on the telephone. Gave me quite a scare. I thought something might have happened to you."

He saw her retreat cautiously into herself—even her shoulders seemed to lift in a turtle effect—and she stuck out her lower lip.

"What made you think that?" she said.

For Christ's sake, he thought wearily. Only that she was having a long-distance fit of hysterics, that was all. And threatening to leave the country.

Russell lay back on the sofa and put his feet up. His eyes felt as though they were going to jump out of his head.

"Well, good," he said, not really giving a damn. "I'm glad to see you've changed your mind about going home."

That was the magic phrase, evidently, because Judy flopped down in the kitchen chair and started to cry with a loud, soggy noise, wiping her eyes with a large ball of Kleenex.

George Russell looked at his wrist watch painfully—it hurt his eyes like hell to try to focus on anything close up—and thought, This is going to take a long time. And in the long run, it's not going to accomplish a damned thing. I've got that feeling in my bones.

He was surprised that his watch said six o'clock. In spite of the storm he hadn't made bad time at all.

About an hour later Judy Hoggenberger woke him by saying that she didn't know who had given the Foundation the idea that the Peace Corps was going to cooperate with her down here in Sousse, but they had certainly been all wrong about that. The Peace Corps kids were really a very limited sort of bunch; some of them didn't even have their college degrees, and they seemed to be proud of being dropouts.

Russell stifled a groan. Miss Hoggenberger's voice was not loud, but it was definitely nasal and a little shrill. He had dozed off, but the few minutes of sleep hadn't done him any good. His eyes weren't hurting so much now, but the pain had spread to a general ache all through his skull.

As for the work at the public health clinic, Judy was saying, that wasn't what you'd call satisfactory at all. Most of the time she didn't *do* anything; she just helped Miss Mejdoub get the babies undressed for the doctor, and as a result she caught everything. She had already had impetigo twice and, in spite of the fact that penicillin ointment cleared it right up, it was disgusting. She never wanted to go back to the clinic again. When she tried to help the mothers in the Child Care class they only laughed at her and asked her how many babies she had had of her own.

"They really don't want to learn anything." Judy wept. "They're not at all responsive, even when you'd think they'd *want* to have healthy children. Some of the babies have sore eyes, probably trachoma, and they won't even bring them to the free clinic to have them treated.

"The worst part is going to see the women who have just had another baby after nine or ten already and trying to talk them into using the IUD, the thing they call the scoobey-doo. What a stupid name!"

"It's a British term," he told her.

"I have this little speech memorized in Arabic about coming to the clinic and having the scoobey-doo inserted because if they already have six or seven children they just can't afford to have any more. But they don't listen. They take one look at the coil and start screaming that if they go to the clinic the doctor will cut the nerve —whatever that means—and they won't get any pleasure from sleeping with their husbands, and if you put the scoobey-doo inside of them it will do the same thing! They even think it will scratch their husbands during intercourse or something. They don't even know where it *goes!* And then they always tell you that if they don't have lots of children their husbands will run off and leave them. And some of them really shouldn't have children any more; Miss Mejdoub says they're so worn out from having babies they need operations to keep their bladders and rectums from falling out—underneath," Judy said delicately, "and things like that. And they have awful varicose veins."

Russell sighed.

But worst of all, Judy insisted, was sitting around the flat at night with nothing to do. She couldn't go out; if she went out on the streets there were boys, just hundreds of teen-aged boys with nothing to do who raced around the street at night in gangs. And who followed you and treated you like you were a pickup.

"The country's got a lot of young people," Russell murmured. "Seventy per cent of the population is under twenty-one. They get a little restless. And as you say, there isn't a hell of a lot to do."

And the PCVs weren't any help, she continued relentlessly. They had their own little cliques and went to the beach every week end but they never bothered to come around and see if she wanted to go, too.

"What we need," Russell said, sitting up and swinging his legs to the floor, "is a drink. In fact, a couple of drinks, and some dinner. No, not here," he said quickly, as she began to look toward the kitchen. "We better go to the Sousse Palace Hotel. It's got to be open—the tourist places never close, khamseen or no khamseen."

Russell was determined to get out of the airless, dusty little flat. His head hurt abominably, and he had to go to the hotel anyway to see about a room for the night. The trip down the hill through the city and out to the Sousse *plage*, however, was another nightmare. With the wind, it was like a tour through a blast furnace of a steel mill and the streets were gloomy-dark in spite of the mercury vapor lamps lining the drive along the Corniche. But the Sousse Palace Hotel, a Moorish castle out of Howard Johnson's by the French architectural team who put up most of the government tourist resorts, stood bathed in Hollywood-brilliant floodlights. The *fata morgana* of the storm driven beachside. The parking lot was jammed with tourist buses. Russell cursed when he saw them. All the holiday trippers who had been on the road had ducked for shelter at Sousse. He knew the hotel would be hopping

It was. There were over two hundred people, it looked like, in the lobby alone. And a line of red-eyed and perspiring Europeans led from the dining room door and snaked past the reception desk and overflowed into the ornamental patio, where they stood patiently ankle deep in gravel and beds of blooming aloes. The hotel was shut up like a box as the central air-conditioning system had obviously broken down.

The dining room, when he finally got Judy Hoggenberger into it, was a hell of a placé, hotter, if possible, than the lobby and twice as crowded. A sweating, surly Arab waiter squeezed them into a corner where they were obliged to share a table with two Swedish engineers driving back to their jobs at Metlaoui. The storm, the Swedes explained solemnly, had forced them to take a layover for an extended lunch. And they remarked on Russell's eyes. Yes, he had been in it, he admitted. He had driven down from Ez-Zahra that afternoon in an open jeep, and as he explained about the *keshta* and the rest of it he could see that they were properly impressed and thought him some kind of lunatic.

"Fortunately, we are driving a Saab," the older one said. His face was as lined as a board of gold fir wood and folded into deep, agreeable pleats when he smiled. "We are lucky to have the fog lights installed on it. They are good for all sorts of weather, including sandstorms."

The younger Swede, who seemed to be in his well-weathered forties, could remember a famous khamseen of the past that had blown for eight days. He had been oil prospecting down near the Algerian border that year, and it had been a memorable experience. After the first few days of intensive wind and record sand accumulation, the camp had an epidemic of *hasheeshet simoom*, the flaring quarrels that sprang from raw storm nerves. The Berber laborers had started dosing themselves with *takruri*, the Saharan form of hashish, to see them through, and the hash had turned them crazy. They had started seeing flying cobras and the vipers of the desert, seductive houris with the wrinkled faces of crones, and phosphorescent scorpions crawling up the walls of the tents. All hell had broken loose. The Swede had worn a pistol in his belt for days until the storm finally abated.

The noise level of the packed dining room made it hard to hear unless they shouted, and Russell was fully sorry he had ever had the bright idea of taking Judy Hoggenberger there at all. But she seemed, he observed, to be having a hell of a good time in spite of it. She was certainly more animated than he had ever seen her, and her face was flushed beet red with excitement.

Maybe, he told himself gloomily, little Judy Hoggenberger was one of those perverse females who didn't really come into their own until disaster had worn down everybody around her. He had known women like that. He bet she would just shine in an epidemic of plague or a major earthquake. And she was just the type, now that he thought of it.

When a waiter in a dirty apron who looked as though he had been recruited from the kitchen garbage detail finally got to them, he shouted that there was nothing left on the menu but couscous. Take it or leave it. And if they wanted anything to drink they would have to go out to the bar in the lounge and get it themselves. The Swedes, who spoke the Sfax dialect perfectly, sent him off with some choice and hair-raising curses to bring some whiskey, and to search and find soup and *entrecôte*, with descriptions as to what they would do to his mother and sisters and all female relatives under the age of fourteen if he was not quick about it. After a long wait they got soup but no drinks, and Russell went out to the bar and brought back six bottles of *vin ordinaire*, which was all he could wangle. The waiter hadn't been putting them on. There was damned little left to drink in the hotel. The Swedes broke open the first bottle.

"In the khamseen, to drink is healthy," they said solemnly, lifting their glasses.

The *vin ordinaire* was very ordinary stuff indeed, they found, the kind they used to supply to the Foreign Legion. A cupful in the morning and it left hair on your teeth. When the main course arrived it was an indifferently fried fish, but certainly better than the sloppy-looking couscous being served around them.

"I suppose," Miss Hoggenberger commented artlessly, "it makes a big difference when you can speak to the waiters in their own language. It certainly seems much friendlier."

Russell was so hungry he had bolted a mouthful of fish and was trying to open the second bottle of wine at the same time when they heard the disturbance coming up behind them. He half turned his head and out of the corner of his eye he saw Norman Ashkenazi plowing through the crowded tables, carrying a chair at full arm's length above his head.

"Christ!" Russell said, nearly dropping the wine bottle.

He hadn't seen the Jewish boys for months and this was the last damned place, he told himself, he expected them to pop up. And with Norman—forever Norman—trying to start a riot, it looked like, by carrying the Sousse Palace Hotel dining room furniture around. From the look of Norman's sweating face, he appeared to be pleasantly lit.

"Hey, El Rosul," Norman was yelling, "make a place for us, will ya, baby? We've been trying to get your eye, and finally I decided the hell with it. Say, what did you do to your eyes?" he said, wedging the chair down in an impossible space between their table and two others, much to the consternation of the *maître de* and a party of beefy Germans on their left. "You come in on safari with the *bedu*?"

Norman's partner, Chaim Dayag, was right behind him, carrying his own chair in the same manner. And behind Chaim, the Arab *maître d'hôtel* was screaming that it was not allowed, any of it, and they would have to leave.

"Tell the bastard to go away, Chaim," Norman said out of the side of his mouth. "Your Arabic is more elegant than mine is."

Russell jumped up and caught Chaim's chair as it wavered over the heads of the German party and managed to slam it down next to his. Norman had left a veritable parting of the Red Sea through the jam-packed dining room, and now all he wanted was to get them tucked inconspicuously out of sight—if it was possible—and get the hotel *service* off their backs.

"They are friends of mine," he told the howling *maître de* in Arabic, which sent him off eventually, with a few backward glowers. He introduced Norman and Chaim quickly as they liked to be introduced: Chaim as a British Jew and Norman an American one, operating a phosphate-jobbing business out of Metlaoui. They both knew the Swedes, who nodded and smiled with pleasure, so he figured he had got it right. Norman promptly pulled a bottle of wine out of his bush jacket.

"Beware of Jews bearing gifts." He grinned. "I see you've already started." He pushed the other bottles out of the way, put his down, and announced, "*L'chaim!*"

"You're crocked, Norman," Russell said evenly.

"Don't you believe it, baby. I'm only slightly buzzed but I'm making the most of it."

Norman, short, swarthy, and with a thick black military-style mustache, was much more the typical Israeli than his companion, Chaim Dayag, who was a six-foot blond *sabra* who could have passed for one of the Swedish engineer's sons.

"What in God's name brings you here?" Russell wanted to know.

"You got it right the first time." Norman said with mock solemnity. He raised his finger ceilingward. "Always on His service, chum. Actually, we got in this morning from one of our villages, a real pisser of a trip in this damned Sahara zephyr, and I feel like I've had it. But after a week of knocking around out there in the garden spot of the world, namely, Bab-el-Fellah, anything looks good, you know? I told Chaim if we didn't get out of our little field of good works and quit eating sand kosher-style, I was going to be ready for the shrink. So against his better judgment, we abandoned the brethren to the scorpions and zipped on in to civilization. Which is, now that

I get a good look at it"—here Norman turned around in his chair to survey the bedlam of the dining room—"pretty bad Karma. The Sousse Palace, frankly, is pure *drek*. But better, man, better than where we have been. Did you know," he said, whirling suddenly on Judy Hoggenberger, "that these Jewish villages in North Africa don't date back to anything we know, like the Diaspora? Hell, they go all the way back to the damned Babylonian exile! I was expecting the congregation any minute to drag out the old Ark of the Covenant and we'd have a trek through the nearest wilderness. With sand-covered manna. But Chaim really digs it. That's, of course, because he's a very strict Hassidic type. I really had to plead with him to get him to cut off his side curls."

"That is not true at all," the blond *sabra* said stiffly. "I do not understand why Norman feels he must say things like that."

"Look at him," Norman said, indicating the other with a jerk of his head. "He's pissed off because I made him leave and bring me into the big city. Chaim is a very dedicated Jew."

"We were in the middle of some work," the blond boy said in his slightly British-accented English. "It was not time to leave the village, not for just a storm. We have just started working in this small place and one must go slowly, you know? It is difficult work. First you talk with the young people because they are the most receptive, they have the most education, and they know that they must leave eventually. And then we talk to the young married, who must think of their children and what kind of future they will have. The old people—that is very sad. Most of them will stay because they cannot bring themselves to change their lives. But when we leave abruptly because of a sandstorm, they do not understand it. Maybe they think we will not come back. They do not have much faith in promises."

"I told you he was very dedicated, didn't I?" Norman said to Judy. He had gotten the cork out of his bottle and he poured wine into her empty water glass. "Frankly, I don't mind selling the free trip and pep talks and the family-living counseling and the whole bit; what gets me down is when we coffee-break for prayers every two hours." He hiked his chair closer to Judy's. "And when we're not praying, somebody is trying to marry me off to a nice girl who's a very good kosher cook and who has a dowry of fourteen beautiful goats. And man, do I ever hate goats."

"It is not easy for these people to make decisions," Chaim protested. "One does not think of prayer as an obstacle."

"Norman," Russell began, "hadn't you better soft-ped—"

"But what makes it rough," Norman said, leaning closer to Judy, "is that when you come right down to it, Tunisia is actually a hardship territory. Don't let these glorious tourist hotels and running hot water and Coca-Cola fool you. In our work we have to cope with not only the problems of the Babylonian-exile brotherhood but also our cousins the Arabs—may Allah protect us!—and the second German invasion, courtesy of the West German tour services. Never trust men in *Lederhosen*," Norman said suddenly, leering at Judy, who drew back in alarm. "They invented Dachau and Belsen, remember?" Norman lifted his glass quickly and winked at the engineers, who were smiling. "I drink to the Swedes, a neutral, uninhibited, fun-loving people!"

The Swedes smiled and nodded and lifted their glasses in return.

"You must not take Norman seriously," one of the Swedes assured Judith Hoggenberger. "Norman makes many jokes, but he is a very able and brave man. And his friend, also."

"I don't understand," she said doubtfully. "What is it they do?"

"They're potash jobbers," Russell said quickly. "And Norman, why don't you try to be a little careful, hmmm?"

"You're kidding. You think this whole damned country doesn't know what we're doing? Actually, baby," Norman said into Judith's ear, "we're Canadian philanthropists. We help people go to Canada."

Russell caught Chaim's eye and read a signal of irritability but no particular alarm. Well, he thought, Norman had said he was a little blasted, but it didn't seem to be too serious. Probably most of it put on for Chaim's benefit. Norman couldn't resist pulling the stolid *sabra's* leg.

And by now, Russell thought, as Norman gazed soulfully at a flustered Judy, he had to take his word for it that there was no heavy secrecy involved. As long as the Tunisian government continued to look the other way, they evidently knew what they were doing. With English and American passports they were technically not Israelis.

"Trust the Swedes to appreciate philanthropy," Norman was saying. "People, I give you the Swedes, peacemakers of the world!" He lifted his glass and then leaned back and put his arm along the top of Judith Hoggenberger's chair. "Are you Jewish, doll?" he said huskily. "You could pass for Jewish."

"Norman has been drinking," the sabra said, looking uncomfortable. "Boukhar before, and now this wine."

"I'm a boozing Jew," Norman said over his shoulder. "A very rare and convivial type."

"You better take it easy, Norman," Russell warned him. To his annoyance Judy Hoggenberger giggled.

"I'm not bombed," Norman said, turning to her. "You know I'm not zapped, baby, don't you? It's just that I'm fed up with this place. And these damned storms get me down."

She giggled again. "Just what do you do, that everybody keeps talking about?"

"Oh, baby, I'm so glad you asked me that." Norman poured some more wine into her glass. "Because actually I have lived an interesting life and I never get anybody who wants to listen to it any more. You see, I have lived a lifetime of extreme peril and confusion in my short years—in fact you might call me the original Wandering Jew. Citizen of noplace. Without identity. Mysterious and tormented. I do look tormented, don't I?" he said, leaning to stare into her eyes.

She giggled again.

"Well, if you want to know," Norman went on, "I was born into a Russian-Jewish family in a German-Jewish neighborhood in the Bronx. Step Number One. Already I got trouble. Then my father moved from the Grand Concourse when I was ten years old to set up a swimsuit factory in Tel Aviv. So boom—all of a sudden I'm a Bronx-born Israeli and I haven't gotten over being a Russian Jew yet. O.K., so there I am, I'm a Bronx-born Russian Jew going to school with Chaim, who's a third-generation sabra. You know what that means, don't you? I'm a poor, screwed-up Yiddish-speaking Russian-Jew kid from a German-Jewish neighborhood in New York, living with sabras who think I'm some sort of decadent Western-obsessed nut, but by this time I'm speaking Hebrew like a native. What can I do? I have to prove something to myself, right? I have so many identities I can't get through a revolving door. So here I am today, baby, overcompensating for my life of peril and adventure by working as a potash salesman and doing a little social work among the Jews here who might want to emigrate to Canada."

"Don't you live in Israel any more?" Judy asked curiously.

"Baby, you must be kidding. I just told you—I defected. I left. I had personality problems in Israel; I just couldn't take it any longer. I am now anti-Zionist like crazy, and," Norman said, looking deep into her eyes and stroking her hand, "I got bunches of papers from Moshe Dayan to prove they don't want me any more. Besides, I'm an American citizen. I'm going to spend the rest of my life getting this Jewish thing out of my system. Starting right now, I'm crazy for *shiksas*. Will you marry me?" he said hoarsely.

Judith Hoggenberger dissolved into a truly alarming paroxysm of giggles, but Russell was not amused.

"Norman, sometimes I think you may have sneaking suicidal tendencies," he growled. "What the hell are you trying to do? Can't your buddies here keep you shut up?"

"What the shit," Norman said, and the corners of his mouth turned down suddenly. "I've had it with this goddamned place. And Chaim's no help."

"It is late," Chaim broke in impatiently. "George is right; this is too much talk here, Norman, even for you to have your fun. And we must let our people in Sousse know that we are staying for the night."

"Do Jewish people really want to go to Canada?" Judy Hoggenberger piped. Her face was shiny red and she looked a little glassy-eyed.

Russell tried to remember how much wine she had drunk and couldn't. He had had a bottle or more himself and was really feeling it.

"Wouldn't they rather," she said brightly, "go to Israel?"

"Shhh, baby," Norman told her, putting a finger to his mouth. "Israel is a dirty word here, you ought to know that, even in this moderate progressive little country. Don't you know no Arab government recognizes an Israeli passport? We got no Israelis here, baby, except those who have been kicked out and hate the place, like me. Chaim's never been there either, have you, Chaim? Canada's a much better country, take my word for it. I love Canada; they got snow there, and it's a healthy, invigorating climate. All Jews love Canada. And the Tunisian government doesn't mind Jews going to Canada so long as they don't go to that other place you mentioned. Canada's great; we got it all fixed up for Jews. We even got a special Hadassah division of the Canadian Royal Mounted Police. They knit bootees for dog sleds."

"Does Miss Hoggenberger," Chaim said hurriedly, "work for the Peace Corps, perhaps?"

Russell was damned if he knew at that point what Miss Hoggenberger did. Right at the moment she was gurgling and sniggering enough to choke and batting her eyes while Norman clowned. Russell said that Miss Hoggenberger was currently assisting in the Sousse public health clinics and maybe she would teach English in the fall.

"Oh, that is very fine, worthwhile work," Chaim said solemnly, watching the girl.

My God, he's interested, Russell thought. Chaim is interested in dumpy little Judy. And he's hacked off not only because Norman is high—or pretending to be—and horsing around, but because Norman is cutting him out. He's on his *sabra* dignity.

The Swedes had opened two more bottles of wine. All of them at the table with the exception of Chaim were getting a little tight, but the Swedes drank steadily, only their eyes and the tips of their noses slowly turning red. They had taken so long with dinner that the crowd in the dining room was beginning to thin out. Beyond the plate-glass window at the far end of the room the night was as black as a *bedu* tent except for a fume of white spray which hit the pane and the light and then fell back.

I'm more than a little blasted, Russell told himself. And goddamned tired. The pain in his eyes and head had washed away with his share of the wine, but he couldn't keep track of what the *sabra* was saying so earnestly, something about since they were now working at Bab-el-Fellah would it be possible to call upon Miss Hoggenberger and see if they could be of any assistance? Would Miss Hoggenberger be studying Arabic, perhaps? He, Chaim, had some small fluency in the local dialect; it was not too difficult in spite of the many Berber words incorporated in it. He had a book on Tunisian Arabic which might be of some use to Miss Hoggenberger.

"Help yourself," Russell said. He couldn't be bothered explaining that Miss Hoggenberger might not be studying Arabic, might not even be in Sousse when Chaim got around to calling. He didn't know what in the hell she was going to do.

Chaim continued to talk and Russell stared at the last bottle of wine and thought: If I didn't have Judy Hoggenberger to take home, I'd split the last of this with the Swedes and then we'd go back to town, to the Rue Général Riu and a place I know, and we'd take it from there. An evening of *maloof* music and a little quiet companionship while the khamseen howls outside, and then to pass out quickly on some nice, comfortable bed.

Chaim wanted to know about his eyes.

Yeah, well, his eyes. He didn't like to think what a damned fool stunt that had been. All for lovely Judy.

"That was a very dangerous thing to do," Chaim said, frowning, "even if, of course, it was very daring. It is lucky your eyes are not worse. I think you took a chance on being blinded for a few days, maybe, after something like that."

"Well, hell, I had to come down," Russell told him. "I was up in Ez-Zahra and there was nothing to do but push on." The Swedes were pouring the last of the wine and their aim was bad; they spilled a great deal on the tablecloth. They were all pretty pissed. One of the Swedes forgot and apologized at length in Swedish, which no one understood. "I had a delay of a day, anyway, and had to stay overnight at Moreau's. The hotels were full up. You know old Moreau"—Russell added cagily—"always has a houseful of people?"

"No, I do not know him." Chaim's face had quickly gone smooth and expressionless. "But of course I have heard of him. And his friends."

I'll bet you have, Russell thought. He held out his glass for the rest of the wine the Swedes were passing around.

Norman had Judith Hoggenberger's hand and was showing her how to count to ten in Arabic on her fingers. The Swedes were talking Swedish and trying to mop up some of the spilled wine with their table napkins.

"Interesting people staying at Moreau's this time," Russell said. "Going down to Nefta in the desert again."

The *sabra* gave him an unreadable look.

"It is out of season for a sightseeing trip now, I think. That is, it is very uncomfortable down there this time of year. But I suppose there are some who will go down no matter what the weather."

"Oh, they like it any time," Russell said carefully. "Any time they can arrange the trip without too much trouble, that is. Won't many be going—just the owner and his friend. And the friend's friend, a Greek or Italian boy."

Chaim smiled a chill, slight smile. "Yes, the friend always has a boy."

It may not be news to them, Russell thought; they may know as much about it as I do already. Whatever their system is, it's damned fast and accurate and doesn't miss much. But probably he's looking for some little piece he can fit in with what he's already heard, that might have been overlooked, because they're still working like hell on it. "I understand they'll stay a while, a good long while this visit. Same old business. Archaeology. Digging around."

There were damned few digs down there, as they both knew. Unless you wanted to chop around the roots of the date palms.

"That is a very strenuous hobby for amateurs, archaeology," Chaim observed. "And not very rewarding, I think, where they are going."

"It all depends, doesn't it? A person could be interested in ancient history."

The *sabra*'s smile became more sharply indented. "Oh, yes, there is some history which becomes ancient very quickly, one could say. And it is a very interesting occupation. One can always hope for a find that is very rich. One always thinks of Schliemann, and all the gold that was discovered in the ruins of Troy."

"But you don't think he'll find anything."

"I? I am afraid I have no opinion." Chaim turned slightly away, allowing himself to watch the waiters clearing the tables, the sea throwing itself at the darkened windowpane at the far end of the room. "It is impossible to speculate about archaeology," he said softly, "and what people will or will not find. And unfortunately I do not have time to keep up with even these very interesting things. You know how it is: Norman and I have our work to do, we try not to—how do you say it?—mind other people's businesses. Because after all, as you must know, we are only allowed in this country under sufferance, especially with what we are trying to do in the Jewish villages. We always have to remember this. It is not easy, any of it. No matter how many jokes Norman makes."

No, Russell thought, it's not easy. I'll go along with that. It's damned dangerous. One slip and you're not only in trouble but you lose your precious Jews, all the brethren waiting to be shipped to the Promised Land. Which damned well isn't Canada. Every step, you have to be sure the Arabs are looking the other way. And they owe you no favors. The only favor you get is the one they're granting you now, to let you come into the country at all.

And, he knew, if the Israeli boys went down to Nefta and ever got anything on the old man, they'd have a hell of a time pulling it off. The General hadn't acquired his reputation for nothing. The desert, it is a very nice place for settling things quietly. You take your little problem out in the evening when all is quiet, and you make your problem kneel down on the cool sand, and then you give your problem one shot right through the skull. Then you shovel the whole Sahara over it. Makes a nice, smooth sand dune without a trace.

As the story went, that's what the Reichsführer of the SS had recommended before Kassérine when there was nothing left in the retreat anyway but the sheer mastery of it and more glory for Rommel. It would have been easy to do, because after all the great General was sick and had enough enemies at Berchtesgaden, and a little accident would have been easy to arrange. But by that time it was a little late; Hitler adored him, and the Reich needed every hero it could get.

But the SS command had thought about it, and von Lehzen, according to the old gossip, was the one who had been proposed for the job.

Norman and Chaim turned down Russell's offer of a lift, as they were staying in the Jewish community in Sousse and had, of course, brought their own car. The Swedes shook hands all around; they were going to try to make it back down to Sfax in the Saab with the aid of fog lights. A sudden sprinkle of rain in the parking lot made Russell get the canvas top to the jeep and go through the struggle of putting it up, not for himself but for Judy Hoggenberger, who didn't offer to help, but stood inside the glass doors of the Sousse Palace safely out of the way of the scattering raindrops until he was through.

When he let Judy off in front of the Monoprix and the door to her apartment building, he told her, "I'll come by in the morning and we'll talk it over. Things will look better then."

"That won't be necessary; there's nothing to talk over," she assured him rapidly. "I'm sorry you came all the way down here, I really am. Your eyes look terrible."

As he pulled away from the curb she ran back downstairs to yell, "And thank you very much for the dinner!"

Russell cursed all the way down the hill. None of this damned youth business made any sense, and the way things were turning out he was the one taking an awful beating. Now here he was in Sousse, a little tight and in the middle of a goddamned khamseen, not sleepy enough to go back to the hotel, and pissed off royally with Miss Hoggenberger's shilly-shallying around. She was, he had discovered, not going to leave in spite of the hysterics and the long-distance telephone call; she just wanted to have somebody come down so she could bitch. She had dragged him all the way down there just for a lot of nonsense.

These goddamn kids and their half-baked problems. Life had been tougher, it suddenly occurred to him, when he was their age. He hadn't had their damned options; there had been nothing much for him to do when he got out of state college except pick out a Nebraska county and apply for a job as assistant county agricultural agent promoting pig-feeding programs and chaperoning kids to Four-H camp. After that, the Army, and damned glad to get out of Nebraska. And then damned glad to get out of a stateside army base after two years, when everybody else had been lucky enough to be stationed in Germany or Korea. One day, looking for a way to keep from going back to Nebraska again, he had found an ad in the *Chicago Trib* offering a job in North Africa for someone with an agricultural degree. Not a particularly exciting job, as it had turned out, not helping to establish communications between American youth and the youth of underdeveloped nations or anything like that, just an agricultural engineering job in the desert with the Foundation, helping the Bedouin dig out and renovate dry wells and raise sheep production enough to keep themselves from starving to death. It had either been that or a semiskilled two-year contract in the oil rigs of Kuwait. He had chosen Tunisia. And it hadn't been bad at all for someone raised on a sharecropper's spread near Table Rock; those had been good years, then, when the Foundation wasn't so concerned with projects that looked good in the annual reports.

He bet those damned wells were silting up again, all those damned wells he had worked on with the *bedu* to get flowing at a decent rate and producing water that was halfway drinkable for the first time in a couple of hundred years. But nobody cared about that sort of work any more. The government was busy trying to round up the Bedouin and get them settled into permanent concrete-block villages in a way of life they didn't like and didn't understand, and fix them up with jobs in the alfa grass industry and the phosphate mines. And the Foundation had moved from decent ag work to archaeology and writing nutty "studies" and now promoting kids.

A few more drops of rain spattered on the window of the jeep.

I might want to go home, Russell told himself. But not back to goddamned Nebraska. That was out.

Of all these kids, only the Negro girl, Genevra Coffin, seemed to know what she was doing. George Russell counted back slowly, surprised that it had been only last Wednesday, five days ago, that he had seen her. He had gone with Miss Genevra Coffin down to the waterfront shed on the Bizerte docks which had been turned into a ramshackle community center of sorts by the PC and then abandoned in the way the PCVs had of taking up projects and then dumping them when their two-year stretch was up. But Miss Coffin had got the old shed cleaned out once more, and she had shown him the four hand-operated sewing machines appropriated from a former dressmaking shop, and the stack of *English as a Second Language* textbooks. Only four of the local women out of an original fourteen had stuck to working with the machines, but they were coming along, mostly middle-aged and with their kids underfoot, but crazy about Miss Genevra Coffin.

Russell suddenly decided he wasn't ready to turn in.

It was raining softly, a fine, dripping mist, when he found a place to park and went into the cul-de-sac just off the Général Riu. Raining enough to make his hair wet and his shirt stick to his back. The bright yellow nail-studded door did not open at once to his knock, although he could hear a record player going loudly inside and a woman's astonishingly voluptuous voice, like glistening honey, threading through the latest love song from Cairo.

Anyone from Damascus to Marrakesh would know that voice, he thought, listening. The singer on the record was Oom Khalthoum, the Barbra Streisand of Egypt. There was a joke circulating in Tunis about the Egyptian passion for Khalthoum which went: Why aren't the Egyptians doing better in the war with Israel? Answer: Because the Egyptians are busy lying around listening to Radio Cairo and Khalthoum and jacking off, and they don't have any strength left to crawl out and fight.

Russell rubbed his face, smearing the dust and wet, and grinned to himself. Tired as he was, the goddamned thing struck him as funny. Inter-Arab humor. The singers of the Maghreb had real gutsy voices. It wasn't the same thing at all.

"*Ashnouah?*" a voice asked, from behind the door.

"*Ana.* Me," he answered. "Russell. Open up."

As he spoke, the rain began to come down in earnest.

In Ez-Zahra the sound of rain woke Sharon Hoyt and she struggled into wakefulness; it was long moments before she realized what was the matter.

But rain—real rain, after so long! She could hardly believe it.

She got out of the bed to close the shutters, and it was raining hard enough to come through the windows and collect in shallow puddles on the tile floor. When she stepped in it, it was warm and wet to the bottoms of her feet and felt just beautiful. It even splashed a little through her toes.

She had gotten out of bed completely stoned out of her mind.

Wow, she thought, leaning up against the wall for a moment and smiling blissfully, it's that freaking hash; I really don't know what I'm doing. And it felt as though it was still coming on strong and would continue to climb and come on even stronger. No telling how long it would last. But she had never felt so beautiful, really beautiful, in her life. It was hard to remember what had happened during an evening which lingered, somehow, in her thoughts as vaguely miserable.

She had gone to bed early, eight o'clock—Cripes, it seemed to her that the sun was even still shining!—because there was nothing else in the damned place to do and she had had it up to there with walks and swimming and trying to talk to the ben Omrane girls, taking with her a piece of Gruyère cheese and a hunk of French bread from the refrigerator, most of a bottle of Koudiat rosé wine, and the book on General Rommel, *The Desert Fox*, which Mr. Moreau had sent over that afternoon by his houseboy. What you might call dinner and a good book. But no better and no worse than most of the evenings she had been spending in Ez-Zahra. It had actually been some dreary satisfaction, knowing how dull and square it was. Judy Hoggenberger couldn't do any better. Or Genevra, with her socked-in obsession with community action work up there in Bizerte.

She had started the book indifferently, intending mainly to get bombed out on the wine and go to sleep without caring about the boiling heat and mosquitoes which settled in the room after dark, but *The Desert Fox* had proved pretty interesting in spite of being all about the military and a couple of wars. Because actually the main subject was General Rommel—or as the dust jacket put it— one of the most fascinating legends of this or any other time. Which rather surprised her, the legend part, as she had practically never heard of him before. However, as it turned out, if you were used to thinking of generals and other military types as strictly paranoid uptight nonthinkers dedicated to whatever kind of military-industrial establishment they represented (in this case, Nazi Germany), General Rommel was something of an interesting curiosity. An independent mind, amazingly enough, working outside of channels. A real person.

The author, somebody named Desmond Young, an Englishman, was obviously hooked on Rommel. Although Sharon hadn't been too impressed at first that Rommel had personally conducted a battle or whatever it was in an open car with shells bursting all around him while his commanders crawled under their tanks or jollied up behind the lines. And World War Two was a kicky little war, especially in the desert, where everybody observed the Geneva Convention and exchanged prisoners and let the Red Cross zap about with parcels and a post office. It was actually sort of archaic when you compared it, for instance, with Vietnam. And General Rommel, although a part of the Nazi war machine, was amazingly human. He called Hitler a damned fool several times, which apparently was a big thing, and made a point of treating Allied prisoners well and feeding them the same rations as his own men and giving them the same medical treatment, and once he even burned Hitler's orders to execute prisoners because he didn't think that was humane.

Halfway through the bottle of wine Sharon thought about putting the book down and going to sleep as she was getting somewhat smashed, but she decided to go on, because by that time it was explaining that Rommel had come from a very ordinary German background: his parents had been schoolteachers, which made them sort of intellectuals, at least according to the German way of thinking, and he wasn't the sort you would think of as a military type at all. But he had been. He had never wanted to be anything else but a career army man, apparently; he had served in World War One and then stayed on after defeat even when the German Army was cut down to almost nothing. That was only the first part of the book. By then the bottle of wine was finished and she was feeling wakeful, not sleepy at all, although a little lit, so she pulled the filter off a Crystal cigarette and stuffed it with the last of the *kef* she had on hand and went on.

The rest was a real shocker. After World War Two started, this Rommel turned out to be something of an all-time military genius, according to the author, who sort of flipped out over the whole thing in spite of the fact that Rommel had been fighting for the other side. There was this really wild campaign in Africa where General Rommel took over from the Italians and brought in the Germans and started beating everybody with lightning dashes through the desert, with really a much smaller force of men. When Rommel was on the verge of capturing Alexandria the *kef* was coming on strong and she was pulling for them to do it, which was, she realized, laughing, really out of sight. Because who ever heard of rooting for a Nazi, for God's sake!

But by that time, as the book was beginning to make clear, there were Germans and there were Nazis but they were not one and the same thing. Especially in the German Army. Because someone like Rommel, who had been a professional soldier all his life, split with the Nazis early and developed a dislike for Hitler which eventually turned to hate. Especially when he found out the truth about the gas ovens and the extermination of the Jews. As a real person, naturally he couldn't go for that.

Because of the *kef* and the wine it was a little hard for Sharon to be completely objective about the book, but it seemed to her that when you looked at it in one way the story was definitely a modern morality play, an example of a man in conflict with his job and his conscience over his country's eventual destiny. Rommel began to see that losing the war in Africa was inevitable not only because of the odds but because he couldn't fight Hitler's political machine at home. And on top of it all, when you began to identify with him, there was the real agony you had to feel for a man who knew the whole thing was a fiasco, that Germany was following a madman like Hitler to destruction, but who felt it was his duty to keep on fighting.

For a while there, fantastically, it seemed there was some hope when the German Army generals had this conspiracy to kill Hitler. Erwin Rommel was going to be head of Germany if the plot succeeded, and the first thing he was supposed to do was contact the Allies and bring about a peace.

The excitement was so great reading about the bomb plot that Sharon felt she couldn't go on without doing something. The *kef* had only brought on a mild high and the wine was waning. But there was nothing in the house, her supply was out, and even though she searched through her stuff on the table and turned out her pocketbook and beach bag, it was empty. There was nothing in the drawers of the wardrobe, either, except a weird lump of majoon candy which somebody in Tunis had given Genevra for a joke weeks ago, telling her if you hadn't actually *eaten* hash and and felt it that way, you had really never had it. The majoon was a gummy paper-covered mess of jelly and nuts that had gotten a little dusty and didn't look too good, but Sharon jumped back into bed and picked up the book and ate while she read. Paper and all, because it was too much trouble by that time to peel it.

Perhaps it was the mixture of wine and *kef* and whatever kind of hash there was in the candy, because the book ceased to be any fun at all after that. There was this ghastly photograph opposite page 204 of Rommel's death mask with a horrible expression which gave her a pretty nasty shock. It came unexpectedly, as she really hadn't thought Rommel had *died*, that is, not in the way the book explained he had. Toward the end of the war Hitler had been hounding Rommel, believing he had been in on the bomb plot to kill him, and General Rommel seemed to realize what was happening. Finally, when Rommel was home on leave recuperating from some pretty bad wounds he had received on the Western Front, Hitler sent the Gestapo to him, and the Gestapo gave him a choice of taking poison or being dragged through a public trial which would prove that he was a traitor and all the other things which Hitler had rigged up.

It was insanity. The book was the truth, but that only made it worse because it showed once again how really crazy the world could be and how things happened that nobody in their right mind would willingly want to think about. Sharon was so freaked out on the mixture of wine and majoon that she was reading and at the same time crying all over the bedsheet and using it to wipe her mouth and eyes so that she could see.

He only took the poison to save his wife and son. He said, "I will never allow myself to be hanged by that man Hitler. . . . I only tried to serve my country, as I have done all my life, but now this is what I must do." And the Gestapo took him away in a car.

She hadn't, she remembered thinking, been so really dragged out by anything in a long time. It was only a book, and Rommel was only a German who had been dead a long, long time, but perhaps part of it was being alone so many weeks in Ez-Zahra where nothing really happened to anybody and there was no real contact with anything important in the world. She had flipped out, she was crying so hard; she couldn't read any more, she couldn't look again at the death mask of Rommel with its terrible expression and at the other photographs in the book—some of them interesting because they had obviously been taken right in the desert there in Tunisia. When an envelope fell out from between the back pages she only opened it, saw there were some yellowed photographs in it, and put it back again. Nothing else was important. She was in a regular crying fit. She bent over double in the bed sobbing and thought, Lay it on them, Erwin, you did good. It was beautiful. The sneer on the death mask was beautiful; it sneered at all the shit that had ever been in the world.

She went to sleep crying, so flaked out she couldn't remember having been that way since reading A *Death in the Family* by James Agee when she was a kid.

Of course it was all, as she was to realize later, a definite reaction to a type of cultural shock. Because although it was generally acknowledged that Rommel was one of the true heroes of World War Two (in spite of the side he fought for) and a genuinely admirable character, what was really happening was that she was finally feeling the effects of being in an environment in which things suddenly no longer made sense and in which the signs, customs, cues, and rules were all switched. And, worse, she had absolutely no way to find anything to do. Rommel was a great guy, but he needn't have set off quite that much of an emotional explosion.

Or so she felt when she closed the windows and shut out the rain which had waked her. Still, although the world had turned calm and beautiful because of the growing warmth of the majoon hash, the whole beautiful sequence of the story still lingered. She remembered the real photographs which had been in an envelope Scotch-taped to the end papers of the book and went back to look at them.

Nothing is seen through a hash high clearly, but she was really charged up with what she had found. It was something, maybe, she would want to keep to herself, but she really couldn't be sure. Perhaps if she hadn't been stoned she wouldn't have thought of it, but it occurred to her that there was only one man in Ez-Zahra who was bound to know just everybody.

. Our old good buddy, who looks out for people.

As usual, trying to do anything while really gassed was so spaced out she must have spent a good half hour just walking around in the room before she could remember what she was trying to do. But it was beautiful. She put a raincoat on over nothing because it wasn't absolutely necessary to get all the way dressed as the raincoat covered everything, but she was halfway down the beach road before she realized she had forgotten her shoes. She had walked barefoot all the way. But it didn't really matter. She checked the photographs and after going through nearly all the pockets of the coat she found them, still safely inside the old envelope. The rain was like a warm dirty shower bath with all the dust that was still in the air, but the mixture was so strange it was really very turned on. It was a long walk to the village and very dark most of the way along the road; a couple of times she must have forgotten what she was doing and just drifted off into the fields because once she found herself standing under an orange tree where the ripening fruit was as big and glowing in the night as golden lanterns. Really beautiful to look at; she hated to pull herself away.

No telling how long the hash in the *majoon* would last. Hours and hours. While it was going on it was superbly lovely: the whole dark, rainy, dusty night was like velvet hands holding you and caressing you and lifting you gently on.

The police station with its broken-down jasmine vine which sagged over the porch and the cement jardinieres with geraniums which had once belonged to some French family was the first house in the village. A villa like that was a pretty strange place for a police station, and the only way one could be really sure was the sign which hung over the steps and said ‎بليس‎ in Arabic. The lights were on inside because there was always someone there, night or day, and just before midnight that somebody was usually the Ez-Zahra Chief of Police, who usually waited until the man on the last shift arrived.

Sharon went up to the porch, deliciously silent in her bare feet, and leaned to look through the window to make sure. The anteroom with the high wooden counter where the village people went to sort out their troubles was empty, but the door to the inner office was open. She moved to the next window and there she saw the Chief of Police sitting at his desk with his jacket off, in a khaki shirt with the sleeves rolled up, smoking a cigarette and writing. There was lots and lots of paper all over the desk; he looked very, very busy. She leaned her elbows on the window sill and smiled at him, even though the rain water was dripping through the bougain-villea vine, plastering her hair down and falling off her eyelashes. She knew she was really stoned and had to be careful not to be caught doing anything too freaky, but it was just great and lovely to watch him through the window when he had no idea anybody was around. The Chief was writing and smoking his Gauloise cigarettes like crazy, and she really hadn't realized up to that time that he had to work so hard. It was a shame, she thought, pressing her nose and mouth against the wet pane, that he kept his hair cut so short, though. Because the back of his neck above his collar was brown and smooth and sort of strong and muscular looking and nice, and his hair was thick and black and turfy, like grass. He bent pretty far over the papers as he wrote. Maybe, she thought dreamily, he's near-sighted.

She actually felt at that moment, standing there in the rain, a valid, intimate warmth for the Chief sitting there inside; it was as though there was this almost psychic sense of relating to him. Some-day, she thought, smiling, she would have to make a real effort to get to know him better and find out what his job was really all about. What he really thought about things.

That is, besides sex.

The front door was unlocked and she went on through and he looked up as she came into his office. She wasn't watching what she was doing and the hash made her float a little, naturally, so that she banged her shoulder against the doorjamb coming in, but it must have been the police training or something like that, because he didn't show any surprise at all to see her standing there at that hour. Only his eyes sort of narrowed. He looked at her without saying anything and then he looked down at her feet and continued to look down at them so that finally she had to look down, too, to see what was wrong. No shoes. She really had to laugh.

"Hi," she said, lifting her hand to wiggle her fingers at him.

Ordinarily that was one of those cutesy gestures she hated, but she was feeling so great she just had to do it.

"It's all right," she said. She was sorry about the shoes because police stations were very uptight places and usually people who had shoes didn't come there without them.

But fuck shoes. That wasn't what she had come to talk to him about at all.

"Don't lose your cool," she said, "because I'm working on something. I've got something to show you."

For some reason he got up from the desk and went into a side room that must have been a bathroom, because she could see a toilet and washbasin through the open door, and came out with a towel.

"I'll just sit down," Sharon said. She lowered herself carefully into the chair beside the desk and got out the envelope with the pictures. "You're really not going to believe this," she said, as she spread them out on his desk.

There were four pictures and they seemed to be similar, almost copies of each other, and very like the ones facing page 76 in Desmond Young's book. They might have been taken the same day and with the same camera. The first photo showed four men standing beside an armored car somewhere out in the desert, and she was pretty positive one of them was none other than General Rommel.

It was the other one, though, that really shook you up.

"Now look," she said, and she hoped she was speaking carefully because she wanted to come on very straight and clear in spite of being almost stoned out of her head. "That's General Rommel, right? But who does that remind you of?" She bent over the photo and managed to put her finger right in the middle of the chest, so he would know who she meant, but without obscuring the face.

He wasn't paying any attention. He came up behind her and put the towel over her head. Her hair was dripping on the desk.

"Hey, watch it," she said mildly. She tried to get him to look. "You know who this is, don't you?"

But he leaned over her, not looking at the picture, interested in something else.

"You have been drinking," he said in French.

"Knock it off, will you?" She tried to throw the towel back, out of her eyes. She wasn't aware that all along she had been speaking English. "It's hash. I only had some hash in some sort of freaked-out candy." She didn't want him to take it seriously.

But as she lifted the towel she was startled to find his face right in hers, his nose only about two inches from her own. He didn't look too great, either. His eyebrows were jammed down and he showed his teeth, exactly as he had done that day of the big row with the policeman in front of the Restaurant de la Poste.

"Jesus, don't yell," she murmured. She couldn't imagine what had made him crash out like that. "What's the matter, don't y—"

"*Takruri*," he said in this very unpleasant and peculiar tone of voice.

Actually, she wanted him to look at the photographs. They were what was important, considering the people that were in them.

But he reached down suddenly and pulled her out of the chair by one arm and got the envelope and scooped up the photographs and even the towel, which had fallen on the floor, and sort of rushed and stumbled her along, pushing her into the side room which was not a bathroom after all but some sort of little room with a chair and a bed in it, too.

"Fantastic," Sharon said. She had to lift a handful of her wet hair out of her eyes to see, but she could already tell how incredible it was. "Cripes, I really am in jail!"

He still wasn't paying any attention to her at all. He began to yell.

"Imbecile girl!" He took her by the shoulders and started shouting so that it really hurt her ears, and shaking her. And as her head wobbled back and forth Sharon tried to remember that she really hadn't done anything to make him jam up this way. Actually she felt very warm and friendly and turned on for him. Only there was something she had been trying to tell him, and she couldn't remember it, with her brains being shaken up like that.

She started to laugh, and she thought, Cripes, it's just like being laid, he's so strong and he's putting so much into it. It's like he's trying to get it all out of him at once.

She wasn't very surprised when he stopped shaking her and began to unbutton the raincoat and pull it off her in a big hurry. It was practically the same thing, because he wanted her hands out of the way and he kept pulling her around and dragging her. It all ran together at once; she was suddenly very, very far out, and little pieces of time broke up in disconnected bits. The light bulb in the ceiling grew and wavered and filled her eyes and head and she wanted to turn away from it but that wasn't possible. She was out, out; she had gone all the way out of sight. The light bulb kept blinking like a strobe flash and then she knew it was because he kept moving in between; his body was moving very evenly and rhythmically and it was happening. They were on a bed, because she remembered a bed being in the room, and the majoon with the hash in it made it seem as though it lasted a very, very long time although she was pretty sure, as these things went, that it didn't last long at all. It was just like being beaten up, he wanted it so much, and it was pretty wild.

He was still saying *uh, uh, uh,* in little bursts under his breath, when they heard the night *boliss* come in, walking around, and the scraping sound of his shoes on the concrete floor of the anteroom.

6

There was the palace
of the Chief
of the Vandals
at Ez-Zahra Gamila,
and the most beautiful
paradise we knew.

—*Procopius*

On July twelfth Norman Ashkenazi drove the old
Ford of the Israeli relocation team from Sousse to Ez-Zahra to tell
Sharon Hoyt that it was Bastille Day and they ought to celebrate by
having a picnic and going to the beach.

Sharon came to the door in a man's shirt and the bikini pants
from her swimsuit, her long legs bare, her hair rumpled up in back
in tangled threads.

"Oh, it's you," she said, and yawned. "Cripes, for a minute I
didn't remember."

She had just gotten out of bed in answer to Norman's pounding
on the downstairs door, but she wasn't so dumb, she told herself
foggily, that she would buy July twelfth as Bastille Day when everybody knew the French holiday fell on the fourteenth.

"You look great," he said appreciatively, watching her scratch her
bare leg.

"Yeah, you're pretty cute, too," she said, yawning again.
"Norman?" When he nodded, she added, "Any friend of Judy's is a
friend of mine. Maybe."

While he was still pushing the business of July twelfth being

Bastille Day, Sharon shuffled into the kitchen and made Nescafé instant coffee, and then they sat in the courtyard between the kitchen and the outside stair, grateful for the shade of the bougainvillea vine which laced back and forth overhead. The day was bright and cloudless, the temperature even at that hour in the low nineties Fahrenheit, and the heat, as tangible as steam, rose from the citrus gardens beyond the high mud-brick wall.

"O.K., so it's not Bastille Day," Norman admitted cheerfully. "It was just a come-on. You flitted in and out of Judy's that night so fast I didn't have a chance to offer to drive you back up here, which I would have."

"I had something on my mind," Sharon murmured. And that was true enough; she had hardly noticed Judy's friends, she had been in such a big hurry to get away. She had had to get the last train back to Ez-Zahra, and by then she had realized what a nutty idea the whole thing had been. You couldn't talk to Judy. She had been crazy just to think she could try.

"So today is my day off," Norman was saying. "Why can't it be Bastille Day for a change? Tomorrow I'll be back in Bab-el-Fellah, where every day is Bastille Day in a literal manner of speaking, so have a heart and go to the beach with me."

Sharon smiled a sleepy grin. She didn't remember Norman whatever-his-name-was too well, but it was great to have someone around who could talk English. American English. And why not? It was Saturday, and she had nothing else to do.

After they had finished coffee she went upstairs and found the top to the bikini suit in a damp lump on the bathroom floor and put it on. The day was stinkingly hot, and Sharon couldn't find the energy to do more than run a washcloth listlessly over her face and get the hairbrush to snag the tangles out of her hair. The comb was lost somewhere in the usual clutter of the upstairs room, and she didn't feel like looking for it. While she was working somewhat futilely with the brush she flipped on the cassette player, and the Rolling Stones came crashing out into the room.

"It sounds good," Norman's voice came up from the courtyard.

"Just an old tape of the Stones. Everything I've got is old by now," she yelled down to him. She leaned her elbow on the open window and watched him sitting at the table below, chasing ants over the oilcloth cover and squashing them with his thumb. He was wearing British walking shorts and Israeli leather sandals but no shirt, and with so much of his body exposed she was fascinated with how hairy he was, his arms and legs especially.

You can really tell he's Jewish, she thought, yawning again. He looks it, being so short and heavy-set, but with those really big shoulders. And all that fur. The Arabs, even when they're short, are usually sort of slender and not that hairy. So there *were* differences. Showed that there was much more to it than just the story of Abraham and Ishmael. Unless Hagar was carrying an un-hairy gene when she got kicked out into the desert to found the Arab race.

She leaned out the window a little farther, wondering how much shorter Norman was than she. He must, she decided, be about five-six or five-seven. Which would make him about an inch shorter than she was.

No, that didn't sound right. She figured he must be about five-eight. Ali ben Ennadji was over six feet. Which was not unusual in the Arabs from the south.

"How's Judy and your friend what's-'is-name getting along?" she called down.

He didn't look up. He had just caught an ant and was regarding it curiously, holding it up between thumb and forefinger.

"Great. What else but great? He's really teaching her Tunisian Arabic, too, the *schlemiel.* That's where they are today—he's over at her place and they're studying Arabic, writing it down like crazy in notebooks and the whole bit. And they'll be at it all day, too. That's some way to get your kicks."

"Don't they even hold hands?"

"Nah." He let the ant go. "They sit on the couch and put the books on the coffee table and when they're not careful they bump knees. That really shakes them up."

Sharon had to laugh. "Oh, come *on!*"

"Listen, baby, I've watched them. If Chaim ever made out with this chick I'd have to come and lead him away; he'd blow his mind. Don't ask me why—I go for girls with waistlines myself. Not," he added hastily, "that she isn't a perfectly nice girl, one hundred per cent nice. A little shapeless, but nice."

Sharon held her hair back with one hand to look down at him.

"Is your friend a virgin?" she asked. "I thought those big sexy *sabra* types tried it out early, in the cactus."

"Chaim was raised in London," he said quickly, looking up, "no matter what else you may have heard. And as for the other—I never asked him. He's Jewish, isn't he? Well, we're all virgins, one way or another. It's a racial hang-up. Hey," he told her, "put some steam behind it before I come up and rape you. We've got to go down to the village and buy some food."

"No, we don't," she said. She took her elbow off the sill and pulled back inside. She didn't want to be seen in Ez-Zahra with Norman; it would mean too many complications. "I've got some stuff in the refrigerator."

Sharon knew a beach that was well away from the Ez-Zahra hotels, a place down highway G.P. 1 toward Enfidaville and past the first *sebkhas*, or salt marshes. It was a beach she had discovered one day while taking one of her usual walks, a small strip of white sand dropping steeply into water as clear as blue glass and backed by high sand dunes. The day was going to be blisteringly hot, but a small breeze was blowing. Norman dropped the picnic basket and towels at the water's edge and looked around appreciatively.

"Lovely, lovely," he said. "A nice secluded spot, baby. Nothing here but sand and sea gulls. I hope," he told her, "you brought me here to seduce me."

"Absolutely." He didn't think she was serious, but Sharon was watching him thoughtfully. It was an idea, anyway. It would be just great to have somebody around. He could drive up on week ends.

They spread the towels and sat down on them, and after a few minutes' silence in the baking sun he remembered something and brought out a package of loose *kef* and some cigarette papers.

"You freak!" she screamed.

She had forgotten all about it, but at Judy's that nutty day when he had tried to come on so strong and invite himself up to see her and she had been so busy trying not to miss the train, she had made some remark about not forgetting to bring a supply of grass. She thought he had acted very turned off by the whole idea, but there it was. He had taken her seriously; he had remembered.

"How much have you got?" she wanted to know.

"Easy, easy." He was trying to cover it, but he was obviously somewhat uneasy. "I hope you're not hung up on this stuff. It's not much, just a souvenir. You were so persuasive, I couldn't resist you. It was sort of insurance to keep from getting thrown out."

"I wouldn't have thrown you out," she purred.

"I don't know about that, baby," he said, eying her. "You know, Sharon, I don't know anything about you—so O.K., I'm not going to tell you how to run your life—but you know you can't keep a habit here; it doesn't work. For one thing, it's against the law, and foreigners with a hang-up for hash or *kef* sort of get on the government's nerves. Even the PCVs have to drop it; the administrators put plenty of pressure on them until they do, or they try to ship them out. If you get a little high and start showing it in public the local people will jump all over you. It makes a very bad image. The Arabs are great gossips; they love to get something going. And this isn't exactly a college dorm out here."

"Nobody's going to say anything. Listen, half of Ez-Zahra smokes. Hash, too. *Takruri*, the heavy stuff. Not just *kef*."

"The hell they do," he growled. "That's the sort of crap foreigners rap about because they don't know what in the hell they're saying. For your information, all the new Arab governments are trying to shake the habit of junk. They want to knock out all the corruption left over from the old days when the Turks and the French liked to keep the starving part of their population dosed and happy. So it doesn't exactly make them hilarious when they see somebody like you setting a bad example for the younger generation."

"Blah," she told him, but she deliberately avoided his eyes. She was remembering a little accident that had happened, and that she had promised herself she would forget. "Around here even the gardeners smoke. Out in the groves. You can see them any day. When they knock off for lunch the gardeners sit back under the trees and light up a pipeful of *takruri* in those little clay pipes. You can smell it all over the place, and it ain't oranges."

"That's different. The country people still hang on; most of them need a little jolt to turn in a good day's work. But by now they've learned how to handle it. Besides, women don't smoke. Well," he said, seeing her look, "if they do it's only around the house. Strictly private."

"O.K., I only smoke it around the house, too." She had rolled the *kef* and lighted it; now she held it out to him, but he shook his head.

"It gives me asthma," he said, and she couldn't tell if he was joking.

"I smoke it in private," she went on. "I just sit upstairs in bed and have a stick while I'm reading. The only difference is, I'm reading and they're doing the wash. O.K.? Besides, it really makes me sleep good, and around here life is so dull you need your sleep."

"O.K., O.K." He lifted his hand in surrender. "I won't argue with you. Smoke your brains out. At least let me bring you a small supply now and then so you won't get caught buying crap, twigs and garbage and goat shit soaked in opium and other junk."

"Really?" She opened sea-blue eyes wide. "Can you really get it with opium here?"

"You can if you're not careful. And don't be so goddamned silly."

"I love you, Norman," she said, laughing. "You really are so straight. This *kef* is really turning me on. Where did you get good stuff like this?"

"I grow it in my little herb garden," he told her.

He looked down at her. She had sprawled back against the towel, the paper parcel of *kef* in her hand. The straps of the all-too-revealing bikini were pushed down her shoulders and the swell of her breasts showed a strip of paler, untanned skin. A deep breath, he thought, and it wouldn't matter. And from the increasingly dreamy look in her eyes, he knew damned well she wouldn't care. He could feel his face growing flushed and heated, and he knew it wasn't the sun.

"You know," he said, "when you've got your mouth open like that you have exceptionally big teeth."

"Oh, you're far out, Norman," she said, and sat up. She got up from the towel, put the paper package under the edge of it, and walked away to the edge of the sea. Norman rose and followed her. "Let's go skinny-dipping," she said suddenly, looking down into the clear amethyst water which curled around their feet.

"Are you crazy? What if a fishing boat came along? And hell, we're right on the highway."

"No, we're not, the sand dunes are in between."

"I don't know you that well," he said with mock seriousness. "You might say we haven't been properly introduced."

"Honestly, Norman," she said, turning to look full at him, "you don't have to *know* anybody to go skinny-dipping with them. You don't really mean that, do you?"

"Let's say you might stir my animal passions," he said quickly.

"O.K., turn your back if you don't want to look!"

She got out of the bikini before he could stop her, throwing it behind her up on the beach. She cut a flat racing dive into the water, and he saw the white flash of her buttocks before she went under. She came up spitting in deeper water, throwing her long hair back from her face.

"Come on in," she yelled.

He followed her more slowly, and when he got near her he said, "You know how clear this water is, don't you? I'm not exactly blind."

She spit a mouthful of sea at him.

"Come on, Sharon," he said, "quit horsing around. In case you don't know it, I'm actually a very serious type."

"Why don't you take your shorts off?"

She looked, he thought, like something that lived in the crystal sea, brown and glittering, her hair smoothed down as wet as a seal's over her shoulders, drops of water hanging in her eyelashes. Her breasts, buoyed by the water, floated before him.

"I better not. I'm getting a hard on."

"Beautiful." She gave a deep-throated gurgle. "You really *are* a serious type." She swam around him quickly and put her arms around his body, pulling close so that he could feel the pressure of her breasts and belly, her legs twining around his knees. "Come on, Norman, take them off." Her hand moved across the front of his shorts and lingered. "Hey, you're not kidding."

"Listen," he said, trying to reach around to get a grip on her and feeling her slippery as a fish in his hands. "Listen to me a moment." He got her arm and managed to drag her off his back, but she slipped and went under the surface. When she came up she was sputtering.

"You don't have to try and drown me, you bastard." She coughed. "God, you're strong!"

"If this is the way a little *kef* turns you on, you're going to have to be damned caref—" he began, but she had already twined her arms around his neck. Her mouth was soft against his, her tongue moving against his lips.

"Don't you like me?" she whispered.

"Oh, hell," he said, knowing it was on his own head. He put his arms around her and kissed her with full ferocity, but she was completely submissive in spite of his roughness, enjoying it. He felt himself draw and tighten painfully.

"That was pretty nice," she said after a while. "I like it with a mustache. And you can stop squeezing me now. I'm getting flat-chested."

"I can't help it," he said. "I don't play games too good, that was what I was trying to tell you. I hope you thought about that, because I'm going to have you. Right here in the water, if you want it that way."

"No," she said. "Let's go up on the beach."

But away from the cover of the water she started shivering and he had to put his arms around her.

"It's the wind," she complained. But the sun was hot as a furnace on their heads.

When they got to the towels he held her away from him deliberately and looked at her. Unlike most girls, she looked even better with her clothes off. In the damned men's shirts and shorts she looked leggy and somewhat boyish, but she actually had admirable full, curving hips and long beautiful legs. Her breasts were sun-tanned but still lighter than the rest of her skin, and the nipples, thrust out tightly with the chill, were wide and palely pink. And she really was a blonde: in the white V crotch of the bikini mark, beige-colored hair curled wetly.

"That's pretty," he said, touching it.

"Let's do it rough," she told him. Her eyes were quite vague and blissful with the *kef*, now, and she was smiling. "And lots of stuff. Anything you want."

"Don't talk dirty," he told her. She was so cleanly, gracefully appealing with her long, smooth body that her words really put him off. "I don't like it. And I don't need it. Just stand still and be quiet."

But she wouldn't be still. She tasted of the salt sea, turning her body for him and then pulling away quickly so that his teeth raked her breasts.

"Dammit, Sharon." He tried to hold onto her.

Her hands explored the shorts, found the zipper, and her wet fingers went inside.

"Oh, goody. Norman, you've got such a big one. You're going to have a lot of trouble getting in."

"I said shut up, will you?" But his flesh was pounding in her touch. "And let me do it, will you? Stop climbing."

He would have preferred something softer and more gentle; he didn't want to go out of control. But there was no stopping her. She couldn't know, damn her, how long it had been since he had had time to enjoy a woman. As her mouth closed on him he suddenly thought of the little priapic statues the *bedu* dug out of ruined cities and peddled in the bazaars: a gigantic organ hung between the legs of a little crouched clay man, ready to tear up the submissive female earth. He couldn't wait any longer. He pulled away from her and took her down onto the towels and they came together with the urgent smack of wet flesh.

"Uh, be careful," she managed, breathlessly.

But he was past being careful. He wanted to take a minute to ask her if she took the pill, but he couldn't even do that. His body smashed against her and she gave way with difficulty, squirming. Then she gave a little shriek against his mouth. He wanted to stop, to make it easier for her, but she pulled against him.

"More, more," she whispered.

It was almost more than he could take. He could never remember making love that way before. The air seemed to turn a bright red and his eyes fogged. The priapic man crouched and drove home, making her cry out. More, she told him. There was no control left. The air and the sky were blotted out; he was not even aware of her face beneath him. The sand beach was ripped out from under them like an antic rug; he wrapped his arms tightly around her so that she could not elude him and they tumbled down through blazing air and heat and away from the towels onto the hot sand and he made sure it was more and more and more until her body began a long, ecstatic quiver under him and the thing which drove him exploded in a shower of fire. When he finally lay still he thought his back had been sprained, a beautiful sprain, spreading and hot and lovely. Maybe, he thought, his eyes closed, he had pulled a muscle.

There was no sound for a long time, only his groaning efforts to get a breath, and then he discovered particles of sand on his mouth and teeth.

"Oh, God," she murmured, "I'm going to be so sore. You nearly killed me." Her hands caressed his back. "I'm even sore now. And it's going to be worse tomorrow."

When he had got enough breath to speak he said, "I didn't want to hurt you, Sharon. It was a damned surprise, that's all. I didn't think we'd get around to this—all of this, right away. I told you I was a pretty serious type."

"Don't make such a big thing of it," she said. But her fingers touched his cheek. "You're really great. I was wondering what you'd be like. You're not," she said quickly, "through, are you?"

He regarded her for a moment. Her face was turned to one side, and she was staring off across the brilliant blue sheet of the sea.

"Sharon," he said suddenly, "you sleep around a lot, don't you? Who else is there besides me? Are you sleeping with George Russell?"

It was as though she hadn't heard him.

"Let's do it again," she said, trying to pull him back to her.

"No, quit it." But he brushed away a piece of red-gold hair that had fallen across her eyes and smoothed it back gently. "You're a great girl, Sharon, you really are. So I'm not going to ask any questions, O.K.?"

"I don't care if you ask questions. Don't make such a big thing of something great like sex, will you? It's only one way people get to know each other. Besides, what is there to ask?"

"Jesus," he said under his breath. There was no answer to a thing like that. "Well, listen, be a little careful, will you? Sleeping around is not exactly a smart thing to do here. I don't care what you think, it's a lousy way to get to know people right off the bat. And for Christ's sake, don't try out your theory on the Arabs; they wouldn't understand! It's a whole different thing for them, is what I'm trying to say. You give some of them the idea you're—well, let's put it this way. Sex is an old and dirty game in these parts. We're in the sodomy belt, to begin with, and then there are lots of other little games that can come as a big surprise to a nice fun-loving all-American girl."

She was looking at him with a very direct regard that he didn't especially care for.

"Cripes, what gave you all these hang-ups?" she said clearly and distinctly. "There's nothing dirty about sex. Are you trying to tell me about anal intercourse, Uncle Norman? And all those games like the one I did to you before?"

For a moment he couldn't think of a damned thing to say.

"What I'm trying to get across to you," he said, when he was sure he had his voice under control, "is that sex as you know it is one thing you can't fool around with in Arab countries. You don't understand the position of women over here."

She broke into screams of laughter, and he felt himself turning red.

"Look, I don't want my girl sleeping around, you crazy chick," he told her. "If you want to play the field, just don't count on me."

"Oh, who said I was your girl, anyway?" she said. "Boy, male sexism crops up everywhere!"

"O.K." He sat up quickly and ran his hand over his face to take away the last of the sand. "Let's have some lunch. I'm hungry."

There had been a couple of cartons of yoghurt in the refrigerator, a bunch of grapes past their prime, and half a bottle of wine. She had put them in a woven mat shopping basket along with a tin of Tunisian paté and a loaf of French bread which they found was still reasonably fresh.

"Jesus, you're some cook," he told her, as they got to the can of paté. "Where's the can opener?"

She was busy with the transistor radio she had brought along and looked up, suddenly contrite as a child.

"Oh, shit! I forgot it, I guess."

"O.K., don't flap. I brought my trusty Boy Scout equipment." He got out his knife and cut around the lid while she watched his arms and hands admiringly.

"Jeepers, Norman, why don't you just squeeze it open? Hey," she cried, "that's an army knife, isn't it?" She took it out of his hands and held it up. "What is it? An Israeli army knife? It's got Hebrew writing on it."

"It's a religious knife," he told her, taking it back. "For circumcisions. What you see there are instructions on how to cut carefully."

She made a face and laughed. "Why do you have to be so funny all the time? You've really got some sort of comedian complex, you know? Listen, I won't tell anybody you're an Israeli."

"That's good. Because I'm not."

While they ate he asked her what she did in Ez-Zahra and how the work was going. She shrugged.

"What work? I've been goofing off, that's all. The Foundation doesn't know what in the hell they want us to do; the whole Tunis office is is really freaked out over having us here in the first place. It was New York's brainstorm, not Uncle Charlie's, man. And George Russell really hates us. We give him acid indigestion. You should see him bringing us Tampax and toilet paper. It jams him up so bad I think it's going to kill him."

"I thought you had some sort of youth discussion group going with the kids here. At least, so Judy said."

"Yeah, good old Judy, she really likes to make things sound big. She doesn't know what she's doing, either. Until Chaim came along she was telling everybody that she was going to go home."

"What's the matter—couldn't you get the Arab kids to talk?"

"Oh, yeah, I could get them to *talk*, that's no problem. But it's sort of a weird setup. The first time it was really disorganized. This old man that lives here, Mr. Moreau, he arranged everything because his butler is related to everybody or something; whatever it was, I don't think George Russell really bought it, but he couldn't stop him. He got this bunch of boys to meet down in the garden and it was hot as hell and full of mosquitoes and the kids sort of came on very cool and far out about everything, you know? And we had this great big beautiful communications barrier. I mean, it's very hard to describe. Also, nothing but boys showed up."

Norman lifted his eyebrows.

"Don't look at me that way; I didn't do it! I can work with girls, I don't have any hang-ups, it's just the way it turned out. They got this group of youths from the village—doesn't that just break you up? 'A group of youths'—anyway, this cool group of kids from about sixteen to twenty. Most of them have a year of the *lycée* or the *école normale* and there's anywhere from eight to twelve of them; they sort of come and go. Including the houseboy who works for Moreau, Salem. Two of the kids speak French about as bad as I do, and they translate for the others. But I really think the others speak pretty good French, you know? I think they're putting me on. I say something in French and they say something in French back to me which half the time I don't understand, and then we wait while they fight over who's going to relay it in Arabic for the rest. It's a gas."

Actually it wasn't that bad, but Sharon wasn't terribly enthusiastic about explaining it to Norman Ashkenazi. The sun was making her a little sleepy and she closed her eyes.

Not bad—but not all that good, either. Crazy kids, no matter who they were or what country you were in, they were always so tough to work with. She had had to fall back on the little skill she had picked up that summer in social work, trying to get the group to open up a little and relax. They had come shuffling into the garden in a clump, looking very resistant and turned off by the whole idea. Not looking at her, but at each other. That is, when they weren't trying to look up her skirt and making remarks in Arabic about it to each other. Exactly like the 127th Street Community Center, the same scene, only with Arabs instead of black kids. "Somebody told us to come in here." Group solidarity working, sitting back on the stone benches in the garden waiting to see what she was going to do. If anything. And who was going to talk. If anybody. That first meeting they had just sat and stared for about fifteen minutes before they decided Salem and his cousin Shedli Zouhir were going to head it up. With Salem very nervous and uptight, probably remembering Mr. Moreau's instructions to keep things going.

Mees Aweet is from America.

That was just great. Absolute silence.

One of the boys had got a pack of cigarettes out and passed them around and they started talking as if she wasn't there and this infuriated Salem; he jumped up in a yelling rage and snatched the cigarettes and threw them into the rose bushes. Then they all started to yell and it looked as though there was going to be a big fight until the cousin, Shedli, put a stop to it and got them to sit back down. Shedli was older, about twenty, and he seemed to have a thing going with them. When he said cool it, they cooled it.

They were all very poor kids, not a middle- or upper-middle-class type among them, which made it very interesting. They wore scruffy white hand-me-down shirts and the cheap black slacks that were sort of a village uniform, and a couple wore white rags Apache Indian style, wrapped around their heads and down over their eyebrows, which she had already learned was the style of the Bedouin, too.

And they all looked alike. No, that wasn't right, she corrected herself; it was just that they all had a beautifully similar look. They didn't look yellow and smooth like Egyptians, and they didn't resemble the beaky Saudis and Syrians. They had North African heads and faces, skulls sort of round and leopardlike with narrow foreheads and wide cheekbones and long eyes and heavy eyebrows. It was a great look, very intense and smoldering, especially in the kids. The ones with the Bedouin head rags were a little taller and fiercer-looking and didn't say so much. She had liked the way the kids looked at once; she had fallen in love with it. They were really beautiful. And she had remembered thinking then, I'm going to make out somehow. I don't care what they think of me today or even next week. We're going to make it go. At least they're young and alive and really beautiful and sort of wild—they're not like the older ones. They don't suck up like the pharmacist in the village, who greases over anybody that can speak French. Or the man who yells at you and is snotty in the Nabeul bank. Or the Mayor and his wife who try to snow everybody with their "cultivation."

"Ask them," she had said to Salem in French, "what they think about the assassination of the brother of President Kennedy. The one who was shot."

O.K., so it was sort of a bomb to drop right in the beginning, a real shock effect, but what did they expect her to start with—how many TV sets there were in the good old United States? It had really rocked them, too. For a minute they had sat in absolute silence, just staring at her, and then they had all looked at Salem.

"Oh, yes," the kid Salem had stuttered, when he finally got around to it. "Oh, yes, we know of the President Kennedy. *Un homme très populaire.*" But he had given the signal to his cousin Shedli, the cool one, for help.

"Listen," Sharon had said, "we can talk about Sirhan Sirhan. I want you to."

She had just wanted to let them know that any discussion they were going to have was supposed to be very open and free, but they had come off the benches yelling and swinging their arms and for a moment she had the distinct idea they were going to have a riot. Right there in old Mr. Moreau's rose garden. But they only wanted to yell. And all of them suddenly able to speak a little French.

"It was a bad thing—"

Whoever had said that was a fink; they shouted him down.

"He didn't do it alone."

That was a crazy thing—they kept insisting that Sirhan Sirhan didn't do it alone. You will see, they kept saying, they told him what to do.

They who?

There were so many of them shouting at once she couldn't follow it.

"To show the world; you will see, there will be others!"

"To make the world see that the Arabs—"

"Do you know the *fedayeen?* Do you know what they are doing?"

It had been a whole new thing. Mentally she was absorbing it all with a sort of shock because it wasn't what you heard in New York, it was like nothing they had ever touched in indoctrination, it was crazy and fantastic, and yet it might be true. But Salem and the cousin, Shedli, were frantically trying to get them all to sit back down and have the nice conversation about televisions and refrigerator production in the nice United States.

But it was too late for that. The discussions in the youth discussion group were never going to go that way at all.

"Maybe I can do something with it," Sharon said, yawning. "Who knows? I really want to get inside their heads, though. I don't want to crap around with the old Establishment line; that's a waste of time. It bores me and it bores the shit out of them. Hey," she said suddenly, "did you notice these grapes are sort of putrid? I mean, sort of rotted."

"Only after I ate about half," Norman said, lying back on the sand and stretching out comfortably. "You mesmerize me, baby. I was watching you and I didn't know what I was doing. But I can tell you one thing—my mother would never look after me this way."

"You can say that again," she said, leaning over him.

When they got back to the ben Omranes' house Norman carried the picnic basket into the kitchen and she went upstairs and got the book and the envelope with the photographs in it, because the whole thing still bugged her and she wanted to see what his reaction would be. She had to return *The Desert Fox* to Moreau pretty soon, but she hadn't found the answer to any of her questions.

"Look, Norman, here's a book about General Rommel. You know about Rommel, don't you? World War Two and the fighting in the desert around here and all that?" She opened the book to the photographs on page 76 which showed General Rommel of the Afrika Korps and somebody identified as General Speidel reading a map, with another German officer in the background. Under that photo there was a whole page of Rommel and Captain Aldinger in peaked Wehrmacht caps and other very German-looking types. Then she put the envelope on the table and took out the real photographs. You could see that they were identical, that they had probably been taken the same day, at the same spot in the desert. "It's old Mr. Moreau's book; he lent it to me. But I found this envelope where somebody had sealed it with Scotch tape and the Scotch tape had come loose and folded back, so that it stuck to the page. And even when you held the book up it wouldn't fall out. I had to peel it off the page. I guess somebody put it in there and forgot to take it out and then looked for it later, maybe, and couldn't find it. But listen, I need to know something—do you know the man they call the General? I met him once and he's really a freaky type, von Lehzen?"

"Never met him."

"Oh, come on, Norman, you know him. He's an old German Nazi or something. There can't be too many of them around."

In spite of his words, Norman seemed quite interested. He turned on the overhead light despite the bright afternoon sun and drew a chair up to the table, sat down, and looked at the photos she had pulled out of the envelope until he had them all spread out in front of him. Then he went back over them carefully.

"That's General Rommel, isn't it?" She held the book up for him to compare the photographs with the book's pictures. "They're practically the same; it looks almost like the same day and place, but with sort of slightly different people arranged in each one. That *is* Rommel, isn't it?"

"It looks like it," Norman commented. "It certainly does."

"O.K., you know more about World War Two than I do. Is it true that Rommel really wasn't a Nazi, that he was more like what you might call a professional army type? And that he ended up hating Hitler and all that jazz?"

"They were all Nazis," he said, holding a picture up to the light. He turned it over and examined the back of it.

"There's no writing on the back, I checked. Oh, Norman, you're so goddamned Jewish! You really ought to read this book. Rommel was really a very groovy person for a military type; they even wanted to make him President of Germany or something after they bombed Hitler. Only naturally it didn't work out. Even so, the Gestapo made him take poison because he was so anti-Nazi."

"He was only doing what he was told," Norman said evenly.

"Oh, crap. You know, you're really incredibly bigoted. It's too bad you don't know von Lehzen. Because I'm sure that's him in the picture you're holding."

"Since I don't know him, I can't say."

"But wouldn't it be out of sight if it was? I wonder if he's trying to hide it, that he was here with Rommel? Also, look—he's not wearing the same type of uniform as the others. It's sort of different. Do you know what that is?"

"Looks like SS."

"What's SS, for God's sake?"

"Forget it," Norman said quickly. "It's probably not."

"Oh, knock it off, Norman, you don't have to play cool with me. What's SS? If you don't tell me, I can always look it up in the Foundation library."

"Ask somebody else. I wasn't around then. Or if I was, I was playing ringalevio on the Concourse. Actually, I remember very little about World War Two from personal experience. Like, I was about three or four years old when the war ended." He tilted the chair back on its legs to look up at her. "Have you got a camera?"

"Nothing great. Just an Instamatic."

"Go get it, will you?"

She went upstairs, and when she came down she said, "What do you want it for?"

"Good, it's got a flash attachment." He took a picture of her before she could say anything, and she was half blinded by the flash. "Just a little souvenir of a lovely day," he said. "I meet this beautiful chick in Sousse who's a friend of a friend's friend and I think maybe I'll drop by and pay my respects and the next thing I know I'm making love to her on a beach. I never knew the world could be so good. I'm beginning to enjoy life, baby, thanks to you. I'm going to love it here in this great, progressive little country."

"You're a bastard, Norman, you really are," she said covering her eyes. "At least you could have warned me! I'm seeing green spots, now. Cripes."

"And a couple of General Rommel, just for luck," she heard him say.

He sat the photograph on end against the empty flower vase in the middle of the table and crouched down and took three careful pictures, winding the film rapidly.

"You *do* know the General," she accused him.

"Doll, I couldn't pick him out of a crowd if my life depended on it. I'm the enforcer, not the finger man."

"Very funny. You're a real gas, Norman. You really think you're a comedian, don't you? But you don't have to fake it, I know you wanted my camera. You're taking all those pictures of the people in the photograph for the Israeli Army or something. But you're wasting your time—I'll bet they're all dead, anyway. I know the Irgun or somebody goes around looking for old Nazis. I'm not exactly a pinhead, you know."

"The Irgun is dead, sweetheart. They operated against the British."

He wound up the camera until all the film was in the cartridge; then he opened the back and took out the plastic case and slipped it into the pocket of his shorts.

"Baby, you amaze me," he said, opening the door. "Forget I said anything. Forget everything until I get back. Forget the SS and stick to the youth discussions, huh? Don't go around looking for trouble."

When they left the beach, carrying the picnic basket and towels up to Norman's old Ford parked at the edge of the highway, Salem slid down from the crest of the sand dune which had been hiding him and kept sliding until he rolled into the hollow at the bottom filled with stiff beach grass. The dune grass was tall and waved over his head and he dug his fingers into the stalks, trying not to touch himself. In spite of what he had seen he did not want to give way to his own body; since he had worked in Monsieur Moreau's house he had grown to detest his own flesh and did not like—nor did not need to—touch any part of it, because that was taken care of in the house of Moreau to the point of sickness.

But this day it was impossible to hold back. He had come upon them from the highway at the moment the girl had left the water naked, and at first he had been only curious to see who it was. He had heard the voices on the small piece of beach that was used only by the *bedu* and even then he could not believe his own eyes. It was as though the sun had dazzled them and he had walked too far in the heat. But his eyes were not deceiving him, it was no trick of light and air; it was truly the American girl coming out of the shallow sea in the brightness of full day. A picture of her hung in his mind; he could see it clearly when he closed his eyes: the American Mees

Aweet astonishingly, unbelievably naked, brown all over except for a pale triangle where he could see her sex like a narrow slit as she walked. The hair there was a pale gold color like wheat.

Then, astonishingly, the girl put her body against the man's and did certain things to him so that he seized her and put her down on the towels spread for them, and he took her there in the bright sun on the little beach for anyone to see that could come wandering by, like himself. As he had wandered along between Enfidaville and Ez-Zahra on the highway. He could not take his eyes away from them; it was a madness. He had only seen a man and woman making love together twice in his life, and both times it had been dark and unclear: once through an uncurtained window, and once his own mother and father together on the bed, remembered dimly. But now he was seeing it all in the bright burning madness of the afternoon when the sun was high, the man putting his hands under the body of the American girl, to lift her, and thrusting at her violently, then this shudder and her small cry.

He remembered that he had started shaking all over, that the sand had poured from between his fingers as he clutched at it and he thought he would slide from the crest of the dune. His mouth was dry, his eyes burned in his head because he saw everything so clearly. He would never forget it.

At the bottom of the dune, in the hollow of beach grass, he could stand it no longer and he groaned and rolled over on his stomach. Now it was coming, his hands would no longer obey him; they were seeking out his flesh which screamed for the touch. He seized himself and it was an act as sudden and explosive as a fit. His eyes shut upon the picture; he thought he would burst with it. Now, and now and now! He plunged and the sand churned around him as he thrashed against the grass and the earth and back again, until the sun and sky met under his eyelids and burst into sparks. He could not help it; he yelled out as the seed left his body.

When he came back to his senses he was ashamed, but marvelously empty and at peace, although he had ruined his clothes. He knew he would have to go down to the sea and clean himself. But when he got up his legs were shaky and he staggered all the way down the slope of the beach like a drunken man. Never had there been anything so powerful. He was wrung out, exhausted, and yet, as he lay back in the shallow water and kneaded his trousers with his hands to wash them out thoroughly, he closed his eyes and saw once more the American girl coming out of the sea in exquisite detail. Again he looked, realizing that there was no guilt in it, realizing for the first time that now this was his own picture, his own property which he could keep with him always. And then there was the other, the man pushing her down and spreading her thighs and raking her powerfully. He could not say which of his mind's pictures he preferred. The naked girl was more his own; he could enjoy her without the tinge of hate he felt for anyone who would have her. He would have to think about it again and again. It was not a matter which would let one alone.

When he got back to the highway he was dripping water, and his cousin twice removed, Haif m'Zali of Nabeul, coming along in his truck to give him a lift to Ez-Zahra, marveled that he had gone swimming in his good trousers and shirt, the only clothes in fact which he owned.

"It was necessary," he told his cousin Haif, because he did not wish to be questioned further. "I was coming from Enfidaville on an errand for my mother's brother, and I was afraid of the heat sickness. I was getting too hot, dizzy, walking on the highway, so I swam for a moment in the sea merely to cool off."

They drove down the narrow streets of the back *quartier* of the village, crowds of children following Haif's truck as they always did for anything that moved, but by that time he was fairly dry and could get out of the truck with dignity and thank his cousin for the lift.

His mother lived inside the house of Ladgham Charchour, a distant relative of his grandfather's; it was an old house, a mud-brick compound with rooms leading off an open courtyard shared by many people. Charchour did not bother to whitewash the outer walls, although the inside of the house was kept clean enough by the forty-odd persons who lived in it. Salem sat down on the doorstep of the room in which his sister and brothers and his mother lived, to stay a little longer in the sun and dry his clothes completely so that his mother would not remark on them. His little sister, who was three, heard him and came out to meet him as she always did, asking him if he had brought her anything from Sidi Moreau's kitchen. Sometimes he took raisins and other things to eat from the house, and his sister always begged for them. She put her arms around his neck and kissed him fondly. There was nothing new in this, and yet he smelled her body smell which was so sweet and familiar—dirt from the courtyard, and a faint urine odor because she was not yet old enough to be careful, and the olive oil which his mother rubbed into her skin—and he began to tremble.

It would never be the same, he realized. All was changed now; he could not even hold his own baby sister, to his everlasting shame. He did not know how he could sleep in the same room with them, his mother and his sisters, any more. Not with the pictures he now carried in his head.

7

The blue sky
is covered
with star flowers;
two young girls
one by one are
always crossing it.

—*Tunisian riddle*

It was generally agreed in Tunis that there had never been a summer like that one, at least not since the French had set up the original meteorological records. The heat advanced with deliberate cruelty during the month of July until finally it hung in incredible readings Centigrade, and the secretary of the American Embassy who converted the temperatures into familiar Fahrenheit for His Excellency's daily information could not believe her eyes or trust her arithmetic; it simply could not be that hot. She sent the Centigrade-Fahrenheit conversions down to Bookkeeping and had the staff there do the figures over again on the machines, and it turned out that it really was that hot, indeed.

Do you know, the Embassy staff said to each other as they came in for work in the mornings and stood unashamedly in front of the window air conditioners with their clothes lifted up, do you know that it never got below ninety degrees last night? And they groaned when they heard the United States Information Services were only working three hours a day, from seven in the morning until ten, whereas the Embassy and the Consulate put in full hours from seven to one-thirty in the afternoon. The USIS's excuse was that their air conditioners were old and always breaking down.

The city, as they grew tired of saying to each other, was just like a sweatbox. A memo went the circuit of all offices warning that a steady consumption of salt tablets could be detrimental to one's health, tempers were short, there had been several more-than-usually drunken cocktail parties in the suburb of Carthage, one of the Consulate's minor clerks had gotten into a messy tangle with the Tunisian Department of Tourism, and over at the USAID offices someone had put up signs which said WELCOME TO DEATH VALLEY and GOD BLESS AMERICAN FOREIGN POLICY, which no one thought particularly amusing. Time was turned crazily around; the Arab help adjusted to the heat by being only half awake by day—sometimes even sleeping on the job—and then staying up half the night gamboling on the beaches at Sidi Bou Said and La Marsa. There was more traffic in the streets of Tunis at 3 A.M. than there was at midday and then, to complicate matters, the Bedouin started bringing in their sheep long before dawn. Something had to be done about the Bedouin, everyone agreed, but of course no one knew exactly what; the countryside was burning up and there were no pastures left for the nomads and their animals and no market in the city, but still they came, these tall, silent people with fierce faces and a look of death in their eyes. One morning in the Avenue de Paris some tribe of the Yussufiya of the awled Ali took the wrong turn in the city streets and hundreds—thousands—of sheep backed up onto the steps of the Majestic Hotel, making a solid wall of animals even the police could not budge. Charlie Benedict had been forced to get out of his car and wade through cursing Bedouin and fat-tailed sheep for two blocks in order to get to the Foundation offices.

In these mornings Radio Tunis hurriedly gave the weather forecast in French and Arabic and then mentioned it no more for the rest of the day, as though the subject was too depressing to repeat. The weather was always the same, anyway: "Fair, southerly winds [straight from that seat of Hell and throne of Eblis, the Sahara] and very hot. The same expected for tomorrow."

In Ez-Zahra, Sharon never managed to get up in time to hear the weather, as she, too, stayed up during most of the cooler night and slept well into the morning. By the time she turned the radio on, the Arab storyteller was well into the day's chapter from the Arabian nights which started at ten o'clock, and the news and weather forecasts were over. Not that it mattered. More than in Tunis, time in

Ez-Zahra was turned around to escape the heat, being almost suspended during those hours of baking silence from noon to early dusk when the population slept, or tried to, and even the birds were silent in the trees. Over the fertile triangle of the valley of Ez-Zahra there was only the steady, complaining noise of the windmills turning in the sea wind, bringing up water from the wells into the cisterns like the one in Haidi's garden where the spill carried it down through pipe sluices into hundreds of shallow earth channels set around the citrus trees. The last thin trickle of water at the very back of the orchard drained into a ragged millet patch.

The opening and closing of the water channels was the very rhythm of time in the citrus country. Every morning at dawn the Bedouin gardeners, in blue denim smocks over their *pantalons* and wide-brimmed straw hats (in place of their usual *keshtas*), came to break the dikes with short-handled hoes and direct the water from one tree to another and then seal them up again, while the *bedu* women in gypsy-colored clothes and painted eyes, clanking with silver chains that served as the family banking systems, picked off each yellowing leaf from the trees and grubbed out of the ground any blade of grass or weed which might drain off a precious drop of moisture, until the earth was as bare and finely grained as flour. Sharon liked to go down in the early morning with her transistor radio tuned to the thumping Arab music of Radio Tunis and stand and watch the *bedu* at work. It was amazing, she found, the exquisite care the Bedouin took of living things. None of the growers used commercial sprays to keep down pests, as the *bedu* women and children hunted down the beetles and caterpillars and killed them on the spot. Each orange, each lemon, was lovingly inspected day by day to assure its eventual perfection. Sometimes, if she stayed long enough, the *bedu* men would talk to her and answer her questions, especially since they found that was a way she liked to practice her Arabic. From them she learned the names of all the tribes (or at least part, as there seemed to be hundreds of them and subdivisions of subdivisions of families and relationships) and how they migrated from the desert to the north to stay sometimes for years, before they returned, perhaps a little richer, to their black tents in the desert.

The *bedu* were always beautifully polite and seemed to be pleased to see her coming in the mornings. To think, they marveled, that she was taking the trouble to study the language of the people and not the usual French! And oh, *bahi, bahi,* they told her, her Arabic was very good. They smiled and nodded. Yes, it was coming along, was it not? Little by little.

Her Arabic, as Sharon knew, wasn't good at all, in fact it was pretty lousy, but it was nice they encouraged her. At least the *bedu* were openhearted and friendly and didn't seem to mind having her around. Perhaps it was the hot weather and the slow pace of the village, or because the newness of her presence had worn off in Ez-Zahra, but the ville Arabs were almost invisible now. The ben Omranes stayed very much to themselves, the people in the village were strictly businesslike, and, except for the regular meetings of the boys in the youth discussion group, she didn't even see Salem and the rest very much. And when she did, she had the uneasy impression that they were in a hurry to get away. It was odd; once or twice she had tried to think if she had done anything which would cool the local people to her, but nothing came to mind. But actually at times it seemed as though she was living in a very peculiar vacuum. She had mentioned it to George Russell, but he had only shrugged, told her she shouldn't expect to fall over Arab friends the moment she arrived, and to study her Arabic and see if that would help.

The Bedouin women, Sharon noticed, never said anything at all. When she came down to the groves it was always the men who carried on the conversation. Their women listened, squatted on their haunches in their outlandishly fancy clothes, digging with muddy fingers under the lemon trees, their faces unreadable under masks of geometric blue tattoos. The Bedouin women never wore veils or haiks, never covered their faces, and in some subtle way seemed to have more than a little contempt for the fat and ugly ben Omrane girls and the flabby Arab women of the villes, slopping along in their rayon-tablecloth coverings. The facial tattoos made them look a little savage and surly. One, the palm tree of Tanit—which George Russell had told her was a leftover from the goddess of the Carthaginians—was a special mark of the tribe which worked for Haidi.

Sharon's early-morning conversations were mostly limited to the subject of the crops. And ah, yes, the terrible weather! There was never, the *bedu* said, a summer like this one in the whole history of the world, perhaps, and pray Allah there would never be another one like it. Of course it was understood that there was never any rain in the countryside in the summer; one had to rely on the deep wells in the earth and the towers which turned in the wind and pumped the water to the surface. This is how, always, one lived from June to September. But this year! They rolled their eyes and grinned at her. The wind, it continued to blow from the south, bringing the desert air and heat with it. Now that they were well into the summer, one could only pray for a breaking of the temperatures, a chance shifting of the wind to come from the northward, across the sea, to bring a little cool and give the trees a chance to expand their root systems and recover from their burns. The *bedu* showed Sharon how some of the leaves were blistered from the sun, just like human skin, as they told her. They touched her arm and then the orange leaves, to make her understand. It was very bad, this drought. They swung their arms to encompass the whole country. Bad in Ez-Zahra and Cap Bon, and also very bad in Pont du Fahs and Beja and many other places. Did Mees Aweet know of the places in the Tell perhaps? The wheat crops were ruined. The grain had not formed properly in the rainless spring, and now what was left was bleaching out like hay, and poor hay at that. Almost useless for fodder, almost useless even for goats, which would eat anything. It was very bad out there in the Tell; there was no work for any of the tribes of the Bedouin, and the flocks were dying. All the men were leaving to go north to search for work in the cities of Bizerte and Tunis, but there was no work to be had. One could see the *bedu* of once proud people sitting on the curbs of Tunis or begging from the tourists on the Boulevard of the President where the Police usually did not allow such things to be done.

Strangely enough, as they told her, it was not too bad in the south, which was always heat-stricken, anyway, and where such weather was considered normal. That seemed to be something of a joke, and they all laughed at that. In their own country, as long as water flowed in the oases it did not matter how hot it would get, for there were still the date palms.

They asked her: did she know the saying in Arabic about the beautiful date tree? the palm, which is a gift from Allah to all those who are strong enought to dwell in the desert, is an example of the desert dweller's spirit and endurance. This is how it is said: The date palm has its roots in heaven (this is the sweet oasis water) and its head in the fires of hell (the burning sun). So it is, all the brown faces around Sharon murmured, sighing, with life itself. The good and the bad mixed together. And life is only for the free and strong.

Sharon had decided that she liked the Bedouin better than any of the other Arabs. She always came away from the groves with her arms full of oranges. It didn't seem to matter that the oranges belonged to the ben Omranes and that she had stacks of them around the house as it was; they were the *bedu's* gifts. Once, when she came down during midday and found them eating, they made her eat with them. It was couscous, a grainy stuff made from flour with a slop of red pepper paste on top which sent her running to the cistern to put out the fire. By that time they knew her well enough to howl with laughter. Ordinarily they would have been too polite to do such a thing, but as they explained to her, now she was a friend, and it was supposed that she would understand. They liked jokes. And they were superstitious to the point of madness. Gradually she found out that the women would not talk to her because— among other things—she had blue eyes. Pay no attention to it, the men told her, it is a crazy, old-fashioned idea, but what can one do with women?

The men might not object to her eyes, Sharon was finding out, but they agreed with the women in their explanation of the drought. The terrible summer had all started with the big khamseen of June, a very bad omen. The great storm had been a very bad sign, one of the worst possible, and it had loosed a very powerful force upon the earth. But this, perhaps, was to be expected, for was it not true that no man could know the terrible things which dwelt in the vast desert of the *sahra?* Djinni and afreets were only a part of what one could expect to find there. And when the wind stirred up the evils of that place and blew it northward in a great cloud such as the *r'hia skhoun,* then such terrors were let loose. And they all made the sign against the evil eye.

No, it was true, the *bedu* told her, and they had proof of it. There were strange things which now lived in the lemon trees, they said, their voices dropping to whispers. Strange things in the branches which had not been there before. In the night one could hear them rustling and moving about. And it was the khamseen which had transported them there.

On the other hand, they said, almost in the same breath, there were things being done to counteract this, for the ulema of all the mosques in the country had announced that prayers would be said without stopping, day and night, until the dread spirits were past. Also, the Ministry of Agriculture had announced on the radio that the government was considering the situation and that the President of the country would shortly announce what was to be done, probably during one of his weekly radio addresses to the nation.

It was amazing, Sharon thought, looking at the ring of fierce brown faces, what faith the ordinary people had in the old President. In Tunis it was sort of a game to make fun of the President and his radio speeches, delivered not in classical Arabic but in the most common idiom of the local dialect, as he gave advice on everything from the importance of washing one's feet and brushing one's teeth daily to how to be a good sport and behave properly at public soccer games. But the *bedu* weren't kidding. The President, hero of the war against the French, was the Father of Them All as far as they were concerned; if the President planned to speak on the weather, the weather had better learn how to moderate itself or at least know it had official disapproval. The same thing went for those weirdies in the trees. Whatever they were.

One morning the *bedu* were gone.

Sharon woke, and it was a moment before she realized the creaking windmills had stopped. The same sort of strange silence that people described when a ship's engines were shut down at sea. She grabbed a hurried cup of coffee and ran down to the section where the Bedouin had been working last in a stand of *mandarines*, but there was no one there. The whole place had come to a stop. Munseff, Haidi's oldest boy, had trailed down behind her.

"They are gone, the *bedu*," he announced in French. Even when she spoke Arabic to the ben Omrane kids, they answered her in French. And Munseff was proud of being an honor student at the *lycée*.

"But *why?*"

He shrugged. Like the rest of the ben Omrane family, he couldn't understand why she had any interest at all in the low-class Bedouin people or of the drudgery of orchard work.

"Oh, it is a thing which has happened," he told her. "In the village the district commissioner has come to inform the Mayor that the government engineers say the water level in the ground is dropping and so the pumping of water must be restricted to the night hours only. This saves water, as the sun draws it off by day.

By evaporation," he added, to see if she understood things. "So now we will pump only at night and there will not be so much work to do. My father and I will open the ditches as required, and Fati will help us. Maybe my mother, too. The *bedu* will not come for a while, perhaps not for the rest of the summer. Perhaps not until the olive harvest in the autumn. If," he added, "there is an olive harvest."

Now who, Sharon wondered gloomily, am I going to talk to?

She was surprised the next morning when the *bedu* came anyway, and for a few mornings after that, collecting at the gate in the still, airless dark of the hour just before dawn. They sat down under her window and waited, listening to the sounds of Haidi and his family getting up, fixing their morning meal, and letting the chickens out, Munseff going to the back garden to turn the valve to fill up the cistern so that there would be water for the house. At the last empty whirr of the windmill, the *bedu* squatting in the road gave a loud sigh. So it was true, after all.

Then they went away in a stir of rattling anklets, the *shush* of bare feet in the dust, and the choking, protesting gargle of a camel being kicked to its feet.

Once Sharon went to the window, but it was still too dark to see them.

The poor bastards, she thought mournfully. She hoped the Ministry of Agriculture and the great All-Father President in whom they had so much faith would see that the *bedu* at least had something to eat between then and the olive harvest. "If there was an olive harvest."

A few days after the Bedouin had left for good, Mr. Moreau sent his houseboy Salem over with a note. At first, hearing Salem at the gates arguing with the ben Omrane girls to let him inside, Sharon thought it was only another damned silly luncheon invitation from the old man and took her time coming downstairs. But she found Salem in the kitchen, silent and shy, studying his bare feet. He handed her a note without looking up.

The letter, in the old man's shaky script, asked if she would consider giving Salem a day's work once a week. Salem had Fridays off and was looking for extra work to do. His family needed the money. Salem's mother and brothers now had no work in the orchards and the family was dependent solely on what he could earn.

But don't overpay him, the note went on. The proper wages for a day's work in the house are one hundred sixty-five milliemes. And quite sufficient.

One hundred sixty-five milliemes was about a quarter in American money. Sharon could just picture Moreau fretting that she might be dumb enough to bust the labor market by paying maybe fifty cents. And making the natives restless.

The old fart.

Moreau had written down at the bottom of the page: "This is Salem's idea, my dear. He seems to be quite anxious to work for you."

Well, naturally, she supposed. Salem was a part of the youth discussion group that met in Moreau's garden; she was pretty sure he would rather work for her than wash dishes or sweep the walks at the hotels. But she had forgotten; there wasn't even that kind of work to be had any more.

"*Je ne suis pas religieux,*" he was muttering, still looking down at his feet.

It took her a moment to realize that he was telling her that he was not religious. That his extra day, Friday, didn't matter to him. He was willing to work on the Moslem Sabbath. But it was so roundabout and kooky, she had to laugh. When he heard her laughing, he lifted his head for the first time and she saw how really beautiful he was, more so, even, than the rest of the kids. A face like a beautiful, hostile cat, brows drawn together in a frown.

"I'm not religious, either," she told him quickly.

Cripes, what was she going to do with him?

Everybody had houseboys; she supposed it was all right. God knows it was cheap enough. And she was a lousy housekeeper. The place hadn't even been dusted since the khamseen, and there were dirty dishes all over, even upstairs in the bedroom, that she never got around to. But on the other hand, he was sort of a whole new bag, you might say: as tall as she was, and he came on pretty strong. The looks he gave her were pretty swinging.

Still, she reasoned, it was a really shitty proposition for a nice kid like Salem to have to go begging for a day's work at twenty-four cents a day, to have to support his family! Maybe she could give him fifty cents and lots of food to take home to his family, if he would just keep his mouth shut about it.

But she found that he wouldn't take it. He understood her offer well enough, but one hundred sixty-five milliemes for Fridays was all he would accept. She didn't know if he was afraid of Moreau, or what it was.

Actually, the arrangement turned out better than Sharon expected. She found she liked having Salem in to clean the house the one day a week; he worked quickly and silently, and he kept the floors clean, washed out the refrigerator for the first time since she had been in the house, and cleaned up most of the khamseen dust. He could, it seemed, do almost anything. He fixed the mysterious wiring for the light in the courtyard and even plastered up the hole in the kitchen wall with a ordinary mixture of dirt and water which, when it hardened, turned into the usual stucco of all the Arab houses. There were a few goofs, but they were her fault, as she admitted. Twice he walked in on her upstairs while she was half in and half out of her bikini suit; the second time he went lurching back downstairs without remembering to give her the mail. But it didn't seem to damage him permanently. One Friday morning he showed up with a bird in a wicker cage, a lark which promptly keeled over and died of heat prostration.

It looked very pitiful.

"*Il est mort*," he told her, and shrugged, and carried the corpse off to the garbage can.

"What happened?" she wanted to know.

"All the birds are dead," he said. "In the trees, they die."

"Salem, tell me—" She really wanted to know if he believed in the bad spirits, too. "Are there things in the trees? Djinni, afreets, which came with the khamseen?"

For a moment he kept his head turned away as though thinking it over, but when he looked back at her his face was scornful.

"There is nothing in the trees," he told her. "If there are noises, it is only small insects and frogs." He used the Arab word, *jrana*. "The wind brings nothing from the Sahara. In the *sahra* there is only emptiness and stones. My teacher," he said, lifting his chin proudly, "in the school, said so. All the rest is superstition."

It was three o'clock, the full blistering heat of the day, when Norman and Chaim Dayag drew up in front of the ben Omranes' gates. The radiator of the old Ford was gushing steam.

"Now you see," Chaim said, "we will have to get some more water for the car. Don't forget to ask this girl if there is a garden hose here. We can't go five kilometers without water, and if we are talking and forget about it, we will be in trouble on the road. I would not want to have to walk for water on the highway in this heat."

"Don't be such an old nag," Norman said. "And talk English, not Hebrew. You know better."

"Does it make any difference?" Chaim took out his handkerchief and wiped his face. "I can't see that anyone is around to hear."

"Never can tell." Norman got out of the car and went to the heavy iron gates and rattled them. But the place was, as he expected, deserted and shut up tight. Everyone asleep. He cupped his hands around his mouth and backed away a few steps. "Hey, Sharon!" he yelled to the upstairs windows. "Get out of bed and come down and open the gates!"

They waited, the heat shimmering around them from the asphalt road.

"Sharon!"

He picked up a handful of pebbles from the roadside and threw them against the blue-painted shutters up there and waited. There was no answer. But after a minute or two a small fat girl about fourteen years of age, barefooted and in a cotton dress, came across the courtyard, ducked under the ornamental orange trees, and padded up to the gate. She was wearing a cotton scarf pulled across her mouth in a dainty show of teen-aged modesty, but she grinned like a fat Cheshire cat.

"May your day be blessed," Norman said formally in Arabic.

"May your day be fortunate, also," she shot back. It was the right response, but she was giggling with every syllable.

"I wish to see the American lady, Mees Aweet. Is she at home?"

More idiot giggles. "Who wishes to know, please?"

None of your damned business, fatty, Norman said to himself.

"I am Mees Aweet's friend. You have seen me before."

"Oh, yes." Her eyes took him in, unimpressed. "Well, she is not at home."

When did she expect Mees Aweet to return?

Who knows? Mees Aweet did not leave messages; she came and went as she pleased. The fat girl waited by the gate, still curious, but Norman got back in the car with Chaim and lit a cigarette. She watched them for a while with the unblinking stare of small Arab females; then the sun became too uncomfortable and she turned and waddled off across the courtyard and into the house.

"She's not there," Norman told Chaim, "but I want to wait a while. If you don't want to wait out here in the heat, we could go across the road to the hotel and have a drink in the bar."

But Chaim looked at his wrist watch. "No, I do not want to go into the bar. We had better go on now, Norman; it will be late when we get to Tunis. Let us stop in the village and get some water for the car and some petrol. Besides," he added, "I am not in favor of giving this girl her pictures today. Why do we not wait a little longer? Why must we give them to her at all? I think you should tell her the films were ruined in processing."

"You don't know this chick. I don't think she'd buy that."

Chaim gave a small groan.

"Why does it have to be this girl who finds any pictures which might be important? I understand she is extremely neurotic. She will cause trouble, I am warning you. This is the first time we are close to making an identification after all these years, and it is a disaster to find this girl in any way involved. I do not like it. I do not know who this von Lehzen really is, but the uniform he is wearing is of the Waffen SS, and they answered to Himmler."

"How can I forget it? Look, Chaim, don't be so goddamned obsessed with this thing, will you? Nothing's happened yet; we just have some nice pictures, that's all. We'll give the girl back her film and I'll make sure it cancels out. I'll spill coffee on it. I'll accidentally set fire to the pictures with my cigar. What's the big sweat? You've got the negatives, haven't you?"

"Yes, but that is another thing. Suppose she asks about the negatives also?"

"I'll tell her I forgot them, and that I'll bring them another time."

"No," Chaim said stubbornly. "We must keep the photographs and the negatives at least until we get to Tunis and see what Michel says. If we are lucky, perhaps Michel can make an identification. He has a head full of pictures; that is what he is here for. If Michel can make an identification and get it cleared, then it will all move very fast and we will not have time to see Miss Hoyt again at all. That would solve many problems," he added hopefully.

"Don't be a nut, will you? Nothing's going to move that fast. I don't care if Michel's got a complete ID. I'm in charge; I call the shots. I'm in favor of keeping Miss Hoyt happy until we know what we are going to do."

"You must talk to Michel first, Norman. He is the base, he made the arrangements for the car, he has been there longer than anyone, and he will know better what to do. And David has arranged for the arms. I think we should have a conference with David and Michel in Tunis and ask their advice."

"Forget it. We don't have to have a conference with anyone. The less David and Michel know, the better, at this point. I'll take care of the girl—I'll even pinch them back from her, if necessary. But I'll do something."

Chaim gave a loud sniff. "Do you think then, Norman, that you can keep her so interested that she will not have time to think of other things?"

Norman's teeth flashed under the thick mustache.

"Chaim, baby, you overestimate me. I couldn't keep this girl that occupied if my life depended on it. The *shiksa* is dynamite. If I threw myself in her path body and soul, I wouldn't have any energy left even to write the folks back in Tel Aviv. But," he added, "I regret that I have but one life to give for my country. I can make the ultimate sacrifice, can't I?"

"You are not being serious," Chaim said severely.

"Oh, for Christ's sake, lay off, will you? You're so goddamned single-minded."

Norman stared through the windshield of the car at the gates of the ben Omrane house, then bent forward to look up at the blue-shuttered windows on the second floor.

"I wish she were here," he muttered. "With this thing, we're going to have to play it by ear. And man, do I hate to do that."

Ordinarily the train trip from Ez-Zahra to Tunis took a little over two hours. The government timetable listed the journey from Nabeul to Ez-Zahra to the junction at Bir Bou Rekba and from there to the terminal in Tunis as one hour and forty minutes, but this was well known as an optimistic estimate, a hopeful goal which even in the days of the French had seldom been attained. On the Saturday Sharon started for Tunis to see Genevra Coffin and hunt up some information on the SS in the Foundation library, the connector which ran from Nabeul to Ez-Zahra was late, and then at Bir Bou Rekba the mixed crowd of Arab farmers with their baskets of produce, women in haiks with children going to the movies or to visit relatives, and sweating tourists from the hotels stood by the tracks in the listless heat of morning waiting to transfer to the northbound express for the better part of an hour. The news at the junction was that the continuing heat of the drought had warped the iron rails and caused damage to the track beds in the south; when the express at last came limping in behind a repair engine, its sick and exhausted passengers were hanging from the car windows like nothing so much as crated and despairing fowl. At Grombalia, midway between the coast and Tunis, there was such a crowd waiting for the much-delayed train that ticket holders tried to force their way on board, creating a near riot when those inside tried to throw them back off.

Tunis, under the noonday sun, was little better. A fine white light of heat and dust hung over the city, a luminous, chalky haze of diffused sun and steam from the lakes so that city had its own peculiar radiance, its own version of light and air quite different from that of the countryside. A heat-sodden, blazing Tunis. Tunis of the enchanted tales. Tunis the white. Tunis the fair. Pearl of Ifrikya, full moon at midday, pale blossom of flawless beauty rising by the mirror lakes. Lustrous as samite. Mother of poets.

Also, a pervasive out-of-focus cinema-verité shot with a wobbly hand camera, smothered in humidity, steel-shuttered for the *sieste*, cats crouched in the slivered shades of doorways, inescapable glare, Coca-Cola signs in Arabic, *bedu* curled under the bushes by the railroad station, the plane trees of the Place de l'Indépendence ash white and full of whirring locusts. There were no taxis, no people; the crowds that had emptied from the train evaporated like steam in the empty streets.

Sharon made it as far as the Rue Portugal and then stopped. All the cafés were shuttered and there was no place to go, but the top of her head was burning from the sun and her clothes felt like lead. After the hellhole of the Tunis express she had to slow down for a minute. She sat down suddenly on the curb between two parked cars and rested, holding the woolen Greek bag she used as a pocketbook over her head for a cover, stretching her legs out in front of her.

Nice young girls in clean yellow knit nylon dresses didn't sit down on the curb in Tunis, she knew, but to hell with it. There was no one around in the emptiness of that hour to see or care, and she certainly didn't want to drop over on the corner of the Rue Portugal with sunstroke.

I'm going to have to give up coming to Tunis, she told herself, if it's going to be this way the rest of the summer. The damned train trip not only takes forever but it's enough to kill you. The temperature in the cars must have been close to one hundred and ten or twenty, she thought gloomily. Not to mention the people that were heat- and motion-sick and vomiting all over the place. And that, by God, was in Première Classe; no telling what it had been like in second with all the real grotty poor people, where it was always rough.

Actually, she thought, staring across the street at the shuttered *boulangerie* and rows of hardware stores that clustered along the back of the *gare* and the railroad tracks, if I can't get to Tunis now and then, I might as well be in jail. There's nothing going on down in Ez-Zahra; it's just a funny little backwater with no real need for any work. Nabeul or some village way out in the Tell would be much better. And the way the village people have been treating me lately I might as well be the Invisible Woman.

There was something going on, she was positive of it. The whole village was weird, with all its past secrets hidden away in the villas behind the oleander bushes, but in her case she was sure there was something else involved, too.

She had been sitting on the curb for only about four or five minutes at the most when out of nowhere there appeared a large *boliss* about six feet tall in a tan and red Tunis police uniform. Sharon got up at once and slunk away, the *boliss* following her for about half a block just to make sure she wasn't in any difficulty, or going to cause any. The damned ever-present police—even when the streets were deserted they were always on the job. So much for the government's lovely, free, socialistic society. And of course you just didn't come along and find nice young American or European girls sitting on the curb between two parked automobiles every day.

They were, Sharon saw in the reflecting glass windows of a dress shop, the only people in the silent street: the briskly strolling, interested *boliss* with thick shoulders and a heavy black mustache, and a sun-tanned girl with long flapping hair, yellow dress, long bare legs hurrying to get away.

At the Boulevard of the President he stopped and stared after her, but Sharon continued down the center of the median park where the trees gave some lilac covering from the sun. But in the Rue Mohammed Cinq all was nicely bare and *moderne*: white sidewalks, white office buildings and villas, glass, an inferno of light. At the intersection of Mohammed Cinq and the El Aoui road which led to the airport there was a large red and white AGIP station, but she could barely make it out; the air fairly quivered with thermal waves, like a desert mirage. The entrance to the Foundation villa was in the middle of the block and, like the embassies farther on, surrounded by a high stucco wall with the shiny bodies of broken bottles stuck into the cement on top to discourage intruders. The villa number, 27, had once been painted on the wall over the bell, but the numerals had faded away. To the left was a new brass plaque which said in French, English, and Arabic, PLEASE RING BELL. But the bell was never used. The electric wiring was broken somewhere between the wall and the house, and it didn't ring. In order to get in one stuck a hand through the ironwork gate and turned the latch from the opposite side. The small garden was filled with concrete urns of neon pink and red geraniums, two struggling baby palms, and a border of dead Bermuda grass. But a gorgeous rare red bougainvillea vine climbed the porch and made a lovely shade.

The bell at the front door was out of order, too. Sharon pushed the door open and went in. After the furnace of the street the long bare entrance hall with its cool tile floors, dim light, and faint, drafty pull of the air conditioners was like a pleasant mausoleum. Absolutely silent, not even the sound of Miss Guffin's typewriter. But it was Saturday, Sharon remembered. She opened the door to Miss Guffin's office and the shutters were closed, the typewriter covered.

Someone was around, she was pretty sure. The villa was certainly open. And she had written Miss Guffin to say she was coming. Probably Miss Guffin had just gone out to lunch; the train had been two hours late, after all.

Well, she told herself, she had to wait.

There were no chairs or benches in the hall, and Sharon wandered down the length of it, looking idly at the framed photographs of Foundation field workers from stations all over North Africa. They were mostly old photos, pictures of irrigation canals running through the desert with the Arab laborers posing in nightgown robes and large grins, the Field Rep standing in front in crisp khakis and solar topee. A real honest-to-God solar topee, she thought, bending to marvel. Just like old Tarzan movies. And more framed photographs: a mud-brick schoolhouse with Arab children standing in neat rows outside, a Tunisian public health nurse giving a baby an injection— the baby's mother a fierce-looking *bedu* woman with a faceful of blue tattoos. A roomful of women at sewing machines. A vegetable garden down in the oasis country, children standing between rows of cabbages with a woman in a long nineteen-thirties dress and drooping canvas hat.

No new pictures at all, everyone of them pre-World War Two.

Like old textbook pictures long out of date. Happy native faces.
Model gardens. The field engineers in Rickenbacker pants and laced
boots. "Progress is our most important product."

Now, instead of all that, they had Wendell and herself and Judy
Hoggenberger and Genevra. Interpersonal relations and discussion
groups instead of irrigation ditches to make the date palms grow.
Well, what was progress, after all?

A door opened at the end of the hall and the noise startled her
for a second. Sir Charles stepped out into a square of electric light.

"Hul-lo," he called down to her. "Thought I heard a noise. Admiring our pictures?"

For a moment Sharon found herself at a loss for words. She had
just been staring at all the dim and brownish pictures and there was
Sir Charles Benedict wearing British walking shorts, which showed
his deeply tanned, knobby knees, and a sport shirt with a loud silk
scarf at his neck.

Cripes, he looks like he's going to play shuffleboard! she thought,
and it was all she could do to keep from laughing.

"Come in, come in." He waved her down the hall. "I'm back here
in the library. That's what you wanted to see, wasn't it? Hope you
won't be disappointed, coming all this way in the ghastly heat. I
say," he said, sharp-eyed, "you look a bit done in, you know."

"The train was late. It took four hours. People were sick."

"Ah, poor child. Damned trains, they're not all that good even
in decent weather."

Sharon tried to apologize. She was sure Miss Guffin had waited
for her and then left.

"Not at all, not at all. Cynthia had a chance at a holiday up in
the hills this week end and I urged her to go. She never gets away,
works like a Trojan. But holds up admirably," he added.

The library was a small room with file cabinets shoved into
corners, looking as though it hadn't been used for years. The books
climbed one wall. Sharon took one look at them and knew it was
hopeless; they were nearly all bound volumes of reports of Foundation work. The end of the shelf nearest her said 1954. There were a
few agricultural manuals, a geology of the Sahara in French, some
books on Arab history.

"Sit down, sit down," Sir Charles told her agreeably. "Well, now, how's it going down in—ah—Ez-Zahra? George Russell tells me you've been most enterprising; you've got an English class going isn't it? With some young boys?"

"Actually it's a current events discussion group," Sharon murmured. She hadn't come to Tunis to get prodded into making any sort of informal report to Uncle Charlie. That sort of thing had to be carefully thought out and edited in quarterly reports—which weren't due yet—and she didn't want to blow it by any chummy talk. Besides, the last meeting of the Ez-Zahra youth discussion group had been so crazy and disorganized she really preferred not to think about it at all. Just an outline of what had happened would give the Tunis office running fits. Most of the kids who worked in the orchards had been laid off and, because of it, were pretty steamy about their situation, and it had all been at a pretty high emotional level. Like liberating their country and the whole Arab world from feudalism, imperialism, and reactionary forces and economic slavery, and the puzzle of how American girls could find men to marry them when, as they had heard, most of them were not virgins.

"It's all coming along," Sharon said. "A lot of real interacting ideas."

Sir Charles drew a chair up to the library table and sat down, tilting the chair back, apparently in no hurry, his eyes twinkling in a very friendly way.

"Now, my dear, what is it I can do for you?"

Oh hell, Sharon thought. The Foundation library was a total loss; she didn't even have to go near the stacks to find that out. But she began talking and the words seemed to come out all right. Like, how great it was that the Foundation had this wonderful collection of books and records and stuff, but they were not exactly what she was looking for. She thanked him for being there and taking up his time. Actually, she needed what you might call a general library.

"Oh, trying to find a decent library in Tunis is a dreadful business," he assured her. "There's not anything in English, anyway." He stuffed some tobacco in his pipe, held a match to it, and the small room filled quickly with a heavy rum-and-honey smell. "Now, let's see, I think we've got some books at home. Becky and I might have"—puff, puff—"something you'd like to read."

"I don't think so," she said quickly. "Actually I'm looking for books on World War Two. I want to look up some local history. On the fighting here, and the Nazis."

She hadn't meant to say Nazis; the word had just slipped out. He looked up from his pipe quickly and gave her another sharp-eyed look.

"Local history, hmm? I understand you've met the General. Interesting old bird, isn't he?"

Shot down, she thought. But she really couldn't believe it. Uncle Charlie really didn't look that smart.

"Perfectly natural," he was saying. "Everyone wonders about these old boys still cropping up here and there with their shady pasts. Comes down to Moreau's a lot, doesn't he? George tells me the old man has quite taken you under his wing. Needs a bit of company, I should imagine. Not a bad thing to have a place to pop over to every once in a while, even if most of his friends are rather old fossils. I wouldn't believe half of what von Lehzen says, if I were you. Full of stories. What's he doing now? Still looking for Rommel's gold?"

"I didn't know you knew him." Now, she found, she couldn't think at all. He was way ahead of her, sitting there with his impeccable British cool, puffing away on his pipe.

"Who, von Lehzen? Oh, he's been around for years, you know. Comes and goes. Don't really know them—can't say the Ez-Zahra crowd's my cup of tea. So they've set you onto World War Two, have they? Going to read up on Rommel's campaigns and the glory of the Afrika Korps?"

"I don't know much about it." She was getting oddly nervous; her hands were sweating and she had the feeling Charlie Benedict knew more about things than anybody gave him credit for. "I got sort of interested—I know there was fighting in North Africa and the troops landed in Oran, but not much more."

She wasn't going to tell him she had read Desmond Young's book or anything about the pictures.

"Good heavens, I tend to forget," Sir Charles said. "The war must seem like ancient history to someone your age. By all means do read—we must get you some books. The Tunisia campaign had all the colorful chaps in it, Rommel, Montgomery, Desert Rats, Aussies, New Zealanders, Gurkhas, too, if I'm not mistaken." He stopped to see if she was following him. "Rommel nearly made it, you know. Got right to the gates of the city of Alexandria, trying for the Suez Canal. Would have changed the whole course of the war if he had. Rommel's sort of a god with the Germans, now. Only authentic hero, you know, not a dirty Nazi and all that. The desert's a positive mecca for German tourists—but I suppose you've already noticed that. Von Lehzen can tell you quite a bit. Umm, but watch out there." He looked more amused than ever. "I think he rather likes blonde young things. Make sure he sticks to history."

"I'm going to read books," Sharon said.

"Well, all right then. But I don't know what books are around. Have you tried Moreau's? He's got an excellent library, from what I hear. House is a veritable museum, anyway. Inveterate collector."

"Nothing on Rommel," Sharon said faintly.

"Really?" Sir Charles raised his eyebrows. "I'd have thought he would have. Well, if Moreau doesn't have anything, I'm afraid I can't be of much help. Pretty vague myself, you know. Rommel must have been down around Ez-Zahra—part of the Afrika Korps surrendered at Enfidaville, and that's just down the road. I've always heard Rommel spent a good bit of time at that magnificent place, belonged to the Roumanian chap, what's-his-name, next door to Moreau. The house the government confiscated. Used to be friends, Moreau and the Roumanian, but Sebastian Ghrika—that's his name —wasn't much help during the war. Moreau made no attempt to butter up the Germans, got into a spot of trouble, and the authorities packed him off to jail in Tunis, then on to Italy, and I believe he finally ended up in a concentration camp in Germany where he had a bad time of it. Starvation and pneumonia; nearly died. Whereas the fellow next door managed to parlay his house into a carte blanche of sorts, entertained Italians, Vichy French, all the German military. Quite an interesting story, how he made out. Moreau might tell you about it some time."

"You don't mean the man next door sent Mr. Moreau to jail, do you?" she said.

"Oh, I wouldn't say that. Moreau was—is—an American, and his wife British. I suppose they were on the spot from the start as enemy aliens. Queer little pocket down there at Ez-Zahra, anyway. I gather it was a colony made up of special cases. Collection of international oddities settled down on the African shore to do some rather elaborate sinning. Dabbling in black masses, *bedu* magic, soliciting the local boys. Cocteau and his crowd shooting—umm—surrealist films. Had the locals positively terrified, I understand. But then I suppose you understand Arabs love to be terrorized; breaks up the monotony of life. Anyway, all gone now. Old Colonel Wembly died just last year. That fantastic Irishwoman, friend of the Webbs; miscellaneous gaggle of French hanging about. Friend Sebastian sat tight during the war and played revolving host. Being Roumanian certainly didn't hurt him any, Roumania was part of the Axis. Don't know what became of him—he must be dead now."

They sat for a moment, and Sir Charles looked at her expectantly.

"Question?" he said finally.

She looked hesitant. "Well, I don't know much about it, of course, but I was just thinking. If the Germans put Mr. Moreau in jail during the war, you certainly wouldn't think he'd have the General around. As a friend, I mean."

"My dear, I simply don't know about von Lehzen. Man seems to be a bit of a mystery, as I said. Very keen on Rommel and the Africa campaign, like most of the Germans, but on the other hand swears he spent the war on the Russian front. You really can't rely on what these old dogs say; they all claim they were in Düsseldorf during the whole thing, dodging bombs and knitting stockings for the war effort. Explains how they got their Iron Crosses, of course." When she looked baffled, Sir Charles smiled. "My dear young lady, it's a bit difficult twenty-five years later to know what many of the German military did. Wouldn't expect them to advertise it, would you?"

"You mean," Sharon said cautiously, "somebody might be looking for old Nazis."

"Not necessarily. They weren't all Nazis, you know. One could very well be a member of the German Army and not be a Nazi; in fact, I suppose the majority of them weren't. Being a Nazi meant you were a member of Hitler's political party, and there was always a tug of war between the Wehrmacht and Hitler. Matter of history. The German Army went underground, you might say, after the Treaty of Versailles and conspired to keep German military strength alive while Hitler was still house-painting and making speeches in beer halls. Of course when Hitler started coming up, the Army went along with him. He couldn't have made it without their support.

But as far as the Wehrmacht was concerned, Hitler was a Johnny-come-lately, a political means to an end, which was the restoration of a powerful Germany. Rommel, for instance—he was an army man who managed to hang on during the lean years—never gave Hitler a second thought, I suppose, until there he was, large as life. But you'll really have to look all this up if you're interested. I'm afraid I'm no authority. India was my field of service, and Burma. Different thing entirely."

But Sharon had been listening to him with her mouth open. Sir Charles, she was just beginning to realize, was the man who would probably know about the SS. She asked him.

"Good Lord." He didn't look up; he was busy with his pipe, which had gone out. "The Shutzstaffel," he murmured finally. "Ah, that's a rather grisly footnote to history. The SS, hmm? A thoroughly bad lot. Haven't thought about them in years. A lot of dangerous nonsense connected with it, too, future prototype citizens of the world, pure Aryan strain, that sort of rot. Not regular army; the Wehrmacht couldn't do anything with them. Don't think they're anything you might turn up, I don't think there were any SS divisions in the Afrika Korps. The old Field Marshal wouldn't have stood still for it. The whole idea of the SS was a bit much for the Wehrmacht to cope with, you know: an army within an army, if you can imagine such a thing. Amazing that it worked at all. Hitler's own invention, of course. When he first came to power he had the Storm Troopers, but his bully boys were such a nuisance the Army raised a stink, didn't want any uniformed corps around competing. So Hitler got rid of the Storm Troopers and invented the SS. Devilishly clever— an elite corps designed to be the instrument of political action. Sounds a bit familiar, doesn't it? Sounds like Red Guards. By the time the Wehrmacht generals knew what was up, the SS had been established right in their laps. And not answerable to the Army command, either, only to the Reichsführer, Heinrich Himmler. The Wehrmacht bucked but there it was, sugar-coated with politics. And, as expected, the SS turned out to be a damned octopus, finger in everything. They not only had armed divisions right in the Army, but they headed up the Secret Police and ran the concentration camps. Everything nice and tidy. I remember a sweet lot called the *Totenkopfverbände*—the Death's Head units. They ran the concentration camps and did all the flogging and torturing, nice jobs like that. And the *Einsatzkommandos,* the extermination squads. Disposed of people in places like Auschwitz and Belsen."

"I know about Auschwitz and Belsen," she said. But she began to feel very strange; it was as though a door was opening onto something terrifying and she had only this last second, this last chance to turn back. "I suppose it just goes to show you how many really crazy, really insane people there are when you want them for something like that. To join the SS, run the concentration camps. But the world's really crazy, anyway, isn't it?" Sharon suddenly wanted to stand up, say good-by, and get out of there, but found that she couldn't.

"Crazy? Oh, I'm sure they weren't all mad. Himmler was certainly more than a bit mental, and one assumes that Hitler was a lunatic. But some of the SS were fine young specimens. The SS had its pick of recruits, and the armed divisions, the Waffen SS, were given the best in equipment, handsome uniforms, best duties, and reserved for the more spectacular operations. I'm sure they thought of themselves as bona fide heroes. Not only that, you know, but they were promised more important things after the war. They weren't just going to be a superstate police, you understand, but the nucleus of a new culture, a new breed for a finer world. Within their ranks the finest Aryan blood would flow. Not the finest German blood, either—the master plan encompassed more than that. It wasn't going to be confined to Germans. After the war was won the SS was going to recruit from all humanity—Aryan humanity, that is. The SS was going to sift out from foreign populations all those who had the proper Aryan characteristics and absorb them, too. I don't know if Hitler had decided about Americans. I gather he thought Americans a bit mongrelized. I'm sorry, m'dear, his own words. But the SS was going to be open to Englishmen, if I remember rightly. Lot of good Aryan blood in the English. Look at me." Sir Charles gave her a bright smile. "If the war hadn't turned out as it did, I'd have been a prime candidate for the SS. Marvelous Aryan type, nothing but Angles and Saxons and a few renegade Norman-Irish in the Benedict line. You can't do much better than that. And Becky—good lord, her family goes right back to the Ardens, only documented Saxon family in England. Blue eyes and blonde hair for centuries. Both our fathers over six feet. I'm afraid they would have conscripted us for certain. And come to think of it, mustn't forget the dear Queen.

I'm sure she would have qualified; family's solid German right back to old Victoria and Albert. To say nothing of Philip's crowd. The damned Mountbattens had to change their name from Battenberg during World War One so Londoners wouldn't attack them in the street. Gives one quite a turn, doesn't it, to think of our young Prince Charlie as an SS *Oberleutnant?*" Sir Charles had amused himself thoroughly; he took out his pipe and tapped the bowl with his finger and laughed.

Sharon didn't move. It was as though she had been nailed to the chair. Naturally he had no idea what it would mean to her, or how frightened she was. It's nothing, she thought, closing her eyes. It had nothing to do with me. I can just forget the whole thing. I really haven't done anything, have I? If anybody ever asks me about any photographs I'll deny it.

It was twenty-five years ago. Nothing to be afraid of now.

The social studies textbooks had said that the Jews were given bars of soap and told to line up for showers, long lines of men and women and even small children four and five years old waiting patiently. But some of the women had sensed something, humanity's sixth sense, and they had hung the babies up in their clothes on the hooks outside. The SS found the babies anyway and threw them in with the rest. When the handles of the showers were turned, out came the gas.

"We caught them all." Her mouth was suddenly full of salt, and she tried to swallow. "We had war crimes trials. They didn't get away."

"Oh, unfortunately a great many of them got away." Now Sir Charles wasn't fiddling with his pipe; he was watching her. "I'm sure you've read about the Eichmann chase. And somewhere around, all over the world, I'm sure the little ones, the rank and file, are still hiding their dirty secrets. Rather galling to think of, isn't it?"

"They're crazy. The way they act would give them away." She tried to swallow again.

"Wish that were true. I suppose a great many of them are living quietly now, turning in a good day's work and playing with their grandchildren. You must remember, after all, the appeals that were made to them in the name of patriotism to do their duty to the Reich. I remember reading one of Himmler's speeches to a group of concentration camp guards, a good, rousing, morale-raising speech.

Keeping people like that pumped up wasn't an easy thing to do. He said something to the effect—'Most of you know what it means when a hundred corpses are lying side by side, or five hundred, or a thousand. To have stuck it out and at the same time to have remained decent fellows, that is what has made us hard.' And—um—adding something about a moral duty. Always add moral duty, gets things done. Comparable to talks to sewer cleaners, don't you know. 'Sewer cleaning's not a pleasant job, but for us to remain good fellows after eight hours in the muck shows what fine stuff we're made of. Not everyone can do a dirty job. Got to give us credit.' Perhaps those who escaped still think of it that way. I say," Sir Charles said suddenly, "are you all right? You look a bit peaked."

"The train, heat," she mumbled. "I'm really O.K."

"No, you're not. Your system's still adjusting, you know. Takes years, actually. Here, I'll go get a Coca-Cola," he told her. "I believe the machine's plugged in."

9

Israel is a danger.
For the Arabs,
it is even a catastrophe.
But the negative attitude
of the Arab leaders
has no effect
but that of strengthening
the status quo.

—*Habib Bourguiba*

In Tunis, Liebman's Garage was known as something of a landmark. Located just off the Place de Pasteur in the *moderne* French part of the city, Liebman's was famous for the finest European-trained mechanics, the best equipment, and the most efficient repair service to be found between Algiers and Tripoli, if not Algiers and Cairo. Most foreign businesses and all the embassies in Tunis sent their cars to Liebman's and recommended him to foreign travelers—if with certain reservations. Liebman's work was good, but one paid for it. His prices were two and three times the going rate in the city, but then on the other hand his work was guaranteed, and that was something of a rarity in North Africa. Most importantly, Liebman had developed a system for getting replacement parts (that bane of all car owners) for a variety of makes of automobiles that was nothing short of magical. In one celebrated coup it had taken Liebman only twenty-four hours to find another dashboard cigarette lighter (after the first one had been tossed out the window by a visiting sheik under the impression that dashboard cigarette lighters were as disposable as a pack of matches) for the Saudi Embassy's highly customized Cadillac.

The reason for Liebman's success was simple. He was one member of a far-flung Jewish-French family that owned and operated garages and Renault dealerships in many places, including Tangier, Casablanca, Beirut, and Rome, as well as the home offices in Lyons and Paris. Whatever one needed, Liebman's could supply. In Tunis the American Ambassador had put his stamp of approval on Liebman's establishment by declaring it as good as any of the Volkswagen places back home in Houston. And as everyone knew, you couldn't get much better than that.

On Saturdays, of course, Liebman's was closed to observe the Sabbath. However, Norman Ashkenazi and Chaim Dayag were expected. As the old Ford rolled up to the workshop entrance on the Rue de Mauritaine side, the overhead garage doors rolled up, controlled by an electric buzzer from within, and then came smoothly down behind the car. Michel bustled out of the glass-partitioned inner office with his usual air of harried impatience, the perfect French *homme d'affaires* in a summer-weave suit fitted neatly to his slightly drooping paunch, a four-in-hand tie, a linen handkerchief rolling nervously between his palms.

Norman leaned out of the window to ask, "You want me to put it in the inner sanctum?" There was another room behind the main workshop which Michel reserved for special work.

Norman spoke in Yiddish. Language was something of a problem at Liebman's as Michel spoke Yiddish and French fluently, had a typical Gallic reluctance to use his serviceable English, and understood no Hebrew. Chaim's French was adequate but he preferred English or the Israeli tongue. As for Norman, his French was good but no match for Michel's slang-filled Parisian. All of them knew Tunisian Arabic but had agreed for the sake of security not to speak it too often. Usually they resolved the difficulty by switching back and forth in five languages, using David ben Yaakov, Michel's assistant who spoke everything, to bail them out. The younger man, a slight Tunisian from one of the Sahel Jewish villages, came out of the back of the shop in a mechanic's coverall.

"No, that is not necessary, David will move it." Michel allowed himself an expression of annoyance. "This is the second time you have come on a Saturday, when you know we are always closed on Saturdays. Really, Norman, you could have waited until tomorrow. It is difficult to make excuses to my family; they know I cannot work on the Sabbath. Besides, when people know we are closed, a car coming into the garage attracts attention."

"Sorry, Michel, we came when we could. Your note said everything was ready so we buzzed on in. Besides, we didn't get the message until last night, just under the sundown line. The kid was very orthodox—didn't even want to handle it after the candles had been lit."

"What are they saying?" Chaim asked David in Hebrew.

"They are arguing about why you always come on Saturday." The dark boy, thin-boned as an Arab, slid behind the wheel as Norman got out, took the car out of gear, and let it roll quietly toward the back of the shop. Michel opened a fuse box over a rack of wrenches, pulled a lever, and released the rear doors. They slid up, revealing another workroom beyond. The car rolled noiselessly in.

"Well, it does not matter," Michel said fretfully. "Yes, of course it matters, but it does not matter. You have probably made the trip for nothing."

"Nothing, hell! You said you had everything ready for us."

"Yes, yes, everything is ready, Norman, it is always ready. This is Liebman's, is it not? For what good that will do us. When I sent the message, how was I to know that we would have another catastrophe on our hands when you got here? Yes, a catastrophe, Norman, do not smile. It will be in the Tunis papers tomorrow; the government is only holding back the news now, tonight, to see what action they will take. But a catastrophe, a catastrophe, you can rely on it!" Michel waved them toward the back, to follow the car. "Hurry up, I will tell you when we get inside."

When they had filed into the inner workroom, Michel turned on the large standing fan to give them some cooling breeze, then released the lever which closed the overhead doors. They slid down as they had rolled up, well-oiled and silent.

"I will speak Arabic. It is safe here, no one can hear us, and it is the one language we can all use quickly. There has been a large strike into Egyptian territory. Friday—no, Thursday—the Egyptians lifted commandos by air into the northern Sinai for a little raid. Well, a little raid but naturally the Egyptians are saying that it was a magnificent operation and that they did a lot of damage. But it is something, anyway. This is the first time they have been able to mount anything of importance since the six-day war, so you must give them credit. Naturally, we struck back. I am told we hit everything that we could find, or that was worth hitting, in the southern

sector of the Suez Canal and along the Gulf of Suez. Tel Aviv radio
has announced that we retaliated in force not only because of the
Egyptian attack but because of all the Egyptian aggression in the
Suez Canal this month. Nevertheless, our retaliation was massive—
it may still be going on. The Cairo radio is screaming that it is the
opening attack of another war."

"That's what they always say," Norman told him. "We lose any
planes?"

Michel raised his hands in genuine anguish. "Planes—Norman,
am I a medium? Do I get messages by telepathy? Does Moshe Dayan
tell me his plans?" When upset, Michel fell into Yiddish. "Does
Golda Meir write me letters? I am only a cog in a wheel. I sit here in
Tunis, monitoring the radio, and I know as much about the war as
anybody. No, no planes lost, as far as I know," he added. "But
please, Norman, don't ask me to speculate. This situation is a very
fluid thing; war could happen any day. Don't ask me this and that—
read the Tunis newspapers tomorrow and then tell me if the Algerians are going to send a brigade, if the Americans are going to bring
in the Sixth Fleet, if any of us are going to be here tomorrow."

"O.K., Michel, you don't have to hold a Bar Mitzvah. I hear you.
We'll probably all be here tomorrow."

"That's easy for you to say; you don't live right under the nose
of the police as I do. And if we'll all be here tomorrow—who knows?
Would you like me to tell you that I have already had one disaster
as a result? Nothing has been announced yet, but already disasters!
That fool Elias went out of his mind in Nabeul; such a *pakhdn* you
couldn't imagine! I have been suspecting that they have had their
plane tickets in their shirts for months down there, waiting to panic,
and so what do they do? They panic. They cleaned out the entire
place, destroyed the receiver—my God, have they no brains?—and
packed up the whole tribe and came into Tunis last night. Screaming and yelling, yet. One little war scare and they go out of their
heads. So what do they do? They check into the Tunisia Palace.
Mon Dieu, the Tunisia Palace! Why don't they print it on their
foreheads? The *schlemiels!* But I'm glad to get rid of them. They're
hysterical, all of them, they won't cooperate, they're not willing to
help their own people here, they look down on them, so of what
use are they? It's better they should go to Marseilles, and good
riddance. I tell you, these are not Jews; they've been here so long

they have the mentality of *colons*. So maybe Marseilles is the right place for them; there they won't have to eat kosher any more and act like Jews. Elias the gourmet! Pfah! I hope the Sabbath prayers should dry up in their mouths, along with the French pork they eat. Better they should turn French Catholics and get it over with. I ask you, what good are Jews with French stomachs? No good, that is what I'm telling you! I will recommend that we never use them again. Never, under any circumstances."

"We won't," Norman said. "Relax. Just hope they get their damned plane out of here quietly. I'm glad he's your contact, baby, and not mine."

"I do not understand," Chaim said to David, unable to follow the Yiddish. "Is Elias going to Israel?"

"I think they have decided France is better," David said diplomatically. "They have money in France. In Israel they would be poor."

"Calm down, Michel," Norman told him. "It's a raid and a strike in retaliation. As far as I know, we're still on a holding basis. Anything else would get through quick, to help us at least try to save our asses."

"Will they suspend our visas?" Chaim wanted to know.

"Are you speaking to me?" Michel said, putting a hand across his chest. "As I said before, don't ask me anything. We are living on top of a time bomb. Actually, a real live time bomb I would prefer, instead of having to deal with hysterical fools like Elias. Even if, as Norman says, it is only a retaliation, a big retaliation but only a retaliation, now I am without an agent in Nabeul. I have to start all over again, with the same problem; there is not a good Jew among them. They are all rotten bourgeois clowns, living in the past. My God, they think some sort of luck will save them. They love the French; they don't believe the French are gone—as if the French ever did them any good! So quickly they have forgotten how anti-Semitic the *colons* were. Even the Arabs were better in the old days than the *colons*. Don't forget, when the Arabs settled in Spain the Jews were honored citizens. So what have the French had to offer? Burning at the stake and Dreyfuss!"

"Yeah," Norman said. "No sweat, Michel, you'll get another radio. We've been through these flare-ups before. And as for the visas, Chaim—hell, we never know when they're going to take them up anyway, just for the fun of it. The last two times we got them back, didn't we?"

"It's a madness," Michel muttered. But he took his handerchief and wiped his face. "You had better stay in Tunis for a few days. We will put you up with the Families."

"Let's speak English," Norman said, "and get down to business. The message didn't say anything about the pictures."

"Oh, yes, so now we come to that." Michel lapsed into Yiddish again, to Chaim's visible annoyance. "Norman, you're a good boy. So much business you bring me, I can't tell you how much I appreciate it. But this is a good one. For this, I thank you, for a change. So good"—here Michel allowed a note of satisfaction to creep into his voice—"so good maybe we can't handle it alone. Ah, now Norman frowns! He doesn't want anyone else in on his little *shpil*. Lift up your heart, *mon petit*, I am about to make you happy, regardless."

Michel turned to David and signaled him to bring the film.

"I have made a microfilm, and I have destroyed your original negatives—I am sorry, Norman, but this is a matter of security—and also the blow-ups of the prints which we have already examined. Only one I have saved, and I will dispose of that when we have looked at it together." He took the enlargement which David brought and the small roll of microfilm. "Too bad we do not have the equipment to make microdots; it is much safer. The film goes to Tel Aviv, as we must wait for final confirmation of our findings from there. But I think I can tell you some interesting things now." Michel held up the enlargement of the photograph which showed General Rommel and his aide, Spiedel, and in the background the head and shoulders of an officer in the uniform of the Waffen SS. The features of the officer behind Rommel were not too distinct in the blow-up, and Michel held the print at arm's length and away from them so that their eyes could adjust to the larger grain.

"Rank," Michel said, pointing to the collar and shoulder tabs and the sleeve of one arm showing. "The SS buttons, the double lightning bolts on the collar, the hat. These are the places we look for identification, so we decide that this is a colonel in the Waffen SS, the armed divisions which were inserted into the body of the German Army. Notice that we are lucky, for once, and the face in the photograph is particularly clear and bears a startling resemblance—in spite of the changes of age—to the man we have known for some time as General Heinz von Lehzen. But here we have something of a puzzle. General von Lehzen is in SS uniform, is he not? Photographed as we see him here, obviously in the desert, and obviously with General Rommel, who is unmistakable. So General von Lehzen is a colonel in the Waffen SS and he is with the Afrika Korps in the desert during the campaign of World War Two. Now, we know from General Rommel's own records that no Waffen SS divisions were attached to the Afrika Korps. Rommel had no affection for the SS, particularly the armed divisions, and his staff general, Bayerlein, has even gone on record as saying that Rommel was opposed to them, and thank God they had no SS with the Afrika Korps or it would have been a different war. We can appreciate this, for it was the Waffen SS who beat up their prisoners and shot them and did things which Rommel definitely would not have countenanced."

"O.K." Norman said. "So what's a Waffen SS colonel doing hogging the camera with Rommel, then?"

"Ah, yes, that we would like to know. Now, from Tel Aviv we find a record of an SS 'observer' with Rommel's staff. This at least was his official title, but we may be sure that this 'observer' was with the Afrika Korps to follow Rommel as closely as possible and send back not only official reports as an 'observer' but also to report very nicely to Herr Himmler any material on Rommel which would be interesting enough to go into SS-Gestapo files. It was a very routine procedure, it went on in many levels of the Army, and you may be sure the Wehrmacht generals were not deceived, Erwin Rommel least of all. Now, we may ask ourselves, why would anyone want to file secret reports on the so-admirable General Rommel? Well, if one consults the Gestapo dossiers, it soon becomes apparent. General Rommel at the time of the desert campaigns was enjoying a large German press and being hailed as a new Reich's Hero. Sending someone to keep an eye on Rommel was routine procedure. The duty of the 'observer' was to take down what the General said, report what he did, and most particularly to evaluate whether General Rommel did indeed deserve to be a new Reich's Hero with a great and unshakable loyalty to the Führer and the Nazi Party. It was not enough, of course, to be a military genius—one had to be a good Nazi, too."

"Doesn't sound like Rommel," Norman commented.

"Exactly so. We are certain that Hitler was very admiring of General Rommel's talents and sincerely so. Hitler adored Reich's Heroes; they were his own creation, as he saw them. But we know that Rommel was an individualist, a Wehrmacht man to the core, and that he had feelings about Hitler which were hardly those of a loyal party follower. What a contretemps! And how much this SS 'observer' must have had to write home about! Poor Rommel, it is believed that even at the time of the desert campaigns he already had a sizable Gestapo dossier. You remember there were black marks against him when von Schirach complained to Himmler that Rommel was not a good enough Nazi to be entrusted with the training of the Hitler Youth. Rommel's friends took this seriously, they tried to warn him, but Rommel was an army man; he was not impressed. He was a Wehrmacht officer, not a political creature, and like many of the Wehrmacht of the old school Rommel did not care or, maybe, understand the importance of keeping his mouth shut. He was not deceived by our SS 'observer'; he kept our colonel shunted about in the rear and out of staff meetings for the most part—you may be sure our colonel stuck his face in this photograph so that he had some proof he was somewhere near Rommel at least once—but the SS man was able to do some of his business, anyway. In one of his reports in the Gestapo file he announces that he was present at Benghazi when General Rommel lost his famous temper and called General Halder, the Chief of Staff, an incompetent ass and the beloved Führer a Louis the Fourteenth with delusions of grandeur. Down it went in writing, with some of Rommel's other intemperate remarks. It is sad, is it not? Here is a general in the field saying what any general has a right to say at some time or other, and it goes—*ziti*—into a little file which later is used to kill him. For we all know the sad history of General Rommel, that his dossier was used to implicate him in the bomb attempt on Hitler's life—a charge never proved—and that the Gestapo were sent to offer him the honor of suicide. From such things we get some small idea of our SS colonel's contribution to history."

"Rommel was killed later—committed suicide, whatever you want to call it," Norman said impatiently. "What does it mean to us?"

"Well, of course, we are not here, as Jews, to avenge the death of General Rommel," Michel said. "He is now, we all hope, in some sort of Wehrmacht heaven, yes? It is the SS colonel who draws our attention. As Jews we are always interested in the SS, but in this colonel especially. Not for what he may have done to bring about General Rommel's downfall, you may be sure. Our SS colonel is only an example of what we have been doing for many years, in many parts of the world, to locate certain people and not only find them but identify them—not an easy thing to do twenty-five years later. Von Lehzen we have had under surveillance for some time. Who is von Lehzen? Do we know him? Is he important to us? Ah, look at the photograph. Here he is as an SS colonel with General Rommel. Is he the SS spy who was making reports to Himmler while posing as a military 'observer' with the Afrika Korps? As far as we know, there was no other. We know of only one, because we have his reports in the copies of Gestapo files. We don't know his name, since the signature was a code word. Norman, we also have another picture," Michel said suddenly. "We have a picture of an *Obergruppen Führer* of the Twenty-third Waffen SS, Ukraine, which is a very poor print, very exasperating, as it has held up identification for some time, but which I think will compare very strikingly with the photograph we have now discovered. Enough for us to know they are one and the same man."

"Can we speak English, please?" Chaim broke in.

"Yes, of course. We are talking now of the Twenty-third Waffen SS in the Ukraine and its commander, a Silesian by the name of Gustav Hauk."

Norman whistled softly through his teeth. "It never rains but it pours. Michel, baby, I could kiss you."

"Please, Norman," Michel snapped. "I am not through." And then, "*Merde*, but I detest speaking English! It is incredible, this difficulty with languages, when we are all Jews. The tragedy of our race. Thank God I am not trained as a linguist—I would be a lunatic by now!" Michel took out his handkerchief once more and wiped his face. In spite of the fan, the closed workshop was breathlessly hot.

"Hauk," Chaim said. "An SS labor camp *kommandant*."

"Ah, Chaim, that is close, but not quite accurate. The Twenty-third Waffen SS served for a time in the Ukraine preparing Jews for shipment to Germany and labor camps and the extermination camps. Hauk was commanding officer, yes. And it was his boast—

we have this in a letter to Himmler—that he made the job simpler by packing as many Jews into open railway cars as could be pushed or shoved into them. Fitting them in was done very efficiently; there were squads who clubbed and prepared their passengers before they were loaded. Open cars these were, in the wintertime. Those who did not starve or freeze to death by the time they arrived at labor camps were the strongest and hardiest by natural selection. Or unnatural selection, if you wish to put it that way. It does not turn our stomachs now, does it, to know that those who survived ate the corpses to stay alive, and sometimes ate each other before they were corpses? *Non?* However, it may be said that Colonel Hauk was very proud of his methods. And at this stage of the war on the Russian Front there was not enough time to be selective; thousands of non-Jewish Ukrainians died the same way."

"Wonderful, wonderful," Norman agreed. "we've got ourselves a real beauty. But it figures. To think that General Heinz von Lehzen, our Prussian highbrow we've been tailing for the past six years just to get a taste of international high life, turns out to be some crummy Silesian mass murderer by the name of Hauk. These old birds never cease to amaze me, the way they have a yen to rise in the world. They get on that *Junker* bag the first thing, but a monocle and a snappy blazer, and give themselves all the old aristocratic Prussian names. It's a real Nazi hang-up."

"Norman, Norman, be careful," Michel said. "I have warned you that our identification is not complete. Do not get ahead of me, please. We still must wait for Tel Aviv to confirm it. I am only telling you that the chances are very good that Tel Aviv will agree with our findings when they get the microfilm and compare it with the photograph they have of Hauk in the Ukraine. I do not often fault myself. I remember the Ukraine photograph very well, and I think we have nothing to worry about. I hope I do not boast unduly when I say that I would not be here with you today if I did not know my trade. With ordinary eyes one does not notice the resemblance between the General as we know him today and the Ukrainian *kommandant* of twenty-five years ago or more. As I have said, the Ukrainian photograph is not good; it only gives an approximate idea, not enough for a proper ID. But ah, when we put them all together—the man as he is now, as he is in the Afrika Korps photograph and the Ukrainian one—it is something to be excited about, *non?* I may be corrected by Tel Aviv—" Michel struggled with caution, then burst out, "No, it is Hauk, I would put my reputation on it!"

"Congratulations," Norman told him. "Everybody knows Liebman doesn't make mistakes. And if you say so, that's good enough for me. Let's have a beer and celebrate."

"Norman!" Michel was sincerely shocked. "On the Sabbath?"

Norman laughed.

It looked promising, he told himself. Hell, it looked more than promising, it looked as though they had finally run their fake Prussian bird to earth. The funny thing was, von Lehzen-Hauk's buddies had set him up for it in a way; they'd given him a dog's job the past few years. How many times had the old General trotted down to the desert looking for Rommel's gold? At least three times that they knew of. When even the Tunisian government didn't believe in that old fairy tale or they'd have dug up the desert themselves a long time ago. God knows the Tunisians needed the money as badly as anyone.

Also, surprising how little new there was in any of it, nothing they hadn't known in one way or another for years. Their work was always a matter of waiting, hoping some small thing would happen to fit the pieces together from Tel Aviv's collection of odds and ends. In this case, an American girl had found a photograph left in a book, and suddenly the center piece of the puzzle had been laid down and all the other formerly useless bits had fitted around.

Sometimes, he told himself, you sit and wait for years, praying you'll get lucky. A crazy business.

One thing they did know was that the middle of everything was always Ireland. Michel had some briefing on it, Chaim a little, David ben Yaakov almost nothing, but Norman's position in the scale of operations always allowed him to know what center they were working outward from. And the center was always Ireland and the damned untouchable ring of "respectable" retired Germans living there quietly on their big estates, raising purebred cattle and participating in the very social county hunts. Charming people, one couldn't fault them at all, except for the high proportion of suspected ex-Nazis among them. Every one with a tail on them from Tel Aviv, but so far not one substantial ID. Nice, affable German country gentlemen with no pasts, meeting from time to time in their

Irish baronial halls to conduct the business of what had become known as Group One. Von Lehzen belonged to Group One—or at least they claimed him—and his assignment for a long time had been his none-too-mysterious trips into the Tunisian desert to look for Rommel's gold. The gold was a pretty silly business, in Norman's opinion, but obviously Group One believed in some sort of Afrika Korps cache left from World War Two or they wouldn't keep sending von Lehzen-Hauk back to look for it. The General, one was supposed to believe, was another homeless Prussian gentleman living off some small income while passing himself off around Tunis as an addition to cocktail parties and pursuing his hobby of archaeology down in Nefta when he could get around to it. Well, it was no better or worse a cover than most of the ex-Nazis living abroad. Group One pulled all the strings, kept an eye on all the projects, doled out living expenses when necessary, found little jobs for all idle ex-Nazi hands to do, and never lost an opportunity to hit the faithful for funds if they seemed to be getting prosperous. Money was what interested Group One. That, and the promise of a return to power some day in the homeland.

Michel Liebman had done quite a bit of work through his family's contacts on the existence of a financial pool to promote the neo-Nazi Democratic Party in West Germany; thanks to Michel they had been able to spot accounts in French and Swiss banks. And the fact that the National Democratic Party was getting funds from outside was no secret: most of the NATO countries had been following it for years, and several magazines in Europe and American had published articles on what they knew. The publicity had produced a distinct lack of intimidation as far as Group One was concerned. So interested Germans living abroad were making contributions to a bona fide West German political party—and so what? Didn't the world Zionist organizations collect funds for Israel? The neo-Nazi party was legal, even if it didn't smell so nice. And Group One went right on with its business, ferreting out old Nazi Party sympathizers all over the world, particularly those known to have gotten out of Germany with a hunk of cash before the Allies moved in, investing in real estate and aboveboard business operations, and getting funds into Germany to support its projects. One division of Group One handled still-uncovered World War Two loot. If there was any chance of unearthing money left by Rommel's defeated Afrika

Korps, they would go after that, too. Group one hadn't overlooked even the long shots.

Norman never made the mistake of underestimating any of them. Their ideas might sound crackpot—give to a good neo-Nazi cause, support your world-wide Nazi community chest, keep your bags packed for a trip to the homeland just in case—but there was a hard core of political logic in it. The Nazi Party had made it once against all odds; you could never completely rule out that they might not be able to do it again, given the proper lunatic time and place. Of course there was nothing spectacular as yet, the neo-Nazis weren't exactly ready to take over the Bonn government by a long shot, but they were *there* when civilization had never thought to see them raise their ugly heads again. Quite an accomplishment. They were nothing if not a real pain in the ass to Bonn, and quite an international embarrassment, especially when the world liked to assume that all the old Nazis were dead and gone, or the West Germans too repentant or too young to be interested in the hard-line Nazi pitch. But the National Democrats hadn't been booted out of West Germany, they were still holding meetings in beer halls, just like the good old days, and still getting the cash lifeblood from abroad thanks to Group One. They even had a good aristocratic name to head them up—Von Hadden. Fat old bastard, looked a little like Hermann Goering. Which probably didn't hurt.

The whole idea of a neo-Nazi party should have been wild as hell, Norman thought, and yet he supposed there was some sort of appeal in it to Germans worried about the Russian occupation of Czechoslovakia and the noisy Russian war games in Poland. Not to mention those old-timers who weren't exactly enchanted with Von Hadden's line but who wanted to see an end to partition, the two Germanies united, and might be persuaded that a new Reich would do it.

The whole damned German thing just wouldn't lie down and be quiet. Look at West Germany's crazy economic comeback.

And now they had one chip out of a very large operation: Von Lehzen-Hauk. He, Norman, was in charge of that. He had lived with the General's history for six years, and to know him, he told himself, was not to love him. When Tel Aviv had first picked up his trail after World War Two, von Lehzen had apparently appropriated a large slice of negotiables before he made his escape from

Germany and was living high in Rio. Before agents could feel him out, he had skipped on to Caracas, one jump ahead of an Israeli team dedicated to getting IDs on all the German military types. And in Caracas the General had really lived it up, apparently blowing the whole stack and having a ball. Then Group One found him, as they found a lot of the others who didn't have the True Spirit, and ran him over a table a couple of times, trying to beat it out of him with rubber hoses. But the money, she was long gone. From then on, von Lehzen had been in Group One's loving hands and definitely on the shit list, serving as errand boy and courier for a while, then being given second-class jobs like trying to come up with the Afrika Korps' legendary lost gold. And on short rations, too: once von Lehzen had run out of money and had had to bum around Tunis until he could scrape up the fare to report back to Ireland. Four months ago, Norman and Chaim had come into Tunisia to take over from the regular relocation team and wait for the General's return to the desert.

"That's what bothers me," Norman said suddenly. "The goddamned gold. Tel Aviv tells us the gold is strictly a bust, that they've checked it out thoroughly and there's nothing to it. But Group One doesn't give up. Are they just being stupid for a change, or do they know something we don't know?"

Michel waved his hand in a gesture of dismissal. "Believe me, Norman, don't give it a second thought. What can anybody add to it, a silly business like that? You hear the same old story over and over again; it's a real romance like James Bond should be involved in. Stupid people keep it going because it is just that, a romance. Believe me, there are some cretins here in Tunis who do as much as anybody to keep this ridiculousness going. Last year some of these writers in the U.S. Information Service were all talking about taking a vacation together down at Kassérine with mine detectors. They were not only going to find the gold yet, they were going to make a fortune writing a book about it! Is this not a real lunacy?"

"What keeps it going, then?"

"Norman, I am just telling you! It is a real mystery thriller; there is a little history to build on, so people make a whole romance of it. Because of course we all know what happened, that Rommel flew out of North Africa to confer with Hitler and never came back; that's why. People go around asking, Why did General Rommel fly out of North Africa? You have to know your history. That madman Hitler would not realize that the war was nearly lost here, and he was still sending Rommel letters about a new offensive—possibly against Casablanca, possibly here, possibly there, he really didn't know, he couldn't make up his military-genius mind. And Rommel was going crazy, naturally. So Rommel takes a plane out of Tunisia on his own initiative to try and talk some sense into Hitler and, if not sense, at least try to persuade Hitler to salvage the Afrika Korps and not abandon them. But Rommel gets nowhere; not only is Hitler so crazy he won't listen to what Rommel is telling him, but he decides that Rommel shouldn't go back to North Africa, that the Reich's Hero should stay and keep him company until he can make up his mind what he is going to do. So you can imagine how Rommel felt. There he was, stuck in Germany, cut away from his command, while Hitler is brainstorming and driving the Wehrmacht crazy. So from March until the first of May the poor Afrika Korps is getting its brains beaten out, and finally when Hitler gives the order to abandon North Africa it is too late, the Afrika Korps is split up and surrounded, and it surrenders in several pieces here in Tunisia on May twelfth. That is the story. That much is true. So then, because some of the Afrika Korps that are captured keep insisting that they knew Rommel would return to lead them on to victory, there begin the rumors about the gold. I think when the Afrika Korps surrendered they were dead broke, you know? But because Rommel wasn't in Tunisia, and because some of his men were sure he was coming back, people begin to believe that the gold was buried in the sand in the desert to keep the Allies from getting it. Or that it was hidden somewhere because the Afrika Korps had faith in Rommel and they believed he was coming back somehow to win. This is what makes these people dream of vacationing in the desert with mine detectors. Pfah!"

"What do you think, David?" Norman said to the younger man. "What do the Tunisians say?"

"Oh, Norman," David said softly in Arabic, "I am afraid that if I have ever heard anything in the villages, you have heard it, too. In this part of the world there are always stories. When you go to Sousse you hear that a large cache of gold was left by the German soldiers in the war, in the Sahel. But where? And under what olive tree out of thousands? Ah, that is something no one can tell you.

But it is there, they swear, if one only knows where to look for it. Which unfortunately no one does. It is a nice thing to say, that is all; it makes life more interesting. And when one goes to Tozeur, the people there say there is gold somewhere between Tozeur and Nefta in the desert, left also by German soldiers. But I think the people in Tozeur say this because, as they see it, why should Sousse have something which Tozeur has not? If Sousse has buried gold, then naturally Tozeur has it, too. Is theirs not just as interesting a district? Kassérine has the same stories. But Norman, the Tunisian government even back in the days of the French looked for any money or gold and decided there was nothing in these tales."

"O.K., I don't believe in it either," Norman told him. "But it bothers me. In a way, there's something about it that doesn't make sense. Group One's long shots aren't as dumb as this. Well, most of them. O.K.," he said again, "that should take care of it. I just wanted to make sure."

"However"—here David ben Yaakov shot a hesitant glance at Michel—"it is strange that maybe the Algerians, they might believe in the gold."

"*What?*"

"Yes, that is true, Norman. It is strange, is it not? Maybe you would not think it important."

"There is no proof, either," Michel put in. "Only rumor. No one has been down to check it."

"Never mind, never mind. What Algerians?" Norman wanted to know. "Come on, David, everything's important. Every little crazy thing is sometimes what kills people, if they don't listen."

"Well, yes, Norman, that is why I thought you should know. Although it is not probably important. I think they are ALN. They have money; they are living very quietly, dealing in dates, they say; but there is an ALN look to them, I am told. It is odd how people will put such things, it does not make sense to describe a person like that, but this is what people say and they are usually right."

"They are watching the house of this man you were talking about, in Nefta."

"Have they tried to contact him?"

"Oh, no, they would not do anything like that! What would they want to do a thing like that for? He is not the sort of person the

Algerians would contact. But maybe the Algerian government believes in the gold, even if the Tunisian government does not."

"How many?"

"Two. They are from a Kabyle tribe which goes back and forth over the border. This is not legal, of course, but it is done, anyway, down in the desert."

"Somebody's got to be putting me on," Norman said. "How many fingers have we got in this fairy-tale couscous anyway? Has everybody gone nuts?"

"Well"—David smiled apologetically—"everyone needs money, do they not? Even governments. And the ALN is very active in the Arab world now. The Algerian national socialism in Cairo and Amman and Morocco. Not to mention Peking, and in Russia, too. Every place. The Algerians are very poor, the war of liberation destroyed much of their country, and they take money from the Chinese and the Russians, but it is still not enough. They need more money to buy arms and planes and have meetings with other revolutionary Arab nations, so maybe they feel they are willing to look anywhere for more. Even in Nefta, for this gold which no one believes in."

There was a moment's silence.

"I don't like it," Norman said flatly. "I don't like unnecessary stuff. We don't need a bunch of Algerians mixed into our business. It's things like this—the unpredictables—that really mess up operations."

"Well," David said again with another apologetic smile, "it is difficult to avoid the Algerians down in the south. The *bedu* tribes and the Berbers, they cross back and forth over the borders as they have always done, so therefore it is easy for other Algerians to do it, also. A lot of it began in the days when the Algerians were fighting the French, and the Tunisian government allowed the Algerians to take refuge and even operate guerrilla bases from Tunisian territory down there. Now the Tunisian government is not so friendly to the Algerians because the ALN is more revolutionary, and the Tunisians suspect the the ALN does work among the old Youssefists, making trouble against the President and one thing and another. The situation changes. One day the two governments are friendly; other days they are not. They do not trust each other now. So the Tunisian police work very hard on the borders to keep an eye on the Algerians. Still, the problem is—the desert, it is wide."

"*Ja*, David, you can say that again," Norman muttered. "The desert, it is indeed wide. All the more reason for us to attend to our business, and quickly. Michel," Norman said, switching to English, we'd better square things away today and get ready for our shipment."

"Norman, there may be a war—"

"Nuts. War or no war, we get our Channukah gift out of here. That's what we agreed on. First things first."

"Channukah gift?" Michel was momentarily baffled. "What is that? What does one give on Channukah? It is only a minor holiday."

"Christmas gift, then, you slob of a Frenchman. *Joyeux Noel*, remember? A nice present for Tel Aviv all wrapped up and kept quiet with sedatives, airmailed out of the Wilderness." As Michel continued to protest, Norman said, "Knock it off, will you? We're only going to do a check-out. It won't hurt to get the extra car lined up anyway, I'm getting tired of the Ford; it's like riding around in a Greyhound bus. Everybody knows it. I want the other lined up and ready to go in case we have to get off our asses in a hurry. Besides, I don't like carrying the stuff around in the headliner; it puts me off. It never pays to keep anything in the same place too long." He turned to David to ask, "What have you got for us? Something good?"

A flash of a grin crossed the Tunisian's dark face. "Oh, something very nice, very beautiful. The motor is a concealed jewel—you could not tell it from the outside, but it is very fine. A special job. And fast! You should be able to get to Ishmael in the Wilderness without any trouble, and in a matter of hours. It is that good."

Ishmael was the cover name for Israeli agents working in the Wilderness, the code for Libya.

"It had better be good, O peerless son of a gifted race of artisans," Norman returned in flowery Arabic. But he was grinning, too. "When we get going, it'll be miles of desert track all the way. You got us fixed up with some special tires?"

"Thick, voluptuous beauties. I will bring in the car. It is outside, under a canvas, behind others. I will have to move several cars to get it."

While David was in the outer room getting the car from its

place, Norman and Chaim opened up the battered Ford and began to pull loose the headliner on the seat opposite the driver, over the door.

"Come on, Michel," Norman called out, "get us a screwdriver and some other tools, will you? This headliner's gotten soft from the weather, and it's going to tear."

"It is torn already," Michel said mournfully, but he fetched them a small toolbox.

"Well, no need to tear it up further."

"We can dirty over the tears some," Chaim said helpfully, "but you are right. It is better to have some patience and be careful."

"Transferring the stuff to the other headliner is going to be tricky. Hey, Michel," Norman called again. "Did you get the metal snaps like I wanted? I hope to hell you fixed us up with some metal snaps. I don't want to take this stuff out more than once, but if we have to, I want to have a way of closing it back up again, and closing it up smooth, like the original factory job. These damned headliners are a real bitch."

"David has made everything just as you want. The boy is a genius. The headliner goes in and out very smoothly; it is a matter of adjusting the cord, which seals it in. Norman, you should watch what you're doing if you hope to use this car again," Michel said critically. "You are rubbing the dirt in, which is very difficult to blend later."

"Hell." Norman's voice was muffled; he was up in the headliner, reaching into it. "It can't be choosy about the dirt. The whole damned thing is full of crap, left over from the khamseen in the spring." They heard the sound of coughing. "You know what this dust means, don't you? We've got to clean the equipment before we can put it into the other car." He handed down two bundles of plasticized cloth to Chaim, who crouched on the seat beside him. Chaim backed out the Ford, took the bundles over to a large work table which Michel had hurriedly cleared, and unfolded the wrappings.

The first gun was Norman Ashkenazi's Beretta, which had been issued to him in the Israeli Army. The markings had been filed off.

"How's Gladys?" Norman said, sticking his head out of the car. He was trying to get the dust out of his shirt and pants by beating at his clothes with his hands. He coughed again.

"Dirty," Chaim said shortly. "At least on the outside. It is remarkable how the dust has come through the coverings, when they were tied so thoroughly. We should have checked them before this."

"Couldn't. You should see the mess in here. I don't know how we're going to get the headliner back together in the Ford without leaving marks all over this side. Looks like elephants have run over it."

"It is not all that bad," Michel said, craning to look. "David will brush it and then spray all of it with a mixture he has. It is a very good concoction, with soot and other things. I told him he should be a faker of antiques, you know? He could make a fortune."

Norman had gone to the table. "Hey, what the hell are you trying to do, Chaim, you *shlomozzle?* This only strips down into five pieces. You trying to make twenty-four?"

Chaim was at work with a collection of fine gun oil in tins, Q-tips, and wads of cotton, cleaning the disassembled Beretta.

"Then here, you do it. Make love to it. Did you ever see a man make love to a gun?" Chaim asked Michel. "It is an ordinary pistol, also, this Beretta, only an army gun. Nothing very important. But he thinks it is his mother."

"It is," Norman said. "My mother's name is Gladys." He took the Beretta up carefully, examined it, and then began to clean it himself. "Not as much dirt as I thought. She's seen worse." He pulled the slide group forward and off the receiver several times, testing it for grains of sand. "The only trouble with Gladys is that we have to be selective with her, only use her as a back-up. We all have our faults, and Gladys' is that she doesn't speak very softly. Can't put a silencer over her big mouth. I think I'm going to have David modify her for this job. Maybe."

The gun Chaim was unwrapping was the one Norman often referred to flippantly as "Frankenstein," as the BSA was a V-43 prototype never put into mass production. The BSA had several assets, however, and one was that the ammunition was interchangeable with the Beretta. The submachine gun was Chaim's weapon; the BSA, unlike the Beretta, could be fitted with a silencer, which Chaim was just then doing, could fire single shots as well as bursts, and the *sabra* had had it fitted with a folding wire stock so that it could be put into a shoulder holster.

"Very interesting machine," Michel murmured, looking over Chaim's shoulder. "A really beautiful weapon. So original."

"It ascends," Chaim told him.

"It climbs," Norman corrected him. "That's how you say it. Can't you get it straight?"

"Yes, it climbs," Chaim continued. "But if I can brace it against something, a wall or the trunk of a tree, it is accurate to one hundred yards or more."

"He braces it against his belly," Norman said. "Don't let him kid you. And he sprays everything in sight."

Chaim reddened, and he tightened his lips. "Naturally, I always hope that it will not be necessary to fire on a small target from that distance," he said evenly. "I always try to stay close to Norman; that is always better. Look," he said to Michel, "see how the British have made this safety feature. If the gun is dropped, the magazine housing along with the magazine becomes unlatched, and it swings out of the way. To prevent the bolt, see, if it accidentally rebounds, from picking up the cartridge and firing the weapon."

"So you don't shoot yourself in the leg," Norman said. He wiped his face with the back of his wrist, getting gun oil in his mustache. He made a face. "The gun's not so great. I don't like the ribbed sleeve; it's awkward. But it plays sweet for Chaim. You should see him, Michel; our *sabra* cantor looks mean as hell with that thing braced against his gut. Judas Maccabeus with a burp gun."

Norman had cleaned the Beretta to his satisfaction; in an offhand way he slid the gun across the table to Chaim. "You check it out, baby. You always find the fly specks, don't you?"

"You will make it dirty again, throwing it around like that," Chaim said disapprovingly. But his face relaxed. In spite of his manner, Norman always referred the final check-out to Chaim, relying on his delicate touch with weapons.

"The boy works on them like a Swiss watchmaker, doesn't he?" Norman said to Michel. "But when you get right down to it, God forbid the guns should do the work. Only in a pinch, and it has to be a real pinch. We always try to operate neat and quiet, no fuss. That's the real test of a good job, to get in and get out without anybody knowing you've ever been there."

Norman had gotten a strip of three-inch adhesive tape out of the first-aid kit in the glove compartment of the Ford, and now he opened his shirt and slapped something against his flesh, quickly covering it with the tape. The object rested between the rise of his chest muscles, in the breastbone depression. Norman looked down at it.

"I got to get it on right; don't want anybody to think I've got three tits," he observed. "And after a while, man, does it itch! Have to get used to it again. Sonofabitch!" He made a grimace. "Why do I have to be built like King Kong?" He had torn the strip away quickly, and the adhesive side was thick with black hair. "Well, that took away some, but not all. I'm going to have to shave my chest again like a damned fairy. Always have to do it."

The underside of the tape held a length of piano wire wound around compactly and fitted with small wooden toggles for handles. This was the guerrilla weapon more useful, as he had said, than the guns. It was Norman's garrotte.

"Ugh, put it away." Michel winced. "I hate the sight of the wire; it makes my flesh melt. I have seen what it does, and it is not nice. The head is always half severed."

"You've just been watching sloppy operators, baby; when it's done right, it's quick and it's quiet. Not even a squeak. The head comes right off. Sssssszack!"

"*Quelle horreur!* Thank God," Michel said quickly, "here is David with the car." He released the garage doors and David drove the Mercedes into the room. The motor purred, hardly making a sound.

"Sweet mother!" Norman put his hand up to his head. "Why didn't you get us a gold Rolls-Royce? How are we going to get that thing south without attracting a crowd?"

David ben Yaakov got out of the car, grinning happily. "Don't worry, I am going to fix it up. I am going to put a German Touring Club sticker on it, and we have someone who will deliver it. He is coming in specially to do it, with the German passport required and everything. And with a little dirt, it will be perfect."

"What did you wish us to get you," Michel added crossly, "a Land Rover? David is right. It will be fixed up very nicely. A German tourist will bring it south, a very nice German tourist with his wife. The car is even registered under a German name."

Norman shrugged. "I leave it to you; you ought to know what you're doing." And, as David came around to open the hood and show him the engine, Norman put his arm around the slender boy and said in Hebrew, "David, you are a good friend and a fine crafts-man; we are indebted to you. Remember, I want Michel to make good arrangements and get you out right after the operation. No delays, understand? Michel has his work here to cover up afterwards, but as for you, we must make careful arrangements. You are too important to lose."

David continued to grin confidently. "I will be all right, Norman. Everything is good. How can I be unlucky? I am full of happiness. Miriam is expecting a child, I learned this only last week."

Norman dropped his arm and backed away so quickly he nearly hit his head on the car's open hood. He turned to Michel.

"Yes, David is married," Michel said hurriedly. "I thought you knew this." Again flustered, Michel fell into Yiddish. "We will get her out right away, Norman, I promise you. We will send her to Rome, yes? Via Alitalia. Vittorio will make special reservations, as a favor to me. But you know, we have been busy, and with this war scare—" His voice trailed off.

"You little bastard," Norman said, turning on David. "If things got tight, you wouldn't think of leaving without her, would you? Now, you cooperate with Michel and get her the hell out of here. This week."

David's face lost its grin. "But why so soon? We were counting on another mo— at least two more weeks."

"You get her out *now*. I'm not going to run this job according to any maternity time schedule. Put her with some Jewish family in Rome and get her out of sight. And then," he told Michel, "I want for you to move her on. Just as soon as you can get her trail covered."

"Rome—how will I find her?" David whispered. "She is expecting a child, Norman. She is a very orthodox girl from the villages, very old-fashioned. She is not very independent; she has always been with her family, or me."

"I could break your neck," Norman told him. He looked at Michel and gave his head an angry jerk in the direction of the Tunisian boy. "You see what I mean, Michel? Get it taken care of."

"Yes, Norman, I hear you." It was Michel's turn to redden. "He knows what he is doing," he said rapidly to David. "Norman has seen what can happen; yes, of course Norman is right. You love your wife, don't you? Of course you do. Miriam is a sweet, lovely girl. We will get her out right away; we will give her a nice vacation in Rome with a lovely Jewish family, very orthodox, Hebrew-speaking; it will be all fixed up. You will see, she will enjoy herself. And then, after that, we will move her on to very nice people, maybe in France, yes? I give you my word, she will have nothing to be upset about."

Michel took a deep breath.

"Yes, Norman, I will take care of everything," he muttered. And then, "And Norman, while we are on the subject, you must consider your own affairs, too. Now tell me what you intend to do about your friend the American girl."

At that moment Norman's friend the American girl was descending the steps of the Sousse-Sfax express at Bir Bou Rekba junction with the rest of the passengers who had come down from Tunis. The little connector train to carry them to Ez-Zahra and Nabeul had not arrived, and the junction was singularly black and empty, unlighted except for the strong electric lamp which shone over the closed station-house door. As the diesel express pulled away for the south, the handful of heat-weary travelers, mostly tourists from the hotels and a sprinkling of Ez-Zahra gardeners returning from the Tunis markets, stood by the tracks and watched its lights disappear into the thick and humid night with varying expressions of dismay. The station house was locked and dark, so there was no one to ask when the connector train was bound to arrive, if at all. And Ez-Zahra was a three-mile walk.

Well, that was a possibility, Sharon told herself. A few short weeks ago she wouldn't have considered such a thing. She would have been too chicken and too inexperienced to think of walking down a dark highway in that part of the world between thick citrus groves and open fields, without a flashlight, even, in a totally strange and foreign place where the only people you were likely to meet in the pitch black were Arabs who could speak only a few words of French and certainly didn't know who you were or what you were doing. But she didn't have that sort of attitude any more. Gradually everything was growing more familiar and because of this, when she stopped to think about it, so much easier.

Little things, but they counted for a lot. It was almost as if, for a while at least, she belonged there.

As soon as she got a few feet down the highway she intended to work the tobacco out of the paper of a Crystal cigarette and pack it with some of the good and heavy Moroccan kef she had been smoking on the train. To walk along in the country night like that, turning on, would be a blast. But she was hardly away from the maze of tracks and switches and iron rails which intersected with the asphalt road when a car came tearing up from the direction of Ez-Zahra, caught her in the headlights, and then made an abrupt U turn. As it drew up beside her she saw the Arabic word for POLICE on the door.

"Oh, shit," she said under her breath.

"*Allez.* Get in," Ali ben Ennadji said peevishly. His elbow was resting on the car door window and he did not bother to get out. "I met the train before this, and now I almost miss this one. It has been very annoying. Why did you not tell anyone you were going to Tunis?"

"You know, I think you're about the only person who could really spoil my lovely high," Sharon said in English as she got in the far side. He didn't pay any attention to her, didn't ask for a translation, so she slumped down in the seat and braced her knees against the dashboard. It showed a lot of leg, practically up to her crotch, but she didn't care. Let him run off the road looking, she told herself; if he wrecked the town's one police car maybe he wouldn't follow her around so much.

"I have been searching for you all the day," the Ez-Zahra Chief of Police said to her. "Since this afternoon. In the morning the boy Salem Gueblaoui comes to your house many times with a message from Monsieur Moreau to remind you of the dinner tonight and the guests he is having, since you often forget. But you are not at home. Finally, I must go to the house myself, and the stupid ben Omrane girl, she at last remembers that you have gone to Tunis."

Well, Sharon thought, she had forgotten one of Moreau's things again, which was just too bad. She had finally got the paper shell of the Crystal stuffed and was trying to get it lighted.

"What is that?" he said quickly, and gave a loud sniff. He said something in angry Arabic, rolled down the window, and grabbed the stick of kef and threw it out. "*Décadente!*" he shouted.

It was sort of a funny word, even in French, and she had to laugh.

But there was no time to argue about it; the car had already turned into the road to Moreau's driveway, under the thick, whispering trees.

"I don't want to go here, dammit," Sharon told him. But old Tewfik was waiting under the terrace light and lurched forward to open the car door.

"Oh, mademoiselle, you are late, you have missed dinner," he exclaimed. "Now they are having the entertainment."

"Lovely," Sharon said. She was back in her own crazy world, which was beginning to grow comfy and familiar, too. When you walked into Moreau's house there was an Aubusson carpet on the floor of the salon. It was rotting in the North African sea damp, but it was there. And there was a woman—his wife—who looked exactly like something out of an old Dracula movie. Down the road the ben Omranes were eating couscous out of a community bowl spread on a mat on the kitchen floor, and in the fields the Bedouin were still camped helplessly waiting for some work in the terrible drought. But here there were lights and the house was blasting with music.

In the outer courtyard a brace of parrots flashed by squawking in the cassia trees. Against a black and white striped pillar a peeled, elegant Arab woman in a sheath of gold paillettes smoked a cigarette and talked to a white-haired man in a dinner jacket. Two blonde faggots in nylon slacks and jerseys were standing by the open door to the bath.

In the long hall there were French women with their coiffures arranged like plastic sculptures and Young Nationalist Arabs in snowy djibbahs. A handful of Americans or French from Tunis in business suits. A *maloof* orchestra was playing in front of the fireplace where ordinarily two sofas stood, and the salon chairs had been moved back to make room for a line of jingling Tunisian belly dancers. But the place was a madhouse of cigarette smoke, bodies, and noise.

It was great. Sharon supposed it was an honor to have been invited to all this. At least Ahmed, the butler, gave her a sharp look-over which included the all-day yellow dress and the still-floating kef smile that she wore and inserted her into a crush of French standing by the dining alcove. He went away before she could tell him to bring her a drink.

There must have been a hundred people in the house. The noise came in gusts, people screaming out conversations at the top of their lungs, French-style, the crowd in the salon tightly packed around the belly dancers, urging them on with imitations of the high-pitched *lululululu* of Arab women. The *maloof* orchestra climbed higher to get above the racket. Over the heads of the crowd Sharon could see the occasional flash and glitter of the belly dancers' gold coin headdresses and painted eyes, the flutter of red and purple scarves. The dance, with its monotonous undulating glide, was the same old dance, the great social turn-on of the Arab world.

But while she was standing there with some Frenchman's elbow practically in her face, Sharon slid away. One moment she was there, and the next moment not. The *boliss* in the town square put out his cigarette and strolled around the midnight streets. In a dark house someone wakened, and heard the train roar away. The spattering of the train lights was exactly the same; she could even feel the hot wind from the vestibule door blowing on her face. The North African towns were so beautiful in the dark because there was a deathly empty stillness over everything: flat streets with whitewashed curbs, the clacking palms, white walls of secret, enclosed houses.

I'm having a flash, Sharon thought with mild surprise. There was something more than kef in that Moroccan stuff, because it's still coming on.

The *maloof* orchestra rose high on flutes and thumping finger drums, the girls spinning around caught in psychedelic veils. The music built to a pyramid of sound and then fell with a crash. The girls took smirking bows, there were a few whistles from the Europeans in the crowd, and then there was a general surge down the hall toward the bar for drinks. Sharon backed against the dining alcove wall to let the dancers through.

They were a pretty strange-looking bunch, she told herself. Not that it was really important, but the leading girl had pretty thick shoulders and, under the gauzy sleeves, really muscular forearms. The girl behind was better, running and hopping along to keep up with the first and giggling, her face smeared with eyebrow pencil and kohl and dark red lipstick, coins rattling by rouged cheeks, still shaking her hips as though she couldn't stop. Her face was a few inches from Sharon's before she realized who it was.

The girl with the still-swinging hips was Salem. The girl behind him, mascara'd eyes downcast, was Shedli.

It was practically all of the Ez-Zahra youth discussion group.

10

Woman is like a fruit,
which will not yield
its sweetness until you
rub it between your hands.

—The Perfumed Garden

On Saturday mornings Cynthia Guffin went to
the British Women's Club from 9 A.M. to 10 A.M. (in the winter from
10 to 11, but set back an hour from July to September to allow for the
dreadful heat) to sew sacques and receiving blankets and toddler's
denim coveralls for the Government Child Care Clinics and the
Children's Villages. It was pleasant work, making children's clothes,
and Miss Guffin rather looked forward to it. The sewing group of
the British Women's Club of Tunis had begun more than forty
years ago under the chairmanship of a more than usually energetic
Consul's wife when it had still been fashionable for the ladies of the
English colony to gather once a week in the clubrooms of the Avenue
de la Liberté to practice the gentlewomanly art of hand sewing and
share a companionable morning cup of tea. The volume of work
turned out had never been impressive but the quality of the sewing
had always been high, and in some years (particularly under the
French) there had been a gracious note from the Department of
Public Health acknowledging their contribution. One spring shortly
after independence, when a massive effort was being made to collect
the street beggar children and get them into the supervised Children's
Villages, the British Women's Club sewing group had produced a

record sixty-nine articles of clothing and ten purchased layettes donated by women too busy with their families to make them.

Lately, however, the sewing group had rather lost its genteel sociability. Time and a shift in the British colony (all the colonial people out and the new industrial people in) had brought an influx of younger women, impatient and a bit too restless in temperament for the quiet business of needlework. The younger set had begun to press for the purchase of electric sewing machines so as to "get things popping," as they put it, and this had caused much distress among the older members. Personally, Cynthia Guffin rather hated to think of the clack and rattle of machines replacing the gentle quiet and good talk of morning tea, but the revolt in the ranks of the younger members had followed hard on the heels of the recent scandal with the Ministry of Health when it had been revealed that blankets and layettes which had been turned over to the Ministry had actually ended up for sale in some village shops instead of being distributed through the free clinics. The director responsible for the sale of clothing had been dismissed but, coupled with the dissension over the electric sewing machines, the group had been through an unhappy time.

For a while Miss Guffin—who detested rows—had toyed with the idea of giving up the Saturday morning group, but she had decided against it. The sewing *was* pleasant in spite of all and kept her in practice (once learned, she had always felt, skills should be retained at full efficiency), and she did have a soft spot for the nice things which could be made for babies. And the sewing group did get her out of bed on Saturday at a decent hour and set her on her feet in a climate where, especially in the summer, it was all too easy to give oneself over to lassitude and late hours. Once up and going, she was able to make her Saturdays most productive. Nine to ten was set aside for the sewing group and eleven to twelve (more or less) for calls. To have a definite time each week for visiting old friends was really the only way to keep them; one certainly couldn't rely on chance encounters or Tunis' lax summer social schedule. In fact, without a certain time for it, she probably would not get around to seeing those of her friends, like Zuleika Khaznadar, who led somewhat restricted and secluded lives.

The rest of her Saturday afternoon was usually left open and dependent upon the heat for shopping and running various errands.

But after the shops closed, Cynthia Guffin felt free to luxuriate in the long afternoon *sieste* with a totally free conscience. On Saturday evenings she sometimes joined Nancy Butler for an American film at the Embassy.

On this Saturday morning in July, Cynthia Guffin left the British Women's Club and boarded the Number Twelve bus, which took her down the Avenue de la Liberté and into the Boulevard of the President, where she then changed to the Number Forty-four. The transfer was in abrupt contrast to the Avenue de la Liberté line: one left the modern city and glass-fronted shops and foreigners of the newer districts and boarded a bus crowded with natives which went through and beyond the vast working-class districts to the west of Tunis. Miss Guffin seldom, if ever, encountered a European face among the passengers of Forty-four. An extremely tiresome, jolting ride (the Forty-four route never seemed to have any new equipment as in the more modern parts of town) of more than an hour finally delivered her to the suburbs and the end of the line. From there it was a fifteen-minute walk through bare and blazing dirt alleyways to the villa of the Khaznadars.

In spite of the difficulty in getting out to see her, Miss Guffin would not have given up her friendship with Zuleika Khaznadar for the world. Zuleika was growing quite old and had been in poor health for the past year, but she was still a delightful person and a window into a world, as Miss Guffin often reminded herself, that one seldom saw any more: the circle of the old and secluded aristocratic families of Tunis.

Mustafa Khaznadar was a *khadra* of the Moslem law courts attached to the Great Mosque of Tunis and from an extremely respected and well-to-do Tunis beylical family, and yet the Khaznadar villa always reminded Cynthia Guffin of a small, rather lackadaisically kept English country vicarage. There was too much left about to her critical eye (that morning a wheelbarrow and a spade lay directly in her way in the middle of the garden path), too much left undone (the flowers underfoot were shockingly weedy and the trees in obvious need of pruning), for it to be as pleasant as it should. The comparison with a country vicarage was perhaps an apt one, though. The Moslem judge with his measured, unhurried speech, his gently drooping jowls, old-fashioned clothes, white Turkish-style mustaches and vague air of scholarly distraction did remind her of a village parson. Not Anglican—there was too much rock-bed puritanism in the Moslem religion for that. Methodist was more like it. Or Scottish Presbyterianism. The view of man's sinfulness was exactly the same. Mustafa Khaznadar regarded card playing, dancing, music, films, and the consequent light-mindedness of modern Arab youth as a shocking example of earthly corruption. And of course one did not mention liquor. As for Zuleika—woman's place was in the home, where she shone with her crown of modesty and virtue. It was positively Victorian. Miss Guffin had often observed that the *khadra* would not be at all out of place in some Fundamentalist chapel in the Midlands.

Across the littered yard an old-fashioned buggy was drawn up by the stable wall. When the new law requiring compulsory automobile insurance had been enacted, Mustafa Khaznadar, like the rest of the conservative Moslem community attached to the Great Mosque, had decided that insurance was too closely connected with the Qur'an's prohibition against the lending of money at interest. One paid the insurance premiums, but then there was the problem of dividends and claims for amounts which might be larger than actually invested. He had promptly sold his ancient Citröen rather than be obliged to buy the government insurance and now used the Khaznadar family carriage, which dated back to the days of his grandfather's service at the court of the beys. The selling of the car was very hard on Zuleika, of course. With her heart condition it had virtually precluded all trips or visits. But the *khadra* had been much admired in the city for his stand. The more liberal and *moderne* Moslems with their Renaults wouldn't consider giving them up, naturally, but they were loud in their praise of Khaznadar's unshakable virtue.

Mustafa had come out on the porch in a snowy, flowing djibbah and old-fashioned Turkish pantaloons, open-backed slippers upon his feet, and now he held the door open for her. "Your visit is a blessing upon us," he said formally.

"And may Allah bless you and your house," Miss Guffin responded.

The formalities of classical Arabic which seemed quite interminable to foreign ears never bothered her; the exquisitely detailed inquiries as to health and fortune and the frequent invoking of God's blessing—which she had just been through with Moulay, the man of all work who had let her in, in the more abbreviated colloquial form—were after all, so courteous and charming.

May your day be blessed.

May your day be fortunate.

May your day be good.

Be in good company, also.

The One God with you.

May Allah grant you a happy evening this day.

May the Lord grant you peace, and a happy morning tomorrow.

But as soon as Miss Guffin entered the porch Moulay rushed forward with a large pump-type apparatus filled with *le Flit*, with which he proceeded to decimate the flies there and fill the air with visible clouds of insecticide as powerful as tear gas. Cynthia Guffin quickly put her handkerchief to her mouth and nose and tried not to do anything so impolite as strangle.

The insecticide sprayer was something new, and the ultimate in hospitality, she judged from Moulay's beaming face. And of course they were certain that as a foreigner she would prefer asphyxiation by *le Flit* to the one or two houseflies buzzing about.

The *khadra* drew up a battered metal porch chair and Miss Guffin sank into it gratefully. It was past noon and the heat was overwhelming in the airless flatlands of El Zeitouna, and she rather wondered why they didn't go inside; certainly at that hour it would be much cooler in the thick-walled rooms of the house. But she could also plainly hear the soft drone of male voices from the window just beyond. The *khadra* had male guests; that was obvious. And of course he did not wish to discomfit her, a woman, by putting her in among them.

Nevertheless, it was awkward. It meant she would have to pay her respects to Zuleika—no long chat that day, she thought regretfully—and get off as soon as possible.

As Miss Guffin took off her hat and wiped her forehead delicately with the handkerchief, she sensed a distinct air of unease in her host. He had known she was coming; she usually did on Saturdays. Had the others inside the house been unexpected?

Not to worry, she told herself. She would make her visit brief.

However, there was to be more than one awkwardness. Zuleika was not well at all. In fact, she was at that moment sleeping, the first good sleep in many days. As the *khadra* talked on gently, softly, signaling to Moulay to bring small dishes of raisins and almonds and glasses of Coca-Cola, Cynthia Guffin found herself following his words with growing dismay. The phrases were well chosen so as not to alarm or upset her—my dear friend, my dear Miss Guffin, my dear wife's beloved companion—that she did in fact become quite disquieted. Mustafa talked of the summer drawing to an end and the slow drifting of the sun, now, to a gentler orbit, the yellowing of the leaves in the trees. One had to listen carefully. There were sedatives now for Zuleika, and so much trouble with the breathing which could not, alas, be solely attributed to the heat.

Why, she realized with a start, he's telling me that Zuleika is dying.

For a moment she felt a rush of grief more painful, perhaps, than if he had told her so quite bluntly.

Zuleika was dying very slowly, as her heart was failing slowly, as the summer was waning all around them in slow death. And as all things must die eventually.

They sat with the fallen flies buzzing on the concrete porch floor at their feet in a long silence. The ultimate cruel courtesy, the offer to wake Zuleika so that she could speak to her, Miss Guffin rejected out of hand. Of course, she told herself, the signs were all there and one had known it was coming all along. But Zuleika was such a dear. Gentle, reserved, warm, she was still, at the age of sixty, one of the city's most beautiful women with her masses of auburn hair and buttery skin, the fairness the old Arab families prized so much. And it was a shame, really, that so few foreigners got to know the women of the Arab aristocracy. All that nonsense about their being ignorant hareem creatures, fat, lazy, little better than hysterical human cattle! That might be true of some of the dreadful Ghigas and their crowd in the past, but never the families of substance. It was ridiculous to assume that the old conservative households of the ruling classes had been given over to women with no cultivation. Zuleika Khaznadar was a perfect example: her father had been a professor of Islamic law at the University of Baghdad and a noted Qur'anic scholar. The family was Syrian nobility. The marriage with Khaznadar had been arranged, but then no more arranged than marriages of European nobility, one might say; there were the same sort of blood connections, the same sort of intermarrying, crisscrossing relationships. The Khaznadars had originally been Persians in the service of the

Turkish beys, money men in the Tunis beylical system for centuries. Their women were especially famed for their beauty and allowed to be as cultivated as they wished. For many years Zuleika Khaznadar had written delightful poetry in the classical style, some of which had been published under a male nom de plume. And she had, as Miss Guffin knew, a quite wicked, irreverent sense of humor which she had somehow managed to conceal quite successfully from that old sobersides, the *khadra*.

They had been madly in love. Mustafa had never reproached her for her childlessness, nor had he, as far as anyone ever knew, considered any other woman.

The porch was, Miss Guffin realized suddenly, quite unbearable and still permeated with noxious gases from the Flit gun. She was really not up to staying any longer. The thought of her own cool flat in Tunis and an hour or two with a cold compress on her head in a room with drawn shades was overwhelming.

But when she tried to use the excuse of the other guests waiting for the *khadra* she inadvertently made a small blunder. One could not do it that way; it reflected on his hospitality. At once Mustafa insisted that he had been terribly remiss; she must not under any circumstances think that he was anxious to join the others. How distressing, that his household was in such disorder that it had given her this impression! She must forgive him; she must come and be properly introduced so that those inside could enjoy the pleasure of her inestimable company.

Oh, *damn*, Cynthia Guffin thought. She was in a tear to get away; she was afraid she was getting a headache, too.

The men all stood up dutifully as she came to the door, rising in a flurry of summer djibbahs and *gandourahs*, dressed in impeccable white street oxfords (how did they manage to keep them free of the terrible dust? she wondered), nylon shirts with silk ties under their tentlike garments. Several politely stubbed out cigarettes. The tables of the small, rather bare salon with its wicker chairs and rickety bridge lamps were littered with coffee cups and the remains of fruit-and-bread breakfasts, so Mustafa had had their company since an early hour. Although their dark faces were all held as smooth and expressionless as the *khadra*'s, Miss Guffin sensed the commotion. Remarkable—some sort of subterranean consternation that took a moment to die down. As she had crossed the threshold they had been speaking rapidly in Arabic, and she had understood perfectly well what they had been saying.

Well, quite a pother, she told herself. And there was no way for her to mend it. She could have greeted them in French, of course, but that would have been ridiculous. No need to pretend she couldn't speak Arabic; the *khadra* couldn't speak anything else. In the tradition of the families associated with the Great Mosque, the Khaznadars had refused for eighty long years to learn the language of the oppressor.

Yes, she told herself, viewing the sulky faces, quite a bit of fuss and an equal effort to hide it. And they did so want to get rid of her! They were quite bursting with excitement, waiting to discuss among themselves who she was and how much she had overheard.

As she shook hands with them European-style Miss Guffin smiled her best gray-mouse smile and ducked her chin. But her eyes were busy.

Khefacha *ibn*—junior—she would expect to find in a household like the Khaznadars'. His background made him quite acceptable. The old Khefacha was one of the Berber powers in the south, though of course that meant less now, with the northern Arabs running the country much to the south's resentment. Anyhow, like most of the sheiks down there, he was something of a religious leader. At least he could make the *imams* hop when he wanted to. And young Khefacha, despite his rapid rise in that ungentlemanly profession, the Secret Police, had enough breeding to keep his thumb out of the coffee cups. The blue eyes, she noted, were quite striking; a falsely angelic look.

But Monji Yacoub—good heavens! The crassest of the crass, mixed line of Algerian shopkeepers and *nouveau* Tunis opportunists. His presence at the villa was most peculiar; the Great Mosque people never mixed with the self-made crowd of the Air Force.

Little Tahar Basti was quite explainable, though. No great shakes socially, but presentable enough. His wife's family was impossible, but his mother had been related to the old Mufti of Jerusalem and had come from one of the great old Palestinian families of Hebron.

But the other two were as ridiculous as Monji. Suffering tortures the moment they opened their mouths, desperately struggling with classical Arabic (why did they insist on it when they couldn't manage it?) with the heavy Berber accents of the south.

"You must not allow me," Cynthia Guffin murmured, taking an unaccountable pleasure in her own impeccable pronunciation, "to disturb you. A thousand pardons." She waved them back into their chairs and for good measure kept talking. She had been so distressed not to be able to see Zuleika, quite upset to find her condition unimproved. She allowed her genuine concern to show, and she saw some of the unease begin to dissipate. But she continued in the same vein until she was sure they were satisfied and even began to look a bit bored and restless. Just another woman visitor. That was enough. She shook hands all around again.

When the *khadra* escorted her down to the gate, she saw that he had had Moulay harness up the horse to the buggy in order to drive her back to town. Well, she would not go all the way back to Tunis in the blistering heat in that amazing contrivance; she would dismiss Moulay after a mile or so and take the bus at some point along the line. She thanked Mustafa Khaznadar, and their farewells were no longer, nor shorter, than usual.

I leave you in the care of God.
May the Lord be your safe conduct, also.
Rest in God's protection.
Rest in peace.

But as soon as the buggy had turned the corner of the dirt road and the Khaznadar villa was out of sight. Cynthia Guffin leaned back against the old cracked leather cushions, yanked off her hat, and shook out her thoughts impatiently.

What a nuisance to have had to be bothered by trivial things when she so much wanted to think! It was positively enraging.

At the top of her mental list she put:

Saharan accent. The "z" sound is always reduced to the soft Berber "d"; they can never quite cover that. But where were they from? And why?

And under that:

Dolphin. They were discussing Norman Ashkenazi when I came in.

Ali ben Ennadji had been sitting on the low stucco wall which enclosed the back terrace of Monsieur Moreau's house when the boys in the entertainment came bursting out. The Ez-Zahra Chief of Police had not been expecting any such thing; he did not even know that the boys were inside. He had just struck a match to light a cigarette, and the flare of flame before his eyes momentarily dazzled him. But one could not overlook such apparitions. As he took in the garish costumes, and the full realization of who these boys were and what they had been doing came to him, he froze, his hand still lifted. They charged past him in a flurry of snorting laughter, almost tripping over the trailing *bedu* women's clothes.

At the steps to the rose garden, one of the boys paused long enough to pull off his gold headdress and wipe his sweating face with the back of his hand, smearing the paint, before bounding off to join the others. The sound of boys' barking laughter went off in the direction of the *tabia*, the cactus hedge which surrounded old Moreau's property. The lighted match, forgotten, burned down to Ali ben Ennadji's fingers. He opened his hand to let it drop.

He had not been so blinded by the flame and the suddenness of it all not to have recognized Salem Gueblaoui and Nourredine Tahar in their preposterous veils. And from this he could well imagine who the rest had been.

Fools. Idiots! Dupes! The words were in his mouth—it was a wonder he had not shouted them out. As it was, a sudden burst of rage so strong that he shook in every muscle of his body came over him, and it was all he could do to force himself to remain seated on the terrace wall, so strong was his desire to run after them.

There was nothing that could be done now, anyway, he told himself after a moment's struggle; the obscene display was obviously finished and it was best to let it be. But he threw the unused cigarette away without realizing what he was doing and shook out another Gauloise with angry hands. If he had run after them and caught them, he thought grimly, he would have cracked their heads together in a way they would not have soon forgotten.

He wondered how much they had been paid to make this stupid spectacle. Not much, he would lay his soul on it. The old Moreau was notoriously stingy, and Ahmed m'Amouri, his butler-pimp-arranger, was not above selling his own sister's son at bargain prices. So these brainless boys could not have gotten more than a handful of milliemes. The rented dancing clothes from Tunis would have cost a hundred times more than they had been paid.

But m'Amouri would see to it that there were also the little extras which would tempt them into making greatest fools of themselves, too: all they could eat of the food left on the plates from dinner, a bottle of *boukhar* and perhaps the privilege of drinking the foreign whiskey which had been left in the glasses. The garbage. Like goats.

But above all the whiskey, and before the dancing, so that they would be a little drunk and congratulate themselves that they were doing nothing which would be degrading to themselves, that it was all a big joke. Very sophisticated. And, after all, were not their own fat bourgeoisie, officials of their own government, swilling whiskey and champagne before the eyes of the foreign guests? So why not a little of this for themselves? And why not also a little of this unspeakable display which threw away their pride as Moslems and their respect for themselves as the youth and hope of the Arab world?

He was just raising a second match before his face when Mees Aweet came rushing out, almost falling over him in her hurry. The lighted match dropped down on his knee and burned a small hole in his uniform trousers before he could brush it off.

"Cripes, did you see that?"

He was so infuriated by the accident of the match and the second burn and her clumsiness on top of everything else which had occurred that he could not gather enough breath to ask her what, in the name of Allah, she wanted now. And to speak French, not English.

But it was not necessary. She bent over to peer at him, and he saw that she was unsteady on her feet. She had been smoking quite a lot of kef.

"What are *you* doing here?" she said curiously. But now in French, slurring the words.

It was a very stupid, annoying question, but then she was a very stupid, annoying girl, as he was well aware. He was sitting outside on the terrace of Monsieur Moreau's house because he was still wearing the greatly sweatstained uniform of the Sûreté Nationale which he had worn since morning, and one did not appear before the old Moreau's guests, the French-educated Mayor of the village, the wali of the *gouvernat*, the foreign embassy people from Tunis, and others like them, in such clothes. Besides, this dinner with its crowds of formally dressed people was not such an affair to which the police, even the Ez-Zahra Chief of Police (which was, after all, only a very minor government position) would be invited. One should know these things. But then, as he told himself, being an American she would not.

"And what was all that?" she demanded in French, jabbing a finger in the direction of the garden. "The boys—in all that SHIT."

Merde was a word, as he had observed, that she used with wearying frequency. As well as other expressions. She knew at least two very vulgar sayings in Arabic which, although correct insofar as they went, were so blunt as to make him flinch. Where did this girl pick up such things? One would think that she would have to have a much better command of French or Arabic even to inquire about such words.

Now, as she stood with her hands upon her hips waiting for him to answer her, he could not help but notice, somewhat sourly, that as usual she did not make a very good appearance. She had not, in spite of the elegantly dressed people inside the house, made any attempt to comb or smooth her hair, and it hung, as it nearly always did, partly over her face. It was very beautiful hair, and of an extraordinary color that was both gold and red, but she had not once in all the time he had known her cared enough about it to go to the hairdresser's and have it arranged in a proper coiffure of piled ringlets and curls such as other women did. The nylon dress was dirty, stained, with red marks which resembled spilled wine, and the jacket-blouse top was not even buttoned all the way. Part of her bare stomach showed.

But naturally the way she looked would not bother her. She was oblivious to it in the manner of most young Westerners. As an *Americaine* she could look like this, go anywhere, and be accepted where others—like himself, he thought bitterly—would not.

Also, she was disgustingly drunk on kef. That did not matter, either. She had the unfocused, faintly witless look which showed it clearly.

"Did you not like the dancing, then?" he asked her, knowing that she was in no condition to appreciate his heavy sarcasm.

"Dancing? Are you crazy?" A slow expression of indignation came to her face. "The old prick paid them to do all that SHIT. My kids." She had to stop and think about it. "My whole damned youth discussion group!"

She leaned so close to him that even in the dim light of the terrace he could not help but notice that the damp and rumpled dress was drawn very tightly across the upper part of her body in such a way that it revealed the outlines of her breasts in distracting detail and even the small, thrusting points of her nipples. She wore almost no underclothes; he could make out only the lines of the bikini underpants against the clinging nylon.

"It should not matter to you," he muttered. He jerked his head in the direction of the house. "These people think such things are very entertaining. I do not see why you do not like them. Always, when the important people and especially the foreigners come to Monsieur Moreau's house, they are expecting to see something a little *audace*—something which he has prepared for them. He has a reputation for such things. And naturally everyone wishes to see the spectacle of the Arab dancing boys. It is very typical, very *folklorique*, as any of them will tell you." He paused, waiting for her to say something, but she only stared at him as though she did not know what he was talking about. "Oh, yes," he assured her, "all foreigners are much fascinated by our depraved customs. Before, in the days of the beys and even under the French, this entertainment was an accepted profession, and some of the boy dancers were very famous. In some of the professional families, if a boy was fortunate enough to be handsome and inclined in such ways—and even if he was not —he was trained to be a dancing boy. It was a very desirable way to make one's living and perhaps to become rich and famous. And when these boys were dressed for the performance, they resembled exactly the beautiful young girls. It is an exciting thought, is it not?" he asked, wanting her to agree with him. "Boys dancing very sexually and provocatively and dressed like girls; it is considered to be very tantalizing and stimulating. And naturally the most beautiful of these boys, they were the favorites of the beys and the pashas, and many rich men had such youths for lovers. All foreigners find this a greatly fascinating subject. That is, how one uses the professional dancing boys exactly. Well, I will tell you," he said savagely. "This is what is called the Arab degeneration. It is very well known, as doubtless you have heard. Of course men make love to boys in other countries, but it is not so refined and artistically done, such as to make an open business of it and offer entertainments. However, this is the reason foreigners came here to this village and built these fine villas here. They wished, naturally, to be artistically degenerate with the Arabs!"

He came to a stop then because, as he well knew, it was useless to talk to her. This girl took nothing seriously; she probably had not even been listening. As for instance now, she was swaying with *kef* and frowning as though thinking something else.

Many times in the past weeks he had told himself that he was not going to have anything more to do with her. That he was going to shut her out of his thoughts entirely. Even as women went, she had a temperament willful and perverse enough to drive one mad. Even now, as he looked at her, it was difficult to believe that he had made love to this crazy, impossible foreign girl and could remember very clearly and intimately what she looked like naked and in his embrace. And that also, she had wished to pretend that nothing at all of such a nature had ever happened, that she had no thought of him at all and was busy with other matters. So that he spent much time following her from place to place in the village and watching her house while speculating as to how, if ever, it could be arranged that he could have her again.

But—as he told himself so suddenly that it nearly swept all other thoughts from his head—she was still insanely, illogically worth all the trouble and exasperation she had caused him. Even now he could remember her lovely body with the small pointed breasts, the long sweep of her smooth belly, and the surprisingly full and heavy feel of her hips in his hands as he pulled her under him.

How could this one girl, he asked himself, be so maddening? She was enough to drive a sane person to the limits of his patience. One did not give oneself to a man as she did, and then appear just to forget about it. Even foreign girls were not known to do such things so casually.

Well, he was not finished with the matter. He had seen to that.

"Would you like," he said abruptly, "to see where they have gone? All these boys in your youth discussion group?"

They went through Moreau's small grove of orange and lemon trees in the impenetrable darkness and felt their way through a back garden waste of bricks and broken fruit baskets and abandoned chicken coops, making for the *tabia* that marked the boundary of the Sebastian estate. At the *tabia* Ali had to search for a few minutes to find the break in the earth bank to let them through. It was literally so black that one could not see a thing until one was right on top of it. The girl stayed close to him, still unsteady from the kef and now a little uncertain because of the dark and she allowed him to take her by the hand to guide her.

"Do you know what you're doing?" she demanded in a loud whisper.

He found the gap at last and took her by the arm to let her scramble over it. But somehow she stumbled and came against him in the blackness so that he suddenly had her completely in his arms. They slid down the far side of the *tabia*, and he held onto her tightly and she did not try to get away. Instead, he heard the gurgle of her smothered laughter and felt the tantalizing press of her warm body slipping in his hands, with her legs between his as they went down, her warm breath against his lips. He quickly seized the chance to find her mouth with his own and kiss her fiercely, clumsily, while he pulled the skirt of the dress above her hips. They came to rest half reclining against the soft sand at the bottom and, in those few seconds with her yielding body against his own, he was already aroused and on fire. He would have taken her right there except that she managed to squirm out from under him and say, "You were going to show me something, remember?"

"Yes, of course."

He got up at once, cursing a little under his breath that the evening had already been so hard on his clothes; he was now covered with damp sand from shoulder to knee all down his left side, and of course he had already burned a hole in his one pair of uniform pants with the stupid match. But whatever doubts he had had about the wisdom of taking her into Sebastian's place were now dispelled. She would want to see the house, he told himself, and that was easy enough to arrange. He would show her everything; it would be a very special *passe-temps* for her, since the public was not allowed in there, and he knew she would be very curious and interested. And then, when he had shown her all that was to be seen, he would have her full cooperation and attention at long last. She would learn how.

There was no path beyond the wire fence. In the blackness they pushed their way through a wall of daturas with the giant white horns of the flowers brushing against their faces. But, once through, they came upon a wide tarmac path, one of the many walks hedged with giant cypresses, the faint murmur of the sea breeze in their tops. Also, quite distinctly, they could hear the click and thump of a finger drum and voices in chopping Arabic singing the lilting rural songs.

"My God," he heard her whisper, "it's like Versailles! This old guy must really have had delusions of grandeur!"

"Wait," he told her. A small unpaved side path went through oranges and heavy stands of cassia and pepper trees. Then, quite suddenly, there was a break in the foliage and they saw the sea, breathing and flowing like a deeper pool of night. The water was spangled with the bobbing lights of night fishing boats, hoping for a good catch on such a calm sea. The rim of the moon was just appearing on the horizon. And to the left, on a small rise, was the summer house made in the fashion of a *marabout*, the square, white-domed tomb of a Moslem saint. On the terrace to the side of the *marabout* the boys were gathered, with lighted candles in saucers and a collection of bottles and plates.

He quickly pulled the girl back into the shadow of the trees. They were close enough to hear the voices, but it was enough, he told himself, merely to watch. The boy with the drum was Shedli Zouhir, and he was tapping it experimentally, testing its tone against the damp sea air. The boy Mounir sat beside him with a flute. But, he also observed with a frown, that was a bottle of *boukhar* they were passing from hand to hand, and there were several other bottles of the same stuff on the mats. Some idiot at Moreau's had given them not only enough to drink at the house but plenty to carry away with them, too.

He did not like the looks of it. They had made fools of themselves once that night with their ridiculous performances, and from the way they were rolling on the mats now and behaving it looked as though they were going to carry on their nonsense in the same vein.

But it was too late to go. Shedli had got the drumhead tuned by holding it over the warmth of a candle flame, and Mounir began the music on his flute. It was a slow, throbbing *bedu* dance, and the raucous sound of their voices drifted up on the sea wind.

"They have been drinking," he said angrily. "That is some of the old foreigner's doing."

"*Décadent, décadent,*" she murmured, watching them, and gave a throaty laugh.

He did not find it funny.

One of the boys who had been sprawled on his back with a bottle of *boukhar* to his mouth got up and stumbled to the center of the mats. As he came, he lurched about comically, pretending to be drunker than he was, and the others applauded. He had taken off his *bedu* skirt, but he still wore the coin headdress and had tied one of the gauzy dancing scarves over his jockey underwear. As the circle of boys began to clap in time, he glided in front of them, shaking first one hip and then the other seductively. The finger drum with its *chock-thump* rhythm punctuated the frankly erotic movement, and the purple scarf drifted back and forth. One could not miss that face, that delicate, thin nose and mouth and heavy black brow, even in that light, it was Salem Gueblaoui. His body was as sinuous as a girl's as he rotated his hips about the circle at the level of their faces.

"They are very drunk," Ali ben Ennadji said disgustedly. "Drunk, and with their heads full of filth, still, from what they have done before. I can smell it on them. Let us go."

"No, I like it." She was watching fascinatedly. "This is really decadent. Don't be such a sore loser."

He did not find that funny, either.

The accursed dance was a woman's dance, acting out the story of a desert girl who comes to her lover to show him what delights await him if he will only come inside her tent—a woman's invitation to marriage. "Come under the black walls of the *bedu* house," the words of the song ran, "and I will show you the pleasures of Paradise between my thighs." The boys' voices broke gleefully as they sang. "Ah—unh!" they groaned with the drum. Salem began long, slow thrusts of his pelvis, hesitating at each outward movement with a delicious quiver, then withdrawing. "This is how you will feel to me, my beloved," the song trilled. The drum slowed for the prolonged, luxurious plunges which seemed to drag his body after them. The drum picked up, and his hips shot back and forth with increasing speed. Now it was a snapping contraction of the whole body, his loins inches away from the boys' faces, the gauze floating over his hips and thighs. The Y flap of his underwear was protruding with his erection, and the boys whistled between their teeth. The body simulated an approaching climax.

"It is enough," Ali ben Ennadji said. He took the girl by the arm to try to pull her away, but she braced herself and would not move.

Now the drummer, Shedli, had looked up, and the drumbeat faltered. Salem had put his hands behind his head and with half-closed eyes was moving in controlled, writhing circles, knees bent, lowering himself to the ground.

"Oh, man," Sharon Hoyt was saying in tones of pure delight. "This is so turned on and decadent it's out of sight!"

"What are you saying?" he wanted to know, raging. The boys were making fools of themselves; they were acting like pigs when they knew perfectly well not to do these things. He not only wanted to throttle them but this stupid girl, too, who was watching them.

The boy was on his heels, a few inches from the ground, still gyrating in a perfect demonstration of balance. The motion of his hips changed to a churning back-and-forth motion. The handclaps rose to a storm and there were yells of "Ya, Salem!" as he imitated a girl lowering herself upon the body of a lover. Then some humorist threw an empty soda bottle along the terrace and it rolled under him. He sprang up.

"Don't pull at me," Sharon murmured over her shoulder.

He had put his arms around her, but now he was not trying to draw her away. He had gotten the buttons of the top of the dress unfastened, and now his hands, still shaking somewhat with anger, were against her smooth damp skin.

The cousin had stopped drumming, a disapproving frown upon his face. But Salem held the soda bottle up for all to see and then slowly he pointed it toward his thighs and even more slowly closed his legs over it. There were more piercing whistles. His free hand tried to push the imaginary ravisher away. But the lower part of his body rolled toward the bottle. It began to disappear realistically, Salem's face twisting from side to side, grimacing. There was no drumming; his cousin Shedli Zouhir was scowling with disgust. The soda bottle pressed onward. Suddenly Salem arched his back and gave a sharp cry of penetration. The soda bottle disappeared between his legs. Several of the boys cried out excitedly, and one of them rolled over on his stomach convulsively on the mats.

Shedli stood up abruptly, kicked the drum away with his foot, and started away from the terrace toward the beach. The others called to him, but he made an angry gesture and kept going.

"You have seen enough," Ali ben Ennadji muttered. He had pulled her against him roughly, and now the soft flesh of her backside was pressing in his crotch. He was angry with her and the others, but he wished to get away from there. There had been nothing in the whole evening but infuriating stupidities, and now he did not intend to be thwarted by a giggling girl.

A boy staggered into the circle, stopping long enough to pull off his trousers and join Salem in his ragged underwear. Salem had begun a bawdy pantomime of all the lascivious possibilities to be found in the Moslem attitude of prayer, his forehead pressed to the ground and his rump high in the air. The other had taken it upon himself to play the lecherous imam of the mosque. Salem began to pray, shifting his backside anxiously out of the way of the other, who was craftily trying to approach him. There was a storm of whistles. But when the other boy pulled down his underwear quickly, the whistles changed to shouts of warning, and Salem hitched along the ground, praying fervently. The audience rolled about on the terrace, clutching their bellies in ecstasy at this burlesque.

"I want to watch," Sharon was protesting.

But her words were lost in the noise which had broken out below them on the terrace of the *marabout*. One of the other boys had gotten up to join the lustful imam, who was now more or less in earnest and was trying to hold Salem down by his shoulders. Salem succeeded in getting to his knees, but the imam put his foot in the middle of his back and forced him down again. The other boys were scrambling over each other, some trying to come to Salem's aid, and Salem himself was shouting desperately for his cousin. There was another grab for the underwear, and the cotton pants came down around his knees.

"Jesus, they can't do that!" Sharon Hoyt cried. "This is the freakiest place I ever saw!"

Ali ben Ennadji did not understand what she had said, but to his amazement she was starting through the trees toward the *marabout*. He caught her just in time.

"What are you doing?" he hissed. "Are you mad?"

By this time Shedli Zouhir had run back from the beach. He threw himself upon the imam and dragged him off. The terrace by the *marabout* was full of struggling bodies.

"Now they are fighting," he said, dragging her back up the path. "So there is nothing more to watch. They have been through all their idiocies and they are finished—and it is to be hoped they will be drunk enough to vomit their stupid minds out. That is what comes of rolling oneself in the shit of foreigners!"

"It wasn't a foreign dance, after all," she protested. "It was a damned Arab dance!" Then she started to laugh again. "I thought it was great. *Formidable!*"

He wanted to strike her. She had been a witness to two exhibitions of filth that evening which any good Arab in his heart would desire to see long buried. And also the drinking and what it had done to these youths, who were not bad boys, only foolish. And still she thought it funny.

"You were going to show me the house," she complained as she stumbled along, trying to pull her hand from his grip.

"Yes, I am going to show you the house," he said savagely.

"My God," she marveled, "where did they learn all those dirty dances?"

"All boys learn stupid things to do. In every country, not just here. In our case—in the case of Arabs—it is necessary to see that they unlearn them, that is all."

When they got to the avenue of the cypresses he drew her into the light to look her over and measure how silly and perverse she still was from the effects of the *kef*. But he could not tell, he thought irately. Silly and perverse was a permanent part of her nature; that was what was so exasperating. The top of the dress was still unbuttoned, and she allowed him to pull it down and away from her shoulders so that he could see her half naked in the moonlight. But she regarded him calmly.

"You like it, don't you?" she said, and moved one hand across her breasts slowly.

Yes, he watched her and he liked it very much, he thought somberly. Her body was very lovely and her skin gleamed in that pale light.

"*Ana aheban*," he said roughly. He tried to put his arms around her and kiss her as violently as he wished, but she pushed him away.

"No, I want to see the house first," she insisted. "You said you could show me the house. Sebastian's house."

"I want you very much," he repeated. "I want you to understand this, so that you will not try to run away from me any more."

"*Bon, d'accord.*" She shrugged. "I know what you mean. I don't want to fight about it any more. But first you must show me this fantastic house and all the stuff. That's what I came over here for."

"Wait for me," he said quickly. "I must go and get the key."

He did not really expect to find her standing there in the middle of the cypress path when he came back, but she was.

11

Oh, children,
From the ocean
to the gulf
you are the blossom
of hope,
The generation
which shall destroy
the chains.

—*Nizar al-Quabbani*

August 10

Sharon, where are you? This is the third time I've been by and still nobody home. Right now it's 2:45 a.m. and your bed is empty. I know, because I looked. Hopefully. Don't flap—I let myself into your side of the house with my Orphan Annie Secret Code Ring without waking your Arab landlord, so there were no riots and your reputation is still clean. But I've been sitting here in the dark for about an hour and now I gotta go. But I keep asking myself, where are you? As I am writing this by the light of your refrigerator I keep thinking violently jealous thoughts, which kind of surprises me. I will have to take this up with you later. Anyway, I wanted to let you know that there are no pictures except a great shot of Genevra Coffin in a mini standing in front of the Foundation office that must have been taken a couple of months ago. Either your camera got busted, or the film got old.

(OVER)

Look, I'm running out of paper. Besides, I need to talk to you, not write letters. Get your camera fixed. I want some shots of you, and not sexy Jenny, no matter what you may think. Be back in a couple of weeks, Maybe.

N. A.
(mild-mannered Clark Kent)

P.S. I drank a coke. Why don't you put some food in this thing?

Norman left the note under the remaining bottle of Coca-Cola, where she would be sure to find it in the morning when she came down to have it for breakfast, and closed the refrigerator door.

197

Missing Sharon was a stroke of bad luck, but there wasn't much he could do about it. He couldn't risk another trip to Ez-Zahra until the current pressure eased off a little. His visa and Chaim's had been called in for another "review," as had been more or less expected, and while their passports were in government hands they had decided to play it very cool and clean, staying out of the Tell as much as possible and working their prospecting franchise and even jobbing a couple of small orders at the potash plant in Mezzouna. Not that this activity really fooled anyone, but it did help to bring out their official cover and flap it around a bit, to let the powers that be know that he and Chaim were listening, baby, and sticking to the rules. That was more important than the damned cover itself.

They had even shut down most of their work in the Jewish villages. They still made some calls and visited the brethren, but about all they could do for the families while the situation was jumpy was to advise everybody to sit tight and not panic. It was, Norman told himself, a lousy, mealy-mouthed way of screwing around, and he was getting tired of telling Jews who were sitting in a sea of hostile Arabs that there wasn't anything he and Chaim could do for them at the moment, because Tel Aviv thought bombing the trolley lines around Cairo was more important.

The current deep air strikes into Egypt were supposed to be worth all the trouble they were causing; even Michel Liebman was very gung-ho about the Israeli raids shaking up Nasser's back yard. But Norman wasn't impressed. Right now the raids were a pain in the ass, kept going, in his estimation, by the hawks on the general staff who had this thing about toppling Nasser. *Yeah.* Norman knew staff operations pretty well, he had put in his time, still had his commission, and, as the Army used to say, there was a time and a place for grandstanding for the Hadassah. The air strikes might look good in the press, but they were endangering all the T-X-12 operations and everybody in the field. And who was going to look out for the brethren if they couldn't?

Lately, that didn't seem to be important to Tel Aviv. The priorities had been thrown into a grab bag, and it was anybody's guess. Michel's request for a confirmation on von Lehzen-Hauk had been received and acknowledged, and that was the last they had heard of it. For shit's sake, how long did Tel Aviv think they could wait?

As Michel said, they could only assume that the office was busy with other things.

Norman wished to hell he could show the Office some of the Tell villages where he had to get the *twansa* Jews out, and fast, before they got their heads knocked in. The kids were nearly all gone, and there was nobody around to protect the old folks. O.K., so they weren't kibbutz material, but they were still Jews, weren't they?

And then there was the real business, the Group One stuff. It had always been one of their A-level priorities. But lately he was getting the sneaking impression that, as far as Tel Aviv was concerned, it was a case of forget about the old war and concentrate on the new one.

O.K., but if that was what they were going to do, at least they could tell him about it.

In his last briefing with Michel, Norman had been pissed off enough to tell him that the only way he could figure to grab anybody's ear any more was to report to Tel Aviv that Adolph Hitler was alive and well and living in Abdel Nasser's guest room, and that they had pictures to prove it.

O.K., so it wasn't funny. But he had a feeling that nobody wanted to listen to anything else. The point was, the way things were going, with the dead silence from the Office, the situation didn't offer much hope for wrapping up von Lehzen-Hauk.

But regardless, Norman had promised Michel that he would tuck in the edges and fix Sharon Hoyt up with a phony excuse about her roll of film. That much he could do. Still, up to the moment he had let himself into her house in Ez-Zahra he hadn't had any firm idea as to what he was going to tell her. He was the last person in the world to figure out what went on in Sharon Hoyt's head. She was a real, living, absolute kook. For all he knew she had forgotten about the roll of film entirely. Maybe even forgotten about him. Sure, he hoped she attached some importance to the intimacy of his lovemaking—he had, anyway—but he wouldn't be willing to bet on it. She had this perfectly serious idea that if you liked somebody, even a little, or was even curious about them, you started screwing. He had heard that, seen all that before, and there wasn't any need to argue with her about it; she was only one of a lot of crazy kids who felt the same way. It was only that it really bugged him, for some surprising reason, to think that she could be that stupid.

In a lot of other ways, she was really a very intelligent girl.

As he was writing the note, trying to think of something to say to her, the idea of the camera just fell into his head. It was better, perhaps, than anything he could have told her, and with luck he figured it would hold her until he got back.

Norman went upstairs in the dark and searched her bedroom thoroughly. There was a lot of junk around; it was incredible how untidy she was, but he finally located the camera on the table by the typewriter under a pile of papers and magazines. It was a quick and simple matter to insert his knife between the back cover plate and the view-finder housing of the Instamatic and pry the cover up and out gently so that the hinge bent from the inside. He struck a match to make sure he hadn't left any telltale scratches. He had bent it just enough; the curve wasn't visible unless you examined it closely and even ran a finger over it to make sure it was there. The cover plate could have sprung from dropping it. And from now on when she used the camera it would leak enough light to blacken the film, convincing her that it had been broken when he shot the last frames.

Even if she had used the camera since then, a light leak was one of those things. It could come and go. Anybody who owned something as simple as an Instamatic would believe that.

He put the camera back on the table by the typewriter where he had found it and pulled a magazine over its face. As he was doing so his thoughts unexpectedly drifted; they changed course, and in rapid succession he thought of a number of things he had left undone that day and still had to do, mental notes and pictures, and at the very last the note which he had left for Sharon Hoyt in the kitchen. In one of those sudden tricks which the mind will play, he was realizing very clearly and for the first time why he hadn't made any real plans, why he hadn't gotten any real story together when he was making arrangements to come there.

He stood in the dark close-smelling room that still carried the odor of her bath powder and cigarettes and unwashed clothes and knew that what he had written in the kitchen downstairs for a joke was quite true. Subconsciously, he had been depending on her to be there, in the house, asleep in bed, when he came upstairs to look for her.

Christ, he had been counting on it! All that time when he had been operating under the delusion that his moves were calculated logically and conclusively, he had been really expecting to climb in bed with her, wake her from her damp and rosy sleep and make love to her, and then figure out something to tell her afterward.

He was damned surprised at himself, damned amazed to find that he should know so little of his own mind. And the crazy thing was, his desires had been sneakily laying in wait for him, ready and full-grown. It definitely gave him, in a minor way, something of a jolt. He supposed that he had been thinking that if it had been good on the beach it would be even better with her in a nice big bed where one could take one's time. Savor, as it were, the fine nuances of lovemaking. None of the crap with the scratching and the dirty talk and the things she seemed to regard as necessary to the full blossoming of passion. Blossoming of passion, hell! He didn't need any stimulation; since that time he had had a real struggle to keep her out of his mind, to tell himself that Miss Sharon Hoyt's brand of free-love-for-everybody was not only distasteful but downright dangerous for what he planned to do. An absolutely *verboten* luxury. And yet to have found her in bed—he could have had control in absolute degree, to calm her down and make love to her slowly and satisfyingly, as he knew she would be more than enough to satisfy any man, and afterwards lie there in the dark with a cigarette and the soft, warm, feminine reality of her in his arms. His whole damned soul unexpectedly lusted for it. He wanted to take her and have her, many times, and then by God he wanted to talk. He wanted to hold Miss Sharon Hoyt and talk American until his tongue and head ran dry. Like, tell me about the filthy subways which I remember now so much. And Simon and Garfunkel. And do they still have concerts on the Mall in Prospect Park? And what do you do in your crazy head and why do you think these things and why do my thoughts keep turning to you when you mean absolutely nothing to me and I have only slept with you just once? And do you dig Dustin Hoffman? I saw *The Graduate* but they tell me all his other pictures are great, too.

All the things, baby, you don't keep up with in places like Bab-el-Fellah.

He was just discovering how lonely he was. In the dark room, standing there, he had never even considered before that he was particularly lonely; it came as an entirely new thought.

Entirely as a goddamned new thought, and a hell of a bad sign.

I'm tired and I've been stupid enough not to realize it, Norman told himself. The biggest professional blunder I could make. This shit with Tel Aviv is getting me down more than I've been willing to admit. I'm not the type to sit on my ass for long; I'm an action man, an enforcer, and that's what I was sent here for. I was sent here to get von Lehzen-Hauk. Now I've got the signal to move at the tip of my fingers and the goddamned Office has gone off and left me sitting on the pot. All of us.

And furthermore, he told himself firmly, it's not Sharon Hoyt; it's not this kooky, toothsome, long-legged chick with a warm and loving snatch that's bothering me, but my own wandering head. And if I don't watch myself I'm going to be turning myself in for a voluntary R and R. That is, if I don't get it shot off before that. Trouble starts in this business when you begin to think about the wrong things and don't even realize you're doing it.

And if he knew what was good for him, he wouldn't hang around in a room that smelled like a sweet, warm body even when that body wasn't in it.

At least a busted camera would take care of that problem for a while.

CONFIDENTIAL

August 18th

To: Sir Charles Benedict
FROM: George Russell
SUBJECT: Blowing up fish canneries

You will be glad to know that previous reports that our Youth Committment Representative Wendell Falck blew up all or part of the Belle Mer Fish Cannery in Tabarka have been grossly exaggerated.

For some reason which I still haven't figured out the Belle Mer plant is still there and in one piece and so is our boy Wendell, but this is not, you might say, for want of trying. I have been given a personally conducted tour of the Belle Mer operation by Plant Manager Mr. Abdelhamid Mahjoubi, and it is my opinion that, given the odds, both all or part of Wendell and the Belle Mer should by rights be floating around in the Mediterranean or washing up on the shores of Sicily.

According to the folder submitted to us by the New York office and which I remember reading pretty thoroughly, this boy is a Catholic seminary dropout and not a mechanic, but, as the lady said when she found the crocodile in the bathtub, I suppose nobody ever thought to warn us about that. However, if we've got any more secret machinery lovers in the crowd I want to know all about it, because one explosion (this one) is going to be about all we can afford. You will see by the attached bill which was drawn up and waiting for me when I got to Tabarka that we are going to have one hell of a time justifying this item of expense on our monthly budget. Or, for that matter, explaining why, without actually going into the whole story, we are now buying one slightly overage World War Two type compressor which I guess now comes in about 500 separate pieces including V belts and what's left of the housing.

At this point I want to bring up the fact that in the recent past there has been some discussion about all of us taking a strong, constructive attitude toward the Youth Commitment Project and not letting their little adventures get in our hair. And I just wanted to let you know that this trip to Tabarka has given me a lot of opportunity to work on my strong, constructive attitudes about pretty nearly everything, and I think I've finally got my natural instincts under control. As for instance, I have not at all been put out by having to spend the whole morning listening to Plant Manager Mr. Abdelhamid Mahjoubi, who, by the way, is a cousin of the undersecretary to the Minister of Transport and a nephew of the secretary-general of the National Party, and who once visited the United States where, he tells me, he got snowed on, chased by blacks in Central Park, and cheated by Jewish taxicab drivers. On the contrary, after looking over the 500 pieces of our compressor with what you might call the enthusiastic help and cooperation of Plant Manager Mahjoubi, I had such strong, constructive attitudes that it occurred to me that if we do this thing right and throw Mahjoubi his cut for keeping his mouth shut, we might be able to pull out of here O.K. and come up smelling like roses. What do you think of gathering up the 500 pieces and sending them out next Christmas as souvenir paperweights from the Tunis office? If you like cast iron, some of these pieces come in pretty interesting shapes. And you can't say that four or five pounds of pre-World War Two metal (they don't make cast iron like they used to) wouldn't hold down a hell of a lot of paper. Before you get really sold on this, let me say now that it's not going to be easy. Getting a listing of roughly $1,500 American for an item like paperweights past the New York accounting office is going to take some doing. But I'd like to suggest that we split them up and list $750 for strictly office use and the other $750 for business gifts. That might do it.

Right now I think you might as well tell Miss Guffin to take the lock off the confidential file and open up another box of memos, as something tells me the Youth Commitment Group is finally going to help us fill up all those empty spaces.

For a starter, let me get down approximately what happened up here. . . .

When Wendell walked down to the cannery on Sunday, August seventeenth, the boats were still out and the canning sheds were empty. There was no one around except for a few women in the large room, cleaning and crimping machines. The bell was chinking in the cutting room. When he stepped in, the place was full of heat and gray light and the cloying stink of fish, stronger here than anywhere else because this was where the tuna carcasses were butchered. And the two boys he knew, Beji and Said Klibi, turned on their heels to see who it was. They were squatted in front of some machinery, working on it, and their faces showed no surprise to find him there, but then their faces never showed anything much, as he well knew, only a tolerant, blank politeness when he was around.

The Klibi boys, like the other kids in the plant, had made it plain that he, Wendell, had nothing to offer them. Not friendship. Not youth groups. Not community organization work. They belonged to some sort of local youth group sponsored by the government, and that was enough. Or so they said. And they said they were not interested in rich young Americans. Not even rich young Americans who wished to work in the cutting room in the lowliest of jobs, for some unexplained reason, but who vomited at the first sight of an opened tuna belly.

Oh, in the beginning they had asked him all sorts of questions about where he had been to school and what he had studied, and about America, especially the West with the cowboys they had seen in the movies. And about American girls. Lots of embarrassing detailed questions about American girls. Wendell couldn't explain, wouldn't try to explain, all those years he had spent in the seminary.

If they were interested in anything, the boys in the plant were interested in the newspaper and magazine accounts of Palestinian youth guerrillas their own age. At lunch time the boys in the plant ate together outside in one special place on the shady side of the docks and passed the magazines, with their color photos of young guerrillas carrying automatic rifles, from hand to hand.

The tough young fighters of the Al Fatah and the Palestinian Popular Liberation Front would never vomit at the sight of a gutted fish belly. It was a standing joke.

Wendell smiled at them. This day was going to be different because he knew all this, he had thought it all over, and he had decided to break through the barriers anyway. He had come to that decision by himself. Here, with Beji and Said, he was going to start over again. Maybe they didn't want him—maybe they really despised him as much as they seemed to, but that wasn't important. It had occurred to Wendell the night before that the world was full of hate, the real evil, and if you hated wars and evil you had to do something about it. All the saints had had to make a beginning. And they had realized that people despised them for it, for what they believed.

Wendell squatted down beside the boys and for once he didn't ask any questions, he didn't try to start a conversation, he just let them feel his openness flowing out to them. It made them uneasy. They kept looking at each other.

Finally Beji said, "What do you want?" in an unfriendly voice. He kept his back turned to Wendell. They were both working on a piece of machinery as big, actually, as a safe deposit vault, and they were using a box of beat-up little wrenches. You could tell they weren't going to get anywhere.

The machine was an old compressor. Wendell looked at it with calm recognition and knew it as the old compressor that was never used; it was just a junk piece of machinery too heavy to throw out. And he also knew, with a fine sense of detachment, that the brothers didn't know what they were doing. They were sweating with frustration.

Yet it was a beautiful moment. They had spoken to him. They both had very large black eyes, and as they stared at him resentfully the full force of their vision struck and made contact, and something entirely new enveloped them all. You could feel it. They were looking *at* each other. They were seeing each other for the first time.

"You look sick," Beji muttered. "What is the matter with you?"

"The valves are stuck," Wendell said. It was an inspiration. He didn't know much about compressors and this was an old one, a real monster of a French-made piston-type compressor that wasn't used much any more, he supposed. It probably hadn't seen action in years. But Wendell knew how compressors worked. He had studied compressors in General Science. In fact, he had done better than that; at one time he had been interested in all sorts of motors, just as a hobby, and had studied them in the central library of the St. Louis library system.

Actually, he had gone much further into botany and astronomy that year than motors, but he still remembered a lot. He was safe in saying what he had said. On old compressors the chances were that the valves were stuck. Valves were always full of junk.

He could see Beji and his brother considering this.

"What we are doing," Beji said carefully, "is of no importance. It is not the real work of the cannery. It is only something we do in our spare time. If it works, then the foreman has said that we can repair other machinery."

"Nobody knows how it works," Said put in. "You cannot get into it."

Of course you could get into it. At once it was all beautifully clear to Wendell. A mechanic made much more money than a fish cutter. That is, if a mechanic could ever get started.

"The valves are stuck," Wendell said again. He was communicating very clearly and directly now. "And you can get into it. I can show you."

They were not very happy about that.

"Let's us go home," Said said, and began to pack up the wrenches. But his brother put out his hand to stop him.

"How?" Beji asked him.

After that it all went so quickly, it was amazing what could be accomplished once they got started. Of course Wendell fumbled once or twice and this made them more cooperative. He didn't know everything; there were a few things they could do, also. They handed Wendell the wrenches and they all worked together.

"Once, I took a clock apart," Said told him. "But it was already broken. However, it was very interesting."

Wendell really had to laugh at that. He had taken clocks apart, too, when he was a kid. They were surprised to find out that they had done the same things.

But this was no clock.

No, they agreed, this was no clock, it was really a serious business. If they fixed the compressor, ah, that would really be something!

Wendell knew how they felt.

After an hour they were all working very closely together, their shoulders even touching at times. The machine was old and dirty and they grew covered with grease. The wrenches slipped out of their hands and they laughed. They were all the same lovely black oily color after a while. They wiped their faces with the same rag and smeared themselves with the same brotherly dirt. It was one of the best afternoons Wendell could remember.

"If we fix it," Beji said, "we will say that you worked on it, too."

When they got the valves out they were all pretty tired. They had so much trouble getting them out and cleaning them that when Wendell asked if he could put one back they let him do so. It was sort of an honor. Maybe it was Wendell who put the valve in upside down. He remembered later at the time that it bothered him, and he wanted to check it, but the brothers didn't want to. The heat was very bad in the cutting room, it was past lunch time, and they wanted to finish. They didn't even want to clean off the outside of the machine as Wendell had suggested. The whole operation had taken too long, and they just wanted to throw the switch and see if it worked. The outside could be cleaned up later.

And for one brief moment it looked like the day was going to be as beautiful as it had been from the moment Wendell had stepped into the shed. As they stood watching it, the machine came to life. The motor hummed, the capacitor whined with a charge of power, and the flywheel began to do a funny little spastic dance, flipping and groaning, then freezing and flipping again.

"Come on, baby," Wendell whispered.

"It is trying," Beji said. His eyes were wide, fascinated.

It was as though their combined wills were forcing it to work. They stared, and they urged it under their breaths, and the compressor put out a magnificent noise, a symphony of hissing gaskets the V belts squealing, the flywheel making a majestic *KABLONG* as it struggled with its catatonia.

Wendell wasn't really worried about the valve being in upside down. It was a distant thought, not really bothering him. The machine was working. Otherwise, there would be air coming in and no air going out and it wouldn't be working at all. Compressors didn't expand like rubber balloons. They'd stop.

"It is a magnificent machine!" Beji shouted.

"And powerful, too!" That was Said.

But as the words came out of their mouths they were devoured by the noise, a noise such as one could hardly imagine. As the floor shook under his feet and two tons of cast-iron housing rocked slightly on the concrete, Wendell was seeing the diagram of a compressor once more in his mind and calmly reviewing the steps. Capacitor start feature to motor building up for enough RPMs, flywheel, air goes into the cylinders.

"It is not supposed to walk around," Said shouted into his ear.

Truly, it was astonishing to see two tons of cast iron trying to walk about the floor of the cutting room. They marveled at the sight. They were not so sure, now, but they were fascinated. It was awesome, it enveloped them with sound and strength, but as one boy they stepped back a step, then two. This was what saved Beji as the first of the twelve V belts broke. It only seemed to reach out to caress him across the forearm, but he screamed.

Wendell heard the scream. He turned, as perhaps he had known all along that he would turn, and dived at Beji and sent him sprawling on the floor. Wendell was not, at that moment, particularly afraid or even really connected with what was happening; in fact his mind was standing back quite coolly and still reviewing diagrams and working out in detail the results of a valve put in upside down. He could see it all as though he were studying a mechanical drawing. He took Beji by the arms, even though Beji continued to scream, and dragged him to the door of the crimping room. Then Wendell went back for Said, who for some reason was lying on the floor, too. Probably the damned V belts. They were flailing like spaghetti, reaching out for them. But the noise was so much you couldn't think.

At the door of the crimping room Wendell stepped over Beji and Said and yelled for the women to come and get them, but the women only threw down their brushes and buckets of water and ran away screaming.

Can't rely on them, Wendell told himself. He went back into the cutting room, through a solid sheet of sound, to find the circuit breaker. It took a long time to find the circuit breaker, as the box was not in a very convenient place. It was over a table where the rubber aprons were stacked. When he reached up a pile of rubber aprons came sliding down on him, and he had to throw up his left arm to fend them off. His hand was on the circuit breaker, pulling the switch into the down position, when the aprons hit him and Wendell remembered thinking that it was over. The handle was down and the electricity was off. Just like pulling the plug out of the socket. All his life he had heard stories of machinery going berserk and the remarkable few who kept calm when everybody else around them was panicking, to save the day by doing something logical and simple. Once his mother's washing machine had overflowed and kept pumping water all over the house with his mother crying hysterically until the repairman came and pulled the plug out of the wall to shut it off. Something as basic as that.

He was only a little surprised to find himself among that company of cool, efficient types after all. After all his troubles. After all people had come to think of him.

As his hand left the circuit breaker Wendell slipped on the rubber aprons and went down on his knees. So it wasn't over, after all, he thought, somewhat surprised. The rubber apron under him skidded on a spot of fish slime. He was already moving when the compressor blew up. The force of the explosion sent him the full length of the cutting room on his hands and knees, aquaplaning on rubber and fish ooze until the apron tore apart and the concrete bit into the flesh of his palms and peeled the legs of the chinos back from his shins. He rammed head on into the back wall.

Actually, he saw the wall coming with the same odd, expectant feeling that had marked that whole exceptional day. He even had time to remember that his father was fond of saying that you can't put much into Slovak heads but then you can't knock much out of them, either. And that was Wendell's first moment of panic. It broke through the clear detachment like a knife. Because there was the whole trouble in a blinding revelation. He, Wendell Falck, was a fraud. His head had always been easy to get stuff into; all his life people had marveled at what his head could absorb: Latin, Greek, astronomy, mechanical diagrams, litany, botany—the Fathers had kept at him, stuffing and stuffing. His head was still doing it. And it was going to break like an egg, everything spilling out when he hit.

In spite of his terror he didn't make a sound; his teeth clamped together in an agony. And nothing much came out except that his nose started to bleed.

On his way back Russell stopped in Bizerte to check with Genevra Coffin and tell her about Wendell's adventure at the cannery. By then his version of what had happened was pretty well sharpened up for her benefit, and it made a funny story. He had gotten over his peeve about the whole thing, and he was pleased to find that she thought it was pretty funny, too. She laughed at his descriptions of Wendell and interpersonal relations as applied to a compressor until she was crying, and she had to go and fix her mascara.

"You know, George Russell, you're a real funny guy," she told him, coming back from the bedroom with a piece of Kleenex and the mascara tube. "You have a great deadpan delivery. It's something people don't expect to find in you, do they? A great sense of humor."

"It's actually a deep cynicism which passes for a life style," he told her. "How's that?"

"Oh, that's groovy. I like that. You're beginning to sound very hip. You sound just like our preliminary reports."

He had found her dressing to go to the wedding of one of the neighborhood girls that afternoon, and she had already apologized for being in a hurry. She had asked him to please help himself to a beer from the refrigerator, as she didn't have time to stop, and now she stood in front of the mirror, touching up her mascara and watching him in the glass.

"Poor Wendell," she was saying. "He's our mystic. With Wendell, everything's got to be some sort of religious experience. He is our guru. In tennis shoes."

Of course they could laugh at it, but he had spent most of the day before chasing Wendell Falck, as nobody in Tabarka seemed to know where he had gone. Oh, he suspected they knew, all right, but they just wouldn't open up about it. At the hospital, Russell had finally gotten the Klibi's address, a flat on the third floor of an old concrete slum overlooking the waterfront. The inside of the stair well was cluttered with four-year-olds minding toddlers. The four-year-olds had given him the story, and with the story he had been able to persuade Mrs. Klibi to open up and let him in. The Klibis, all ten of them, lived in one room. In the sleeping alcove the family bed, that is to say, the bed for Mama and Papa, was made up with embroidered cotton sheets and massive pillows. On it Russell found Beji with the scratch on his arm bandaged Arab style from wrist to elbow, like a compound fracture, and Said asleep with a towel across his chest. In the middle, between them, Wendell was holding a rag with a piece of ice in it to the top of his head. It was a hell of a way to treat a concussion, but Wendell and Beji were playing cards with the two youngest Klibi girls sitting on their legs.

"We're not hurt," Wendell said at once. The ice was melting and running into his eyes, and it made him blink.

"As long as they've put you in their own damned bed you'd better speak Arabic," Russell growled. "Matter of courtesy."

The little girls tugged at Russell's sleeve to show him the cards. Beji's sisters were identical in black pigtails, black eyes, and home-made cotton shifts like flowered nightgowns. They were enjoying themselves immensely, crawling back and forth over the boys' legs and bouncing up and down in the bed. They loved their brothers and now they loved the *Amrikaneh*, too. The boys were heroes. Beji's arm was cut and Said had been whacked across the back by a V belt and Wendell had a concussion, but they were not very much hurt. When they were well they would all get their jobs back because Wendell was the biggest hero of them all. He had dragged Beji and Said from the smoke and flames of the terrible exploding dis-aster and then had covered them with his own body to protect them from further harm. Also, Wendell had assumed full responsibility for everything. Before everyone—before the doctor in the hospital and Monsieur Othman the foreman of Belle Mer and Plant Manager Monsieur Abdelhamid Mahjoubi (a hard man and very unforgiv-ing, may Allah bring him his just rewards!)—Wendell had sworn that he was alone when the accident happened and that Beji and Said were at home asleep in their beds and had nothing to do with it at all.

Everyone understood. It was a magnificent thing to do, to lie like that, and very noble of the *Amrikaneh*; it had saved them. Most particularly Beji and Said, who now still had their lives. And their jobs.

"You son of a bitch," Russell said. "Thanks a lot. Do you know how much that lousy compressor is going to cost us?"

Wendell's fingers went nervously to the rag on his head with the ice in it. "I suppose you're going to send me home." His ex-pression was resigned. "That's what it says in the contract. That you can send me home without a good recommendation."

Forgetting his own advice, Russell had burst out in English. At the word "compressor" the whole household had started to scream, drowning Wendell's words. Hearing the noise, a couple of married daughters carrying babies came in from the outer hall and, without knowing what was going on, began to yell, too. Even the little girls put down their playing cards and dutifully opened their mouths to wail. Mahjoubi was a bandit; this was well known. The compressor was worth nothing; it had not worked in years. The *Amrikaneh* boy was a genius even to get it to run for a few moments. Yes, this *Amrikaneh* was a pearl of a boy, a lion of courage; one could not praise him enough. With his own body in the smoke and flames, etc. They went through the story again, and now that the married daughters understood what they were shrieking about, they shrieked louder. Without him, Said and Beji would not be alive that day. Mrs. Klibi rushed forward, howling, to throw herself across the three of them in the alcove bed, and her bulk managed to not only cover them but send the little girls and playing cards sprawling.

"I didn't really cover them with my body," Wendell said in Arabic, from under Mrs. Klibi, who was trying to kiss him. But nobody was listening. No one could hear him.

The Klibis had an uncle, a postman, who was going to write a letter to *le Président*, recommending Wendell Falck for a Citizen's Medal. For saving the lives of Said and Beji Klibi, who of course hadn't been there when the explosion occurred. Who had already made a signed deposition to that effect, now on file at the Belle Mer office.

Russell didn't try to argue with that brand of logic. He left while one of the little girls was climbing across Wendell's stomach to pat him on the face and push a piece of slightly used *loukhoum* candy into his mouth. At the door, Mrs. Klibi caught Russell and covered his face with grateful kisses.

12

If only we could
win a major victory here.
I rack my brains
night and day
to find a way.
Unfortunately the conditions
for it don't exist.
Everything depends
on supplies—and has
done for years.

*—General Erwin Rommel
February 26, 1943*

Itzhak bar Shafik was having prayers for the third time that afternoon, and Norman Ashkenazi was getting restless. More than restless, he told himself, he was getting pissed off as hell that Chaim wasn't doing a damned thing to wind up the visit. Norman was anxious to get away. He shifted his aching backside on the hard wooden bench in Itzhak's kitchen and cleared his throat with a loud growl, hoping to get Chaim's attention, but Chaim sat with his head bent, lost in some faraway thought, and did not look up.

Norman shifted his weight again, and this time the bench co-operated by bumping along the dirt floor with a noise loud enough to make one of Itzhak's granddaughters look up inquiringly. But not Chaim. Norman took another look at his watch. It was five o'clock.

There wasn't much he could do about the holdup. The agreement was that he, Norman, left the fine points of family and religious etiquette to the *sabra*, relying on Chaim's tact and superior knowledge of the local variations in language and custom to keep these visits going. But this afternoon his partner was dragging his feet for some reason.

Hell, Norman corrected himself, he knew the reason. Chaim was off dreaming about that Hoggenberger bird in Sousse again, and completely out of it.

I've got a lovesick Jew on my hands, he thought, looking at Chaim's blond head. And I'm damned if I know what to do.

But why Chaim? That was what puzzled him. His levelheaded buddy was the last person anyone would pick to get flipped out like this over nothing. And "nothing" was a good way to describe Dumpy Judy. As far as Norman was concerned you could spend about two solid minutes contemplating Judy Hoggenberger, and that was it. Subject discontinued for lack of material.

But that, apparently, didn't bother Chaim. From the looks of him he was off on the Israeli equivalent of Cloud Nine.

Norman rubbed his hands together, fidgeting, and then the back of his neck where the sweat was accumulating; it was miserably hot in the kitchen and it didn't help his frame of mind much to be reminded of how useless these interminable visits were, anyway. There was damned little they could do for Itzhak's family except promise some vague aid in the future. The past few weeks they had been going through the motions of their work and trying to avoid raising hopes unduly because they couldn't offer anything definite, not with the current Arab-Israeli situation worsening every hour.

Thank God, Norman told himself, for the Tunisian government and its president. For all his faults the old President still deserved his title of statesman and was certainly the only Arab leader who did. The pillar of the Neo-Destour Party and the Father of his Country had kept to the middle way in spite of hell and Nasser and at least five attempts on his life in a country where the majority of the population was under twenty-one and itching to follow the glorious trumpets of Al Fatah.

And, Norman had to add, thank God for the Tunisian people. They couldn't be underestimated. Like the Lebanese—in that other outpost of middle-of-the-road policy—the Tunisians leavened the Arab world with a native genius and a verve and bounce of a very un-Arab character. You had only to put a Saudi and a Tunisian side by side to know the difference; it was like comparing Hatties-burg, Mississippi, with the city of San Francisco. He and Chaim were damned lucky they were in Tunisia and not trying to work, for instance, in Algeria. Morocco was tough and getting tougher, but violently anti-Israel, sometime Maoist-leaning Algeria made any relocation assignment practically a suicide mission. There was none of the business about sliding by on good-but-contrived British and American passports, no I-see-you-and-you-see-me student or business-man covers. In Algeria you were tailed, pinned down, shipped out fast. Everything had gone to strictly cover-of-night and fishing-boat operations, when you could get them, mostly run by native Algerian Jews. And some of the Algerian emergency cases made the Yemeni oppressions look sweet by comparison. If the Algerians caught you, you could always look forward to dying in prison of a "heart attack." That meant they deliberately forgot to feed you. If you were lucky.

The bell on the goldworker's shop in the front of the house tinkled. Norman caught the granddaughter's eye. She heard it, too. The girl was already half out of her seat when there was a soft knock at the entrance to the family quarters.

No customer ever tried that door.

The knock was repeated, the series of threes they had agreed upon, with a space between the second and final set. Norman was ahead of the girl. They almost bumped into each other at the door.

A figure in a ragged jibbah with a rag tied around its head and drawn over the mouth stepped inside. The girl gave a low, frightened wail, and Norman tried to shut her up: in spite of the Arab disguise he recognized David ben Yaakov at once.

"I am sorry, Norman," David whispered. "I did not wish to disturb the family, but I cannot wait any longer."

Norman moved the still-anxious girl to one side and shut the door. And to Chaim, over his shoulder, he said, "Tell Grandpa to knock it off. We've got trouble."

They were not supposed to see David again until they made contact in Tozeur. He was supposed to pick up the car from the Germans in Gafsa and drive it down. And before that, before anything, they were supposed to get the confirmation from Michel. That was what they were waiting for.

"I do not wish to interrupt the worship," David said in English. His face was shiny with sweat. He pulled the *keshta* away from his mouth and ran a dirty hand over his lips. "Is there water? I am very thirsty."

In spite of Chaim's tugging at his sleeve, Itzhak had gone right on chanting. Only a tightening around the old man's lips showed his annoyance.

David glanced doubtfully at Itzhak, but Norman dismissed the patriarch with a brusque motion. "Forget it. Just go ahead, tell me what's on."

"Norman, I am sorry." David hesitated. "But I have brought the Mercedes. I put it in the alley behind this house; there was nothing else I could do. It should be moved soon, I think; it is not in a good place there. I am sorry it has to be this way, but I have taken the car quickly from Michel's garage to get it out of Tunis. Michel is under police surveillance—is that right? Yes, surveillance. The police are at the garage now and they have put a lock on the office. They have confiscated Michel's records. No, no," David said quickly before Norman could speak, "only the garage records. There is nothing else. Everything else Michel keeps in his head."

Itzhak's son Yohannon had taken over the efforts to quiet his father, and now Chaim came up to them, frowning slightly.

"What is the matter?"

"Believe me, Chaim, at first we did not know what was the matter!" The words came tumbling from David in a rush. He took the dipperful of water from Yohannon's daughter and gulped it down, almost choking in his anxiety to speak. "Something has been hanging in the air lately, you know? There is a new man at the Sûreté Nationale, the son of one of the Berber sheiks in the south, a Fendri Khefacha, and it seems there have been many changes because of him. He is something of a mystery. No one knows much about him, but it seems maybe he has been allowed to take over many operations since Mustafa Ali left. Anyway, there has been this and other things to make us uneasy this month. As I say, something has been in the air; it is almost as though you can feel it. But still, I was surprised when Michel came in Tuesday and found that the front window of the garage had been broken by a rock. We find the rock on the floor but it does not look as though anyone has tried to get in. Then, just as we are sweeping up the glass, Michel's contact on Government Hill calls him on the telephone to tell him that the police will be at the garage in a few minutes. That was all the warning we had. I tell you, we did not have much time to do anything, only to clean out the back room of the shop as good as possible." David bit his lips suddenly and looked at Itzhak, who had at last subsided in wrathful silence. "Is it safe to speak English here? None of the family understands?"

"No. Forget it. Where's Michel right now?"

"Oh, Michel he is all right. I think he is still all right. But there is not much left of things. Suddenly we lose contact with everybody. I think the police have seized the radio from the new man in Nabeul, and if so, that is very bad, you know? Because always we were more or less sure that the police, they knew of the radio but they did not think it important enough to do anything about it. And yes, Monday night there is word that the police are watching André in Bizerte. André sends a message by hand, a student brings it, and the message says, *Who is Khefacha?* and that is all. That is all the information André has, just that one name."

Norman had been fidgeting visibly. Now he cut the younger man short. "For God's sake, David, don't waffle around like a goddamned Arab! Get to the point. What the hell's happened?"

"I am telling you, I am telling you," David said excitedly. "But there is so much to tell I cannot put it in a list, one, two, three, like that. Because that is not how it happened."

"Give him time," Chaim said. "He is right; he is telling you."

"What I am trying to say," David went on, rubbing at the sweat on his face with a slightly trembling hand, "is that Michel, yes, he is all right for the moment. The garage is locked up, and the police are guarding it, but Michel is not in such a bad position. He always pays much for the bribes and the protection, and then of course he keeps his French citizenship, so he is not in too much bad trouble right now. And we know his man in the Sûreté Nationale is still speaking with him and is still taking money, so that is a good sign. But even so, it was very close; we almost did not get the warning at all. I had very little time to move the Mercedes. I was really frightened, I can tell you, because the Mercedes has all the guns in the headliner, and it would have been very bad if the police had found them. At first I did not know what to do with the car after I left the garage, so I drove out to the Levy family in La Goulette, thinking that Michel would find some way to contact me and tell me what to do. But at La Goulette it is not Michel who calls but someone I do not know. Still, the message is the code we use; he says it is Dolphin, which is the right word, and to take a tour of Tanit's temple, which means I am to look in Bab-el-Fellah for you, Norman, and you, Chaim. I am not even sure you are here. I tell you, I was very worried while I was bringing the car down alone.

218

I got the djibbah and the *keshta* in La Goulette from Levy, thinking to have some disguise. Then, on the road, I was not so sure. I had to take off the Arab dress because I realized I was driving the Mercedes with a German Touring Club sticker on it and with the German registry. First I drove along wearing the djibbah, then I drove without it, trying to think which is best. But I kept worrying that some stupid *boliss* in some small town who is suspicious of everything would stop me and want to know why I am driving such an expensive car. I was planning to tell them that I was a chauffeur to a rich lawyer and was bringing the car down to him in the desert. It was the only thing I could think of."

"Nobody tailing you?" Norman wanted to know.

"I do not think so."

"I suppose," Norman said flatly, "there's been no confirmation from Tel Aviv on the picture."

David shook his head. "I am sorry, Norman, but this I would have told you right away. This makes it very bad, does it not? That is to say, here I am with the Mercedes and we do not have anything to do. Michel said, 'Tell Norman I still do not have clearance to proceed.' That is what he said. But he gave me this." David dug under the djibbah and produced a package of Tunisian Crystal cigarettes. He split the inner lining of the package with his thumbnail, and a slip of rice paper fell into his hand. "Monday," David said softly. "It came in the *poste* for Michel. It was very funny—it came in a package of dates."

"Lovely," Norman said. He opened the rice paper carefully and examined it, his mouth slowly forming a silent whistle. Then he passed the paper to Chaim. The drawing was simple, freehand, the plan of a rectangular house in the Arab style with an open courtyard in the center and a smaller courtyard beyond that, a main gate marked "S. sta. here" and rooms identified as: "lib.," "sal.," "dining room," "chambre," and finally a part of the roof marked "Ni. G."

"Michel said he could not get it," Chaim said.

"No, he said he didn't think he could get it. But he tried, anyway, and he did. What a doll! I'd love to know who did it. Whoever it is, he or she writes an American hand. But Michel baby got it, and he didn't sit on it. I could kiss him. I was beginning to think we were going to have to use the damned Mercedes for a table lamp. There's a servant stationed at the main gate. Somebody who at least doesn't look as though he's armed. We'd better assume that he is. But 'Ni. G.' means night guard with a gun, and no shit. On the roof. Our pigeon isn't taking any chances for an amateur archaeologist, is he?"

They were silent for a moment, and David studied their faces.

"*Ja*, Norman, I know what you are thinking!" he exclaimed. "I said to myself in the car: this is what Norman will think of when I tell him! But Norman, listen to me: it is better, much better to wait. Let us hide the car somewhere and wait until we hear from Michel. It may not be too long; we will hear from him, I am sure. Michel said—"

"Knock it off, will you, David?" Norman growled. "Michel didn't say anything; that's the whole point. Half the message is what's left out. But you can figure it out yourself. You take it step by step. The heat's on, and Michel is closed up and out of business for we don't know how long. And we're down here in the boondocks with that damned Mercedes and a headliner full of equipment. Sure, Michel didn't say anything. He didn't have to. The house plans are just a little kiss good-by."

"No, no, Norman," David burst out. Within the second he tried to lower his voice, looking over his shoulder at the bar Shafik family. "Michel does not have the authority, I swear. Even you do not." He appealed to Chaim, but to David's surprise the *sabra* slowly shook his head.

"Norman is right," Chaim said. "It is always too dangerous to sit and wait. That is bad tactics. I think now, with these circumstances, there is no way to go but straight ahead. As planned."

"You do not mean that," David said in disbelief.

"No, David, what I am saying is correct. Whether it is the right thing or not to do"—and here Chaim paused for a moment to think it over again—"is just a matter of luck now. If we wait and do nothing we will be trapped by the car and the fact that we cannot contact Michel. And that the police are interested in something."

"That about sums it up," Norman said.

"Also," Chaim went on, "I think it is best that I drive the Mercedes." He broke into his reluctant smile. "Norman is all right in European clothes, but David is too much Tunisian. I will be better than both of you. I will go very well with the German Touring Club and the German registration because of the way I look. Also, I speak a little German. So I suggest that as of now the Mercedes is my car, and we are all tourists."

David looked from Norman to Chaim, appalled.

"But you do not understand," he said. He began to rummage in the rags of the old djibbah. "I have not told you all of it. We cannot go—we cannot go anywhere." He found a folded Arabic newspaper and shook it out with trembling hands. "Do you know what this says? I bought it in Sousse—people were running in the streets to buy newspapers. I paid five hundred milliemes for it just to find out what was the matter!"

Chaim took the paper. A moment later he looked up from the Arabic script, and his face had suddenly gone taut, bewildered. "They say we have burned down the Al Aqsa mosque in Jerusalem." He turned back to the paper. "I cannot believe it; it is incredible. But if it is true, it is almost an act of war. It must be a mistake. We are not insane!"

"No shit," Norman said. He tugged quickly at his mustache, his only sign of surprise. "The Al Aqsa. Jesus, that's like burning down St. Patrick's Cathedral. Not quite the Vatican, but it will do. How the hell did it happen?"

"I cannot tell, that is what is so provoking," Chaim murmured. "This newspaper is getting the news out of Cairo, and of course it is all hysterical, it is not even journalism. But it says that Israel has announced it will burn down and loot all the mosques inside Israeli borders. I know this is ridiculous, but that is what it says. I cannot make much sense from the rest of it."

"Crap. Crap!" They were silent while Norman pulled at his mustache and frowned. Then he looked up. "What are we doing here? Let's split. Yeah," Norman said at David's startled look, "I mean now. And quick. Before the trouble starts around here. I don't want to get caught with these people if there's going to be a Jew hunt. Not with the damned Mercedes sitting in the back alley."

David opened his mouth, then closed it slowly. There was nothing else to do; even he knew that. But David turned to regard the bar Shafik family: the old man still smoldering from the indignity of his interrupted devotions; the polite, questioning eyes of Yohannon and his wife; the younger members.

Something of the sort was running through Norman's mind, too, for he said suddenly, "They'll make out all right." He turned away brusquely. "They're used to it. They're Jews, aren't they?"

12:15 A.M.

A few minutes after midnight Sharon Hoyt stepped out of the shadows of the banyan tree long enough to lift her wrist watch to the bright moonlight which lay in a dazzling silver glare over Sebastian's house and gardens, check the time, and then duck back again. He was fifteen minutes late.

And what the shit was keeping him, anyway? she thought fretfully.

She couldn't stand under the banyan tree forever; it gave her a bad case of the drears. The crazy roots of the thing stuck up out of the ground in knotted coils and elbows so that she always managed to trip over them going in and out, and weird runners dropped from overhead like ropes. Every once in a while she heard noises in there with her. Hiding under the banyan tree like that was about the only time she ever really thought of snakes, all thirty-six North African varieties, including asps and vipers and cobras, that people were so willing to tell you about.

It didn't matter that she had never seen a scorpion or a snake in all the months she had been there; now and then you were forced to think about it and wonder what you would really do if you ever met one. But there was no need to have a nervous breakdown about it. When she was standing under the banyan she always told herself that it actually wasn't so bad and what was worse was to blow your mind being neurotic with all sorts of unrealized fears. The tree was in fact really great, something of a botanical curiosity like all the other junk planted in the endless gardens of the estate, where obviously a small fortune had been spent to make it the ultimate in fantastic objects that other people would never even think of. As for instance, also, the most beautiful house in the world and all that sort of thing.

It was just too damned bad that she hated it so much.

It was really surprising, when you came right down to it, how fast you could become accustomed to what a lot of people in Tunis would give their right arms to see. Because it really wasn't all that much. Unless you dug the weird and very far out. The whole place was laced back and forth with dark avenues under cypress trees where it was usually so black she had to feel her way along between the masses of dark bushes and moving shadows. And in spots there were paths through thick daturas whose perfume was actually narcotic, and where you could get breathless if you didn't walk fast enough. Once she had wandered into some back area with marble statues which had, in the moonlight, nearly scared her out of her flipping mind before she had discovered they weren't ghosts or some sort of living people. She really needed to bring a flashlight, she told herself; the whole thing was getting on her nerves.

But no flashlights. And wait under the dark of the banyan tree. And no noise, please. Because old Hamid, the caretaker, wasn't supposed to know anyone was around. God knows, she told herself, how the Ez-Zahra Chief of Police explained getting the keys to the main house. Or maybe he didn't have to explain, being the police.

Sharon shifted the cassette player to her other hand and shivered. It was dumb to be shivering in all that heat, she realized, but the banyan always had that effect on her. And it was even dumber to be standing there for nearly twenty minutes or half an hour, surrounded by the faintly glimmering whitewashed domes and terraces of Sebastian's imitation Moorish palace. But the reason she was there, of course, was that she hadn't figured a way of getting out of it.

After all, how did you go about getting out of anything which involved the Ez-Zahra Chief of Police?

Il est formidable, the little kids in the village said of him, and ran when they saw him coming.

And in his way he was *très formidable.* Every day she told herself she was glad she was leading a clean, pure life and didn't really have anything else going with Norman Ashkenazi or George Russell or anybody much. Because she had a feeling it could get very rough. The Ez-Zahra Police Chief, he really didn't fool around. As George Russell had once said, apparently there was no such thing as a little friendly, casual balling. Not in Arab countries.

On the other hand, she couldn't see that it had been all her fault. At one point there he had so completely sealed her off from other people—the whole village, practically—that she hadn't had much choice. It was either cooperate or start talking to the four walls, and she hadn't been quite ready for that. And what the hell, it wasn't worth fighting over. She wasn't exactly a virgin.

Still, outside of the actual sex, it could be pretty confining, even depressing. If she didn't show up, he came looking for her. Or he came looking for her anyway, just to check and see that she was still around. And Sebastian's place had really turned her off. She didn't know why she had wanted to see it to begin with; that's what she had got for swallowing other people's stories. It was beautiful all right, if your taste ran to a sort of broken-down Disneyland, an entire Moorish castle with rooms full of junk that the French hadn't cleaned out, crawling with noises and probably filled with ghosts. The house where people had come from all over Europe to do whatever the ancient version of the Jet Set used to do back in the days before World War Two.

According to one of the big stories, the Bedouin used to come along the beach at night and see the lights in the main house and hear the dance bands hired from Tunis for the big parties and then, later, when the lights had been put out, all the screams and shrieks.

What shrieks and screams? she had wanted to know, but nobody seemed to be able to tell her. The ben Omrane girls just rolled their eyes. Oh, mademoiselle, shrieks and screams, that is all! Monsieur Sebastian, he was a very mysterious man. Still, nobody died.

That was the way they put it: "But nobody ever died." It was just old Sebastian and his friends from London and Rome having their fun and games in this nice little quiet corner of the Mediterranean. In, as Ali ben Ennadji had once said, this land of Arab degeneration where no one asked questions.

Charlie Benedict had said black masses and scaring the hell out of the natives.

Even if you didn't believe it, there was still the incredible bathroom with the mirrored ceilings and walls and the Byzantine baptistery which had been converted to a four-seat bathtub. And upstairs, the absolutely far-out *fantasie*, the all-black suite with black painted walls and black marble floors and even a black tile bathroom, and windows with pierced-wood lattices in the style of a sultan's hareem. So campy that if a person saw it in an old movie they would laugh themselves to death. The main rooms had been pretty well stripped by the government commissioners, but you could certainly get a good idea of how it had been in the old days.

Sharon wished she could turn on the cassette player and quit thinking about it all, but she had left the earplug attachment at home and it would make too much noise. When she finally heard the sound of his footsteps on the tarmac path she was just so glad to see anybody at that moment that she came scrambling out from under the tree limbs and practically threw her arms around him. But he didn't even notice it. He brushed past her and put the key in the lock and opened the door.

Not even hello.

"You're late," she said.

"Yes, late." He stepped inside and then closed and locked the door behind them. It was very dark in the dusty, marble-floored hall; she could hardly see. "We have been listening to the radio. It is bad news. A mosque in Jerusalem has been burned."

"What?" She hated the dark, especially in that house, and tried to stay close to him, but he pushed her ahead.

"Upstairs," he told her.

He couldn't bother to say hello or kiss her or take time to be agreeable or friendly; he just wanted her. And quick. He had already slipped off the belt and shoulder strap, and now he was unbuttoning the uniform shirt. She smelled the sharp scent of cologne. Sometime during the day he had managed to take a bath and put on cologne. He was really a gas. He couldn't be too damned polite or friendly, but he had remembered the cologne.

"What mosque?" she said, but he kept pushing her ahead of him. "You don't mean the Israelis set fire to a *mosque*, do you? But that's crazy; they wouldn't do a thing like that!"

"You would not know it," he said, pushing her toward the stairs. "But the Jews are responsible, yes."

Sharon didn't want to go upstairs. Up there was the black suite with the hareem shutters and all the junk she had seen once before.

"I hate this house," she complained. "It's a fraud." She used the French word *fraude* because it was easier to remember, but then she added *tromperie* because that's what it really was. A trick. Just an illusion of beauty and taste.

"Nonsense. There is nothing wrong with this house. It is a very beautiful house, the most beautiful in the country. That is why I bring you here."

That really bugged her.

"It's a lousy house," Sharon said in English. "It's an old faggot's whore's dream, and you don't even know it."

But he was hurrying and didn't ask her to translate.

At the top of the stairs Sharon pushed open the door and then stopped short in surprise. It was all different. All the dust and litter had been cleared away; no papers at all. The room was beautifully neat and clean. Even the canvas dust cover on the bed looked as though it had been washed. In the middle of the floor there was a brilliant red gem of a Kairouan prayer rug.

"Oh, wow," she said softly. The little rug was really great. It was such a funny gesture. What American would think of a rug? But she really couldn't picture the Ez-Zahra Chief of Police with a broom and mop, cleaning up. Maybe he had had the caretaker do all that for him, too.

The rug was like the cologne—she really couldn't understand him. That is, he was *there*, and you could read the superficial things, but you really couldn't understand at all. The last time they had been downstairs in the fountain courtyard with only a couple of dirty cushions under them, and the tile floor and everything had been full of old khamseen dust. He had been really furious. He hated dirt. She flipped on the cassette player with her thumb, and the gutsy, wailing voice of Janis Joplin leaped into the room.

"Unnnh . . . nhh . . . I need a man . . . to love me . . ."

The effect of the music in that room was wild. The great Janis Joplin on tape. Her voice filled up the room like funky smoke. The record, "Cheap Thrills," was old, but Sharon liked it. There was no substitute for Joplin; she was the essence of fantastic, resting a bottle of Southern Comfort on the mike as she sang, roaring out the blues, tearing her voice to shreds with a gut-shaking beat. They kept telling her she was going to burn out her voice singing that way, and all she said was, It had to be good while it lasted, didn't it?

"I do not like that music," he said irritably. "It makes too much noise. Turn it off."

"You don't understand what she's singing." Sharon moved her thumb slightly and turned up the volume.

The Chief of Police had taken off his shoes and now, wearing only his uniform pants, he went to open the shutters. As he leaned over the sill, the glare of white moonlight struck his head and bare shoulders and the frowning shadows of his face. Sharon regarded him critically, swinging the cassette player in her hand.

Up close, she thought, he still looks like the rest of the damned Sûreté Nationale. All the National Police looked as though they had been stamped out by some giant government cookie cutter. The Arab version of the TPF, even to the short haircut.

But, she told herself, watching him, he really had great shoulders and arms, really a great body. And his skin was beautifully smooth, not at all rough, and smelled a little of olive oil under the mask of cologne. The Chief of Police went to the hammam, the Turkish bath, at least four times a week, which was almost more than anyone else in the village. She knew that from the youth discussion group because Mustafa, the masseur at the hammam, was an uncle of Shedli Zouhir, who was a cousin of Salem Gueblaoui, her houseboy.

It was incredible to be in a place where everybody knew everything about everybody else, including how many times they took a bath.

Sharon flopped down on the bed and kicked off her sandals. Well, there was one good thing about it—she had only to be around him for a few minutes and she started reacting to him like crazy. She switched on like electric lights. It was the only reason for being there, otherwise it didn't make sense. It was really about as bad as being involved with the snotty *directeur* of the *lycée* in Nabeul. At least she supposed if she went to bed with the *directeur* of the *lycée* she could probably get him to give her her teaching assignment. He was ready.

They were all ready.

"Take off your dress," he told her, turning from the window.

Sharon lay back on the bed and yawned. When he came to her she didn't cooperate; he had to lift her up bodily and squirm the cotton shift over her head. When her hands came out of the armholes she gave a bounce and the cassette rolled away on the bed.

"Hey, watch it!" The cassette player couldn't be replaced. Not in Tunis, anyway. And there was something wrong with the transistor radio back at the house. If she broke both of them at the same time it would be a disaster. Sharon rolled away and ducked under his outstretched arm and got away from the bed. She crossed quickly over to the other side of the room.

"Don't be in such a hurry," she told him. She knew that was

really going to bug him, but she didn't care. She was very turned off by the rush business and wanted to have a moment just to stay away and do something herself. She ran her hand over her stomach, and her whole body felt as though it lifted to respond. It was a great feeling. Every inch of her body seemed to soak up the touch of her hands.

He didn't get up. He threw the dress away from him and sat on the edge of the bed, looking down at the floor, and she could tell that he was really racked up.

That's too bad, she told herself. She liked to see him flip. He covered it pretty well, but he flipped.

Naked, she moved around, making her body, her breasts, sway to the beat of "I Need a Man to Love."

"Talk to me," she said. Because she knew it was the last thing he wanted to do, he was practically choking, he was so pissed off. And yet so ready. He lifted his head and looked at her, and he gave her a sort of dogged, burning look. Really freaked.

"I will talk to you later." He got up from the bed and started unbuckling his belt.

It was amazing, she thought, how visually oriented he was, like all the Arabs. That was a big thing with them. The whole society was wildly sex obsessed, but actually the men never really got to *look* at anything much; the government even frowned on nudie calendars. And of course anything female was kept in the house or wrapped up in haiks, except for a few miniskirts in Tunis. So show and tell was a big deal. Just a bump and a grind from the girl singers on TV, and half the men fell out of their café chairs.

And, as she knew, for all his French-style cool the Chief of Police was no different, either. He had such a hang-up for blondes it was unbelievable. And he had flipped out of his mind to find all that taffy-colored pubic fuzz. Blonde everywhere—it was the eighth wonder of the world.

All she had to do was stay away from him for a little while, move her hips around, put her hands on her breasts, and squeeze them up like she was turning herself on. Real plastic, *Playboy* stuff. And he flipped. He came out of his pants with an enormous hard on. She hardly ever saw him when he wasn't erect, the flesh standing out and away from his thighs like a big rod, flushed a very dark red color with a ragged circumcision scar around the top. Barbers or the imams in the mosques circumcised the kids at thirteen, and they certainly weren't graduate surgeons. His was as rough as though somebody had done it with a pair of fingernail scissors.

The cassette player had gone on to the next song on the tape, which was Janis Joplin singing "Piece of My Heart."

"You know you've got it . . . if it . . . makes you feel goo-ood . . ."

The voice on the tape machine rose high on the drums and gave a sudden long scream. It was only part of Joplin's thing, but she could really yell. When she sang "Piece of My Heart" she threw herself all the way into it. She went wow—wow—oh—wow! tossing her long hair back and jamming the mike into her mouth with a freaky scream as though it was really happening to her. Right up there on the stage in front of everybody. It was wild.

"Come on . . . come on . . . come on . . ." Janis was shouting. The electric beat of the bass pumped so that it shook and sizzled the little cassette speaker. Sharon shook her hair forward, too, and put her hips into it. She knew what she looked like to him; she had seen herself in the mirror often enough naked and practicing to a hard rock beat. Being long-waisted with a fairly big, full butt was really out of sight.

He started around the bed.

She saw him coming but pretended not to. That was part of it. Instead, she lifted her breasts in both hands and looked down at them. Nice breasts; they really stuck out a lot. They weren't awfully big, but they stuck straight out. She stroked them, concentrating. And then she sidestepped at the last moment.

That was peripheral vision. At one time she had made the girl's varsity basketball team because of it. He had gone a few steps past her and then suddenly stopped, still looking straight ahead. Burning. She felt like laughing. She slid her fingers down into her pubic hair, threading it over her fingernails.

Sometimes, when he was really zapped, he tried to take her standing up, but she was too tight and it never worked. As it was, she practically threw her across the bed when she finally let him catch her. The cassette player took a bounce and she reached out and caught it in her two hands, bringing it down against her chest. It was a lucky catch, but it caught him under the chin. He yanked the machine away. When he was excited, she noticed, he never spoke elegant French, only Arabic and pretty colloquial Arabic at that, with a weird accent. She couldn't understand much of it except *bahi*, which meant nice, pretty and lovely. And *mizyeda*, which was even more so.

"Now you've got it . . . wow . . . wow . . . wowow . . . WOW!" Janis Joplin screamed into the bed.

Sharon opened her mouth, and her voice and the voice on the cassette tape were one. It could have been Joplin that he rammed into with all his strength. He used up every inch of her, gripping her bottom with his hands and taking her in long, smashing strokes that lifted her up in the air and dropped her down on the bed again. Just as in the dances. With the same quivering, hesitating moment at the peak.

"*Bahi*," he gasped into her shoulder. "Now I have—" She couldn't make out the rest of it.

But with sort of a frantic detachment she was watching her body go up to meet his, her legs sprawled out sluttishly, submissively, her hands reaching around to touch his shoulders and neck. The back of his neck and his face was all nerves; he groaned when she did that. It really tore him up. She pulled his head to her and explored his mouth with her tongue, and he burst out in big gasps and said things, Arabic words, against her lips. *Beautiful. I will make you take me.* It was great.

She couldn't hold back when he crashed out like that, when he shook all over with what she was doing to him. Sharon started going off in big, rolling waves just like a tumbling surf. The cassette player rolled off the bed and struck the floor with a hard plastic smack, and Janis Joplin stopped short. But Sharon didn't hear it, because for some reason she started over again. She started going off like sky-rockets, one right after the other. Just like the Fourth of July. And he started going off with her. He could really match her every time, and more. He put his head down beside hers, dug his mouth into the bed cover, and she felt an earthquake, just like a convulsion, tearing at him.

Bahi, bahi, bahi.

And wow! *mizyeda* all the way.

She wrapped her arms around his body and let him take her with him, until he finally was still.

Later, when they were sharing a cigarette, she really did want to talk. She hadn't been kidding, before. What was the use of any of it if they finally didn't have some sort of verbal communication, too?

"Let's talk," she told him. "Let's say something to each other."

But he only lay with one arm around her, smoking, with a slight frown on his face and didn't answer.

Sharon was determined not to give up on it. She sat up in the bed and turned to look down at him. It was great, she thought, to look at people afterwards and really study them, especially their faces, because usually they looked so changed—all open and unselfconscious and relaxed. And he did look different, he really did: he looked very young and smooth and crazily sensual since he had such a great body and slightly shiny, sweaty skin. Even in spite of the frown. When he didn't have on the Police Face he was really sort of beautiful, with straight black brows and a straight nose and a very soft, curling, self-satisfied, typically Arab mouth. It was the mouth that changed most. She bent forward a little to get a better look at his face and the rough edge of the scar near his eye. Scars were always interesting, too, she told herself, because they were the evidence that something had happened, sort of a visible record of a person's history. And in his case she was pretty sure this one was.

"Are you," she said curiously, "really a Bedouin?" When he didn't say anything she said, "Well, is that where you had the Bedouin mark cut off?"

It was after all, a perfectly valid question, and only what the ben Omrane girls always said of him. She wasn't prepared at all for what happened. She was sort of reaching forward to touch it and feel it for herself, and all of a sudden he just lunged out and knocked her hand away. He looked absolutely furious. And it had hurt.

"What is the matter with you?" he practically shouted. "Are you an idiot?"

He had dropped the lighted cigarette; now it rolled down between them and they had to move quickly to find it.

"Men do not tattoo their faces," he said angrily, while they were looking. "Only women. It is a decoration, a thing to make them *jolie*." The fire had fallen off the end of the cigarette when they found it, and he looked at the stub as though he didn't know what to do. She was amazed to see him so really flipped out about nothing. His hands were even shaking.

"Cripes," she said, leaning over him. Whatever it was, she hadn't meant to make him blow his cool like that. She didn't want to touch his face and get that started all over again, but she put her hand against his chest and smoothed it because she really wanted to touch him, and rubbed it across his belly and then down onto his leg. He held up the cigarette and looked at her as though he couldn't think of more than one thing at once, and she could tell by his eyes that it was better.

"Why do you ask me this?" he said. But his voice wasn't so angry now. "It is not important." He finally threw the dead cigarette on the floor.

He did not, he was telling himself, wish to tell her anything. Most importantly, he did not wish to discuss himself with her. She was a very annoying, ridiculous girl, interested in only trivial, illogical things. But he sighed. When she wanted to, she could be very persuasive. He knew he would have to say something.

"Arab or Berber?" she wanted to know.

"*What?*"

"Are you an Arab or a Berber Bedouin?" she asked. She was staring into his face very interestedly with her remarkable sea-blue eyes.

He did not understand what she was talking about. But then he frequently did not understand her. She talked a lot of nonsense.

"*Bedu, bedu,*" he said irritably. "I do not understand these other things. All the Bedouin from the south, near ben Gardane, belong to the bu Yahia. They are of the Hammami, of the Kabyles."

"Oh, great, then you're a Berber," she murmured.

Her hand had moved across his leg and he shifted slightly, to move with it, and quickly lit another cigarette. Then, because she was as usual full of questions, he found it necessary to explain where ben Gardane was to be found. He had been born in or near the oasis of ben Gardane, which was the last town on the border before entering Libya. Yes, it was really desert down there.

He could very well see that, in spite of himself, he was going to have a conversation with her. Like most women, she was going to persist. Now she was coaxing him, her hand moving over his legs and thighs, which was very pleasant and distracting. But it was all false, he reminded himself; she was only curious, she did not feel any sentiment for him.

She wanted to know what it was like, in the desert, and he could not remember. It was a silly question. What was the first thing anyone remembers?

If he remembered anything at all, the very first time, it was the desert and the tents moving from place to place following the herds of camels and the sheep. The small black tents perched upon the earth so that at a distance they faded into the sand and the black shimmering tatters of the mirage and one could not tell anything was there at all.

But he could not tell her that. She would find it impossible to believe that people could exist in such a manner, merely herding goats and sheep and camels, squatted against the earth with nothing but a black piece of woolen cloth over them to protect them from the wind and sun. It was a very poor, debased mode of life. But she insisted that she wanted to know everything about it.

Well, his tribe, an *ersh* or family of the bu Yahia, moved by horses and camels. Yes, there had been horses, too, but not many, as they were a small family and not rich. However, his father's brother, who was in charge of things, owned fine leather boots made in Algeria and wore a gold wrist watch. And also he owned a very fine horse which—although they were poor—he would not sell. Even though many people had offered much money for it.

She wanted to know if the desert was beautiful.

Beautiful? He tried to think. It was a large waste, a desert of sand and gravel and, in the far Sahara, barren rocky mountains, and he had not thought of it as beautiful, but he supposed this could be so, at times. Suddenly he was surprised by his own thoughts, as they reached back, and the memory of the purple color. His mother had fed him at the breast until his third or fourth year, as was the custom, and so he had then been old enough to remember dimly being held on the camel's back as the tribe moved with the herds, and the warmth of her body, the feel of her smooth young breast in his mouth, and the sun like a glowing spot in the purple robe which she held over him to protect him from the heat and dust.

It was such an old remembrance that it quite startled him; he had not thought about that in years. It was very strange to think of time and memory.

He was already of an age to go to sleep in the men's side of the tents, which would have made him about seven or eight, when his father left him with his mother's uncle in ben Gardane, and his mother and father had gone away. Where? He did not know. His mother had had another child by then and it had died, perhaps because there was not enough food. He did not remember that too clearly. And perhaps they had left him in the care of others because they had become too poor to feed him. This was not such an uncommon thing, in the south. But his mother's uncle was also very poor and had a large family. He went to look for work with the other *bedu* of the bu Yahia, across the salt lake in the date groves of the oasis of Tozeur, and took his family with him. So once again he, Ali ben Ennadji, was left in ben Gardane with still another tribe so that finally, as it happened—perhaps gradually—he belonged to no one. That was not so uncommon, either, in the desert oases where there were too many poor people and too many children. When he was nine or ten he was given to the French Fathers' orphans' school in ben Gardane.

Actually, he told her so that she would properly understand, it was very fortunate that the French Catholic Fathers accepted him for the orphans' school, for at that time the country was governed by the French Protectorate and there were not so many schools at all, even for those who could afford to pay for them. And especially not many schools for the children of the Bedouin tribes, who were considered by the French government to be too wild and primitive to educate.

But life at the French Fathers' school was not so good. At least when he had lived with the poor families in ben Gardane there had been some thought that perhaps his family might return to claim him. But once he was admitted to the orphans' school it was assumed that he was an outcast, an unwanted person. The French Fathers were not so friendly, either, at least not so much as one would expect. There was one Father in particular who could not bear to have the children come too close because he was always afraid of catching the body lice. They were always given carbolic soap with which to wash themselves for the body lice and the ringworm. Then there were the prayers. They were made to pray each day before the Jesus Christ and the Virgin Mary, even though they were Moslems and not Catholics. There were lessons, yes, in the school, but for the lessons they were required to learn French, the language in which all subjects were taught. No one in the school was encouraged to speak Arabic; the French Fathers did not like it and the French government preferred also that everyone speak French. If one wished to study Arabic it was only taught as a foreign language in the University in Tunis.

When they were not having lessons in the orphans' school, they learned to weave baskets and mats of alfa grass which were sold in the market in ben Gardane. That was called learning a trade. The mats also helped to buy food for the orphans' school. They ate two meals a day, and he remembered that he was always hungry. And at night the boys who were there cried in the dark, before going to sleep, because they were ashamed to be without families. To be without relations was the worst thing that could happen in an Arab country. Except, perhaps, to be without a family and also in the hands of the French Fathers, who wished to turn everyone into a French-speaking Catholic.

When he was thirteen he had had enough of the orphans' school, and so he left to find a job in the north. For a while he worked in the railroad station in Sfax, carrying luggage when the regular porters were busy, and after that he found a man who was also of the bu Yahia tribes—although not a relative—and he was able to get a job with him as a mechanic's helper in a garage. The city of Sfax was a very good place, the second largest city in the country, and it was a better life just to be there. In the beginning he slept in the streets at night, but when he went to work in the garage he rented a room with a poor family because the work was good and steady and he made enough money to allow himself the comfort of a bed. Once, a French girl had allowed him to drive her car to test the repairs that had been made upon it, and when they were in the countryside around Sfax he had made love to her, right in the car, which was difficult. But she was very passionate, that French girl. She had put her hand on his leg and thigh while he was driving to let him know that he could have her, and he had nearly driven the car off the road into an olive tree. He was very poor then, and young, and had not had many women, so he remembered the French girl and making love in the car for a long time.

Then, when the war with the French began, he left his job in Sfax and went to join Salah ben Youssef's guerrillas near the Algerian border. That was very exciting. The war was good; he had no love for the French, and it was satisfying to be fighting for his country's independence. There were a lot of Algerian *fellaghas* with ben Youssef at that time, and he had found the Algerians very tough; they knew a lot of things about guerrilla war because they had been working to overthrow the French in their country for a long time. The Algerians liked him and taught him the art of dynamite, and after a while it happened that he knew enough to become a dynamite expert. Once the partisans dynamited the highway into Le Kef, and he was personally responsible for laying the charge. After the war, as perhaps she had heard, there was a lot of trouble with ben Youssef, who wished to keep his partisans mobilized to form a Leftist wing in the government. But the Army came to arrest him, and ben Youssef was exiled, and the *fellaghas* who had fought with him disbanded. In recognition of their services, however —and perhaps to keep them from making any trouble—the government offered schooling to all the fighters. So that was how he returned to school again, since he was still a youth. And how he finally, when the schooling was finished, took the examinations for the police.

That was all.

Except that long before all of this he had stopped acknowledging that he was a *bedu*. It was not important; it was only that he did not like being referred to by that name. He had his own name. It was not necessary to call him "the *bedu*" and nothing more.

He had become absorbed in his own talk and had almost forgotten her. But she was sitting there before him, staring into his face in a most disconcerting manner, her mouth opened a little with the wonder of it all. He almost smiled.

"They had the worst of it, the Algerians," he said, almost to himself. "And we did not help them enough. That is the curse of the Arabs—that we are never united to help each other. When the Algerians began their real war with the French and were fighting for their lives, we already had our independence and we were busy with our own problems, and so the President announced that in order to survive we could not help them any more. But I think this was a mistake. They were Arabs also; we could have given them an army. Because after the Algerians had won their war with the French they had lost one million dead, and two million to the concentration camps, and maybe half a million more who had fled to Maroc and Libye and Tunisie. That was too much. They bled their guts out; they nearly did not win. That was too much to lose out of a population of only nine million. Our war was easy, compared to theirs."

"Umm," Sharon said. She really wasn't interested in the Algerians, but she had been fascinated with what he had said before, about how he had lived and all the things that had happened to him. It was really very strange; she was finding that he was really a complicated person after all, with actually very complicated thoughts and reactions. And in spite of what he said, the Tunisians had helped the Algerians plenty in their war for independence; it was weird that he didn't really think so. But she knew from the indoctrination course that about a year after their independence the crazy Algerians had tried to assassinate the Tunisian President because they didn't think he was Leftist enough. That was some sort of plot connected with ben Youssef, too, even though he had been living in exile.

It really wasn't important. North African politics were nuts, anyway, really out of sight. She hadn't understood a lot of it, even though they had spent two whole days taking up the subject.

What was important, after all, was individual people, not governments. Like the Chief of Police and his hang-up over being a Bedouin. She hadn't even suspected that he had any sort of trauma about it. Now that she could see how he felt, it explained a lot. It made the whole thing with the police bit and the big black belt and the flashy fake ring and gold cuff links and all the other means of overcompensating perfectly understandable. God knows how much he had to claw and fight his way up the ladder of the Establishment from a desert tribe that travelled about on camels! She had been down to Tozeur with the rest of the Youth Commitment Group from the Foundation for a week before their assignments, and she had first seen the desert people then. They were really beautiful, like hooded hawks with their faces all wrapped up in *keshtas*, covering even their mouths. Except that you knew those beautiful *bedu* really weren't thinking about anything except where their next meal was coming from. It was no fun looking like the King of the Hawk People when you were practically starving to death.

The crummy ville Arabs always treated the *bedu* like dirt. They called the nomads "lice" when they came north looking for the starvation wages of seasonal work. That was probably one reason why she didn't like the ville Arabs so much. Besides the fact that they were always fat and minded everybody's business.

I don't care, Sharon thought, I'm going to touch him, I've got to.

She put her hands against his face and held them there, and then ran her fingers down across his lips. He was really so great. It was like she could understand everything now and really flow into him, mind and soul.

"Poor baby," she said. He didn't understand English, naturally, but she wanted to say it, because she was feeling everything for him in such a large, terrific way. The more she looked at him, right into his eyes, the more she realized that it was a tremendous new thing—he was entitled to his hostilities and his obsession with blonde women and his perfume and his ring. Because of the way he had had to live, coming out of the desert and into the twentieth century, almost.

She would, she thought suddenly, give almost anything to see him in the desert as he had been, in his natural environment. She hadn't flipped out of her mind or anything silly, she didn't believe that people really went around looking like something out of *Lawrence of Arabia,* but on the other hand she could really picture him completely covered in a burnoose, with a *keshta* wound around his head and mouth, only his eyes showing. He had great eyes; they were really fierce and burning like *bedu* eyes. But she knew if she said anything about it, he would blow his cool like crazy. He was too uptight about the Bedouin bit. She guessed he had worked too hard for the police uniform and the French and the Chief thing and all the rest.

Also, he was very sensitive about being dark. Sometimes when they were making love he would look down at their legs side by side and she knew what he was thinking. Even with her suntan she looked white beside him.

She was feeling so much for him at that moment that she nearly couldn't stand it. She put her mouth on the side of his face and kissed him there. He looked a little surprised, but then she gave him little soft tender kisses all over his mouth and chin, just to show him, and then moved her body across his legs and settled down. She saw the change in his face at once. He threw his cigarette away quickly and put his arms around her.

"Poor baby," she whispered, and kissed him on the mouth for a long time. His arms tightened; he was really holding on.

He always wanted her, she told herself. That was the great thing, that he was always crazy hungry for her, and it wasn't fair to bug him about it, under the circumstances. That is, now that she understood his motivations. They were just two different types of people, that was all, two products of entirely different cultures. Up close his eyes were so black and intense she nearly flipped. He was thinking about screwing her again.

It was fantastic, she thought breathlessly, to think how these things happened. Because if he hadn't gone to the French Fathers' school, if he hadn't fought with the partisans and then taken the examinations for the police, he would probably still be riding a camel somewhere in the desert, living the life of a poor Bedouin and probably lusting after blonde girls without ever having a chance to have any.

She could feel him go tense against her. But then that was natural. She was practically sitting in his lap.

"Let me do it," she said against his mouth. She could almost do it without moving, anyway; it was almost impossible to avoid him in that position. And she *wanted* to make love to him, she wanted it to be great, the best he had ever had. She wanted to be all soft and passionate and completely everything for him. Because all he ever wanted was her. *Mizyeda.* All the time he had been saying to her that she was the most, the best. And he had had so little love or tenderness or anything like that in his life; you could tell it from what he had said.

When she pressed herself down upon him it was terrific; it was difficult, but it was wild. But she was sort of inspired; she did everything she could think of, and he just lay back and closed his eyes and let her take her time with it, saying things in Arabic sort of under his breath as though he liked it very, very much and it was blowing his mind. That turned her on, too, and it got even wilder. But then it suddenly must have got to him, and he sort of exploded. He opened his eyes and grabbed her around the waist and went all the way into her so that she almost yelled, and held her down like that. It was almost too much, because he was so big it was like being invaded and totally possessed, physically, mentally, passionately, and emotionally by another person. The absolute ultimate. And she was willing to let it be like that because she was so absolutely helpless, because it was so *real*. She wanted to surrender completely, do anything for him, except it was impossible to make up for a childhood in an orphans' school where the kids cried at night because there was no one to love them. And that made her feel terrible and happy at the same time.

She had to lean forward and put her arms around his neck, and when she did she just naturally burst into tears. The tears ran down the side of his face, and if he hadn't been so busy right at the moment with his hands on her hips, trying to keep her moving up and down, he probably would have stopped and asked her what was the matter.

But nothing was the matter, actually. It was really a very normal reaction. It was just something she did when she got ultimately, beautifully involved with people.

Afterward, too, it was very different. It was hard to believe they were the same people as before. They lay side by side on the bed, smoking and talking about everything, even though it was late and neither one of them was going to get any sleep at all that night. Finally he remembered and asked her why she had started crying like that while they were making love, and she told him that it was nothing, it was only that she had been thinking about him as a really little kid in the orphans' school going hungry and with nothing else to do except weave all those crummy mats, and it had gotten to her. That made him laugh.

She didn't think it was all that funny, but she still loved to hear him laugh. It was so new and crazy it just flipped her out. She raised up on one elbow to watch, not wanting to miss any of it, and his face was just like the faces of the boys in the youth discussion group—it turned all the way on with laughing and went out of sight. Pure, beautiful joy. She put her mouth in the hollow of his neck while he had his head thrown back like that, and she could feel the laughing right through his throat.

"You're so beautiful," she whispered against him. Because he really was.

13

Never say I shall
do so and so tomorrow
without saying also,
"If it please God"
[*Insh'allah*].

—*The Qur'an*

In the last few minutes before midnight on August thirty-first a drenching shower from the Atlas mountains of Algeria swept into the Tunisian desert around Nefta as though some clockwork mechanism, set for the first of September and the traditional beginning of the rainy season, had been released, and, on signal, the deluge commenced. The downpour came not as a thunderstorm, not violently, but heavily, windlessly, as though some celestial river had upended itself upon the desert sands.

I have never, Norman Ashkenazi had thought, watching it through the windshield of the Mercedes, seen so much solid goddamned vertical water in my life. Standing up in it, you could drown. The Mercedes headlights were useless. They had had to pull the car over by the side of the Tozeur–Nefta highway for about an hour while Norman cursed the delay. Fortunately there was no traffic, so they didn't have to worry too much about being spotted.

They had hoped it was a freak storm, a cloudburst so common to the desert country coming down on them from the hills over Algeria, but David ben Yaakov shook his head. No, at this time of the year, the Tunisian boy assured them, this was truly the breaking of the drought. The rain would go on for weeks. It was a good thing —God's blessing, as the country people called it—and only a big rain like this would save the drought-ravaged nomads from starvation.

O.K., Norman told himself, the rain was just dandy and a big lifesaver to the desert dwellers and all that, but as far as they were concerned it was a large pain in the ass, one more thing to make their business unwarrantedly complicated.

David estimated the rain would slacken in an hour or two. It always began like this, he assured them. A big rush, a lot of water, and then it settled down to a soaking, steady drizzle. They did not have to worry; the heavy part would not last for long.

But now, at 2 A.M., lying on his stomach under the palms of the wild oasis of El Hamma with the General's house in sight, it was still raining so hard that Norman could only check the time by cupping his hand carefully over the luminous dial of his wrist watch and practically bringing it up to his nose to read it. Even so, it was like trying to make out the numerals through the far side of a fish tank. There was water everywhere. It not only flowed over his wrists and hands, it dripped off his eyelashes, obscuring his vision, and it made his chin a dripping spigot. And Christ, it was cold! Pressed close to the ground like that, he felt as though he were lying belly down in a cold running mountain stream. After fifteen minutes in that position, the black *keshabiya* he wore was soaked through and about as comfortable as a lead sponge. But the black color and shapelessness of the Arab coats with matching hoods were supposed to make them almost invisible under the trees. All around him in the dark of the close-standing forest of date palms the rain seeped and struck and ricocheted from palm fronds with a thousand chattering voices, so that it was not only cold and wet but noisy. That made it tricky; he had to strain for any sound of movement beyond his spot.

The rain had one advantage: it had not only swept the thinly traveled Nefta highway three miles distant clear of traffic and reduced the danger of their being seen but it had also allowed them to bring the Mercedes, headlights out, right up to the eastern side of the oasis by the salt lake, instead of stashing it in some *oued*. Visibility was less than three meters in the continuing flood; they had just rolled the car right in under the palms. The General's house stood a good half mile inside, by the brackish spring.

You had to admire the General's choice of a desert hideaway, Norman thought. It was quite a place. The oasis of El Hamma was "wild"; that is, the date palms stood too close to the salt pan of the

Chott Djerid so that the date trees were sterile and bore no fruit. Even the ground was too salty to support more than a few clumps of the desert plant the Berbers called, in their peculiar language, *deu gauffage*. So there was no reason for anybody to fool around there for long. Occasionally some *bedu* camped under the trees in the spring while migrating to the Saharan pastures with their sheep and camels, but David ben Yaakov had heard in Tozeur that the General kept even the Bedouin pretty well run off.

Everything nice and private and tidy, Norman told himself, wiping rain from his face with the back of his hand. And O.K. so far as it went. But he would have preferred, frankly, to have picked up their bird some other way. Chaim and he had scouted a very nice spot in the Nefta road where the Mercedes could be turned to block the right of way without too much danger of running off into the sand shoulders. That was much better. Just pick up the General's car as it came bombing along the highway some evening, pass it, and then —over a nice, convenient, shielding dip in the road ahead—make the turn, stop the Mercedes, throw out a lug wrench and a jack as though going to fix at flat, and wait for him to come up. Even if he came up fast he would have to stop, as there was no way to get around a car blocking the road at that point. Not with soft Sahara sand on both sides. And once stopped, it would be fairly simple to hold the BSA on the General's traveling companions (there was at least one Arab, they knew, wearing a shoulder holster under a natty green sports jacket) while they pumped their pigeon with a calming dose of Scopolamine and Nembutal and got him ready for the trip across the *chott* and into Kebili and eventually the Libyan border. In Libya, the Brethren in the Wilderness at Ksar Tkout had them fixed up with a Trans-Sahra Oil Company plane pickup on an auxiliary airstrip.

That was probably the easiest way of doing it, they had all decided, except that they hadn't been able to find the old bastard. They had spent a week circling back and forth over dirt byroads as far north as Gafsa, and sweating out the easy mark of the Mercedes, before David had been able to report that the General was finally at home. In Nefta, David, wearing his burnoose and passing as a peddler looking for work in the date groves, had heard that the General had been down in Bir Romane, hunting. That was possible, but Norman really couldn't figure that one out. Hunting at that time of the year? There were still some addax antelope down in the dunes, but mostly the local sheiks had sportingly shot them out, using high-powered rifles with telescopic sights from the backs of Land Rovers. So if the General had been down near the Algerian border at Bir Romane, in the middle of the thousand miles of that beautiful inland beach, the Grand Erg Oriental, he was probably bringing back nothing more exciting to show for his hunting trip than cobras and a few of the deadly white desert scorpions. They made lousy trophies, mounted.

But at least when the General had arrived home on Saturday he had stayed put. The only time the car had left the house was when the Arab cook had driven it into Nefta for groceries. So much for the plan of waiting for him along the highway. Now there was no telling when he would come out.

They were going in to get him, instead.

Norman heard a sound over the pounding of the rain in the palm leaves, and carefully loosened the Beretta from the folds of the *keshabiya*. David ben Yaacov had modified the gun for a silencer in Michel's shop a while back, and the feel of it was still strange to his hands.

But it was Chaim who slid down beside him softly in the muck.

"This is going to be a little bit difficult, Norman," Chaim whispered. He pushed the hood of his *keshabiya* back from his face. "I have been all around the house. There is a walk along the top, as is indicated in the map, and the place where the night guard should be, in the back, in a wide place with a sun matting over it. But he is not there."

"You sure? Can't see a damned thing in this fucking typhoon or whatever it is. He isn't sitting down somewhere? In a spot where we maybe can't see him?"

"No, the wall is too low for that. This house is built as are all the houses down here in the desert; one just walks along the top without much protection. I think he is inside the house."

"Shit."

Chaim was probably right. In this cold rain the son of a bitch had probably sneaked off for a coffee or a shot of *boukhar*. The desert Arabs hated cold and wet worse than cats. But if that was so, it would put their guard anywhere inside the place, running around with his great little shoulder holster. Or, since the roof spot was a night lookout, maybe he was packing a shotgun.

That made two of them, with the General. It was to be fervently hoped their other pigeon was safe asleep in bed. But even so, they would have to be quick to catch him there. They would have to count on his having a gun within reach, too.

"O.K., go get David from the car," Norman said after a moment. "We still got the same damned problem we started out with. Not enough guns."

The Beretta with its silencer would have brought the guard down from the roof without too much fuss. But then they had been counting on getting him silhouetted against the light of a night sky, not in a stinking downpour.

And now, thanks to the unexpected raid on Michel, they had David along.

It was too damned bad they weren't operating in Texas. They could have walked into a hardware store any time that past week and bought a thirty-oh-six for David and solved all their problems.

"Give David the BSA," Norman said, "and put him out front on the exact angle of the house, where he can spot anybody making a bolt for it either through the front door or the one that opens out from the kitchen. And dammit, tell him *anybody*. Tell him if he sees anybody to just pull down on the trigger and spray. That ought to do it."

"I'm going with you," Chaim said quietly.

"Sure you are, baby." But Norman could not look at him. "We always work together, don't we? It's just a little hairier this time, that's all. Jeez, what the shit is this!" Norman exclaimed, and gave a start as something cold and soft as death touched his hand.

Chaim moved slightly to peer through the rain.

"A frog," he said. "I forget. With the rain, all the frogs will come out now. It is quite amazing, that there are so many, all at once."

"Christ, I don't like the way it feels! Here, get out of here," he said, and picked the thing up and tossed it away from them. It fell in the sands a few yards off with a thick, squashing sound.

"There are thousands," Chaim observed.

"O.K., just so long as they stay away from me. Listen, baby," Norman said, putting his cowled head close to Chaim's, "I'll give you the garrotte now, and you're going to carry the package with the needle. The garrotte isn't much, I'm sorry about that, but it's something. And for Christ's sake," he said earnestly, "back me up, will you? You don't know how much I count on you. I need six pairs of eyes in the back of my head, what with this lousy rain. If you see anything, you've got to let me know, fast."

It was ten minutes before Chaim returned, and he slid down in silence beside Norman.

"Has he got the gun?"

"Yes."

"Can we depend on him to use it?"

"Of course. David is good; he is all right. He said to be careful with the grapple. It is soft palm wood and does not make much noise, but in the wet it will not be as good as steel. It may slide."

The wall of the house was above them. Between the palms and the outer walls there was bare ground for about a distance of four meters, or perhaps twelve feet or so. The made it across the space running crouched, sliding a little in the yellow dirt and sand which was rapidly becoming mud.

The grapple hit above them and, as David had feared, did not hold. The wood was soft but made a sound even so, which Norman silently cursed, hoping the noise was covered by the rain. On the second try the graple held just beyond the angle of the guard's roof station, and Norman went up, Chaim quickly after him. Norman flattened out at once on his stomach on the narrow walkway, looking down into an inner courtyard with a little garden in its center and a bed of drowned flowers. Chaim came suddenly down behind him, and he could hear the soggy sound of Chaim's keshabiya as he flopped against the stucco. The courtyard was ringed with doors. A flight of steps led down from the guard's lookout into the left-hand corner of the house.

It is, Norman thought, studying it, sort of like "The Lady or the Tiger." You go down the steps and start opening doors, praying you get the right one the first time.

There was no sign of anyone. The door to the outer courtyard was open, and they could see a patch of paving there, clouded behind a thick veil of rain, and a courtyard fountain overflowing with rain water. Beyond and to the right, the kitchen and the scullery.

Straight ahead at the bottom of the stairs was, according to Michel's map, an L-shaped library and office. And next to that, a bedroom. Theoretically, the place for the bedroom of the master of the house would be right next to his office. They had to take a chance on it.

As they eased softly down the stairs with the drone of the rain covering their footsteps, a nagging something rose and darted through Norman's head. He didn't have time for it—he couldn't let anything bug him right at that second when he needed all his concentration—but it wouldn't go away. Right there with all his nerves tuned to the dark, his eyes on the cramped little courtyard and the puzzle of the doors, the thing, whatever it was, rang a warning bell. As he had come over the wall there had been so much rain in his face and eyes it seemed as though he had registered a flash, a minute glitter, almost a pinpoint reflection of some furtive light.

Raindrops tricks, he thought. Goddammit, he didn't have time for anything right then! Refraction. Jump of the optic nerve straining against dark.

Yeah, but if a light, where? Had he caught it just as it was being put out?

At the door to the L-shaped library-office they flattened themselves carefully against the wall and stopped. Underfoot, there were things moving in the dark; the damned warm pavement was filling up with frogs. Norman held the Beretta under the front flap of the *keshabiya*. What you did, as he knew, was gently lift the fancy wrought-iron catch of the bedroom door and open it very slowly, staying to one side. And then step in, fast, then move sharp right again to get out of any possible line of fire.

The door came open easily and silently enough. Norman let it swing inward; it was only a matter of seconds. He was watching the large white slab of wood with its fanciful pattern of nailhead scrolls and gauging his move, Chaim close behind him, when the first burst of shot started from behind and to the left. His mind registered: machine pistol. The muzzle flashes lit the entire garden area, the ring of doors, even the tops of the palms above the roof. Chaim fell against him heavily. They must have looked like a single figure then, in the dark, because there was another short, spare burst obviously calculated to finish it off.

Norman bounced the weight of Chaim away from him with a thrust of his shoulder as the second burst was beginning, and aimed low. He couldn't see a damned thing. There were only the strobelike flashes of fire to show where the bastard was. At the door to the library.

Norman spread himself against the wall and moved toward him, firing. The Beretta's silencer spoke thickly, a rattlesnake hissing in the rain. He put six shots into the doorway and there was no answering fire, only the sound of something settling heavily to the puddles of the courtyard tiles. It was raining harder than ever; it was as though the whole damned bottom of the universe was dropping out. In the dark, the things splashed and squatted underfoot, getting in his way.

Close in, he held his fire and got out the Beretta's second clip with his free hand. But it wasn't necessary. An old man in green pajamas lay half in and half out of the doorway. As he had fallen, one of Norman's last shots had caught him above the left eye. Norman gave him a solid kick in the chest to make sure, and there was no response. Nobody could play that dead; there was always an involuntary bounce. He booted the Mauser pistol into the flowery border.

The library was dark, but the place was bare enough—a desk, a couple of chairs—to tell at once that it was empty. The oil lamp was still warm to Norman's hand.

The son of a bitch had heard them coming down the steps, had probably heard the grapple hit in spite of the noise of the rain, and had turned off the light and waited for them.

Outside, Norman heard the fast, hiccuping burp of the BSA slicing the dark frantically. Then, a muffled shriek.

A hell of a lot of noise outside, when there had been so little inside. The Mauser had done most of the talking, with the lethal compressed air snickers of the Beretta passing softly over the dripping garden flowers.

Carefully, Norman crossed the courtyard, easing around the *petit jardin* to the door of the bedroom, directly opposite, and the WC which opened into the courtyard. Nobody at home.

In the other courtyard he tried every nook and chamber meticulously, checking out the oddities of Saharan architecture. Another bedroom to the left, also empty. Another bath and toilet. The front entrance, with antechamber. He left the front doors bolted. The dining room, dark and smelling of garlic and roast meat. The kitchen. The scullery door was standing wide open.

David heard him, because there was a single shot from the BSA across the scullery door.

"O.K., you stupid bastard," Norman snarled into the rain. "It better be clear out there. Because if it's not, I'm going to have your ass!"

A few steps beyond the open space at the back door, two figures lay like fallen bundles against the earth.

"Norman?" It was David, coming up out of the dark cautiously. "What's that crap?"

"I do not know. They are all gone, except these." With the BSA tucked under his arm, David bent and examined the bundles. His face looked up, baffled. "There is another, the guard, who shot at me. Over there."

Norman came out of the doorway slowly.

The night guard had managed to get down into the palm trees and was lying with his face in fallen dry fronds. But the bundles by the door were the Swede, Baron Bergson, and the Greek-Italian boy.

"Norman, I swear, I did not even know they were here!" David stuttered. "How could they be in the house? No one ever saw them!"

"Forget it. How many got away from us?"

"I could not see, exactly. Maybe two. There was a cook and a servant."

"I wish this shitting rain would stop," Norman said.

In the courtyard, Chaim had pulled himself to a sitting position outside the bedroom door.

"Get the goddamned lamp," Norman told David. "Hop it. There's a lamp in the room behind you. Light it and bring it here."

"I covered you, Norman," Chaim said, looking up. "I covered you good. This last time."

"Yeah." He squatted down and began to pull the front of the *keshabiya* open, but Chaim brushed his hand away.

"No, don't look," he whispered. "It is enough. We have all seen this before."

"Don't be an asshole," Norman said. "Where's that goddamned light?" he yelled.

"Norman. Norman, listen." Chaim grabbed his hand, and his fingers were hard and cold. "Listen to me, do not waste too much time here. I want," he said, suddenly, fretfully, "to speak Hebrew. I cannot think in English."

"Sure, you do anything you want to, baby, I'm right here." Norman took the lighted lamp from David and held it up. A beautiful bright crimson, like paint, ran down the front of Chaim's woolen *keshabiya* and streamed across the courtyard tiles, mingling and fading with the heavy rain. Just within the ring of light a brown frog sat, unblinking, the trail of the red stain running under him.

"You are not supposed to leave me here." Chaim frowned slightly. "You must remember that. I do not want to make trouble. You must take the body away and bury it, so that they cannot find it and connect it with us in any way. If they find me—if they think the Jews have done anything like this, in this country, it will be worse than ever. They will blame the murder and disturbances on innocent people, and Tel Aviv can never help. You must wash away all sign, wash away the blood here in the house, and do not let it drip when you carry me."

"Ah, come on, what's the matter with you?" Norman said cheerfully. "We know you wouldn't drip. You're a very nice, tidy kid; you'd never make a mess."

"Yes, that is right. Not to make a mess." Chaim closed his eyes. "Is he dead?"

"I'm afraid so. The son of a bitch turned out the light in the back room there and waited for us with a Mauser. Great weapon, just his style. Old SS gun."

"I am so sorry," Chaim whispered. "This will make it very bad. It has all gone wrong. We did not even wait for the confirmation on the photographs. So we do not know what we did."

"Don't you believe it, buddy," Norman told him. "Everything's coming up roses. There's a whole office full of papers back there with Group One directives written all over them; our baby had the typical Kraut obsession with writing everything down, thank God. There's more stuff than we can use in twenty years. I bet this old bird even saved his old Gestapo medals. Listen, we nailed him, he's dead, but that only saves us the trouble of haulage, you know? Just remember what I tell you—when they speak of us from now on, they will say that we were Chaim Dayag and Norman Ashkenazi, the ones that got Gustav Hauk."

With his eyes still closed, Chaim smiled. "You do not have to say lies, Norman," he murmured. "It is all right. You are a good friend; it does not matter that this did not turn out well."

"C'mon, Chaim, I'm not snowing you." Over his shoulder, to David, Norman said, "Prove to our good buddy that I'm not a liar. Go in and get an armful of the crap that's on the desk in there."

"All the papers?" David blinked.

"Move your ass," Norman said evenly, "and do what I tell you."

While David was gone, Norman leaned over the other. "Are you hurting?" he said in a low voice. "We've still got the hypo if you want it."

"No." Chaim shook his head. "I only wish to sit up, more."

Norman took him as easily as he could under the shoulders and lifted him, so that Chaim could brace his back against the wall. Chaim's nose began to bleed, but when Norman tried to dab at it with his hand Chaim moved his head away.

"No, leave it, please. It is nothing."

For the first time, propped up as he was, he could see the frogs which had hopped into the pool of light.

David returned with the papers from the office held against his chest.

"Here," Norman said. He took the top stack, stapled together. "Feast your eyes on this. The old bastard was writing his memoirs, bragging about how many Jews he had killed in the Ukraine. We got all the documentation the home office could want. They ought to love it."

He held out the papers, but Chaim shook his head slightly.

"I cannot read it. I cannot see too well. You tell me, Norman— is it good?"

"No, it's not good, it's shit. It's lousy shit and it tells about killing people, and it's in German. My German's not so good, it's sort of half Yiddish, but I can give you the important parts. O.K.?"

Norman began hesitantly, his voice muted by the steady rain. He spoke of an entry marked Kiev and dated October 11, 1945. But after a few moments Chaim lifted his hand to make him stop.

"No, that is fine, Norman. I do not want to hear any more. As long as you are satisfied—" His voice dropped away and then, as they watched, he made a sudden urgent movement to lift himself against the wall. "I think—" he began, and his head turned uncertainly. "I think—I want to write a letter to Judith. No," he said, before Norman could speak, "my mother and father. Quick, I wish to write something."

"Sure, baby, David will get you a pencil and a piece of paper from inside. Just take it easy."

"I—I—maybe I cannot write too good."

"No."

"You must write it for me, Norman. But hurry."

"O.K., go ahead, keep talking, David will be back in a minute. Just tell me what you want to write. I can remember it."

"Say that—" His eyes focused now on Norman, and they were suddenly like crystals, reflecting the light from the oil lamp. "You tell me, you must help me," he whispered. "I have forgotten."

"You wanted a letter to your moth—Christ!" Norman exploded.

A round body had landed in front of them with a smack, spraying water.

"Goddammit, where the shit are these things coming from?" Norman's voice had a thin edge to it. "Scat!" he told it. "Jesus, I hate these things. I hate any kind of crap that crawls."

He tried to push it away, gingerly, but the thing wouldn't budge. A fat globe of brown flesh, with curious amber eyes.

That made Chaim smile. "Ah, Norman, sometimes you are funny," he murmured gently. "Leave it—it will not hurt you. Look, it is only an animal, like us."

The thing continued to sit in the light, regarding Chaim with its amber stare.

"Look, it is nothing," Chaim repeated softly.

"You look at it," Norman told him. "If you like it, you look at it. Now listen, I don't want to hurry you, kid, but you were going to write a letter, remember?"

But Chaim was sitting with wide eyes, absorbed in the presence before them, and he could not get his attention.

"*Tod*," he said suddenly, and so softly that Norman almost did not hear him.

"No, frogs," Norman said. "Now look, the letter—"

"Norman," David said breathlessly, "there is paper in there, but I cannot find a *stylo*—whatever you say, to write with."

He stopped.

"Forget it," Norman said.

He held the lamp high. They saw that Chaim sat quite still, with his head fallen slightly to one side, as if contemplating with some private amusement the thing which had come before him.

"Get it out of here," Norman said vehemently. "Get a stick and kill it, move it out of here." He got heavily to his feet. "And the rest of these goddamned things, too—this *drek!*"

He swung the arc of the lamp at them savagely, and they flopped and twittered at the movement of the light.

"It can't be, it can't be," David whispered. His eyes turned from Chaim to Norman and then back again.

"O.K., that's it," Norman said brusquely. "That's it. That IS it. Just clear out a place," he said, looking around. "I can't walk with this shit under my feet."

While David stood staring, Norman went into the library-office and returned with the thick Bedouin rug from the floor.

"Here, help me roll him up. I don't want blood all over the car." Norman spread out the rug and bent and took Chaim by the shoulders. He looked up. "What are you waiting for? We got two Arabs heading for the highway somewhere out there. It's going to take them some time, but we still haven't got all night. Take his feet."

Still staring helplessly, David moved forward, his hands outstretched, but then he drew back.

"The feet," Norman told him. "Take his goddamned feet."

Twice he moved forward, and each time he drew back.

"Oh, Christ," Norman said in disgust.

He had seen it too many times before. Everything O.K. up to the actual second of touching a dead body, and then, no go. A strange damned thing. Sometimes the steadiest, most experienced people, sometimes the toughest soldiers—there was no damned way of knowing when it would happen. No sense to it at all.

Norman rolled Chaim in the rug himself, threw the office papers in on top of him, and tucked it around him as best he could.

"I need a rope." But David only stared back at him with a peculiar horror. "Rope. You want to look in the kitchen?"

But David turned his eyes to the rug-wrapped shape on the courtyard pavement as though he could not believe it.

"Look, you *twansa* son of a bitch," Norman told him. "I hope you're getting my message. Because I can't carry this bundle all by myself, I'll get a fucking rupture. Do you hear me? He weighs damned near two hundred pounds and it's a half a mile to the goddamned car, and mudshit all the way. *David!*"

It was no use to shout. The other only turned dazed eyes on him.

"O.K.," Norman said, squatting down and beginning the slow process of getting Chaim's weight across his shoulders. "I'm not going to forget this. I'll get to you later. Just keep ahead of me— and keep these stinking things away from my feet!"

About six miles south, following the shores of the salt lake, on the crust of clay and sand and salt the Arabs call *dab-dab* that was still firm enough to take the Mercedes, Norman picked a spot and told David to get out and dig a hole with the small army spade which they carried in the trunk. It was still dark as a coal mine, and David fretted for a light.

"I cannot dig in the dark," he complained. "How will I tell what I am digging?"

"Just dig it deep as hell—we don't want him to wash out by morning, for Christ's sake. And about six feet long. Feel around with your hands."

Even where they were, pretty far out in the desert and along the shores of the salt *chott*, where you seldom found anybody even in good weather, except a few *bedu* mining the salt pans, Norman didn't want to risk turning on the car headlights. They weren't far from Algeria and there were border police on both sides, even though, he guessed, the Tunisian Sûreté were probably all at home in the Station Centrale in Nefta, warming their butts over a cup of coffee.

And goddammit, it could be done in the dark if David would just quit bitching and get on with it. Intermittently, through the hiss of the rain and the muddy chunk of the shovel in the earth, he could hear David's weeping.

Tough shit, Norman thought, turning on the dashboard lights. But then, that wasn't the half of it. David would weep even harder if he knew what a royal fuck-up they were in. He spread the road map out in his lap. There was a track across the dead salt sea that ran for forty miles, right through the heart, and came out at the town of Kebili on the other side. It was marked G.P. 16, and the map legend had it down as "poor condition." That meant a dirt road with little elevation, no shoulders, tough as hell to pass anybody coming in the other direction. Norman had been across G.P. 16 in dry weather, and that had been bad enough. The goddamned salt stank to high heaven, the mirage worried the eyes, and after a while, if you were tired, the road seemed to disappear in a haze of light and nothingness. People were warned not to get out of their cars and walk onto the salt pan.

Now, he could just about picture the salt lake in heavy rain, the road sloshed across in places with the flood. They would have to wait until light, he decided. There was no other way. Even he wouldn't chance it in the dark, in such cruddy weather.

No alternatives, either. To the south you had to make a big detour around the Chott Djerid, following the shores, and there were no roads. In places the sand dunes of the Grand Erg Oriental came right up to the lake. It was a great place to lose a car, between the salt flats and the sand traps.

But on the other side of poor-condition G.P. 16 one entered the town of Kebili, where there were a hundred dirt tracks glorified by the name of secondary roads which bypassed the main highways and dipped south of Matmata and Tatahouine and then picked up G.P. 19, a nicely paved road on which they could make good time almost to the Libyan border. Except they had to be careful crossing over. Norman knew a side road at Garet El Makrerouga which went through a very thinly patrolled spot. And once over, in the Libyan village of Ouezzen, they would start to pass among the brethren in the Wilderness, the Libyan Jews who would arrange for the flares on the emergency air strip at Ksar Tkout.

If they waited for light to cross the *chott*, it would take them all day to get to Libya, but there was no other way to do it that Norman could think of. And if it continued to rain as it was doing, he thought suddenly, that would make it just dandy. The rain could be a help. In the fall rains the little mud towns were like cemeteries: not a soul in sight.

Norman reached over the back seat and opened the rug bundle that was Chaim and got the papers off his face. He threw them into the front seat. Then he went through Chaim's clothes quickly, looking for anything they might have forgotten. There was nothing, no telltale IDs. But then you could count on Chaim not to goof up. He really hadn't expected to find anything. But damn, Norman thought, looking down, Chaim's chest was shot to a hash of bone and gristle. He had taken both bursts of that goddamned Mauser machine pistol through the back. But probably knowing exactly what he was doing. He was too much of a soldier not to.

"This last time," Chaim had said.

Norman threw the rug back over the body and sat down in the front seat again. He rolled the window down to let the rain wash the blood off his hands. For a moment, as the cold rain poured through his fingers, he was tempted to throw all of the General's papers and crap into the night, too.

God, when he had time, he was going to sit down and try to figure out what he had done. He had never gone so wrong in his life. Everybody blew it once in a while, but he had just made a masterpiece. Thanks to nothing, exit one suspected ex-Nazi, SS war criminal, nothing proved, dead as a doornail. Thanks to T-X-12 operations man Captain Norman Maurice Ashkenazi.

Make that, he told himself, *former* Captain. *Former* T-X-12 operations man. The former Norman Ashkenazi.

Good-by General, good-by Chaim, good-by Captain. And we hope you do well in your next job with the Katmandu Gas and Electric Company. But this time you get no gold watch.

The papers weren't in German; that had been a lot of crap for Chaim's benefit. When someone's dying you tell them anything. Dying people have weird tendency to worry over nothing: money they owe, where their missing arm or leg has gone to, the car insurance they forgot to renew.

But he had been in real trouble there for a moment. He didn't know much more German than *Eine kleine Nachtmusik*, but he had mumbled around, faking it in Yiddish and, as he had figured, Chaim had been too busy to pay much attention.

Just what the shit, Norman thought, turning the pages idly, was von Lehzen-Hauk doing in the date business? Archaeology was supposed to be his bag. But there it was: bills of lading, manifests, credits, orders, receipts. Buckets, baskets, boxes, tons of sticky Algerian dates pouring into Nefta like somebody was going to make the world's largest fruitcake.

Hell, there was no sort of date called *delfine*.

Norman sat up and shoved the letter under the dashboard.

Delfine was the local Arab-French jargon for *dolphin*, which was their own code name. O.K., maybe it was nothing, he told himself, but here was somebody writing from Bone, in Algeria, warning of a shipment of dates that had gone astray in the *souks de grana*.

Goddamn, had they been that close onto them all the time? The sons of bitches, what did it mean? He couldn't believe his own eyes.

Norman got all the papers and spread them under the dashboard lights, taking them up one at a time and making two piles, those that seemed to refer to code names and delivery schedules, those that seemed to refer to the quantity of merchandise shipped.

Code names, they were all over the place like bedbugs. Nobody ever heard of Marco Polo dates, either. What kind of shit was Marco Polo? he wondered. The numbers didn't make any sense at all. If all the dates listed had been coming into Tunisia—which had enough of its own damned dates to market—Nefta would be six feet under fruit.

It was, he was sure, name-and-number codes or he didn't know his business. And codes threw him; they were not his area. Now he needed Chaim like crazy; he wished to hell he was along.

He is along, he corrected himself; he's just no help at the moment.

Begin again, he told himself suddenly. We may have goofed once, but with luck, we may not do it again. *Insh'allah.*

Although, he added, I wish to hell I knew what I was doing. There's nothing like sticking your neck out twice. Especially if you got most of your head chopped off the first time.

Half an hour later David came up and tapped at the glass on the driver's side. Norman rolled the window down.

"It is a very deep hole," David said bitterly. "It should please you, this big hole I have dug. That is, if anything pleases you now."

"O.K."

Norman dragged Chaim out of the back seat. Chaim was big; his body had sort of wedged in and stiffened a little between the front and the back and Norman had to force his hands down to get him out.

Well, there was one nice thing—rigor mortis didn't last long. If they could just keep the rug around him and bury him deep enough, Chaim ought to sleep by the salt sea forever. Salt was a good preservative; maybe Chaim would end up looking better than any of them on Judgment Day.

Norman shoveled the mud back himself. David sat on the ground by the car, hunched over, the hood of the *keshabiya* pulled forward over his face. Norman tamped the sand mud down as firmly as he could and then walked slowly the length of the grave, packing in his footsteps. While David watched, he took the shovel and carefully roughened the surface, but it wasn't really necessary; the rain would do a good job of blending in the hump in an hour or so.

It was getting lighter. Around them the desert rose and fell in long swells, the clumps of gray-green *deu gauffage* stretching as far as they could see. To the left, the dead expanse of the salt lake melted into a graying sky. Cold dawn. A shroudlike dawn. Coming up through David's long-promised drizzle.

You could even, Norman saw, squinting, find the horizon westward. The dunes over there were the northern end of the sand sea just beyond the Algerian border.

"Arise, O David," Norman said in Hebrew, "and come and stand by me now."

David looked up quickly, the hood of the *keshabiya* falling back.

"Come, David," Norman repeated in Hebrew, "and if you have something for your head, cover it."

David did not move.

"Come on, get up, will you?" Norman said in English. "And get out your *yarmulke* or something. You want to do it right, don't you?"

"What are you doing, Norman?" David said in a suspicious voice.

"You're a good Jew. I hope to hell you know the responses."

"Norman," David cried, "what is this you mean to do?"

"Just give me the responses and don't flap. See if you can do something right for a change."

Norman lifted his face to the sky. There was still enough rain to drift coldly against his eyelids, but the gray clouds were breaking and scudding toward the east.

East to Libya. Where they should be in a few hours, with God's help.

And east, oh Lord, to Thy handmaiden Jerusalem.

"*Yisgadal, v'yiskadesh sh'me rabbo,*" Norman began. The Hebrew words rolled out richly to the desert and the sky.

Well, everybody found God in the desert; that was where He lived.

We are now standing on His doorstep, kid.

"Extolled and hallowed be the name of God, throughout the world which He has created according to His will." Norman closed his eyes against a spray of cold fresh rain. "And may He speedily establish His kingdom of righteousness upon the earth."

Speedily is the word. Because it's got to come soon; the world can't go on this way much longer.

"Amen."

There was a silence, and finally Norman opened his eyes and looked at David.

"Praised be," David said hastily, in a shaky voice. "His glorious name unto all eternity."

A little trembling light broke upon the sand and a gust of desert wind swept toward them.

"Praised and glorified be the name of the Holy One," Norman said, "though He be above all the praises which we can utter. Our guide in life is He, our Redeemer throughout all eternity."

The Kaddish was the prayer for the dead. But strange, because there was so little of death in it.

"Our help cometh from Him, the Creator of heaven and earth," David whispered.

"The departed we now remember—"

Chaim, baby, he vowed suddenly, I'll take care of everything. I'll write your mother and father just like you wanted. Judy, too. Better than that—I'll even take Judy to dinner at the Sousse Palace and break it to her gently. A number-one, top-quality job. You couldn't ask for anything more than that. Could you?

"—have entered into the peace of life eternal. They still live on earth, in the acts of goodness they performed, and in the hearts of those who cherish their memory."

Judy and me. And your mother and father. That's about it. Except maybe in the home office they'll think about you occasionally.

"May the beauty of their life abide among us as a loving benediction."

That was the worst part. A loving benediction. Because he *would* have a damned loving benediction in spite of the lousy thing they had done to him.

A spray of rain marched along the sands and began to melt the ragged signs of the shovel upon the yellow earth.

"Norman," David whispered after a few seconds.

"You shut up," Norman said, with his eyes still closed. "You ought to be happy. That ought to redeem my soul as far as your damned *twansa* heart is concerned. But I just want you to remember that I was the one who had to carry him all the stinking way back to the car."

Going north from Nefta on the main highway they thought they were being tailed for a few miles by a Border Police patrol car, but finally it passed them, doing a straight eighty on the wet road in the direction of Tozeur.

"Stupid bastards," Norman said, looking up from the papers in his lap. "At that speed, they're aquaplaning all the way. I hope they break their own goddamned necks and not somebody else's."

It was raining hard once more, and the clouds had closed in. David turned the windshield wipers to "Fast" position.

"I was thinking," he said, "that perhaps the weather would clear a little for us to get through the *chott*. But parts of the road are probably flooded by now. With the lakes on both sides of the road it is not so good. Salt is bad for the tires."

"Yeah," Norman said, not really listening. He had reached a point with the papers where he couldn't go much farther and he didn't want to make too many guesses. He had made a few, and they scared the hell out of him.

It can't be this much of a mess, he thought. On top, there seemed to be a primary code. He was fairly sure of that. And then, obviously a code under that. Goddamned confusion made it worse, whole pages of key names. Columbia. Marco Polo. The *delfine* had been direct enough and easy to recognize, but then Dolphin was their code name and not anybody else's.

They know who we are. Let's assume that. Also, since the letter was only a week old from the looks of it, maybe they could assume there hadn't been time to do anything about it. But only maybe.

The rest of the stuff really made your head hurt. There were months, weeks, days, as far as he could determine, but it seemed like they were in Arabic numerals—that is, those discarded by the Tunisian government for the sake of modernity but still in use in Egypt and places in the Near East. So naturally, if they were dates, everything dated from the year of the Prophet's Hejira. No B.C. or A.D. Because of this, he had been reduced to counting on his fingers,

writing the Arabic numerals from one to ten, the base, on a sheet
beside him just so he could keep track of what he was doing.

I. ٩ ٨ ٧ ٦ ٧ ٠ ٣ ٢ ٢ ١

And so forth. Then you went up by adding the decimal mark to
combinations.

But shit, every once in a while he got involved and started reading
them from left to right instead of from right to left, and that screwed
it all up!

But he was making progress. He didn't know exactly what he
was doing, but he was making enough progress so that the damned
soggy *keshabiya* he still wore wasn't what was giving him the cold
chills.

David.

"Listen, David," Norman said suddenly, "see if you can take a
look at this without wrecking us. This is a date—a month and a day
—isn't it?"

"Yes," David said, looking back and forth from the road to the
paper, quickly, "but it is in Arabic numbers. Is this the modern
counting, from the Christian calendar, or from the *Issana el-Higriya?*"

"Hell, I'm not sure of anything. But let's say it's the Moslem
calendar, since the stuff's in Arabic. Do you know what the date is?"

"Yes. That is today. The first of September."

The windshield wipers made a clicking sound. They were passing
through a depression, a dip in the road where the rain collected in
pools filled with the knobby brown shapes of frogs.

"Jesus," Norman exclaimed. But he did not look away. The tires
slushed greasily through and there was a long silence afterward.

They were coming into Tozeur, an oasis town set in a bowl of
palm trees that looked from a distance as though a green spot of
algae had settled on the desert floor. At the break in the mountain
chain northward, the oases were like green steps on the valley floor,
leading on into the Sahara.

"David," Norman said abruptly, "you know this country pretty
well down here, don't you? I mean, you know where the cutoff, G.P.
16, is, that crosses the *chott?* And how to get out of the Kebili on
the far side, and the way to find the roads that connect with G.P. 19
and the Libyan border? You know the brethren's name is Mokhtar
Lev. In the *souks de grana,* the Jewish *souks* of Ouezzen."

"Yes, of course." He was frowning. "We had to memorize all that, did we not?"

For long moments Norman stared thoughtfully ahead into the rain.

"David, listen to me," he said slowly. "And don't stop the car, don't swerve, don't do anything nutty. Just listen. I'm going to leave you in Tozeur. I've got to find a telephone."

"Of course, Norman. I will drive you around and then pick you up. There is a café—"

"Listen, David, now for God's sake, *listen!* I'm not going to yell at you, I'm going to speak to you like this because it may be the last time I'll ever see you. You know that's important, don't you?"

David kept his eyes on the road, but his face went suddenly stiff and wary.

"I'm going to leave you in Tozeur and I'm going to try and find a telephone as I have to talk to some friends of mine. Now I'll tell you as much as I can—God knows I don't know much about this crap myself. O.K., there was nothing in old von Lehzen's papers about the SS or the Ukraine; I was just lying to Chaim because I wanted him to be happy about it. So unless Tel Aviv comes across with an identification one of these days, we will never know if we killed the right man or whether he was just some goddamned Kraut who got in the way. Frankly I don't give a shit what he was; if he ever belonged to the SS in his whole life he deserved what he got on general principles. But that's not important. David, are you listening to me?"

"Yes," David said. He was looking straight ahead.

"But the papers have got something else in them. It's a goddamned code; I can only guess at what it means. Some of the stuff is in German, which I really don't know, and some of it is in Arabic, but a kind of Arabic that really throws me. It's really as good as any code you could want, because it's all screwed up with really high-class classical Arabic usages. But I know enough to figure out the numbers. That's what threw me at first; I thought I was bucking a numbers code and God knows I'm no mathematician. I nearly quit then. But finally I realized that what we have got here is a system for bringing in a lot of hardware. Specifically, what seems to be Chinese-make AK-47s."

"But Norman—"

"Just wait a minute. It's not the numbers, I found out. The real key to the damned thing is trying to think like a fucking German. The dawn broke when I realized the methodical sons of bitches were guaranteeing delivery by actual serial number. That's why I was drowning in Arabic numerals. That kind of efficiency really takes your breath away, doesn't it? I couldn't believe it until I remembered all those damned gold fillings from teeth and all the old clothes they inventoried, hot out of the gas chambers. Then I knew it made sense. So if you go one step further, you don't have to exactly be a genius to know what a concentration of AK-47s here means. Group One is making a little money out of the old German profession. Peddling war."

"This is madness," David said. "You must come with me. What will I tell them in Libya? I cannot explain to them why I did not bring you with me. You cannot stay here now, in this insane country, for any reason. Whatever it is these people are planning to do, we are no part of it. Let them kill each other if they want to, it is none of our business."

"David, chum," Norman said, "I don't know what the hell our business is, and that's the truth. We haven't been doing anything that makes any sense for weeks. It looks like Tel Aviv couldn't give a shit where we are, or what our troubles are, they're so busy playing Russian roulette with World War Three for the preservation of the Jewish Homeland. And I'm beginning to lose my sense of identity again—I mean, I'm beginning to feel too much of a Jew again for this military power-structure jazz; I'm beginning to get my usual alienated feeling. Because, David *bubbeleh*, I'm beginning to realize alienated is all I know; I am actually at heart a real loser, a genuine, alienated, high-minded, intellectually brainwashed, poor, fucking Jew, one of God's forgotten Chosen. Like, I was raised not to turn my back on my inborn burden of guilt, and the rest of mankind. My kind of Jew is not supposed to go off and let what's left of the Families catch it in the ass. I am not even supposed to let my fellow Semites—after all, sons of Abraham just like the rest of us—catch it in the ass, either. If anybody is planning some sort of pan-Arab Liberation Front take-over—and what else?—with Chinese-made hardware, I am supposed to go back and stick my head in the cannon for a role which traditionally nobody will appreciate. They will just say I am some dirty Jew who came back to collect interest on a loan. Right?"

"Norman, I do not understand what you are talking about," David exclaimed. "Whatever you have found, it is nothing—these guns come in all the time. And the police, they are always picking them up from crazy people, from those crazy revolutionists, as they picked up a whole truckful six years ago. Norman, if you stay here you will do nothing— you will only kill yourself!"

"You worry too much," Norman said, sliding down in the seat. "Don't disturb my Jewish idealism. Besides, I've still got my passport; I'm still an American citizen. Nothing's going to happen to me. I'm just a nice potash salesman trying to get ahead in the world, and if anybody here gives me a hard time it's because they're a bunch of goddamned Arabs persecuting an American Jewish businessman. I'll get Senator Javits to cut off their foreign aid."

"Norman, you are the one who is crazy, I believe it. You made a big mistake last night—" David could not turn his head, but his hands tightened on the wheel of the car convulsively. "We should never have come here. Even you know this. And now you are thinking of making still another mistake. What will you do in Tozeur without a car? You will be caught. And soon the police will be looking, they will be looking for the people who broke into the house in the oasis and murdered—"

"What time is it?" Norman said abruptly. He lifted his wrist watch. "It's six A.M.! Jesus, where can I find a telephone at this hour? And damned French phones; I've got to buy a stinking token just to make a call. It's got to be a place where I can wait. Not a café full of Arabs. To make a call to Tunis means I've got to wait while they take their sweet time getting it through. I can hang around for two hours like that."

And David is right, Norman thought. I'm one bounce ahead of the Sûreté. I wonder how long it will take the local police to get on to what happened out at El Hamma?

More importantly, what was supposed to happen on September first? Maybe it had already happened.

"Pull up to the curb," Norman said, "when you get to the Public Gardens. There's a newsstand there."

The newspaper, when they got it, was in Arabic, and Norman

read his way through several headlines without ringing any bells. By then he was getting pretty jumpy.

Hungry, he told himself. He needed a cup of coffee and some sort of breakfast.

The item he was looking for was not really the item he was looking for, that was the hell of it. He didn't recognize it until he had read it twice. It was on the bottom of page two, but it would make page one tomorrow.

"Here," he told David, in a big hurry. "You got money, keep going. Don't stop, don't speak to strangers. If I'm lucky, I'll see you again some day."

"Ah, Norman, please," David cried. He leaned out the car window as if to protest more vehemently, but saw Norman's face and withdrew. The Mercedes pulled away from the Public Gardens.

I'm still wearing the damned *keshabiya*, Norman thought, looking down. And going into the Hotel Splendide across from the park I'd be better off in European clothes.

There was no time to do anything. He decided to carry it off as best he could, wear the damned Arab coat and speak French and fill out the thin spots with *chutzpah*. But to his surprise he found that his body was beginning to tighten and he could feel the strain. Guerrilla work, in the dark, he could do; now he was overtired and jumpy. And he had never had a lot of talent—or the delicacy—that this sort of thing required. You needed steel guts and a ready smile, the kind of nerve to see it all blow up in your face and never turn a hair, smiling right down the line.

There were other people who could do it better. Like Michel.

The concierge of the Hotel Splendide was reading the morning paper and taking his coffee at Reception. The mahogany desk looked as though it had been recruited from a close-out sale of the Foreign Legion. A flyspecked globe lamp sat unsteadily on a pile of French magazines in a litter of a half-eaten *croissant*, unemptied ash trays, and an old-fashioned brass inkstand. Even getting close to the desk was something of an effort—the lobby was a maze of interesting house plants in ceramic pots scattered about on the tile floor.

Norman told the concierge that he would take breakfast in the bar while he waited on the Tunis call.

There was no bar, he found out; the bar service was at the courtyard tables where rain now dripped steadily.

Well, the dining room, then.

The dining room had four tables with white plastic tablecloths and four matching ceiling fans. The Arab boys had the radio in the kitchen full up, and the room was filled with the throb of North African music from Radio Sfax. Norman drank a cup of thick black Tunisian coffee and ate fresh rolls with butter while he waited.

"You are in luck," the concierge said, coming in. "Because it is early the lines are not so busy now. I have the Tunis operator on the line, on the little telephone in the hall."

As Norman passed out into the open gallery which ran around the rain-filled courtyard the concierge stood watching him thoughtfully, working a toothpick against his teeth. In spite of the need for hurry and the sprinkles of wet which fell on him from some hidden leak in the concrete floor above, Norman felt alarm bells ringing in his head and nervous system. A plop of water fell on his hand as he lifted up the receiver. There was something wrong and yet he couldn't put his finger on it; it oozed out of the dank peeling stucco walls of the Hotel Splendide and caught at his breath in the same feeling he had had a few hours before, when things had gone wrong at the General's villa. The words crossed his mind: This is it. I think this is where it all ends.

"Hello, Wild Rose?" Norman said close into the mouthpiece.

Jesus, at a time like this he really needed Chaim. A sense of frustration, of mindless anger, swept over him. If Chaim were there to back him up he wouldn't feel like something was happening at the door now where he couldn't see it. Something to do with the greasy concierge.

"This is Dolphin."

"I think you must have the wrong number," the British voice of Cynthia Guffin said.

"I haven't got time for games," Norman rasped. "Now listen to me. I'm going to talk to you fast because I'm in a bind, and I'm going to tell you everything I know. And you stand there and listen, if you've got any interest in your operations. Because they're not *my* operations; I just got into them by mistake."

"Where are you?" the voice said cautiously.

Norman didn't have more than three or four minutes to grind out the whole bit, sketchy as it was, and half of Miss Guffin's questions had to go unanswered because he simply didn't know; he had almost no idea of the scope and import of the stuff he was carrying around and could only guess at it.

"I've got to get out of here. If I still can."

The feeling was really strong now; hair was standing straight up on the back of his neck. From where he stood the Hotel Splendide rose around the courtyard in open tiers. A man leaned his elbows on the iron railing of the second floor, watching Norman through the rain. And there was someone also right over his head; he could hear the scrape of feet on concrete, moving around.

He made himself hang up. He had just stepped away from the telephone—in fact he was in such a sweat to get out of there the receiver missed its cradle and fell and was still dangling when he half turned to slam it back up again—when two of them came running in from the lobby and the man started coming down from upstairs. In the lobby Khefacha was out ahead of a uniformed *boliss*, Khefacha's summer djibbah billowing like a white spinnaker as he ran.

Norman ducked for the dining room, hoping for some way out in there, but he was blocked. The waiter and the cook were standing, goggling, in front of the kitchen door. And Khefacha was right behind him; he caught him by the hood of the *keshabiya* long enough to hold him and then got him by the right arm. For a moment, as Khefacha spun him around by his arm, Norman thought he was being lined up for a judo approach, an *ippon seionage*, and he tried to counter. But that was his error. Norman lost his balance, stumbled into the big Sûreté Nationale who had just come thundering up, and the Sûreté lurched backward over a dining room chair.

What really confused Norman was the awkwardness of it—the little bastard Khefacha hanging onto him by the tassel of the *keshabiya* hood and slinging him around by the arm like a yo-yo. The jackass had lost control of himself; he was having a goddamned tantrum.

"You fool!" Khefacha howled. The Arabic words sputtered and choked. "You turd! We tried to keep you out of this—interfering Jew!"

God knows, Norman remembered later, it wasn't any sort of calculated move. He matched Khefacha's frenzy with his own. He didn't even bother to lead with his left. Instead, he brought a round-house right up from the floor that caught the Berber full in the teeth. Khefacha went down, dragging a white plastic tablecloth with him, and a pepper-sauce bottle and a little vase of plastic flowers. He fell in between two molded plastic chairs and caught his leg somehow over a chair seat so that one foot, with a neatly polished white buckskin oxford, was the only thing left in sight.

The foot struck Norman as funny; he had just enough time to laugh once before the Sûreté hit him from behind on the neck. When Norman went down the Sûreté dragged him up again and turned him around and hit him again. He was still hitting him when the two reinforcements came in, and he bounced Norman over to them and let them have him for a while. Khefacha went out to call a doctor for his mouth. After a while the original Sûreté sent for another uniformed *boliss* standing guard outside the Hotel Splendide, and the new man took over the beating while he went out with the others for a rest and a Coca-Cola with the concierge.

They didn't even bother to take Norman to the police station. The dining room stayed closed until twelve-thirty while they worked him over. Lunch was a little late, that was all.

14

My heart is capable
of every form.

—*Mhi Al Din ibn Al Arabi*

It was still very early on Friday morning, the white steams of a heat-drugged night still drifting among the leaves of the orange groves, when Salem wheeled his bicycle into the lane between Monsieur Moreau's house and the estate which had formerly belonged to Sebastian Ghrika.

He was after one of Monsieur Moreau's roses, a delicate red bud which he had seen the day before (an accursed and eventful day which he preferred at the moment not to remember) while he had been hiding in the garden to escape the eternal problems of that house. It was this rose which he had come for now, and which he intended to take to the house of Mees Aweet afterward.

Salem was breaking the stem of the rose and trying not to stab himself with the thorns when his mother's brother, Ahmed m'Amouri, came suddenly down to the gardens from the house. Salem jumped and raked his thumb on a sticker.

"Are you mad, son of trouble?" his uncle hissed at him. He would have seized him, only his hands held a large pan of kitchen scraps for the chickens. "What are you doing? Why are you not at the *Amrikaniyeh's* house? Or have you not brought enough disaster on your head, that you must also turn thief with the old one's flowers? Do you wish a repetition of what occurred yesterday?"

"That was not for stealing flowers," Salem flung at him, but he retreated a step. "Nor would I look to you, fat one, for help!"

His uncle turned red and angry. The problem was nothing new; it had been growing for some time. For three days in a row Salem had been told to go to the old man's bedroom during the hours of the *sieste* and rub the old one's body down with the bottle of alcohol. It was the usual thing which he was required to do, and certainly no secret. But this time he had made it clear to his uncle that he was not going to do it, as he had in fact refused to do this thing for more than a month now. Then he had run out of the house and had hidden under the datura bushes, a safe place where he could sleep undetected until it was time to go home. But the old one himself had come into the garden with his bathrobe flapping about his legs, to poke into the bushes and under the garden benches with a stick, and eventually he had found him. He had called Ahmed m'Amouri to drag him out and, since he was resisting fiercely, old Tewfik, too. It had taken both of them to do it, and for a brief moment it had been almost funny: Tewfik and his uncle trying to drag him out from under the datura bushes, his uncle hitting him angrily around his head and shoulders with his free hand. But Monsieur Moreau had been enraged, shouting that he was a demon boy and an ingrate, a lazy beggar who ran off and would not do as he had been told. It was time for a beating. His patience had run out.

The beating was unimportant. But this time Salem had vowed that he would not let the old one touch him again. Fools that they were, his uncle and the other one had not understood that. Instead, they held him while the old man pulled his trousers down to prepare him for the beating, exposing his naked body for even the cook to see when he came running down from the house to see what all the noise was about.

At the first crack of the stick, Salem shouted out with all his strength. He was determined to yell and make such a commotion that perhaps some of the tourists on the beach or even people on the road would hear and wonder what was going on. He was not going to be silent any longer. At least the world would know that he, Salem, did not suffer all this willingly.

Then people from the beach had come tramping through the rose garden in great bewilderment, speaking in English and German voices, and among them must have been the American girl. Because she screamed out at what she was seeing. Even in those confused moments as his uncle at last released him and tried to pull Monsieur Moreau away, he was surprised at the remarkable loudness of Mees Aweet's screams, and how much she sounded like his own mother and sisters when she was enraged.

"Do not be a fool," his uncle was telling him, as he gestured with the pan of feed. "*Essma*, Salem Gueblaoui ibn Hafid, there is no trouble now if you do not deliberately bring more upon yourself. It is true the old Moreau is still angry with you for causing this disturbance as you did, and it is not to be denied that you deserved a good beating. But consider, what is asked of you here is very little; it is not as though it leaves a mark for others then to see. Think of Beji ben Chakker, who served in this house for four years and who is now married and with a profitable pottery shop in Nabeul. Did it harm him, that anyone can tell? No, the old one even came to his marriage and gave out many expensive gifts. And think also of Abdel, my own cousin's son, who by virtue of the same generosity was able to attend the agricultural school at Pont du Fahs, and who is now engaged to Abdullah Yacoub's daughter. I am telling you that many have served a good service here and profited well. As I, too, am still here," his uncle added significantly.

Salem backed away cautiously. Yes, his uncle had served in that house longer than anyone. He was growing old and fat now, but in his youth he had been very good-looking, one of the most beautiful boys in the village. In his time, Ahmed m'Amouri had also carried the bottle of rubbing alcohol to the old man's room in the hot afternoons.

"You do no more, no less," he was saying, "than what many others have done before you. If you think perhaps to lose pride because this one is a foreigner, remember that you could be doing the same thing in the houses of rich Arabs, also. If you wish, you can do service in the villa of Abedine Azzassi—he knows you are a handsome boy, he has asked about you and what you are doing now. But Azzassi would make you work hard and he would not let you steal from the kitchen and sleep under the trees, as you do here."

Salem only laughed. "Pimp your offers somewhere else, Ahmed m'Amouri," he told him. "I am not going to work for any of your rotten bourgeoisie, nor will any of my friends. We know that in the houses of these stinking exploiters of people one cannot do honest work for honest money, that one must sell one's body for just enough milliemes to buy a little food! This kind of 'profit,' my uncle, you can have!"

"Good—do not work, then!" his uncle shouted at him. "And you will let your mothers and sisters starve, dog turd! You will go begging in the streets; this is what will happen to you! I know where you hear this filth, this shit, this talk—it is from Shedli Zouhir, this great sage and fountain of all wisdom. This prophet of the Tunis street corners! Like his father, that great and wonderful one who is now an exile from his own country."

"At least Mohammed Zouhir fought with Salah ben Youssef. He was a man and not a whore!"

"Yes, of course, most admirable. A great hero, but dead. The dead are always heroes. I tell you, Salem Gueblaoui," his uncle raged, "you will find it a very hard thing to be a hero, if this is what you want. To go to the old man in the afternoon with a bottle of alcohol will not seem such a bad thing after you have seen some of these troubles! The ideas of Shedli Zouhir will not put food into the mouths of your family, nor keep you from the loving care of the *boliss!*"

"You take my place here, dear uncle," Salem shouted, "since you are so worried about it!" But he was moving away, toward the *tabia* and his bike. "If the old one's money means so much, take your own backside in your two hands and go to him. See if he still fancies it!"

With a howl of rage, his uncle hurled the pan of slimy scraps after him.

It was still so early—not yet seven o'clock, and he ordinarily did not arrive before nine or after—that Salem did not expect to find Mees up and about. But as he let himself into the kitchen he heard her walking around upstairs. By her footsteps he could tell that she went out onto the women's roof, where she kept a small line for her private laundry to dry, and then he heard her come back inside. The machine with the rock music was going very loudly, and in a few seconds there was the roar of the shower.

Salem mixed the Nescafé powdered coffee—always, to him, a very weak and unappetizing-looking brew—and put the rose in a glass of water. The deep red bloom was just opened in the heat, and as he watched it, it seemed that it unfolded and opened back almost before his very eyes. The rose was of such a perfection that it cried out for a better receptacle, but Mees Aweet's house was very carelessly kept, and there were no such things. There was only an ordinary drinking glass.

With the rose in his right hand and the cup of coffee in the other, he ran upstairs. At the door to her room he hesitated, but it was open, showing that she was not dressing, and the shower was not running, either. Perhaps, he thought, she had gone out on the roof as she sometimes did, either to gather her laundry or to sit in the bikini swimsuit in the sun and write letters. He crossed the room and ran up the steps which led to the women's roof, but she was not there. He turned and started back again.

If he had not been in such a hurry and with his mind on other matters—such as what she would say when she saw the rose—he would have known there was some mistake. At that moment she came out of the room of the bath and she had a towel about her head but nothing on her body. She was naked, just as he always saw her in his private thoughts, but now her breasts were fuller than he remembered, the nipples soft and wide as pink mouths. Her body was still shining with bath water, the length of her thighs glistening, the patch of light hair in her crotch tight and curled.

He was numbed, frozen with the sight.

He could not control his eyes, could not make his head turn away. But wild thoughts flashed through his head: was this a dream, now, or was it real? Such a wave of heat and desire for her—if this was true—swept over him in those seconds that he felt faint. He could have her, now. It was as if all the thick, sensuous powers of that hot morning centered in him and drew him inevitably toward his fate. His hands had no strength left in them; he felt the coffee cup roll over on its side, spilling hot coffee on his wrist, and the small crash as the cup hit the floor. A final wash of warmth over bare foot.

The noise jarred him. He was able to move, and he saw that he still held the glass of water with the rose, miraculously unharmed. He went to his knees to begin to pick up the broken pieces of coffee cup on the floor, but it was as though it was beyond him to do so. He reached forward with his right hand, but his fingers were paralyzed; they would not move.

There was only one towel in the bathroom and that was dirty, so Sharon had come out into the bedroom to look for another one. She almost walked right into him.

That really did it. For a moment she thought he had had a heart attack. He went down on his knees and then almost over on his face, and it took her a minute to realize that he was only trying to clean up the broken dish.

She had really dreaded seeing him again after that awful mess at Moreau's; in fact she had thought about the poor kid so much she hadn't slept well at all, and then she had gotten up early with the idea of making an all-day trip to Bizerte to talk to Genevra, to ask Genevra what in the hell she was going to do about everything down there in Ez-Zahra. Living in that damned place. It was getting so complicated and weird that if she didn't get something normal to do, like teaching in the *lycée* on a nice, normal, regular basis, she felt as if she might flip right out of her skull. Seriously.

The scene at Moreau's had been really bad, not just because of what had been going on, with the old man flailing around with his stick and the obvious implications of the whole thing, but because of Salem yelling his brains out over it. Right there, while it had all been going on, she had finally realized what a jam he was in. Right then she had understood that he hated the whole bit, that he was practically a prisoner of the job and circumstance and having to support his family and everything. It had made her almost physically sick; she had wanted to vomit. And sort of hysterical. She remembered screaming a lot, too.

Poor kids. Poor fucking kids! Even after all that time she really hadn't understood the kind of life they had to lead, just when she was beginning to think she understood it all.

"*Maalesh,*" she said, because she didn't know what else to say. It didn't matter about the coffee cup, or anything like that. What was important was to learn that sometimes horrible things didn't matter; you had to shut your mind to them. Good things had to happen. He wasn't going to work for Moreau all his life. Somehow she would have to see to that.

He didn't seem to hear her. It was as though he had fainted. And it suddenly occurred to her that he really might have had a heart attack or a mental blackout or something. He was really a very nervous and uptight kid. Last Friday in the kitchen when he had been sweeping he had accidentally backed into her, and she had thought he was going to blow his mind right on the spot. He had really jumped right up into the air.

"Salem?" she said. She was sort of worried. Should she yell for the ben Omranes to get a doctor?

No, she thought quickly; she didn't want them in on this. They were never any help, and the explanations could really get screwed up if they weren't careful.

She didn't think kids—kids that age, anyway—really had heart attacks over sudden shock, but then you never could tell. Sharon bent over him and gingerly reached into his shirt and felt around. Her fingers flattened out against his chest where his heart ought to be, and it was sort of pleasant because his skin was smooth and warm. His body was awfully thin, but with a boy's hard, solid muscles. He didn't move when she touched him, even though she had to bend pretty far over to get her hand inside his shirt and her thigh was resting against his arm and shoulder. His heart felt normal enough, she thought, with a small frown. At least it didn't seem to be bumping or jerking or anything that she could tell. But then she was no heart expert. His body was so funny and wiry, with his heart racing like that, that it was a very odd experience. She couldn't help thinking what would happen if he really *had* a woman.

Without even thinking what she was doing she just very naturally put her free hand on the back of his head and smoothed his hair.

He turned so quickly, grabbing her so convulsively around the knees, that he almost toppled her over. Water splashed on her legs and something fell. She heard another crash. The whole floor was going to be covered with broken stuff, she thought; it was already a mess.

But it was lucky, the glass rolled away and didn't break.

"Hey, wait a minute!" she exclaimed.

He had her around the knees in this iron grip, his face turned up, chin pressed against her leg, and she couldn't get away. She stared down at him, dumbfounded.

In that second she was trying to realize that this was going to be too much and she was going to be sorry she had ever gotten involved with anybody's problems, because she already had so many of her own she didn't need any more. But he was looking up at her under half-closed eyes, his cheek mashed against her thigh, and he looked so beautiful and flipped out it was crazy. The same look of all the boys; it was what had sold her on them in the first place: that lovely wild look, the high cheekbones, the secret, staring black eyes, the beautiful mouths ready to burst out laughing or turn downward with yelling and anger.

And the other kids treated him so rotten. She remembered the night of the freaky dancing and how his cousin had practically had to come back and fight the others off and they had only thought it was funny.

It wasn't fair. And it was stupid, because sex, straight sex, was no big thing. It was just a beautiful spontaneous meeting of bodies for the most normal human expression. Just a terrifically profound experience. Besides, these kids were so naturally sexy it was unbelievable. But the way they lived, being kept apart from the village girls, was enough to blow their minds.

He started upward with his mouth, first her thigh and then his lips against her hipbone and trailing across her stomach and then down again. Then suddenly trying to part the flesh there with his mouth, his tongue stabbing and prodding.

"Wow," she breathed, because it really rocked her. It had come as a complete surprise, and yet she supposed it was sort of an instinctive thing to do, even for somebody without much experience. But it was fantastic. His lips pushed her open and his mouth came on so strong that for a moment she was completely zapped. With his hands gripping her backside, he pushed her against all that really crazy kissing.

"Oh, hey," she murmured. She ran her hands down onto his neck and shoulders. He had such a great tense, thin body and yet it was pretty strong; she couldn't have gotten away from him even if she had wanted to. But at the top of her thoughts, sort of over everything else that was going on, she was trying to warn herself that this could be really complicated. It wasn't the right way to get the day started at all, in spite of what she was feeling at the moment. Because there was tomorrow. And there was the Ez-Zahra Chief of Police. Cripes! she thought, and shuddered. He grabbed her around the waist and pushed her thighs wider, and it was as though his tongue went right up inside her.

"Oh—ummm," Sharon whispered, and practically melted. She

began to move a little; she couldn't help it because he was turning her on and it was out of sight. But she was trying to think of all the other boys in the youth discussion group and what it was going to lead to. Kids never could keep their mouths shut. Because, after all, one student in Tunis and a PCV ready to go home and a couple of other people and Ali ben Ennadji and Norman didn't quite add up to this. It would probably even make it impossible to get the house cleaned up on a regular basis.

But it was all really inevitable, no matter how you looked at it. He was already pushing her toward the bed. Then they were down on it and he was on top of her, unbuttoning his clothes and pushing them out of the way.

Oh, well, Sharon said to herself. Because she was trying to be convinced that it could be straightened out somehow afterward, and it *was* important for him—after everything that had happened to him—to have a straight sexual experience for a change. Especially the horrible way he had had to live up to now. She put her arms around his neck and stretched out slowly under him and it was beautiful to do because he was shaking and choking like he was going to blow his mind, it meant so much to him. She marveled again that he was so beautiful, really, with those wild black eyes and furry eyelashes and a trembling, wet, soft mouth. Like an explosion. Anybody could tell, she thought dreamily, that he didn't have much experience, because he went off in about one minute flat and then fell upon her, sobbing with relief.

That night, which was Friday, Sharon found she couldn't sleep at all. Which was a very strange experience for her, she realized, sitting up in bed. Her whole mind was in some crazy kind of uproar. Her head was going back over everything that had happened for a month or more, including the way Ali ben Ennadji had tailed her until she finally gave in.

There was nothing in the house—no *kef*; it was long gone and she hadn't been to Tunis to get any more—and she had even forgotten to buy any wine. She had forgotten to shop, and the stores were closed after seven in the evening.

The only thing to do was go to the village *pharmacie* and see if she could get something to make her sleep; she was so exhausted she felt as though she was going out of her mind. She was not only sleepless but she was really up there, high and vibrating, like a thousand-volt current running through her absolutely beat body, whipping it on. Like a high on speed. It was a terrible way to feel. And in the back of her mind she had some kinky idea that she didn't want any more complications; she had had about as much as she could handle.

The next morning wasn't any better. That is, when Sharon fixed a cup of coffee, she vomited it up. It was so quick she didn't have time to run upstairs to the bath; she just barfed it up in the kitchen sink. It was nothing but coffee anyway, so it didn't make too much of a mess.

And she hadn't slept. The pills made her feel just as though she was drowning, they kept pulling her under the dark waves of some sort of horrible unconsciousness that wasn't sleep until she had to fight her way back up again. It was noon before she stopped feeling groggy, and then she had a giant headache, a real disaster.

Even going over the quarterly report didn't help much. It was a great report in many ways and she had worked hard on it the past few weeks, telling all about the youth discussion group; with luck the report would make some sort of splash with the Foundation and show that she hadn't been entirely goofing off in Ez-Zahra all summer in spite of what her own organization had done to screw things up.

At a little before two o'clock on Saturday afternoon, Sharon started for Moreau's villa. This one last time she had to meet with the boys and make some arrangement to have their discussions in another place, because they certainly couldn't keep going back there. The day was burningly empty and still as death; there was no wind and not even any sound of birds at that hour. In such heat, the day turned into one long *sieste*. Sharon sat down on one of the concrete garden benches to wait, and after a while the sun went in behind the clouds and she looked up in surprise, because there hadn't been any clouds in so long it was really something of a novelty to see the sun disappear like that. But the overcast wasn't much cooler. To pass the time, Sharon got out the preliminary report which she had brought along with her to check against this last meeting, and tried to read it through again.

There were a lot of usual things in the report but there were some goodies, too. Like the discussion they had had on Frantz Fanon's book, *The Wretched of the Earth*—which some of them had already read in the original French version—which was really going to jolt the Foundation's Tunis office at least. But then what the shit, she told herself; the time had come for Charlie Benedict and Miss Guffin and even old Lonesome George Russell to get used to something new. Naturally all the Arab kids wanted to read Fanon; the book was all about the Algerian war for independence against the French, and the conversations that had come out of it had been a gas. She had it all down in the report. That wasn't all of it, either. The boys not only were familiar with Che Guevara, but even with Fidel Castro back to his Oriente days, when he had been fighting alone in the mountains. This group of kids was dynamite. And the report was a whole capsule study and an in-depth examination of their lives and attitudes that was exactly like the *lumpenproletariat* that Fanon had said were going to be the real movers of the revolution in the Third World.

But sometimes they really tore you up, she thought mournfully. Like four kids of the group had gone far enough in their education in the *lycée* or the *école normale* to be pretty well up there, before they had had to drop out to earn a living for their families. Some of them had even learned how to use a slide rule and all that. Some of them could do a little trig, and they had still ended up in the groves around Ez-Zahra picking oranges. Not enough jobs anywhere. It was a real disaster. The kids knew enough, they had enough education to be aware of what was wrong with their lives and the society in which they lived, but they didn't have any power to do anything about it.

And, as she had really pointed out in her report, these kids didn't have any reason to have any faith in Western capitalism—the way it always ended up for them was exploitation by the upper classes of their own people. The President's old revolutionary buddies had just taken over screwing the poor where the French had left off. Fanon had been right. The national bourgeoisie of the liberated Arab nations identified plenty with the Western bourgeoisie from whom it had learned its lessons. Like how to keep on making money off the people on the bottom. Business and the old power structure as usual.

It was suffocatingly hot in the garden, and Sharon wiped her dripping forehead with the back of her arm. What was taking them so long? When she looked at her wrist watch it was four o'clock. That was strange. For one thing it didn't feel as though she had sat there that long in Moreau's garden. Somebody always showed up after half an hour. They were late, but they showed up eventually. The garden was very hot and still, and the cicadas had started drumming in the trees.

Suddenly, she knew they weren't coming. She didn't know how she did, but she did. And the realization of it came on her like she was suffocating, simply not able to get enough air into her damned lungs. She could sit there until hell froze over, but they weren't going to show. That was the real nitty-gritty truth of it.

The garden was empty. No one at all. They weren't coming. Maybe never again.

The whole world was starting to fall to pieces, just as she was falling to pieces.

Genevra!

She had to have Genevra because she needed her; there was just nobody else. She had to have Genevra because she was afraid something awful was about to happen.

If she got sick, Genevra could go to Nabeul for the doctor. Genevra could telephone for the doctor, at least.

Sharon went straight down the driveway because she had forgotten about staying away from Moreau's house. She was feeling dizzy again. It was the terrible heat, it was as though it was dragging her by the arms and feet to keep her there. The villa was all closed up, no one around at all. When she got to the road she hailed a little Renault cab and went to the village to the *bureau de poste*. She had to send a telegram.

COME QUICK, she wrote. The letters were in block print and very funny-looking, too big and wavering across the form BIG TROUBLE HERE. I AM SICK.

"I am very much afraid," Nancy Butler said on Sunday afternoon as she came down from the house with the tray of silver tea things, "that this isn't going to work out at all. Look at Cecile." She stood, holding the tea tray tentatively and frowning.

"I am all right," Cecile Lambert protested. "It is not the heat, it is really these incredible—how do you say?—*moustiques*. Where do they come from? I have never seen them before, like this!"

"Gnats," Cynthia Guffin told her. "It's the weather. Beastly hot, overcast and calm, always does it. And they really are bad, Nancy," she added judiciously. "The little brutes are biting like mosquitoes."

"You look as though you have the measles, Cecile," Nancy murmured. "Come inside and I'll put some calamine on you, and we'll take our tea on the porch."

"But we *always* have our tea here." Cecile looked anxiously apologetic. "No, even if there is no sun, I do so like to look at the sea. It is restful."

But Cynthia Guffin stood up. "Nonsense, there's no hard and fast rule; let's not be silly about it. I've got to go up and make a telephone call, anyway."

"I hope you find the damned telephone working," Nancy said on their way up to the villa. "It's gone so well for almost a month I'm sure we're due for one of our periodic breakdowns. When everything's operating the telephone people simply won't do maintenance —on the theory, I guess, that if there's no trouble you don't want to go looking for any. So of course the whole system gives way at once. My line was out for a while this morning, so I guess it's started."

"Hmm, I'll give it a try, anyway. It's rather urgent."

"Pick up the extension in the bedroom, then," Nancy said, holding the door for her.

"Well, the porch *is* nice," Cecile said gratefully, settling into a wicker chair. "And the glass makes no difference today, because there is no wind."

"This damned weather is bound to break; it can't go on forever," Nancy observed, putting the tea tray on a table in front of them. "Tomorrow's the first of September. Don't laugh—Chelli the gardener says we're going to get rain right on time. All the signs and portents absolutely guarantee it."

"Oh, *mon Dieu*, signs and portents." Cecile sighed. She mopped her face with her handkerchief. She had turned quite pink with the exertion of coming up the hill. "Does the gardener draw you the symbols in the sand with the fingers like so? They love the necromancy; all the Embassy people in Carthage are quite enchanted with it."

"Rot. He wouldn't dare, I've been here too long for that. But you know, I do trust him with the weather. He said 'No rain' after we had that awful khamseen, and he was quite right about that. Any luck?" Nancy asked, as Cynthia Guffin came onto the porch.

"Not much. The phone was working, but I can't seem to raise anyone in Tunis. Has everybody completely left town in this heat?"

"Sir Charles is out here in his villa," Cecile offered.

"Actually," Cynthia Guffin said, "I wasn't trying to get Sir Charles." She put down her tea and examined the backs of her hands, a small frown on her face. "I want to know where the General's got to. And I can't find out.

"Is he away from Nefta?"

"Yes, he has been for some time."

"Well, do you want me to call around, see what I can find out?"

"No, I'm afraid your sources are no better than mine at the moment. And of course people are busy with this President of Finland visit. I can't seem to get any one at all on the telephone."

"You *are* worried."

"Not at all. What is there to be worried about?"

"Well, he could have found the gold," Nancy said, and smiled. But, to her surprise, Cynthia did not seem to be amused.

"You know," she said thoughtfully, "I really think I might check again with London on that damned gold. Perhaps they can come up with something fresh on the finances of the Nineteenth Division when they were in Ez-Zahra. And I wonder if there's anything new on Sebastian Ghrika. Though it's not bloody likely. I'll have some more tea now, thank you." For a moment, as she held her cup, she looked hesitant and uneasy; then her face smoothed to its usual composure. "How closely," she said quickly, "do you keep track of Norman Ashkenazi? He's in on one of your passports, isn't he?"

Nancy Butler lifted her hands into the air. "My God, you don't know what sort of passport that is! We don't even talk about it. Those dual citizenship things drive us mad."

They sat for a moment in silence.

"Well, do you want me to check on Norman?" Nancy asked. "The Chain usually knows where he is. They won't say, of course. I'll have to get old Mestiri to do it for me."

"No, it's not that," Cynthia Guffin said, watching the sea. "I don't know what it is, exactly."

"You are right," Cecile put in quickly. "We do not know what it is either. But something is happening."

"That's because the Securité caught some kid with an AK-Forty-seven down in Feriana," said Nancy Butler. "But I can't see why that would cause a flap. That stuff comes in all the time under the bellies of sheep with the Algerian Bedouin. Nothing to worry about."

"What a strange summer," Cynthia Guffin observed, as Nancy refilled the cups. She leaned back in her chair and looked out through the glass porch panels to the metal-shining sea. "I really feel quite worn out this year. Getting on, I suppose."

Sharon had spent her time waiting for the train, which was late, as usual, practicing what she was going to say, which went: "Hi, Genevra baby, you brought the rain with you! How lucky can we get?" And perhaps even, "We put up the little flags and stuff because we knew you were coming!"

She had been repeating it to herself because Genevra really *was* coming; her telegram had said, "Arriving 10:50 train Sunday night," and it was such a tremendous, lovely thing at last that she wanted her welcome to be just perfect. And the rain was absolutely great; if she had planned it that way it couldn't have been any better. The change in the weather, strangely, made Sharon even more restless and jittery, but she was determined not to let it bother her. Something was happening finally; the whole earth was changing. The dry, dusty trees of the drought within the radius of the station lights had suddenly turned a violent green, already drinking in the flowing water. And on top of it all, just to make it crazier, it was apparently some sort of holiday: the station house was decorated with bunches of miniature red and white Tunisian flags. There were more bunches of flags tied to every light pole.

When she arrived, Genevra looked exceptionally beautiful in a white plastic raincoat and white rain boots and a floppy hat. Sharon could hardly wait to throw her arms around her. Genevra felt good, all wet and crackling and plastic, and she smelled of perfume.

But she wasn't smiling. Not even a little.

"Yeah, it was raining in Bizerte this morning," was all she said in answer to the speech of welcome. And then, "All the flags and decorations are for the President of Finland's visit. The whole country is covered with them. God, Sharon, don't you even read the newspapers? What *is* the matter with you, anyway? Your telegram said you were sick."

Sharon wanted to get out the whole complicated story right then, in the cab, but she realized she had to be careful. Although they were speaking English she didn't want the driver to hear any part of it. Especially not to mention names. So she had to change things around a bit.

"Oh, man, I'm really not following this," Genevra said, after a while. "It's really too much. Has this guy been threatening you or something? Why don't you just tell George Russell?"

Sharon knew then that Genevra hadn't understood a word. She was relieved when they paid the cab driver and got inside the house. She was starting over again when Genevra took off her raincoat, then the floppy hat. "Ugh, Sharon, how can you get in such messes! How could you let this Arab guy bang you in the first place? I wouldn't let him touch me. I don't want to be around them any more, I really mean it. I've already written my letter to old Charlie Benedict. It's in the mail."

But Sharon wasn't listening; she was staring straight ahead.

"Wow," Sharon said. "My God, I forgot about that. What time is it?"

"You're really nuts," Genevra said. "You even *look* far out, you know it? I never should have come down here; I have enough problems of my own. What's making you *shake* so?"

"Listen, Jenny," Sharon said in a hurry. "You've really got to help me out. I mean, I'll listen to the rest when I get back. You go upstairs and take a shower and fix some coffee for us and I'll be back in a few minutes. I really have got to talk to you. I'm in trouble here." She was already struggling into her raincoat. "You've got to wait up for me, don't go to bed, will you? Because we can sleep tomorrow. We'll drink coffee when I get back and you can talk to me," she said, holding the door open with her heel while she got the scarf around her head, "and I can talk to you and you'll see, it will be better. But I've got to go for just a minute, because I nearly forgot something."

"Sharon," Genevra said, trying to grab her. "Where are you going? Will you stand still a minute and stop zapping around like that? You're driving me crazy. Sharon, where are you going in the middle of the night? It's pouring rain out there!"

She was so damned late she was really afraid he wouldn't be there, and she searched around for a few hectic minutes by the main door to the villa and even under the banyan tree before she remembered the side entrance where there was a terrace and part of the roof covering it. Running up, in the blowing rain, she still didn't see him until the very last moment: he looked like part of the white wall because he had something white around him and he was standing well back, partly in the shadows. Then, a few feet away, she saw that he was wrapped in a blanket or a cape—she didn't trust her eyes because of the streams of water. Then she saw that it was a burnoose.

Sharon was breathless from running, but she wasn't so rattled that she couldn't tell it was a real burnoose over his clothes, one of the thick natural-wool-colored kinds with yards of cloth that the poor people wore and slept in and used not only for coats and beds but everything else you could think of. He had one side of it looped up over his shoulder to wind it around him tightly and keep the rain out, and the hood was up, just as she had seen the desert *bedu* wear them.

Sharon was so freaked out with lack of sleep that for an instant she had an awful feeling that it might be some sort of trick. Then she saw him move, and she knew it was real.

Her first thought was that she was glad he hadn't pushed the hood back, because the hood shadowing his face made it beautiful and mysterious. He looked so out of sight standing there with the red glow of the cigarette in his mouth that she couldn't move, in spite of the tons of rain pouring down. It was a total mind-and-body experience, one of the greatest things that had ever happened. It didn't matter that she was still high and vibrating, or about Genevra, or anything else.

"What is the matter with you?" he said from the door. He flipped the cigarette away impatiently into the rain. "Come in here, you are getting wet."

But she didn't want to move; she wanted to keep looking at him. He had finally taken shape in her mind and senses as the most incredible thing that had happened to her in her entire stay so far, and she didn't want to spoil it. Absolutely the most. He really knew how to wear the burnoose; he was born to it, as she knew. It was just sort of carelessly slung around and bunched up to keep his uniform dry, but it was perfect. As no one else—no European or other Westerner—could wear it.

It was, in that moment, what she had come all the way to North Africa to experience. Total reality.

"Are you crazy?" he said again. "Come out of the rain. Now this time you are late," he added significantly, "and it is not my fault I have not much time to stay." He came to the edge of the steps and waved her toward him fretfully. "Yes, hurry. I regret this, but I cannot stay. I have to leave for other business shortly."

"Me, too," she said, but she really wasn't listening. Even when he moved, it was perfect. The burnoose flowed and bunched around him in cream-colored folds, and he looked very Bedouin and inscrutable. "I have *une amie,*" she said, "this American friend who is visiting me, and she is waiting." She couldn't really be bothered with French. For the first time in about two or three days she was feeling so great she wasn't out of her mind with a lot of crazy problems.

He was staring at her, frowning. "What is the matter with you? Do you not know you are wet, a mess? Even your hair." He reached out and pulled her roughly under the overhang by her raincoat sleeve.

"You're beautiful," she told him. She always used the formal *vous;* her French was really pretty sloppy, but this time it was right because he looked so mysterious and wonderful. "I love it. It's a burnoose, isn't it?" she said, reaching out to touch the cloth.

That made him very hacked off, and he pulled away quickly. "It is nothing, it is not even too clean, this thing. I have the raincoat, but it is being repaired. This I must borrow in the station quickly, to keep from getting wet." He obviously didn't even want it around him. He pulled the loop down from his shoulder and let it swing free like a cape, and she could see the uniform underneath. "I do not wear old clothes like this. Only tonight, because I am in a hurry, to protect the uniform."

"Don't take it off," she begged him, but he wasn't paying attention.

"It is my fault—I apologize that I cannot stay," he was saying. He got out a package of Gauloises from his jacket. "Also, I do not have the key to the house. I cannot find that idiot, Hamid."

"It's all right," Sharon murmured. Anything was all right. She watched the flare of the match light his face in the dark. He held out the cigarette for her and then began to light one for himself. The little bit of French put-on with the cigarettes didn't bother her now; it was just something that was part of him. "You look so great," she told him. "I wish I had a photograph of you in that thing."

He gave her an odd look. "Do not be ridiculous," he said shortly. "No one wishes to have a photograph made in old dirty clothes. Now listen, I am trying to tell you that there is not much time. I wish to know if you have spoken to Messadi as I told you, and if he has promised you this job at the *lycée* as you wish. Be careful of the cigarette," he said quickly, as she put her arms around him.

Sharon turned her face against the wet woolen cloth and closed her eyes. It was beginning to be great and solid and familiar, now, the way they came together. She had really missed him the past few days. Through the burnoose and all their clothes they made contact, they could feel each other right through everything. He put both hands against her backside and moved her closer.

"What is this?" he said softly, smiling a little, "I think you want me, yes?"

"You want me, too. I can feel it."

His mouth was cold. It slid along her cheek and throat quickly and then back to her mouth. She sighed and wrapped her arms around his neck, giving herself over to it. This was the only place really beautiful and great now, when she was with him.

"You kiss differently, now," she whispered against his mouth.

"Differently?" he said, and kissed her again. "How?"

"As though you really mean it."

It didn't come out right in French, and he didn't understand.

"Yes, and I want you, too," he said hurriedly. "But I can only stay a few minutes here. Do not do that, do not move against me," he told her, but he sighed. "Yes, I want you, but it is raining here."

"Ummmm," Sharon murmured between the kisses. The connection was fantastic, full of wild vibrations. They wanted each other so badly it was as though there was nothing else to think about. Her hands got under the burnoose and the tight uniform belt and managed to get his shirt pulled out so that she could press her hands against his back.

He pulled up the raincoat. "Why are you wearing clothes under this?" he said, and kissed her again. They couldn't stop, not even long enough to talk. Finally he held her away from him and said, "*Essma*, there is not much time—will you listen? Now, Messadi has this job for you at the school. It is all arranged." But he groaned and kissed her again. "There is no time for this—besides, you have on all these underwear clothes pants and things."

"I can take them off," Sharon told him. She couldn't get his clothes pulled away, couldn't get his belt unbuckled fast enough. "I can't help it—I want you." She couldn't stay away from him; it was all of the things of the past few days running together.

"No, listen, there is no—" he began, but when her fingers closed around his warm flesh his whole body jolted. "Yes, all right," he said quickly. "But first take off this coat."

He pulled off her raincoat with his arm still around her and it came off jerking and pulling, taking the sleeve of her shirt with it, because the front was unbuttoned. He put his hands over her breasts quickly.

"Put the raincoat on the floor," he told her.

"We're going to get wet," she said.

"I will put the burnoose over it," he said in Arabic. "Lie down on it."

"I want you to take your clothes off, too," she said, even pulling off her shoes. "Everything."

"Are you mad? I am in my uniform. I do not have the time to get all the way undressed."

"I want to look at you," she whispered, and lay back against heavy wool. "Besides, you've got them half off, anyway."

He sighed again. But he took his clothes off, watching her as she lay there.

"Yes, it is a good idea," he said slowly. "You are very beautiful. Always when I think of you, it is how very beautiful you are. You have very lovely breasts and legs; it is part of the pleasure, just to look at you."

"You're beautiful, too," she told him simply. "I just wanted to see you, that was all."

"Now you have seen enough." But he was pleased. The rain blew in on them, but he deliberately covered her with his body.

"You are not ready for me," he said, with some surprise. "You will have to put your legs very wide."

"I *am*. I want you."

"I do not wish to hurt you," he said all in a rush. "Please—do as I say."

"I *am*. Oh, God! Oh, God!"

It was the greatest. He put his full weight on her, and her mouth was turned to touch his cheek. She could see his eyes close and feel the trembling that shook his body.

Do you want me very much? he murmured.

Yes, always.

Then put your arms around me. Kiss me.

She was with him all the way and yet a little ahead of him, so that she was floating down slowly and could feel him, feel his body contracting and then the warm spurt inside her.

After a while she put both her hands against his back and spread her fingers, to cover him a little from the rain.

"*Mizyeda.*"

"*Mizyed,*" he said, his mouth against her bare shoulder. "That is the way you speak to the man."

"I know, yes. *Mizyed.*"

They were so close, it was really complete now. It was so great—it was as though they had been making love together for years and years.

"Ummmm," she said when he kissed her on the mouth. "*Ente mizyed.*"

"Yes, I kiss you because you are a crazy girl," he said softly. "Because you want me, and you wish to take off all the clothes and do it now. It is crazy to do this, almost on the steps in front of this house. It is insanity."

"Don't go," Sharon said, trying to hold him.

"You do not mean this," he said, looking down at her.

"Yes, I do. Forget the time." She smoothed his hair and stroked her fingers across his mouth, seeing him follow, trying to kiss them. "I want you to make love to me all the time. I want you to come to my house and make love to me in my bed all night, until I can't move. I don't care who knows."

That was the way it was with them now. Sometimes he made love to her so much that after a while she couldn't do it any more, but he wanted her one more time. Like he wanted her to know that he could make her do it, that he could have her even then. Total possession. Sometimes she was so tired she almost couldn't stand it;

she really fought him. They had outright battles and he thought that was very amusing; it only made him more excited. He took her then like crazy.

Only tonight was really different.

"Yes, well, perhaps," he said, somewhat uneasily. "Perhaps some day I will come to your house." But he was looking at his wrist watch. "Also, I am crazy," he said under his breath. "Like a madman. I want you again, you are making me want you, but there is no time. I mean this; I am serious. I have done a foolish thing as it is. Tomorrow there will be more time."

"You promise?" she said, trying to pull him down again.

"Yes, I promise. All the time you wish." But he pulled her arms from around his neck and got up.

When Sharon let herself into the house Genevra was in the kitchen making coffee, but she went straight upstairs to take a shower. She didn't want Genevra to see her for a few minutes; it was like she was drunk, but she still hadn't had enough.

When she came out of the shower, Genevra had brought the coffee up. "Well, you've been with him haven't you?" Genevra said.

"Yeah, well, we have this place every night, but he's been away for a couple of days. I nearly forgot about it."

Genevra sat down on the bed beside her. "You mean, *every* night?"

"Yeah, well, it isn't exactly a record," Sharon said. She was tired, but she still couldn't stop shaking.

"No, it's not exactly a record, but it's getting pretty involved, isn't it?"

"I don't know." Even, she noticed, her voice sounded tired. "It just gets wilder and wilder, that's the weird part of it, and I really want him. I mean, at first it was kind of a drag; he bugged me; it was just a thing, getting balled. But now I'm so turned on when I can't have him I think I want everybody. It's getting complicated."

"I should really have listened to you," Genevra said, still staring at her.

"Oh, don't lay it on, will you?" Sharon said. "My problems aren't permanent. God, I hope they're not permanent. It's just that they go round and round in the most freaked-out way; you wouldn't believe it. Like that crazy kid knows I'm screwing the Chief of Police, but he also knows about Norman, too. And that's really weird because I think Norman knows about Ali ben Ennadji, or least he thinks it's an Arab, and I know about Norman and that crazy thing he and Chaim are into—"

"Oh, wow," Genevra said. "I think I'd better get ready."

Sharon took the little rolled joint and said, "Oh, you're a doll, Genevra!"

"I'm not promising anything. It tastes rotten, I've tried it. But it has hash in it; it's really on."

"I don't care," Sharon said, lying back in bed. "It's lovely. Now I can talk. I can really lovely talk, talk, talk."

15

God is most great!
I bear witness that there
is no god but God
and Mohammed
is his Prophet
Come to prayers
Come to good works
God is most great!
There is no god
but God.

—Mohammedan call to prayer

A little after one on Monday afternoon George Russell fixed himself a plate of fried eggs and opened two bottles of Celtia beer and got back into bed to finish reading the preliminary reports of Wendell Falck and Judy Hoggenberger and enjoy a late breakfast. The preliminary stuff actually wasn't due in until September fifth, as the summer had supposedly been a slow and uneventful one due to lack of firm assignments, but, as it turned out, Wendell and Judy were their early birds, right on the spot via registered mail. And somewhere they had found a hell of a lot to write about; Wendell's epic alone ran to over two hundred pages.

A damned book, Russell thought sourly, moving it away from his knee. No wonder it had taken him all week end to get through it.

He picked up the first bottle of beer and settled back, leaning on one elbow and leafing through Judy's neatly typed pages for a last check-through. There was no real reason to be lying around in bed on a Monday afternoon except that he was taking it easy on himself, and to hell with it. The rain had quit for a while and now the sun was coming steamily through the bedroom shutters, a reminder that summer was far from finished. And with a promise of more rain toward evening. Sluggish weather, a damned steam bath after the crackling dry heat of the drought.

And the reports, he thought, succumbing to a yawn, weren't exactly calculated to stir you to wild enthusiasm. They were a pain in the ass to have to do in the first place. Reports weren't his department at all; they went straight to Charlie Benedict. But this year it looked as though he, Russell, was getting stuck with anything pertaining to the Youth Commitment Group. And he supposed that Cynthia Guffin was pretty anxious to see that somebody went over the Youth Group material ahead of time to keep Charlie from seeing anything that might make him nervous.

Reading and studying every word of the damned reports was interminable, though. By Sunday afternoon he had had to call Cynthia Guffin to tell her that he had read through the week end and was still going strong, and unless she absolutely needed him he wasn't going to go to the office on Monday; he was going to stick with it until he was finished. There was nothing much doing anyway. Nothing much, even, for Cynthia Guffin to do except take a few messages over the telephone and gossip with Cecile Lambert and Nancy Butler.

Judy's report was just what you'd expect from Judy: a nice little layout of what she had said and done in the clinic and environs since May, practically a daily journal. With references to public health circulars, handbooks, and folders neatly catalogued, and figures lifted from the clinic files ad infinitum, down to the last typhoid inoculation. Plus a graphic, utterly fascinating account of Judy's adventures with the scoobey-doo program. There was a whole page devoted to working women's complaints of excessive bleeding with newly installed IUDs that practically curled your hair.

But great for the New York office.

Wendell's little opus was another matter. Frankly, he didn't know what the hell he was going to do with it. He had sort of been counting on Wendell's taking up Mohammedanism and becoming the Foundation's first convert to Islam, but what he had got instead was a totally unexpected load of dynamite that had jolted the hell out of him. Russell had read through it quickly Saturday and had put it aside for the time being. Now, he still couldn't believe it was all there. Wendell's learned dissertation on the corruption of governmental labor practices and the politically expedient repression of the workers in the name of progress and national unity had come like a bolt out of the blue; thank God they had insisted that the kids send their stuff in by registered mail. As it was, every word Wendell had written was absolutely true. And—if it ever slipped out of their hands—could probably get them all deported.

Goddamn kid, Russell thought. He had got into some hot little insurgent labor group up there at the Tabarka canneries, and what had come out was a lot of pan-fried neo-Marxism by way of "accidentally" assassinated former labor leader Feneena Mukhtah. And the government had taken care of the Mukhtah problem by building a lot of statues in village public squares, so that everybody had forgotten about it by now. The report wouldn't make much sense to anyone in the New York office, but it sure would drop like a bomb in Tunis.

Russell was just starting on the second bottle of beer and writing notes on the margins of Wendell's report as to how to tone the stuff down a bit, if they couldn't do anything else with it, when he heard a quick knock on the door of the flat, Cynthia Guffin's brisk British accents urging him out, wherever he might be, and her no-nonsense footsteps on the tile floor.

He recognized her voice, but he sat in the bed with the can of beer lifted to his mouth, telling himself that he was mistaken. What the hell was Cynthia Guffin doing at his apartment, at that time of day? His watch said one-fifteen. She was supposed to be at the office.

Or, for God's sake, at any time of day? He could count on the fingers of one hand the number of times she had come to his place. And now, apparently, walking straight in, without waiting for him to answer the door.

He put the can of beer down on the floor and scrambled out of bed. He was bare-assed naked, and he had to get into his pants, the way she was coming on. As it was, she caught him just zipping up his fly as she got to the bedroom door.

"Oh, really, George." Her eyes gave the bed, the papers, the bottles of beer a quick appraisal. 'Well, do get on with it." The tones were brisk. "And be quick. I'm afraid we haven't much time."

She was wearing a blue and white dress with flowers on it and a funny little British-style fedora straw hat that made her look like a girls' school headmistress done up for the Queen's garden party. Except that the hat had slipped back and to one side and she obviously hadn't had time to fix it.

The first thing that came to Russell's mind was that something must have happened to old Charlie to make her barge right in like that. He bet she hadn't come into anybody's bedroom without knocking in her life.

"This is Inspector Beshir," Cynthia Guffin said. "The Inspector was *directeur* of Department Number Seven before Fendri Khefacha was promoted."

"Regrets for disturbing," the old Inspector murmured politely in Arabic. He came in, too.

The Inspector was one of the few who still wore the old red flowerpot tarboosh with tassel, like some relic of the days of the Turkish pashas.

The two of them made it a masquerade party.

Then a husky uniformed *boliss* with an M3A1 tucked in the crook of his arm stepped in obligingly.

"And of course *he's* along in case of trouble," Miss Guffin said with a hurried wave of her hand. "You have two. That's about all we can get in the car, regrettably."

"May I ask," Russell said politely and in Arabic, "am I under arrest?" It seemed like a pretty logical thing to ask, and at the moment he wasn't sure about anything.

The Inspector gave a visible start, but Cynthia Guffin only shot him a disapproving look.

"Good heavens, George, what made you say a thing like that?" But before he could say anything, she went right on. "Do get your shoes on, please. You can't go that way."

"Right." He sat down on the edge of the bed, watching the *boliss* with the M3A1 out of the corner of his eye.

"Just stick your feet in," she told him, as he took up his boots. "We really haven't got time. And take sunglasses."

"Do you have a gun, perhaps, Monsieur Russell?" the old Inspector inquired.

"Don't bother, they have one for you," Cynthia Guffin put in quickly. "You can pick it up in the car. Just *do* hurry."

She wasn't exactly rattled, Russell told himself, but she was certainly in pretty high gear. Otherwise she would have put her hat back on straight. She had gotten a khaki shirt out of the wardrobe, and now she flung it around his shoulders.

Maybe a total of two or three minutes had elapsed since he had jumped out of bed and into his pants, and he really wasn't with it, even yet. He threw off the damned shirt to get his arms free and put on his boots.

"What the hell's going on?" he growled.

"Now, George," she began. Her face took on a rather prim look. "Libya's fallen. Or is falling—the people here don't know much about it yet, and it hasn't been announced." When he looked up, she made a gesture with her hand for him to keep on with what he was doing. "And we're not sure, either—there's been so much confusion. But old King Idris is out of the country, and they've tried a coup."

"Jesus." His right foot was stuck. His feet were sweaty and his toes had curled up, going in. He took his foot out, to try again.

"Of course it may blow over," she said rather thoughtfully. "It depends on how quickly he can fly back in, among other things. But everyone's in a terrible uproar, you know. Wheelus Air Force Base and the oil fields. Not to mention British installations.

"We also think," she said after a slight pause, "the Saudis are having something of the sort, too. But their censorship is so tight we probably won't know until it's all over with."

He had to stop for a moment just to stare at her and let it sink in. Saudi Arabia. Libya. It looked as though everything was going at once.

They had, he remembered quickly, put together something of an emergency plan in the event things started popping unexpectedly. He was to head south and round up the girls, Sharon Hoyt at Ez-Zahra and Judy Hoggenberger in Sousse, and get back to the Foundation office in Tunis with them if he could. Charlie Benedict was to go north and pick up Genevra Coffin in Bizerte and Wendell in Tabarka.

"What the hell is this," he wanted to know. "Liberation day?"

He had done as she had told him and just stuck his feet into his field boots, but he already had a feeling that wasn't going to work. He grabbed a pair of socks and put them into his pants pocket. He started getting into the shirt.

"Yes, it does look that way, doesn't it," she said, a trifle tartly. "It's certainly no coincidence, I should think. The Libyan business seems to be army and quite Leftist from the way they're going on about it over the radio. And of course there's always the worry they might cross the borders. Everyone's quite holding their breath at the moment. Oh, I do want to warn you," she added. "You mustn't pay any attention to Radio Tunis. They have the station and they're screaming mad things into it."

"The Libyans?"

For a second she fixed him with the very direct sort of look he hadn't seen since his army days.

"My dear George," she said, "we have had a coup attempt here, too. I'm sorry," she said, lifting a hand to stop him. "We *are* in a dreadful rush. There's almost no time to tell you about everything; you'll have to just do the best you can. Now," she said with the air of one picking up the thread of thought with an affort, "you'll probably run into difficulty just getting out of Tunis. The *souks* are already packing up in case of trouble, and the streets are in a ferment. We were able to drive up as far as Ali Azous, although I admit the car is quite wedged in. I don't see how they are going to get it back out again. It was really much more risky than coming into the Medina on foot, but they seemed to think it was necessary. However, things are in a rather chaotic state even now. The President's wife tried to go down to him about half an hour ago by helicopter, but they found that some of the Army people had taken the helicopters off—moved them to insurgent bases, apparently. And had sabotaged the two the President keeps at El Aouina. As a result, we had to change our plans for you, too," she added.

She followed him right to the door of the bathroom and stood there. Russell tried to close the door, but she pushed it open slightly.

"I've got to—" he began.

"Really, George," she said severely, "this is hardly the time to make a fuss, is it? And I must go on with this. Do watch yourself with the Sûreté; they're still counting heads, if you know what I mean. And I'm sure a lot of them are still waiting to see which way to jump. You can rely on old Beshir; he's not terribly clever, but he's honest. And even he will have to feel his way along—he's been out of the department for months, thanks to Khefacha, and I don't think he's terribly sure of his own men, anymore."

"Where's Khefacha?" he wanted to know.

"My word, George—Khefacha was one of the first to declare himself! He's in Sfax, on the radio there, proclaiming all the Kabyle tribes in on the coup and even urging the rest of the Berbers to come over the Libyan and Algerian borders and join in."

He threw the door open, towel still in his hands, and stared at her.

"The hell you say."

"The south's in quite a stew," she said calmly, "but then that's the old Youssefist stronghold, anyway. All they ever need is guns. The Sûreté is at odds with the Army as a result of Khefacha, and the Army has its own problems, so you must watch your step. We had a bit of unpleasantness down on the Boulevard coming over— the Army's thrown up a barricade—until Inspector Beshir finally persuaded them to let us through. Don't assume any friendships today," she said crisply. "Foreigners are always in a bad spot at times like these."

"Please," Inspector Beshir urged them.

"Yes, of course," Miss Guffin murmured. With a firm hand she moved the *boliss* with the M3A1 out of their way, and they went into the bedroom. "One more thing now, George," she said. "Keep your ear open for any word of Norman Ashkenazi."

He didn't pause; he was throwing stuff from the top of the bureau—change, ID, comb, keys—into his pockets.

"Christ, don't tell me Norman and Chaim are in on this, too. What are they supposed to be, Russian spies?"

As soon as his hands were free she produced a roll of dinars.

"You have two thousand here," she told him, "don't hesitate to use them for bribes. It's quite a lot of money; you'll have to make out a chit for it, later. I'm afraid," she said, "Norman and his friends seem to have got right in the middle of things. And Norman—" She paused and looked vaguely reluctant. "Norman may have some papers. Terribly important."

"Please," Inspector Beshir said again. "We must go now. Officer Abdelkrim precedes us. Downstairs, we wait while he goes out to observe the street, yes?"

Russell was still buttoning up his shirt as they went down the stairs.

"The car is at the corner of Sidi Ali Azous and Zeitouna, in case we get separated," Cynthia Guffin was saying. "Just pop right in the back seat with Dr. Kheireddin. Whatever you do, don't stop. I won't be going with you."

"Now look," he said. "I still don't know what the hell's going on. You can't turn me loose like this."

They started into the empty streets of the *souks attarine,* following the slight figure of the Inspector in his red tarboosh. Most of the shops as they turned into Zeitouna had been shuttered up, too. A few loiterers ran when the *boliss* with his submachine gun came trotting into view.

They always go for the old man, Russell thought suddenly. They begin with that. They've practically turned him into a shooting gallery.

"Is the President dead or alive?" he asked her.

"He's alive and absolutely *furious.*" She had been trotting, holding onto her hat with one hand, and she was a little breathless. That's why they're taking Kheireddin down to him. He's the heart man, not the surgeon. I can't get anything out of them about the President of Finland—I suppose they're not particularly concerned about *him* at the moment. But my word, that would be a disaster!" They had to pause for a moment to wait for the *boliss* to check out the intersection. "You'll go down with Kheireddin because they'll see that he makes it if anyone does. Don't forget to get a gun from Beshir. And oh, yes, there's a CIA man with the President's party, but I haven't the foggiest. They're always changing them. I really don't know what you'll find—they were all in Ez-Zahra, in front of the Hotel Miramar going in for lunch, when it started."

It was like a flood of ice water being pumped into his bones.

"Jesus Christ," he began, but she was already tugging on his arm, trying to get him to move ahead.

"George," she said sternly, "pay attention. The assassination attempt took place right across the street from ben Omranes', and somehow Sharon was involved. And," she added, "Genevra Coffin."

There was no time to say anything more. She gave him a quick shove forward, and Inspector Beshir leaned out of the back seat to grab him by the arm. There was hardly enough room to get the door open—the Peugeot was rammed into the *impasse* with about six inches' clearance on both sides, and he damned near didn't make it.

Cynthia Guffin stuck her head in the window to say, "Ask Kheireddin for something. Sedatives, if nothing else!"

"Watch it!" he yelled as the driver put the car into gear without warning. The door wasn't even all the way closed.

He saw her jump out of the way as they plowed forward into the alley, stopped, jerked backward a few feet, and then turned and shot off downhill through the *souks*.

He tried to see her through the rear window, but the street had veered to the right and she was gone.

It was like that all the way, doing about fifty through the alleys of the Medina, nearly scraping the walls. They zoomed out into the Boulevard of the President with a fine disregard for traffic or traffic lights.

There was no traffic, Russell saw; nothing except an army truck far ahead going toward Mohammed Cinq. At the first intersection, flying squads of what appeared to be kids, university students with red armbands, came bursting out of the side streets, raced across the median park and around the trees, yelling, and then ducked back in again. There was some gunfire, but he couldn't tell where it was coming from. Inexplicably, a few hysterical women hobbled along in haiks, probably trying to get home. The flower stalls were open and so were the newsstands, but deserted, as though the operators had fled in panic. Otherwise the city had a clean, swept air about it in the bright sunshine.

The Peugeot was so jammed Russell could hardly move. There were four of them in a back seat that was usually a tight fit for three: the little plump doctor calmly smoking a cigarette in the far corner, Inspector Beshir hunched in the middle, and himself, and the *boliss*, Abdelkrim, half squatting on the floor. In the front was a man in business clothes, another *boliss* at the right front window with an M3A1 propped in his lap, and another *boliss* as driver. The Peugeot radio was turned up loud enough for a sound truck; as they moved down the street they carried a trail of the national anthem with them. Inspector Beshir abruptly gave the driver orders to swing into Sadikia and bypass the army barricade up ahead at the Avenue de Carthage. The national anthem ended as he began to speak, and a voice with a slightly hysterical edge to it started shouting in Arabic, cut on in mid-sentence.

"—have revolted for you, oh, beloved people, in the name of the People's Popular Liberation Front! We will set up Arab peasant's democracies—" The voice choked off, and there was the faint hiss of dead air.

"They do not know how to work the microphones," the doctor observed, puffing on his cigarette.

"It is the other equipment, they do not know how to work the other equipment at the transmitter," the plain-clothes man said.

"Nevertheless, why do they still have the station? I understand the Army was sent out there at once."

"Perhaps the Army has joined them."

"As long as they have the radio," the *boliss* on the floor said suddenly, "it is bad. People will believe anything."

As the car cut from Sadikia into the Rue Portugal on two wheels, squealing all the way, they turned back toward the Avenue de Carthage. A loop around the barricade.

Russell tried his door to make sure it was locked.

After a ragged *wowow* from the radio, the national anthem began again and then was taken off abruptly with a faint shrieking gouge and replaced with a recording of an English military band playing "The Colonel Bogey March."

As they traveled out of the Avenue de Carthage the traffic grew a little heavier, a few private cars headed for G.P. 1 and the south and some commercial trucks, the drivers evidently caught on the road and undecided where to stop. More soldiers, stationed at street corners, but staring as the cars moved by. At the intersection of G.P. 1, though, there was a roadblock of Sûreté Nationale, cars run off onto the shoulders and stopped. A hell of a mess. They stopped, too, and as the doctor rolled down the window on his side the *boliss* came up from the floor of the back seat and stuck the nose of the M3A1 over the edge.

"I think you had better change places with me, doctor," Inspector Beshir said, climbing over George and getting out the far door. "It will be safer with you in the middle."

The *boliss* let the doctor out, and half a dozen uniformed Sûreté Nationale men came up at once with drawn pistols.

"I want to speak to your sergeant," Inspector Beshir said. "We are taking the President's doctor down to Ez-Zahra. It is a thing of most urgency. Also, I need a motorcycle officer. Are you a motor-cycle officer?" he asked a *boliss* in a jacket and white helmet.

The sergeant of the Sûreté came up scowling, shiny with sweat. The sun was growing hotter and the air was like a sponge, leisurely thunderclouds building up in purple pyramids over the bay of Tunis.

There was a roadblock at Grombalia, he told them. A motorcycle escort would not do them any good; they would only pick him off as he came ahead.

"The Colonel Bogey March" ended with the same nerve-splitting gouge, and a voice began to read the names of the inhabitants of such and such a street in Tunis who were supporting the new government.

"Turn it down," the doctor said, "I can't hear what they are saying about the roadblock." But no one paid him any attention.

"Bring up another car, then," Inspector Beshir insisted. "We will take two cars." He was offering his identification to the sergeant, who passed it around for the rank and file to examine.

"Do not be an idiot, Inspector, there is no car," the sergeant yelled. "The cars, they are patrolling the road into Grombalia. We are waiting for the Army to clear this obstruction they have set up there. We call on the radio four times, and they tell us they are doing it, but nothing is happening."

The voice on the radio proceeded to the names of workers of various companies in Tunis and Bizerte who were supporting the coup, and then went on to an interminable list of more workers in Sfax. "And all the workers in the *mines phosphates* in Metlaoui; it is unanimous!" the voice ended triumphantly.

"That is very stupid," the doctor said. "The government is making a recording. They will have all the names and they will catch every one of those fools."

"We will try the motorcycle," the Inspector was saying. "At least we can but try."

"Inspector, there is no motorcycle!" the Sergeant was shouting. He flailed both his arms windmill fashion, in an Arab gesture beyond despair. "Show me a motorcycle—and you will have it!"

"This is your President's doctor! Do you wish to have this responsibility on your head?"

"Inspector, we have heard three times already that the President is dead, and five times that he lives! Who is to know what we believe at this moment!"

After a prolonged moment of dead air, in which hollow studio voices could be heard arguing off microphone, a new voice spoke.

"The Governor of Nabeul has announced his support of the new People's Popular Liberation Front at this moment, and the vote of his *moutamed* council makes the decision of the people of the *gouvernat* unanimous."

"He is not even in Nabeul," the plain-clothes man in front said with a snort. "The Governor of Nabeul is with the motorcade. His name was on the list of luncheon guests."

"Then it is a fraud."

"Things could change in Ez-Zahra," the *boliss* in the front seat said. "You do not know what is going on down there."

Inspector Beshir got back into the car and rolled the window partly up, in spite of the fact that they were beginning to steam inside.

The car started down G.P. 1, picking up speed from the fifties to the sixties to the seventies, passing the cement factory and the miserable mud-house squalor of the workers' district that sprawled along the highway into Hammam-Lif.

"After this, we will get rid of the French and the Americans and the foreigners again," the driver said suddenly. "That is what is corrupting this country."

"Monsieur Russell speaks Arabic," Inspector Beshir announced.

"If they are corrupting it, they will have to go," George said diplomatically. He was in a mood to kiss anybody's ass as long as they made it to Ez-Zahra. Also, he goddamned well was going to get some information out of Beshir, one way or another. He wasn't going to sit for forty miles and sweat in silence.

At Hammam-Lif they were stopped by a company of army troops with their personnel carrier parked in the AGIP station nearby. The atmosphere was watchful, relaxed, and the lieutenant who came over was jumpy as a cat and uncertain.

The lieutenant was not even sure he ought to let them go on. In the café across the street, part of his company were sitting at the tables drinking Coca-Cola and watching with half smiles on their faces.

"Watch it," the man in the front seat said under his breath. At his signal the *boliss* next to him got out with his M3A1 and leaned it on the hood of the Peugeot. The lieutenant rolled his eyes like a shying horse.

Now he was certan they should not go on.

The *boliss* from the back started to get out, but George Russell reached across the doctor and shoved him down.

"Get out of here," Russell told the driver. "And make it quick."

"Beshir!" the doctor shouted.

They were already moving when Beshir lunged in; they just sort of scraped up the *boliss* with the M3A1 as they passed him.

The radio was reciting the names of the tribes in the south who had pledged their support to the People's Popular Liberation Front. The beni Arfa. The beni Ouargla. The beni Khefacha.

"It is that turd Khefacha who is doing it," the man in front said. "They think, because he is in it the whole of the Sûreté Nationale is, also."

"Tahar Basti was on the air before," the doctor said, "but that does not mean the whole Ministry of Education."

"His mother was a Palestinian; what do you expect?"

"Palestinians—*pfah*—they do not have the guts to get their own country back; they want the whole Maghreb to do it for them. And Egypt," the driver added.

"What do you hear about the coup in Libya?" George Russell asked the doctor in a low voice.

The little doctor pulled away from him as much as he could in the cramped space, to stare in astonishment.

"Love of Allah! Do you mean there is also—"

"Doctor, I was told to ask you for some sedatives," Russell said, loudly. In a moment, the whole thing might blow, thanks to him. "You still haven't told me," he said to Inspector Beshir, going right on, "what I'm supposed to find down there."

"Ah, yes," the Inspector said. He took off his tarboosh and wiped the sweat from his forehead and the back of his neck thoroughly with his fingers.

To the east, the Grombalia plain was sliding by: drought-burned fields of grape vines, and the sawback of the Djebel Abderrahman towering over them. The sun shone through a veil of heat and water vapor.

"I think you are asked to be discreet in the taking care of any difficulty with your people there. To be discreet, now, is all important. For all of us. It was the Minister himself who asked for you." the Inspector said, giving his attention to his throat and collar.

"I wish," Russell said, "only to know if the young ladies have been injured in any way. There was shooting, was there not?"

"I really have no further information," the Inspector said, putting his tarboosh back on.

"Libya, too," the doctor was muttering. "Then perhaps there is no hope."

A mile ahead of Grombalia there were plenty of army troops, but they were waved on. The driver stepped down on the gas. Some of the young soldiers in their baggy, sweltering, World-War-Two-surplus ODs threw a salute as they passed.

"That is better," the man in front said. "They see the Ministry plates and the flags on the hood. That is much better."

But beyond Grombalia they charged right into the damned road-block, big as life: a pile of traffic barriers and on top of them household furniture and tree branches. On both sides of the road, mixed police and soldiers and men in blue worker's smocks, and plenty of guns.

"Down!" Inspector Beshir shouted.

"Not you, you idiot!" the man in front yelled as the car swerved. He grabbed the wheel.

"Go on through, you bastard!" Russell yelled.

There wasn't much time to change course anyway. They were doing seventy, and as the wheel straightened they went right on through. Part of a chair or branch which had been thrown up on the right side of the barricade bounced off and hit the roof of the car, and there were a lot of flying twigs and trash obscuring their vision for a moment. They caught some fire: Russell could hear the bullets plowing into the rear of the Peugeot.

After a mile or so the *boliss* on the floor of the back seat calmly changed his clip.

He had emptied the whole damned thing and Russell realized he hadn't even heard him in the excitement.

At Bir Bou Rekba there were about ten cars bunched by the side of the road, mixed police and what looked like part of the President's motorcade. The hood ornaments of the limousines were decorated with bunches of red and white Tunisian flags.

Chief Inspector Beji Essa-afi strolled over. "You will change cars here. Hello, Rosul," he said to George. "You get in another car, and we take you in"

"Are they both O.K.?" Russell said.

"Both Presidents." Essa-afi beamed. "In excellent condition. But both a little *enragé*, naturally. However, now they are finally having their lunch, and this makes them feel better."

"The girls," George said. "The two American girls."

"Over here," Essa-afi said, "in the car with the doctor, please."

There were no marks visible in the downstairs courtyard, but as one began to ascend the outside flight of stairs partly covered by the bougainvillea vine it looked as though the teeth of giant rats had been at work in the whitewashed stucco. There were so many chips and punctures that in spots where they overlapped and ran together large pieces of the wall had given way, making it look like a gnawed piece of cheese.

They must have spattered the whole side of the house from top to bottom, Russell thought, until they either got tired or pretty nearly ran out of ammunition.

Downstairs, in the dining room, he had finally found out from the little government Sûreté Secrète that the girls were apparently O.K., but up to that time he had prepared himself as calmly as he could for anything. Even the possibility that they might be dead.

At least Sharon Hoyt was alive and howling: that was her voice he heard from the upstairs bedroom.

Right at the top of the flight two Sûreté Nationale men blocked him and, in spite of his Arabic, wouldn't by God, let him through. He had to go back down into the courtyard and get the Sûreté Secrète to come up and verify it, and by that time everybody was a little hacked with everybody else and shouting.

A large purple thunderstorm was hanging over Ez-Zahra, too. Not so good for tempers.

"Christ," Russell said as he came in, "how long has this been going on?"

He had expected a lot of things, but not exactly this sort of dismal mess. Sharon Hoyt's radio was blaring the hysterical revolutionary voices from Radio Tunis, and a couple of uniformed *boliss*, evidently from the motorcade, were fooling with the tape player, spinning it to ON and OFF and REWIND curiously, oblivious to the strangled yelps of the recorded rock singer. There were about six motorcade *boliss* in the room, distinguished by their red shoulder braid as

Special Detail, but apparently nobody was in charge. The rest were picking over the things on the floor, slowly, interestedly, and obviously because they had nothing better to do.

Genevra Coffin was sitting on the floor in a bikini swimsuit, smoking a cigarette.

Sharon Hoyt was lying on her stomach on the bed, also in a bikini swimsuit, just screaming.

"Oh, God, am I glad to see you," Genevra Coffin said, and closed her eyes wearily. But her voice was flat, expressionless. She didn't even get up.

"Put that down," he told the two *boliss* with the record player, in Arabic. "It is not something of yours; it belongs to the young *Amrikaniyeh.*"

They stopped, gave him a good looking over, and then went right back to what they were doing. The room was a wreck. It looked as though a high wind had gone through, sucked everything out of closets and drawers, and then dumped it on the floor. The *boliss* were walking around and on top of books, shoes, suitcases, clothes, magazines—Miss Hoyt was not exactly a tidy person, but still Russell was amazed at the quantity of junk.

"Get up, Jenny," he said, leaning over her. He pushed a *boliss* out of his way and reached down and took her by the elbows and gently lifted her up. He was somewhat surprised to feel her body sag against him, almost helplessly.

"Are you O.K.? These bastards didn't do anything to you, did they?"

"No, it's just that you can't do anything with them. You'll see. They got into all my stuff," she said listlessly "I'll never find my clothes."

He sat her down on the edge of the bed. It was hard to talk over the noise of Sharon Hoyt's shrieks.

"They didn't bother Sharon?"

Now she looked at him, as though trying to remember something.

"Don't go in the bathroom," she said finally. "They don't know how to flush the toilet. I've had to flush it five or six times myself."

"Don't worry about the bathroom," he told her. "I'll clean it up. Just tell me what they said and did to you."

"Oh, nothing." She shrugged. "They tried to ask us questions, but it was in Arabic and I couldn't understand them. They all speak different dialects. Then somebody came up who spoke French, but Sharon was having hysterics and he said he'd come back with a doctor, but he never did. They keep running in and out, the officers or whoever it is that's in charge, but then they keep calling them back to the hotel. Is the President dead?"

"No," he said, "not as far as I know. They don't act like it, anyway. You know what's going on, don't you?"

She sighed, and ran a hand across her face and mouth.

"Yes, I understand enough from the radio, and *they* keep talking about it. Is the government finished?"

"I don't think anybody knows, yet. Have you had anything to eat?" he said.

She stared at him. "Where did you come from?" she said strangely, as though just discovering him for the first time. "Why did you come here?"

"Listen, Jenny," he said quickly, "you're a smart girl. I'm depending on you to perk up a little, right? Because it's goddamned important. You're the only one left on your feet."

"I can't hear you," she said, looking at Sharon.

"Now look, I'm sorry I can't give you a full report on what's going on. You'll have to tell me your part of it before I can figure it all out. But right now I get the impression that Essa-afi and the rest of them want me to cool this somehow. There's a coup going on in Libya and one in Saudi Arabia, and you may be sure Algeria is watching this place very carefully. It looks like the whole damned thing is blowing at once, and we may have a tough time getting back to Tunis, just for starters. Christ, on top of everything, I don't know what to do about Judy down in Sousse!"

He had got her attention; now she was looking at him.

"But whatever happened here," he went on, "they don't seem to want you two in on it. If the whole thing passes over somehow and this crowd manages to stay on top, they don't want anybody to remember anything exotic at all, like you kids were around. And I don't blame them. Listen, the old man has had five assassination attempts on his life, and none of the trials were ever made public after they caught the guys. It's a matter of policy to plow everything under, if possible. I'm beginning to think that I'm supposed to shut you two up and make good girls of you if I can manage it, because they don't want any more of a mess than we do. Two foreign girls would make the newspapers all over the world. And it is," he said, watching her closely now, "a pretty big mess, isn't it? More than anybody thinks, maybe?"

"You better believe it," Genevra Coffin muttered. "He shot the other one, and she was screwing both of them."

Both girls had, Russell gathered, when he could get Genevra Coffin to be fairly coherent about it, stayed up pretty late the night before. Sharon was always, Genevra complained to him with her strangely detached air, trying to get her to come down to Ez-Zahra to advise her about some new mess she had gotten herself into, but actually, in Genevra's opinion, you couldn't talk to Sharon; it was a waste of time. She used words like subjectivism and relevance and involvement without having the vaguest idea of what she was talking about. And this time she had been more spaced out and irrational than Genevra had ever seen her.

At dawn Genevra had gone to sleep while the Holy Modal Rounders were just beginning the old *Easy Rider* song, "I Wanna Be a Bird," on the cassette player, and Sharon had just got to the part where the youth discussion group were dressing up in women's clothes to do crazy obscene ethnic dances.

At 11 A.M. Sharon shook her awake, explaining that she had wanted to go for a swim but all the roads to the beach were blocked. The President's motorcade, with the head of the government of Finland, was coming to the hotel across the street for lunch.

When they went out on the open stair-well landing they could look out through the bougainvillea vine which covered that part of the house and see the road blocked with Sûreté from the village and a row of curious tourist spectators lining the shoulders. Some of the tourists had even brought folding camp chairs, as well as their cameras, and were settling themselves comfortably in the sun. The heavy rain had stopped, and while there were plenty of clouds around it was a beautiful brilliant blue day.

Sharon still wasn't in good shape. She hadn't slept that night, either, and she had big black marks under her eyes and she was as shaky as somebody with a hangover, but she seemed happy enough. She kept trying to point out the biggest *boliss* down there in the road directing traffic as the one she had been talking about.

They had decided to get the old folding beach chairs from the back of ben Omranes' house and go up on the high roof, the one above the women's roof, where they would have the best seats of anyone around to watch the President come by. The entrance to the Miramar was right across the street.

"It seemed like such a great idea," Genevra told Russell bitterly. "My camera was even loaded with color film. I thought it would be great to send the pictures back to my father, he would get such a charge out of it."

Sometime during the night or early morning, probably, when the rain had stopped, the hotel people or the mayor's staff from the village had put up strings of thousands of little red and white Tunisian flags, the star and crescent against a red background, and they ran along from telephone pole to telephone pole as far as the eye could see. There was just enough wind to make all the little pennants flutter. Besides the tourists and the village police, there was a straggly bunch of kids in the street in front of the Miramar carrying trombones and drums and a few clarinets.

Sharon guessed they were the band from the *lycée* in Nabeul, but they didn't add much. Especially since they didn't have uniforms.

Every time Sharon leaned over the parapet of the roof in the bikini all the *boliss* looked up appreciatively until the big one came along and made them stop.

"He made them quit," Sharon had declared. "You've got to admit he's really beautiful. It's too bad you can't see his face with that stupid hat on."

"*Ugh*, don't remind me," Genevra had told her. She was busy making light adjustments on her camera.

The sun was blinding after so much rain, but the view was worth all the effort of climbing up, as the roof was the highest spot on the road. They overlooked not only the entrance to the Miramar Hotel, partly hidden in oleanders and gravel walks across the way, but also the vast sweep of newly rain-washed orange and lemon trees which stood like a sea of dark green leaves all around them. Beyond the blue-gray, eroded hills ringing the valley, the big tooth of the mountain of Zaghouan in the south raked a heavy blue sky filled with wandering white clouds. A purple thunderstorm like a mirror image of the mountain hung over Tunis.

Genevra had just finished taking shots of the valley and a couple of frames of the mountain when the *lycée* band below them struck up the national anthem. As Sharon had predicted, it was pretty awful.

"Shit," Genevra had said, rolling the film to Number Six. "How many times are they going to play that thing?"

"This is for real," Sharon said, leaning over the wall. "Here come the cars."

But Genevra had been still fiddling with the camera and adjusting the lens for a long shot when she saw the head of this boy coming over the wall from the women's roof beneath them.

"Hey, some kids are coming up here," she had told Sharon, to get her to turn around. "Are they from your Arab family, or what?"

As Sharon told her later, her first reaction was that Salem Gueblaoui had a hell of a nerve to come through the house like that; after all, it wasn't Friday and certainly no one expected him there. Then the second thing that occurred to her was that he had lost his job at Moreau's and was looking for her to help him out in some way.

He was on their part of the roof by then and bending over to do something strange. He lifted up his pants leg and started un-strapping something tied to his leg. Right behind him, the one they said was his cousin, Shedli, was coming up, too, but he had his gun in his hand. He put it on the roof ledge first and then climbed up after it.

The band struck up the national anthem for the third time, and just as the lead car of the motorcade came round the corner there was a sudden commotion in front of the Miramar. An army officer came sprinting down the steps and shouted frantic orders to his men. The President's car came to a halt.

Genevra remembered thinking, They're getting out of the cars. We're missing everything. And she was still thinking that when the first boy, Salem, rushed to the far side of the roof, almost knocking her down as she got in his way. The gun started firing even before he had it lifted up and in place. A trail of Roman-candle things dug into the concrete roof under their feet and stuck there, smoking.

The gun went bup! bup! bup!—a convulsive choke as though it had caught in some sort of spasm and couldn't stop.

"At the same time," Genevra said to Russell, "I started to scream. I don't know why I screamed, it was just one of those instant-reaction things: I started to really scream my head off."

The other one, Shedli, was cooler. He had got into a corner where the roof lifted to support the bougainvillea vine over the stair well, and he braced his back and pulled the trigger. A whole flock of lights like brilliant birds spilled into the sunshine and sprayed the trees of the Miramar across the road. He lowered the barrel and tried again, and the side of the Miramar Hotel toward the back where they hung the laundry out to dry was instantly dotted with smoking flares that stuck and burned, even in the whitewashed brick.

Salem's gun was jerking him around in half circles, and the firecrackers blew and sputtered through the air like luminous, fuming rockets.

You couldn't really believe they were bullets. It looked like some sort of crazy, absolutely insane entertainment. Something, frankly, that only the Arabs would think of.

A few of the tourists down in the road started applauding uncertainly; then a man ran up and down, shouting in German, and they all started falling down flat in the road or diving into the oleanders of the Miramar. The *lycée* band had gradually stopped playing, until it sounded like only one clarinet going it alone and then even it quit. All the *boliss* and the people from the motorcade had fallen flat or had crawled behind the limousines or jumped back into the cars and crouched down out of sight.

"All the time," Genevra said, "I was just standing *up*. I was standing up right in the middle just like Sharon and we were looking around with the most fantastically stupid expressions on our faces. Then I said to Sharon—and you could hardly hear me because there was so much noise going on—I said, 'Sharon, do you realize those mother fuckers are shooting *back* at us?' It's exactly what I said; those were the exact words I was thinking at that moment. And do you know what stupid Sharon said? She was standing up right in the middle with chips flying out of the part of the roof where we were and silent things just whizzing past us in the air and she said, 'You're kidding,' in the most ordinary, conversational tone of voice!"

The *lycée* band had stood huddled together for a moment with their instruments still in their arms, their faces turned up toward the roof, and then one of the kids started yelling, "*Vive l' revolution!*" and they threw down the trombones and the drums and clarinets all at once and started for the oleanders, too, and they were all yelling it! "*Vive l' revolution!*" Like kids at a soccer game. They just kept on yelling it from inside the oleander bushes.

Then Salem dropped his gun but it went right on firing, lying there on the roof plowing Roman candles into the far wall. He just stood where he was for a moment, holding his hands up in front of him and staring at them. He had burned them somehow. She could see them clearly. They looked like fried meat.

And stupid Sharon, when Shedli shouted out something in Arabic and they turned to run, she tried to *stop* them. She was screaming that it was all her fault, that this kid had blown his mind and if he just stayed behind the most they would do to him was put him in an insane asylum. When they wouldn't stop, she jumped down onto the women's roof with them and went off across the back entrance through the ben Omranes'.

"When they brought her back up she was all covered with blood," Genevra said dully, "and I told you, I thought something had happened to her."

Sharon had been running so fast she had half fallen down the hole of the ben Omranes' stair well, and at the bottom of the steps she did fall, but when she scrambled up she saw that the boys had split apart. Shedli had run off to the right, through the lemon trees and parallel to the road, but Salem was still going straight ahead, down toward the back of the garden. Shedli still had his gun; he was running with it in one hand and it threw him off balance so that he sort of staggered. He looked like a figure from a picture, a boy in a white shirt and black pants and sandals, ducking through the trees with a small submachine gun in one hand. Like a news photograph.

Salem was just ahead of her, running through the ben Omranes' orchard. His hair was getting long, it flapped as he ran, and he was going very fast. But he was limping, having trouble with one foot, and Sharon realized that he must have hurt himself somehow when he jumped down to the women's roof.

There was no one around; the back of the house and the citrus groves in the bright sunshine were deserted. But as she ran, Sharon had seen the Ez-Zahra Chief of Police running now as he had come through the gates, and he was going so fast he got ahead of her. For a moment Sharon had felt a surge of relief; she had thought: Oh great, he'll stop him. And then she saw that he had his pistol in his hand and she realized that he didn't understand that it was only something a crazy kid had done. Because she was sure that Salem was really crazy and hadn't been responsible for anything. She started running and shrieking because she knew something was going to happen; it was becoming more and more real and terrible and unavoidable. It was all her fault, as she had kept insisting afterward, and she couldn't get it straightened out right then; it was coming together inevitably.

Right about then she stepped in one of the irrigation ditches around a lemon tree and slid in mud and water and fell for a second time, so that while she was down on her side, scrambling to get up, she didn't see the first shot, but she heard it.

When she got up she started to scream even more loudly, because Salem was sitting down, holding his leg that he had hurt when he jumped off the roof. The Chief of Police ran up and Salem threw his arm over his face and eyes as though he couldn't look, but as though he knew what was coming. And he sort of cringed back, waiting for it to happen.

The second shot knocked him over. He flipped back under the tree in the middle of the lemon groves where the heavy rain of the night before had knocked the lemons to the ground so that it looked as though the dirt was speckled with gold coins.

Sharon had been coming so fast, running and stumbling, that she really didn't realize what had happened. All she saw was the back of Ali ben Ennadji's uniform, black with sweat, and that he had lost the ugly Police Chief hat with the big visor. He bent over Salem, who was just lying there, and put his pistol down carefully just a few inches from his face, and fired again.

And that didn't make any sense, as Sharon had said. She hadn't been able to get there in time, she knew he was dead, but she couldn't understand why he had shot him again and again, just to make sure.

She was close enough to him so that he could hear her coming through the rain puddles, and the leaves were wheeling around, and she was screaming and screaming until it wasn't her own voice any more, just some ugly rasping sound.

He straightened up and looked at her and his eyes were very black. In that moment it was as though they looked at each other for a long, long time, for years and years and centuries and centuries in a strange and shining silence, even though she was really lunging and shrieking through ditches and lemon leaves and trees. She was locked into his eyes for those few seconds—no words, but something definitely communicating. Only she couldn't understand it, because he wasn't angry.

He seemed to make up his mind. He set his mouth and jaw and kept looking at her.

Then he lifted his pistol up and took aim and shot her.

She felt it hit. It smacked her right across the forehead and she remembered falling a little. That is, just beginning to fall, because actually she went out like a light before she hit the ground.

"Sharon," Russell said, shaking her, but she wouldn't come out of it.

Genevra Coffin stared down at her. "I really tried to help her," she said in the same flat, listless tone of voice. "I even put cold towels on her, but I gave up. It won't stop."

"How long has she been going on like this?" he wanted to know. "Did it just start up? An hour? A half hour?"

"Since they brought her up. You see the bump on her head," Genevra said thoughtfully. "She's been in pretty bad shape. I mean, yesterday, too. This sort of flipped her out. She thinks the one, Salem, the houseboy, did it because he blew his mind. I mean," she said, closing her eyes, "that he suddenly went psychotic. Because she let him—"

"I'm getting the general idea," he said. "I think she's getting that across."

But it didn't make any sense, because he knew damned well that wasn't the way it had happened.

"Tell me again," he said. "She ran after them."

"She ran after them, and the next time I saw her these two guys from the motorcade were bringing her up and she didn't know what she was doing. She couldn't even walk and she had blood all over the front of her and I thought they had raped her. I don't know why you think things at times like that, but you do."

"She ran after the houseboy." He could hardly hear Genevra, Sharon Hoyt was screaming so efficiently. She wasn't even getting hoarse.

"She ran after both of them. One of the guns was going off; it

shot all these rocket things into the wall and the roof and they
stuck there and burned and the whole roof was like the Fourth of
July. I think it wouldn't stop or something, and that was why he
threw it down and then they just ran."

"Do you know what tracer bullets look like?" he asked her.

"No. What are they?"

"I'm just asking. Listen," he told her, "Hold her down for about
five minutes because I'm going downstairs and see if I can get
somebody to make one of these bastards fix some coffee. I'll be
right back. You know I'll be right back, don't you?"

"Yes," she said.

"Stand right by the bed."

When he got back he had arranged for some coffee to be brought
up from the kitchen and he had had a brief, enlightening talk with
the Sûreté Secrète sitting in the dining room.

"I'm going to give her something, and when she calms down we'll
see if she will drink some coffee," he said. "Get hold of her; she's
about to go off that side of the bed."

Russell reached into his shirt pocket and found the money Cynthia
Guffin had given him, and finally the aluminum package from
the doctor. There were two sections, one for now and a repeat if
the first didn't work. He peeled it open and then stared at it.

"Jesus H!" Christ, the fucking obsession of French pharmaceutics
with suppositories!

"What is it?" Genevra asked him.

"Nothing I can get her to swallow, believe me." He held it out.
"Here, you do it."

"No," she said, drawing back, still staring. "What is it?" And
then, in an odd tone of voice, "I don't have to do it; you can't make
me."

It was, he saw, no time to push her. And it could be managed,
he supposed.

"Where's the sheet?" he asked her.

It was under Sharon, twisted like a rope. They rolled her off it
and he had to begin from the beginning and shake it out and tuck
it in at the bottom of the bed.

"Hold it up," he told her. "No, not straight up, pay attention to
what you're doing. Like a tent. I'm not running a goddamned side-
show for these bastards."

He rolled Sharon Hoyt over on her side and moved one knee up and got hold of the back of the pants of the swimsuit.

"O.K., baby," he told her. "Be a good girl. This is the only way to do it."

Eventually one of the *boliss* came up with one miserly cup of coffee and put it down on the table on the far side of the room. Russell went and got it and gave it to Genevra Coffin and let her drink it. Then he went over the stuff on the floor and found something that looked like a bathrobe or a housecoat and got Genevra to put it on over the bikini.

That cut out some of the crapping around. The two *boliss* had run down the batteries on the cassette player, so they went out on the stair landing for a smoke and a conversation with the Sûreté Secréte, who had moved out to the table under the bougainvillea vine in the courtyard below. The others settled down to the radio, which was playing mostly music, now, but interspersed with a lot of dead air.

Russell hunted around on the floor and sorted out the magazines and the newspapers and found all the typed sheets he could gather, and after he had read some of them he kicked around in the clutter and found the rest. From beginning to end—which left off in the middle of a sentence—there were nineteen pages. Sharon Hoyt's preliminary report covering a sample of eleven Tunisian boys with their ages and some personal history sketched in and a chart of the number of discussions, progressing from one topic to another. Conversational accounts of schooling, comments on benefits and shortcomings of certain forms of educational systems in newly established countries, subsequent economic opportunities, or lack of. Attitudes toward pan-Arab movements such as the Al Fatah and the Pop Lib groups, and the validity of dedication to the concepts of Islam for better cultural unity among Arab peoples, pro and con. Fanon. The Castro revolution and Señor Guevara in Bolivia. National Liberation as a part of the Third World's fight against imperialism. The necessity to distinguish between Jews and Zionists in the struggle against Israeli expansion. The future role of the liberated Arab woman, with a clipping of some cute Palestinian chick in a kaffiyeh holding an AK-47, taken from some French periodical.

Russell took the papers into the bathroom and laid them in the bottom of the shower stall and set fire to them. Then he poked the burned flakes down the drain and turned the water on to wash it all away. He opened the bathroom window to let the smell of smoke out.

When he came out Genevra Coffin said, "Look, it's working."

He found a chair under a pile of clothes and pulled it up to the bed and got Sharon's hand and held it in his.

"Hey," he said, "how are you feeling?"

"Pretty good." She was pale and wet with sweat, and he helped her pull most of the hair away from her face and loop it back up on the pillow. "You should have been here," she said, and tried to smile.

"Sharon," he said very gently, "I want you to keep your mouth shut now about screwing Arab houseboys. Even to what good it accomplished and your diagnosis of neurological problems and what size he was and everything else. Do you hear me?"

"I ran after him," she said with a peculiarly unfocused, thoughtful look, "and Shedli ran off to the right, that way. They must have had it worked out. And Salem kept going ahead down to where the lemon trees were."

"You ran out," he told her, "but by that time you didn't see a thing. They were gone by that time."

"Are you nuts?" she said, lifting her head now to try and stare at him. "I was *there*. I saw him shoot him. Then he ran up and stood there and sort of pointed the gun down and did it again. That was what was so horrible, that he did it again, to make *sure*. I was screaming all the time not to shoot, because anybody who knew that kid and knew the life he had to lead would know he was under terrific pressure. He just flipped out of his mind, that was all. They would have put him in a mental hospital, not a prison, anyway. But he *shot* him, the goddamned Chief of Police, Ali ben Ennadji—he shot him! And when he saw me coming he turned around and shot *me*. I mean, I swear to God—I saw his face, he lifted the gun up and aimed, and I saw him. He shot me. I never thought he'd do that. He never had any reason to because I *know* he didn't know; he made love to me just the night before, last night, and he still didn't know about it. About Salem, that is. I mean, we always did *everything*, you know, and I mean he was really turned on for me, and it wasn't like I had any hang-ups or wouldn't go along with anything he—"

"O.K.," Russell said.

"—and if you've got that much going for you, you don't shoot somebody you're sleeping with regularly, do you? I mean, I know he didn't know about Sal—"

"Sharon," he said, patting her hand. "You didn't see anybody shoot anybody. When you got there it was all over, right?"

"He's dead, out in the lemon trees," she said in a small voice. "The poor kid is dead. I saw him afterward. When they turned him over the whole back of his head fell out. The brains in Lab were always gray, but his were pink."

"Nobody shot at you," he told her. "You ran into a tree branch. Here, feel." He guided her hand up to the lump rising above her right eyebrow. "You ran into a tree branch and knocked yourself out. Even Genevra knows that. That's where you got that thing."

"I got shot," she insisted, but her voice was softer and now her eyelids were drooping.

"Nobody shot at you," he repeated. He felt as though he was going to keep repeating it all night if necessary, because a hell of a lot depended on whether he could get her to believe it.

"Why Shedli?" she whispered. "He's such a cool type. He's too cool—sometimes you wonder about him."

"Sharon, listen," he said rapidly. "They picked this kid Salem because he had access to your house, and that roof up there overlooks the road and the entrance to the Miramar. Anybody else wouldn't have been able to get through the motorcade security except the damned houseboy. And he wasn't crazy; you didn't do anything to him, so forget it. He knew exactly what he was up to, and the other kid with him, too."

"Where did they go?" she whispered, her eyes closed.

"They ran away. Don't you remember? They ran away, and they were all gone by the time you got there. You don't remember anything because you hurt your head. You don't remember anything, do you?" he said, patting her hand to get her attention.

But her eyes were closed and she didn't answer.

16

Brute force is out;
this is a thinking
man's game.

—*Dr. George Habash, PFLP*

"Have you heard how Charlie is this morning?"
Willie Crompton said as he came into Charlie Benedict's office.
"Sorry to be late. The breakfast briefing at the Embassy took a little
longer than expected, but it was worth it. They delivered us the
straight poop on what's taking place in Libya. Some of the material
was just declassified yesterday, and it's fascinating, absolutely fascinating. Our briefing officer from Wheelus Air Force Base was a
gold mine, he could have gone on another hour especially with the
question-and-answer session, but the Ambassador had to blow the
whistle on us. Otherwise—as the Ambassador said—we would have
been there for lunch. Incidentally," Crompton said as he circled
the old mahogany desk, "I like the Ambassador a lot; he's really
a great guy. Not at all what you'd expect from the way some of
the people here in the city talk about him, you know?"

Willie Crompton, who had jetted in from New York as soon
as he heard of the kids' troubles, was an engaging stream of sound
and motion; he slung his attaché case into the IN file stand and
settled into Charlie Benedict's chair and then, as Russell watched,
lifted glossy chukker boots up to the surface and leaned back.

"A little circulatory trouble," Crompton said ruefully, catching
Russell's look. "Badge of the bureaucrat. Oh, hey, come in," he

319

called out to Cynthia Guffin, who had appeared at the door. "Ça va, this morning?"

"Good morning, Mr. Crompton." But the British tones descended four distinct notes as she, too, took in the chukker boots resting on Charlie Benedict's blotter. "I hope the American Embassy breakfast went well."

George Russell turned his eyes to the window, where the rain clouds were racing past the Foundation's back garden toward the Lac de Tunis, and deliberately avoided looking at her. He detected a fine ironical edge in Miss Guffin's voice, but he couldn't tell whether or not she was putting Crompton on. However, he remembered all too well that Charlie Benedict had always hated the damned American Embassy affairs and the Big Noise from Texas, and never missed a chance to poke fun at them. Both bored the hell out of him and he nearly always sent his regrets.

"Right on," Crompton was saying enthusiastically. "I appreciate your little memo, and the backgrounding and the filler, very neatly done; it was quite a help. Jolly good show. And say, do me a favor, will you, Cynthia," he said, reaching for his attaché case, "and bring in those Active Youth Commitment Group files? And Russ's Confidentials while you're at it."

Cynthia?

Russell couldn't resist it; he had to see the expression on her face. But Miss Guffin only gave Crompton's boots a particularly thoughtful stare and went out.

"She's quite a girl when you get to know her, isn't she?" Crompton observed. He was riffling through his notes on the Embassy briefing.

On impulse, Russell opened his mouth to say something, then changed his mind.

Let Crompton find his own way, he decided.

The attempted coup and its plenty hectic aftermath had thrown up a lot of interesting sidelights in the city, but none more amazing than the number of covers it had blown for all the operatives who had been at work there. For the past few weeks it had been damned near impossible to get a decent seat on an airplane going in or out of Tunis, owing to the hurried reshuffling. The Russians had dived underground at almost the moment Radio Tunis returned to the air in government hands, and they had sent home a whole office load of operatives for caution's sake. The Algerians, as far as anyone could tell, had completely disappeared. And the West Germans were said to be hot on the trail of Group One's arms-supplying setup to wash that dirty linen and see if any strings led back to domestic politics in the Fatherland. They had beefed up their structure by about 200 per cent. The Americans had unloaded a monster computer programed to the gills with Near Eastern supersecret data and an entire CIA field wing which took up nearly one half of an old customs warehouse down on the docks. But the one item that had everyone talking was that the Foundation's long-time Executive Secretary was now well out in the open as one of British Intelligence's more esteemed lady contributors.

It shouldn't actually have come as that much of a surprise, Russell told himself. The damned British, you had to hand it to them. For a cold, difficult, officially nit-picking bunch who went out of their way to give the impression they were up to their knickers in nothing more important than tennis and tea drinking, they could still come up with some of the craziest and most imaginative operations of any foreign service. He supposed they had to, the way their shoestring budget always kept them cut back.

But Our Miss Guffin. Our Cynthia. It also accounted for the "we" in her conversation which had bothered him so that Monday in his flat.

What the hell, there had certainly been less likely and a lot less qualified agents. But it still surprised the hell out of him to find all those interesting bits of Miss Guffin's past history surfacing in Tunis gossip circles. As Nancy Butler had pointed out, the clues had all been there to begin with; there had just been no reason to grub around in a quiet spinster's background to find out what she had been doing lately, that was all. As take for example John Baggot Glubb, that old Anglo-Arab hand who had carved out the Arab Legion for King Abdullah of Jordan, now retired and knighted for his efforts and writing scholarly treatises on Arab history. But who the hell would have known that Glubb Pasha was a second cousin, and that a whole tribe of Guffins had made the Foreign Service their profession in a string of consulates from Aden to Tangier? All Guffins got, it would seem, their first chunks of the Qur'an with their bottled orange juice.

Add to that the British love for quirky jokes. For years their gray mouse had sat in the same pew in St. George's C. of E. church off the Rue des Protestants under a modest brass plaque like the others which lined the stone walls of that vaguely military establishment, naming great-grandfather Guffin colonel of the Shropshire regiment that had protected the British merchant community of Tunis against the Barbary pirates in 1810. All that had been missing in that Sunday tableau of Miss Guffin and great-grandpa's contribution had been one of those poster hands from the comic strips: ☞ Follow the clue from above to below and find out which Guffin Arab specialist we have with us now. And doing what.

All those years they had been so sure that the only reason she hung on was because of Charlie Benedict and what she felt for him.

Now there was no reason for her to keep up the pretense at the Foundation, but you never could tell. Strangely enough, the British had shown no sign of acknowledging what was known all over the city, and they hadn't moved to reassign her. Maybe they would in good time, as the British always did such things.

At the moment he was having so much trouble trying to clear a meeting with Norman Ashkenazi through Government Hill (which denied even knowing anybody by that name) that he had just about decided to bring up the whole nasty subject with her, gracefully broach the fact that he had heard who she was and knew what she had been doing, and come right out and ask her to pull a few strings. God knows if she would admit it, or even act as though she knew what he was talking about, but he had to try. He was pretty sure she could help him locate Norman, if she wanted to, and get official permission to talk with him. As events of September first had shown, whatever her connections were, they apparently burned a straight line through to the top over there on the Hill.

"You know, Russ," Willie Crompton was saying as he went through his notes, "you'll have to pardon me, but I'm really overwhelmed by the implications of this whole Libyan thing; we had a thorough comprehensive on it this morning, and the entire shake-up across the Arab world which took place out here the first of September is going to be so far-reaching—for the first time I'm beginning to appreciate what people have been saying for the past few years. I can't get over it. Naturally the Middle East has always been a trouble spot, but I think we in the States have tended to regard it as a chronic thing, the Balkans, you might say, of this half of the twentieth century. Now the implications of what's happened are really mind-boggling, and the acceleration of hostilities and this sudden shift over to pan-Arab Leftist governments look as if we're racing to a real confrontation. In my opinion, the U.S. is going to have a tremendous reaction in our foreign policy that's even going to dwarf the Vietnam mess. I don't expect New York to believe it now, this minute, because we're all sort of still rocking over Libya and what happened here, and Indo-China is still on everybody's mind and very much to the fore, but when it's all sorted out, our Asian involvement will be nothing compared to what's evolving here."

"Maybe so," Russell murmured, eyeing the legal pad which Crompton was consulting.

"For starters, the military is admitting that it looks as if we're definitely going to lose Wheelus Air Force Base in Tripoli, lock, stock, and launching pads. According to our briefing this morning, the new Libyan revolutionary government has made our monster air installation their Number One priority, and they have just delivered their word on it. Which is—get out. All that's left for us is to make up a withdrawal timetable. It's going to be a nonnegotiable item as far as we can see, and that's what hurts. You go down the list of our investments and interests over in Libya, and we've got thirty-eight oil concerns wholly or partly owned by American companies, all those oil rigs in the Sahara sitting on the world's second largest lake of oil now hanging by a thread, our banks and financial holdings, and now our multibillion-dollar air base and SAC missile installation up for grabs. And we're just standing around with egg on our faces with no options at all. You know what the guy from Wheelus admitted? That with this little Libyan coup we lost one third of our nuclear striking power! Well, I mean he didn't come right out and admit it, but during the question-and-answer session we sort of ran him to the wall, and you can come to your own conclusions. The U.S. had three command SAC bases: Thule, Greenland; Okinawa; Wheelus in Tripoli. So now, one third wiped out, just like that. Naturally our man from Wheelus this morning wasn't saying anything officially or unofficially about where the missiles or the nuclear stuff is right now, but I bet the Pentagon is really sweating. We know the Israelis have a reactor and are probably capable of putting their bomb together right now; if we've just left a few of our own nuclear devices around for the Arabs to pick up, we may be looking down the barrel of World War Three. On top of everything else, the Libyan revolutionary junta has started flying Egyptian military advisers into Tripoli. As soon as we pack up, the Egyptian Air Force moves in. And you know what that means. Nasser and his friends get one of the biggest, most expensive, and up-to-date American air installations in the world just for the cost of going by and picking up the keys. I really can't be optimistic about the oil, either, under the circumstances. The Libyans are assuring the oil companies that it's going to be business as usual, at least for the time being, but frankly, we can thank God the Saudis put down their little coup on Black Monday, or else we would have lost our other big puddle of black gold."

Since Crompton looked up expectantly, Russell said, "Right," although the Embassy briefing held nothing new for him; the news about Wheelus Air Force Base had been reported in the Arab-language papers in Tunis pretty thoroughly the day before.

"We went over our troubles here in Tunisia to some extent," Crompton was saying, "although naturally Libya was the big American topic of conversation. But as the Ambassador brought out, if this little country here had folded, too, it would have had its own world-wide repercussions, although not on such a grand scale. It would have been a long-range disaster for the U.S., not only for the money we've poured into Tunisia to keep it pro-Western—and which we don't expect to get back out—but also for the fact that, geopolitically speaking, we would have ended up with a solid tier of these wildcat revolutionary countries with Leftist governments all across North Africa and straight through to the Suez Canal."

"We may yet," Russell murmured, but Crompton appeared not to hear him. He had pulled up some white sheets of paper and was transferring some salient points from the legal pad to the others.

"Amazing," Crompton said to no one in particular. "Right on the spot here like this, there's a whole new perspective. Say," he said, without looking up, "I'm right in assuming that this whole series of coups in Saudi Arabia, Libya, and Tunisia was set to coincide that Monday, right?"

"Looks like it," Russell said. "I don't think anybody is trying to pass it off as one big accident."

"There's more to this than meets the eye," Crompton said meaningfully. "It really makes your blood run cold when you think there might have been some master plan behind all this. I smell Russia, personally, although it's hard to tell. Red China is moving up in Arab politics very, very fast. As witness our neighbors next door, the ALN Algerians."

"Actually, that damned *fedayeen* group, both the PFLP and the Al Fatah, are shaping up as more—" Russell began.

"Somebody really had their finger on the Go button, that's for sure," Crompton went right on. He was peeling the sheets off the yellow pad of legal paper and setting them aside now, as he checked them with his white sheets of transcribed notes. "It's going to come as a hell of a shock to the American public when all the facts are made public as to what happened out here. We've been so preoccupied with Vietnam we have yet to learn what a hell of a blow this was financially. To say nothing of the over-all military and political goof. Frankly, Russ, I find it pretty hard to understand. We've been spending ourselves stupid out here in the Mediterranean and North Africa just to stabilize the situation, and now it looks as though we're going to lose our shirts. And what the hell, this has been our sphere of friendly influence since World War Two—I mean, we've been operating on the assumption that the Arabs really liked us and appreciated our efforts for their struggles for independence. Especially in North Africa."

"They used to like us in Asia, too," Russell said.

"But I mean you'd think we'd at least have the situation covered security-wise, if nothing else. *Three billion dollars* is what we shelled out last year in a hidden-budget item for the National Security Agency, our supersecret military spy network that's supposed to be everywhere the CIA isn't. And look what happens. We still don't know what went on September the first over in Saudi Arabia except that, whatever it was, the Saudis got the lid back on their coup before anybody could even take a look. And as for right here in Tunisia—well, I've heard about four different versions of the conspiracy and the attempted assassination of the President and the only thing that makes any real sense is that the Americans here—military, diplomatic, or business—didn't know any more than anyone else. The only people who give the impression they were at least keeping their ears to the ground are the West Germans and the British, but even they got caught sitting on the pot. Say, have you heard this rumor going around that the West Germans are in a flap because they think the arms for Tunisia's little conspiracy were supplied by some German neo-Nazi group?"

"Haven't heard that one," Russell said, looking him straight in the eye.

"Seems pretty wild," Crompton said. "But we really have no excuse for what went on next door, the way I look at it. While Libya was getting ready to blow sky high, the National Security people must have been out playing golf. I mean it, that's the only conclusion I can come to, and everybody says that's a great course they got at Wheelus. It has something, anyway, because we're admitting now that the Wheelus brass didn't have any sort of security briefing from the NSA about a coup, or, if they did, some low-level clerk was sitting on it. When this pro-Palestinian Leftist revolutionary bunch walked in over at Wheelus we didn't even know how to spell their names. Nobody had ever heard of them before, they were just some razorbacked bunch of small-time army officers, as far as anyone could tell. Except for this Colonel al-Maghrebi, the new Prime Minister. That's a dead giveaway. It turns out to our surprise that he was born in Haifa and emigrated from Israel to Libya during the 1948 Arab-Israeli war. And trouble any way you want to look at it. It seems to me Wheelus should have had a dossier on those damned Palestinian refugees in the Libyan military structure from the day they enlisted. We should have had a tail on every one of them. I wonder what NSA's excuse is—that all Arabs look alike?"

Crompton looked up, and Russell smiled dutifully.

"Of course I can joke about it now," Crompton pointed out, "but that doesn't minimize the total dismay that anybody is bound to feel under the circumstances, you know? I mean, according to our best sources back in the States we've had an entirely different picture all along. Tunisia was shored up with American money and coming along as well as could be expected, and the Saudis were rich and quiet and happy, and Libya—as far as we knew—was a solidly pro-Western state, a great example of what could be done to equalize the political and economic pressures here in the Arab world. I personally got the impression that old King Idris was a very corruption-free and enlightened Arab-style monarch, interested in building schools and hospitals and upgrading his backward country, totally revered by his subjects, each and every one of whom had an average income of $1,000 a year, thanks to oil revenues. Which ought to make any formerly poverty-stricken population pretty well off, don't you agree? At least on paper. Ah, great," Crompton said, as Miss Guffin came in with the file folders. "And say, Cynthia," he added, "fix us up with some coffee, will you?"

Cynthia Guffin went out, closing the door behind her softly.

"Well," Crompton said, it's going to be a lot of work for us. I can tell you that. The Foundation Governmental Studies Committee is going to have to update all their papers on the Arab world situation, starting from now. Something tells me the U.S. will start reassessing all their commitments out here immediately. If nothing else, the oil companies are going to be screaming to high heaven in Congress. And our pro-Israel lobby, which has been so powerful these past few years, is going to come up against some tough administration postures on this one. Now you know," Crompton said quickly, "I wouldn't want anybody to get me wrong: those hard-working Israelis have really made a tremendous political difference in the Middle East. Their citizens have come out of concentration camps and ghettos to build one of this century's great achievements, a tough and thoroughly admirable little country. But the question is, what are they worth to us? I mean, this is coming right down to the real nitty-gritty of whether we back Israel and satisfy all those large Jewish urban voting blocks—which usually vote Democratic-liberal anyway—or whether we try to patch up our image in the Arab world and save our oil."

"I thought it was a moral question," Russell said mildly. "The last time you were out here you said we ought to support Israel in the Middle East because it was a moral question."

"Oh, certainly it's a moral question," Crompton said quickly. "I don't think there's a person in the United States who doesn't admire Israel and what they've done in the face of great adversity. But the frightening thing is, while we're behind Israel to guarantee their right to exist as a tiny little island in a sea of Arab peoples, we may be laying our own necks on the line. You know, after all, the Arab Palestinians have a point. They want a strictly secular state, open to all peoples regardless of religious creed or ethnic background. The way, more or less, it used to be."

"It used to be ninety per cent Moslem," Russell muttered.

"And as it stands now, Israel is definitely a racist state with one national religion, and the Israeli government has said they intend to keep it an all-Jewish country with no substantial minority groups. We'd find it very hard to defend that as democratic, you know. And the way things are going now, we're really forcing the more moderate Arab governments into the Leftist revolutionary bag. Listen, the Arabs make it a matter of either you're with us or you're against us, now. You should have a quick rundown on some of this anti-Western propaganda that's flooding Libya already. They've done a complete flip-flop in their attitudes. In just the space of a few hours the Libyan revolutionary government embarked on this all-Arabization program. They took down the English-Arabic street signs and put up only Arabic ones, and don't you think that didn't make for chaos! Overnight the place went strict dietary Moslem. They rushed around cleaning out the bottle shops and confiscating the booze, they even put a police guard on the Germans' brewery when they shut it down. I understand the oil workers out in the desert are going nuts. Anybody caught with an alcoholic beverage gets six months in jail. The official language is Arabic. People who have been doing business for years now have to take an interpreter along, because even those Libyans who know English and Italian perfectly won't speak it any more."

"Well, it *is* their language," Russell said, inspecting his fingernails.

"The government rushed right in and grounded all the planes at Wheelus because they said we were smuggling Jews out of the country or some such nonsense. And they've already taken over the British and Italian banks. But what really scares you is the outright hate campaign for all foreigners, and Westerners especially. So how did this get started, when all along we've had this estimate of Libya as our great, friendly Arab nation?"

"Libya was rotten as hell," Russell said calmly. "I don't care what kind of *Reader's Digest* stories you people in New York were reading about old King Idris being the Most Unforgettable Character We Ever Met, the truth of the matter was that all that oil money in Libya was going into the pockets of a few big Arab families, and the Americans were either ignoring the graft or else going right along with it. While the military bunch over at Wheelus was enjoying the great sodded golf course and the movie theaters and the private beach and the bowling alleys and keeping themselves apart from the dirty natives, the oil companies were paying the big Libyan families one million dollars in bribes just to get their routine paperwork through the Libyan Council of Ministers. I understand one guy skimmed off about a hundred and twenty-five million dollars in just a couple of years in the royal administration. But we didn't mind, as long as the oil kept coming out. Considering the average Libyan counts his fortune in upward of four goats—if he has that many—a hundred and twenty-five million is a nice tidy sum."

"No kidding," Crompton murmured. "That's the straight inside dope, isn't it?" For a moment a gleam of something like well-modified envy appeared in his eyes, and then he smiled. "You know, I can't help it; I have to admit that a real knowledge of a language like yours, Russ, is a wonderful thing. I suppose you hear a lot of things most of us never dream about. So Libya was really corrupt, hey?"

Russell sighed. "Putrid. And you don't need a knowledge of Arabic to find that out. People have a way of believing what they want to believe. The Americans knew all along what was going on; they just didn't want to do anything about it."

"How about here?" Crompton said interestedly. "I'll bet there's a lot of corruption here that no one knows about, either."

"It's not the same," Russell said cautiously. "But it's no damned secret. The country is shaky as hell. There's a real revolutionary pressure here because Tunisia doesn't have any oil and the people are hard up and they're getting a lot of fighting pan-Arab propaganda from all directions, and what the hell—it has its effect. I don't blame them for wanting to line up behind some sort of movement that shows the Arabs aren't a dirty, degenerate bunch of clowns. They used to be a damned proud people; the way they look at it, they're fighting for their identity, too. The Palestinian *fedayeen* call themselves the new Zionists. I can't blame the kids for thinking Al Fatah and the PFLP are romantic as hell. The average age of the Libyan junta is twenty-eight. That should give us a good idea of what's going on."

"So you think the same thing is going to happen here, eventually?" Crompton said. He had picked up his legal pad and was making notes again.

"How the hell should I know? The President is a good old guy; he midwifed this nation after the French were kicked out and made it what it is today. But he's getting old, and the times they are changing, fast. It's just too damned bad that he hasn't got what it takes now, because the same old sickness is still here. You've got an Arab middle class that's taken up where the French bourgeoisie left off—hell, most of the bureaucracy is French-trained, just like that damned thieving bunch in Vietnam we're backing—and while they don't have oil money to steal, as in Libya, they still do pretty good. The middle class is still hooked on turning a quick profit, and they want to put their money into tourist hotels and flashy office buildings and screw the long-range agricultural and industrial programs, which are going to be government regulated anyway. But as always, they're sowing the seeds of their own destruction. Because down on the bottom everywhere, in Libya and Saudi Arabia and Tunisia, there's what you might call a 'silent majority' that isn't getting a slice of anything. On the bottom there's a hungry, partly educated population explosion that's only half waked up to the twentieth century, but it's raising its ugly head and sniffing the change in the wind, and it's beginning to rumble. Nobody believes it, but Israel is only a symbol. Israel gripes the Arabs most particularly because it's a nation made up in the main of efficient, Europeanized Jews. To the Arabs, Israel represents Western imperialism backed by all the Western imperialist powers like the U.S. and Britain."

Willie Crompton was still making notes, but he decided to change the subject. "Frankly, you know I'm very impressed with our Youth Group," he said, looking up with a carefully earnest expression. "I really am. I'm especially impressed and delighted with the Falck kid. I mean, Wendell has been exceptionally responsive to the whole cultural challenge—he's taken to the whole way of life with what seems to be a total commitment on his part, and don't discount his real linguistic achievements. The few minutes I spent with him I couldn't help but be knocked out by this kid's excellent Arabic."

It was on the tip of Russell's tongue to bring up the subject of Wendell Falck's future now, and get it over with, but instead he settled obdurately back in his chair and studied the rain-soaked toes of his field boots and said nothing. He didn't, he told himself, have the heart for it at that moment. Somebody over on Government Hill had managed to keep a finger on the collective labor groups' ferment in the last few months and had spotted Wendell's inestimable genius up there in Tabarka right off. As a lot of the radical-leaning labor groups had been on the wrong side of the coup conspiracy, that had more or less put the seal on it. It had been suggested that this was the time for the Foundation to seek some other field for their prodigy.

"I wish," Crompton was saying, "we had had the same luck all down the line, I really do. Because I hate losing the Coffin girl; her record up there in the Bizerte community action project looked great, really great. But when her father jetted in, I felt we should get on the stick and facilitate the old man's desires to get her home." He sighed. "I don't suppose we managed to pick up a preliminary report from her, either?"

"No."

"Well, that's too bad. I was hoping for a better showing on those reports. But of course I understand the really tremendous pressure of the events of the assassination attempt and the near revolution, and how it blew your schedule. Still, those reports would have helped us to make a valid showing of work to date by this group. But fortunately, the Hoggenberger girl's piece makes up for a lot. She seems to be a very well-organized person, getting her report in early and wrapping it up as well as she did. I'm going to send it on. It's the only thing we've salvaged out here, in a manner of speaking, but it might give New York an idea of what we can accomplish under more normal circumstances."

"Look," Russell said quickly. "I was talking to Sullivan over at the Peace Corps office, and considering that the PC staff is trying to find jobs here in Tunis for some of the hundred and seventy PCVs that got kicked out of Libya last week, and there isn't all that much work to go around anyway, why doesn't New York hold off on this youth group stuff for a while? Dammit, we nearly had a disaster here in this country, and the Tunisian government is not exactly happy with being loaded down with a lot of foreign kids right at this time. Youth is sort of a dirty word, you know. The government has a hell of a lot of headaches squelching this neo-*fedayeen* group that figured in the conspiracy."

But it was futile; Crompton was shaking his head emphatically, no.

"Russ, I wish I could go along with you on that, but believe me, I really can't. If anything, with the Libyan setback and all our chances centered here for the time being, we're more involved in the Active Youth Commitment Group than ever. That was the consensus of thinking when I left New York, and I know it hasn't changed. Especially with the briefings I've been shooting on to them from here the past few days." Rather deliberately, Crompton lifted his watch and consulted the time. "Hey, the morning is getting away from us, isn't it?" he commented brightly. "I don't want to hold you, but there are still a few things I'd like to take up now quickly, if you don't mind. First of all, what is this fantastically complicated role the Hoyt girl played in what happened at Ez-Zahra? I hear that this police captain, Ben Ennadji—"

"Ali ben Ennadji. His name's not Ben."

"—who, from all I can gather from your report and the newspaper accounts, was the actual back-up man in the ambush and the projected assassin who was supposed to get in close enough to the President to pick him off, was into our girl for some really bizarre stuff. I realize how lucky we all were that the whole plan backfired and this ambush crowd blew it. That"—and Crompton picked up his notes quickly—"they weren't counting on the tracer bullets; it sort of threw them off from the start, and the kid lost his head."

"Salem had a runaway gun," Russell said wearily. "But it didn't matter all that much, as he held the covering fire for about as long as it should have taken Ali to get to the President's car, anyway, and that was all he was supposed to do. The kids on the roof weren't supposed to get anybody; they were supposed to make a diversion. Besides," he said, almost to himself, "his hands were pretty badly burned. I saw the corpse, and it looked like he had held onto the barrel of the AK-Forty-seven like a damned fool until they burned all to hell. He had to drop it."

"Well, what do we have to do about all this and how much is the Foundation implicated?"

"It's already been taken care of," said Russell.

He had been all through the matter with the First Minister, and they had both agreed that whatever Miss Sharon Hoyt had done in and around Ez-Zahra during her stay there, it was better to seal it all up and forget about it.

By the time he got to La Goulette it started raining in sullen, explosive bursts, and as he turned into the driveway of Nancy Butler's villa in Carthage the sky opened with a full, angry roar. Nancy held the door open for him as he sprinted from the jeep to the house.

"Oh, damn, will it never stop?" she muttered, looking past him at the leaden curtain of water descending upon the hill. "It's always bad in September, but this year is absolutely ferocious. The radio said it's flooding in the south and the city of Kairouan may be cut off completely in another day or so." As she took his slicker she said, "George, you are a dear to come and do this; I don't know what the damned Foundation would do without you."

"How's everything going?"

"She's all packed." Nancy took him by the arm, as they went down the long tiled hall that led to the front of the house, and shivered a little. The bare hall with its stone floors and ceramic walls was not only damp but turning chill. "She's a sweet child; she hasn't given me a moment's trouble. If anything she's been too quiet. I feel so sorry for her. Yes, I do," Nancy said quickly. "I've heard all the talk, and it's so unfair. She's really such an idiot romantic— all these children are with their silly emphasis on feeling instead of thinking; it quite takes my breath away. How in the world do they expect to survive? It's like Byron and the originals all over again. This time they're going to change the world with love and relating to each other, or whatever it is they say. Pure passion."

"You can say that again," Russell observed. "Listen, Nancy, I want to say thanks for the past two weeks. If you hadn't—"

"George," Nancy interrupted him, "we had a stupid thing happen. It was all my fault, really, but Cecile and I were so sure it would be good for her to get out. That's how it started. You see, only Wendell has come to see her in all this time. He just threw his arms around her and kissed her. I almost cried. I think these two are the best of the lot."

"What happened?"

"Oh, nothing, it's really quite stupid, but it was cruel. Cecile dredged up some junior attaché from the Embassy—well, he did look very presentable—and got him to take her to dinner at the Hotel Reine Dido. It's right down the hill; we didn't think into Tunis would be a very wise move. But even that much was a mistake. He brought her back in less than half an hour in a towering huff, the clod. *His* huff, mind you. And it was so obvious what had happened. Naturally he'd heard all those nasty stories. I'm sure he had decided it was a perfect setup. I was furious. And Cecile is beside herself; you'd think the honor of France was at stake. She wants him fired."

Russell had to laugh. "Don't worry, I'm sure she put his nose out of joint. That is if that's the right expression."

"Oh, don't be a beast," Nancy said quickly, but she laughed, too.

"Well, yes, she did take it rather well. She just shrugged and went upstairs without a word. But really, George, people have been rotten, you know. At least that fool Ambassador's wife could have come out to see her once. Or sent a note. They don't have to act as if she has the plague. I've grown quite fond of her," Nancy added, "and I'm going to miss her. And of course she's terribly attractive. I can see how men would lose their heads over her. She's not beautiful the way the Coffin girl is, but she has this wonderful glowing vitality. And, of course, she *is* sexy."

As they came to the door of the porch, Nancy pulled him aside for just a second.

"George," she murmured *sotto voce*, "something happened, rather odd. A child came with a package for her. Get her to tell you what it was, won't you?"

Sharon Hoyt was sitting with her legs curled up under her in one of Nancy's wicker porch chairs, staring out at the drop of the hill of Salammbo and the expanse of rain-filled sea beyond. She was wearing her long copper-penny hair tied back with a ribbon, and she had on a dress with long sleeves and white collar that made her look curiously like a large, pale, well-scrubbed child. Russell was reminded of some children's book illustration of a heroine with a wide and innocent mouth.

He wasn't ready to buy that. Little Alice in Wonderland was, as he remembered, a pretty obnoxious kid. The author sort of glossed her over, but when you came right down to it, she was a brat, and she did ask a lot of annoying questions.

He only hoped he had all the right answers.

"How goes it?" he asked her.

"O.K., really O.K." The voice was rather small and subdued, too. "I've packed; you don't have to wait."

He eased himself into a chair across the wicker table. "There's lots of time."

Since she didn't say anything, he said, "You look good. You look as though you've gotten lots of sleep."

That was dumb; he regretted it the moment it was out of his mouth, so he added, "I mean, you look rested."

He saw her smile.

"Yeah, it's really been great staying here, I didn't mind it at all. And Miss Butler is a real doll. The rest of the Embassy are pretty much creeps, but Nancy has been cool. I don't see," she murmured, "how she stands working for that old freak. I really don't."

He sighed. "I hope you didn't take it on yourself to tell her that."

"What, that the Ambassador is a fink? No, as a matter of fact, I kept my mouth shut. All the time I've been in this country people have been telling me to keep my mouth shut, so I did. I didn't have any thing to say, anyway, so I just listened. Listening is actually much sneakier, but people think it's sweet. So I listened a lot. I listened even when I was supposed to be upstairs sleeping, and I heard all the dirt. They're a gas, anyway."

"They who?"

Now she looked up and gave him an appraising stare. "Oh, come *on, you* know. Nancy Butler and Miss Guffin and the French Ambassador's secretary, Cecile Lambert. They come here all the time. They call themselves the old hands and they know everything about Tunis; you'd be surprised. Hey, did you know Miss Guffin is really famous as an Arabic scholar? I mean, even the Arabs consider her to be this real big authority. She specializes in pre-Islamic poetry, of all things. And from the way they talk about her when they think no one is around, I think she's some sort of spy or undercover agent. No, I'm not kidding. She was the one who got them to look for Norman Ashkenazi. Otherwise I guess he'd be dead by now."

"Mmmm," Russell said.

"You haven't heard the latest, either, I bet. Judy wrote Miss Guffin this letter. Judy is such a slob. She says she's dedicating her life to Chaim. You know what that means. She's going to resign and go to Israel to work on a kibbutz or something. Nobody is supposed to know about it yet, because the Foundation will really bleed at the mouth when they find out. We were all supposed to be standing around playing with ourselves when the revolution blew, you know? And we weren't supposed to be involved with Norman or Chaim or anybody connected with it or—or anybody."

"Try to keep your mouth shut on that, too," Russell murmured. "Cynthia Guffin has enough headaches right now."

"But the old hands know everything. I've been listening to all the inside stuff, and it's fantastic. Did you know the *directeur* of the *lycée* in Nabeul was in on it, too? Nancy said they caught him yesterday in Sfax and they're trying to get him to tell where the others are. I mean like Shedli and the rest of the kids."

"You're not supposed to know that."

"And then there was some guy whose plane was shot down while he was trying to get away."

"That's true enough. Monji Yacoub, along with Tahar Basti and the bunch from the Grand Mosque and the army people and Khefacha from the Sûreté and the Pop Liberation Front kids, was a prime mover in the conspiracy. Monji took care of the Air Force end of it, and he did a damned good job. The Air Force went over to the revolutionary side almost seventy per cent."

"There isn't really much you can tell me now," she murmured, turning to look at the sea and the rain again. "Because I really have made time with this listening bit. I ought to try it more. Even old Inspector Beshir spilled a lot, because the interpreter kept getting things screwed up and he didn't know I still remember a lot of my Arabic."

"You were lucky to get old Beshir to do the interrogation, because he's not a bad old guy. He thought you were very polite. He thought you were a very sweet, pretty young girl. That's what he told me."

"Maybe the Inspector liked me because I cried," she said. "They kept asking me about Salem and what he was like and what would make him do such a thing, and I cried quarts, I really did. When I thought about him lying there with his head all blown to bits and how absolutely useless and stupid it all was anyway, it got me so down I started screaming. Nancy was there; she thought I was going to flip out, I guess, because she went and got me some hot tea and aspirin, I was crying so much. She's really a gas. Hot tea and aspirin! But she came in and talked to me every night after I was in bed. That helped."

"She's a good one," he agreed.

"I think the Inspector believed me," she said in a very low voice. "He let me talk about it a lot. I mean, explain about the boys and how really shitty their whole life was. Cripes, this is a garden of faggots out here, it really is. They're all over the place. One of the assistant consuls screws every boy he can get his hands on, and the cultural attaché is a closet queen—he's married but he practically grabs little Arab boys off the street—and even one of the Peace Corps administrators has a sort of hareem of houseboys. Like, these are all Americans—not even counting the British and the French and the Germans! It's enough to make you want to puke."

"You didn't tell Beshir all that, did you?"

"Sure, I told him. I wanted him to know that I realized how damned exploited his people were and things like that. It's not the buggery especially, it's everything else, too. And I told him about Ali ben Ennadji being a *bedu* and going to orphans' school—you didn't know that, did you? Well, it's important because you have to know the motivation behind these things. But I didn't say anything about how he used to be with the *fellaghas,* only on Salah ben Youssef's side, because I already know the government is really down on the Youssefists. But Nancy says it doesn't matter, they know about that part, anyway." She stopped for a moment and looked at him obliquely. "He really did shoot at me," she said softly. "Nobody believes me, but he did. Just like he shot Salem. I saw him do it."

"Well, maybe he had to do it. The boy was hurt and couldn't run, and he couldn't let him fall into the hands of the police. He did what he had to do under the circumstances. Nancy told me," he said, to change the subject, "somebody brought you a package."

"They didn't catch any of them," she whispered, her eyes shining. "Nancy says Monji Yacoub is dead. But they didn't get Shedli and the rest of the boys; they just disappeared. They think a whole bunch of them got to Libya somehow."

"They're rounding all that kid group up in droves, Sharon, but that's not your worry. Just quit thinking about it."

"I think *he* got to Libya," she said stubbornly. "That's what you heard, isn't it?"

"Listen, I haven't the vaguest idea and probably the government hasn't either. They've got a little war going on down in the southern desert with the Berber tribes that's giving them fits, started by the Khefacha family. That keeps them pretty busy. And besides, whatever's been going on is going to be pretty secret. Now, what's up? Did somebody send you a present?"

"Yes," she said. But she gave him a wary, covert look. "It's nothing; you wouldn't believe it even if I told you."

"Try me out."

She held out her hand and showed a wadded piece of paper in her palm. "A boy brought it. One of the kids who sells the fake clay Roman lamps and tourist junk from around the museums out here, I guess. At least that's what he looked like."

"You didn't know him?"

"No. Like all the other poor kids. That's what I'm trying to tell you. He had on a sweater and it was raining and he didn't have enough clothes. His lips were blue. They always look like they're freezing to death because they never have any clothes, any raincoats or anything like that. And he gave me this thing wrapped in a piece of paper, and I thought he was trying to sell me some fake junk or a lamp and I said I didn't want it. He kept asking if I was the American mademoiselle and I thought he meant Nancy, because she was at work and there was only the maid around. But he said no, not the American madame, the American *mademoiselle*. Then he gave me the paper and ran. We couldn't even get him to come back for a tip. It was all balled up, not even tied with a piece of string or anything. And I opened it, and it was this." She pulled the paper away and held up a small object. "The ring."

"Whose is it?" he said, squinting.

"*The* ring, you know. The one with the zircon in it that was really out of sight. He loved jewelry. He had this big gold wrist watch and the gold cuff links—he always wore cuff links even with the uniform; it was incredible. But actually he had this small *nothing* house on the highway to Nabeul. I mean he wasn't rich. He didn't even have his own car; he used the police car all the time."

Russell lifted the ring from her hand. "What makes you think it's a zircon?"

"Oh, come *on*. It's a zircon or a rhinestone. But it looks better than a rhinestone."

He gave it back to her. "I'd say it was real."

"Real what?" After a moment she said, "You're kidding."

"No. I left my appraiser's eyepiece at home, but I'd say even in this light it's the real thing. Look at the setting. That's a setting for a diamond. You wouldn't put a piece of glass in a setting like that. The rest of it is gold. Nice, real, yellow gold."

She looked down at the ring, then up at him quickly. "It's too big to be a diamond."

"It's not all that damned big. It's about two carats or so, maybe less. That's not big, but it's respectable."

"Is it worth a lot of money?"

"It's worth a lot of Tunisian money, if that's what you mean."

"But that's sort of stupid." She held it up, frowning. "Why would anybody give it to a strange kid to deliver like that? Just wrapped up in a piece of paper without any string, or a box. You'd think he'd be afraid somebody would—"

Her voice trailed off and she sat for quite a while, holding it up to the light and staring at it.

"I don't know why he gave it to you, Sharon," Russell said finally. "But just to look at it I'd say it represented his savings account. Does that make you feel better? That's an old *bedu* custom, to bank all your money in jewelry. I wouldn't let it get you down. Maybe it isn't paid for, and you'll have to take up the notes." He was watching her face. "You'll have to get rid of it, anyway. Can't take it through customs."

"What did he give it to me for?" she whispered, turning wide eyes on him.

"Jesus, I don't know. Chalk it up to *bedu* pride if you want to. The world's proudest people, damned near. Stiff-necked as hell, just like the English. Maybe that's why the British and the Arabs get along so well together. After all, he put you on the spot, didn't he? He was the one who put the kids up on the roof with the AK-Forty-sevens, and you had a good chance of getting mowed down with them, didn't you? Maybe he wanted to apologize. The Arabs are great on the grand gesture for apologies."

"Maybe he's still around. Maybe he hasn't gone to Libya," she said softly. "He must be still around someplace. This was only yesterday."

"Listen, Sharon, nobody in their right mind is still around here, especially in the suburbs of Tunis."

"He'd marry an Arab girl, wouldn't he? I mean in Libya? He was so turned on for sex he'd have to get married soon."

"They're all turned on for sex, so forget about it. Give Cynthia Guffin the ring," he said abruptly, "and let her get rid of it. You can count on her to keep her mouth shut. Perhaps she can turn it into cash. Then you could give the money to buy a lot of poor kids raincoats, or whatever you want."

"I really don't think," she said staring far away, "that he would get married for a while. I think maybe it would be a long time before he got somebody else. Otherwise he wouldn't have sent me the ring."

"O.K., then, I'll take it," Russell said quickly. "Or better yet, let's drive up to Salammbo and you can pitch it into the sea. That's a very appropriate thing to do, to let it rest where it belongs. The

Romans and Carthaginians were always throwing stuff off the hill and into the water to please the gods; there must be tons of treasure down there. How about that?"

"But he still tried to shoot me," she said in the same faraway voice. "I guess he thought I knew too much, when I saw him kill Salem. It wasn't like Salem was trying to escape. He just fell down and stayed there as if he knew what was going to happen to him."

"Hey," he told her, eying the ring and wondering if he should just reach over and take it from her. "If he had wanted to shoot you he would have. He was a crack shot, had a couple of police trophies. You were in good range. He could have picked you off without a second thought."

But he stopped and just looked at her.

Or could you? he thought. *If you had killed the boy, would you still have enough steam left to turn and put a bullet through her, too?*

"He was so great," she whispered. "You never saw anybody that wanted something so much. And after a while it got like that for me, too. I mean we just wanted to touch each other and be with each other and just the whole total thing. He used to kiss me and kiss me and hold me afterwards; he never just rolled off and that was it. It was like we really belonged to each other, and he was never really finished; he could start over again right away because he always had a hard on when we were together. When I got here to Nancy's I nearly went out of my mind. I could hardly stand not having him. I mean, I couldn't sleep at night, and I really hoped that he was somewhere and feeling the same way and not wanting anybody else. That he'd be climbing the wall and have to jack off about five times before he could get rid of it. I hoped he was really suffering."

"Let's get your coat," Russell said. He didn't want to hear about it. He never liked to hear people tell about what they did, anyway. It was none of his business as long as they let him alone about it.

"I want to see Norman," she said, raising her voice. "Oh, God, I want to see Norman! If I have to leave this country without seeing Norman I think I'll kill myself. I bet you didn't even pay any attention to Nancy when she called you."

"Yes, I did. Cynthia Guffin set it up for me about an hour ago. And we'll see Norman if you'll lower your voice and try to behave yourself."

It had almost been a near miss. But Norman was leaving via Air France for Paris-New York that afternoon, so there wasn't much that could be made of it. It had only taken Cynthia Guffin about fifteen minutes on the telephone, and the permission had been rammed through.

In the lobby of the Hilton, though, Russell had to show the First Minister's card, and even the Reception wouldn't let him talk to Norman's room. The Assistant Manager was called to the desk and telephoned himself to check it out with Inspector Hamedi up there.

"Let's go into the bar," he told Sharon Hoyt, taking her arm. The coffee shop was jammed with the late-breakfast early-luncheon crowd from the African Adventure tour, and he was counting on the bar being deserted at that hour.

They had just ordered beers when Norman came through the door, the Sûreté Secrète man holding tightly to his elbow. Before Russell could grab her, Sharon Hoyt had jumped half out of her seat.

"Oh, Norman," she wailed, nearly turning over the two beers. And then, "My God, what did they do to your face!" It was nearly a shriek.

Russell gripped her by the back of the dress and tried to pull her back down. "Look, you'll have to cut that out," he warned her. "If you don't stop yelling I'm going to take you out, you hear me?"

Inspector Hamedi steered Norman to a seat across the little table and then sat down himself and got out his note pad and pencil.

He hadn't, Russell realized, seen Norman for a long time, and now it was enough to give you quite a start. Norman had a large scab over the split on his upper lip, but what made him such a beauty was his nose. It was flattened out like a squashed purple Easter egg, surmounted by two black eyes that were just beginning to open up in the swelling. But he guessed the eyes were automatic with a busted nose.

"Oh, God, Norman," Sharon moaned. She reached across the table to touch him, and Russell lunged for the beers to move them out of the way. Norman was wearing a white shirt and a striped tie and a navy blazer. "It's the first time I've seen you with real clothes on," she said, and to their amazement gave a wobbly giggle. "You're just not the Ivy League type, you know?"

Norman flushed. At least the part of his face that wasn't purple turned a deep shade of red.

"I never said I was," he said carefully, through the split lip. But his eyes went to Russell inquiringly.

"She wanted to see you," Russell said. "I cleared it straight through the top, so it's O.K."

"Oh, Norman," Sharon Hoyt murmured. She had got Norman by the sleeve and now she was stroking his hand. "Is it true you're going to have a desk job in New York from now on and they'll never let you do anything ever again? That you'll never go anywhere and do what you want to do? Won't they even let you go back to Israel?"

"I'm going to become a rabbi," Norman said carefully. "Cut it out, will you? Inspector Hamedi understands English perfectly."

But she wasn't listening. Her eyes were on his face and her body seemed to be straining forward in an agony of concern.

"Oh, damn, this was all my fault," she wailed. "You see what a mess I got you into—what happened to your face was all my fault, really it was. If I'd never showed you those pictures it would never have happened. And Chaim wouldn't have—"

Norman's look to Russell was cold and baleful.

"I'm surprised at you, you dumbhead," he said stiffly. "How did you let her talk you into this?"

"Norman's right. Pay attention to what you're doing, Sharon," Russell said. "Hamedi's taking notes. How are you, Hamedi?" Russell said agreeably in Arabic. "Everything goes well?"

"Very well, thank you. Good morning," Hamedi said, rising slightly and bowing in the direction of Sharon Hoyt.

She was oblivious to him, still struggling to keep hold of Norman's hand.

"Oh, hell, I wish we were alone," she was saying. "Do they put ice on your face? I wish we were alone, just so I could talk to you, I really do."

"Inspector Hamedi likes you, Sharon. Why don't you sit all the way down in your seat and stop yelling?" Norman said, careful of his lip.

"I don't care!" Her voice rose considerably and the bar boy looked up. "I can't just sit at a table and stare at you, for God's sake! Oh, God. Please, Norman, let me do something!"

"Judy has a message," Russell said loudly. "She doesn't think you got any of her letters. She sent them to the Foundation office and we forwarded them on to the First Minister as agreed, but maybe they got hung up somewhere. You're unofficial, you know; you're not even here."

"That's right," Norman said, putting his hand to his mouth to protect the scab as he talked.

"But Judy wants you to know she's staying on for a while."

"No, she's not, she says she's going to dedicate her life to Chaim!" Sharon burst out. "Poor Judy, Oh, hell, oh hell."

Norman laughed. "Give me a handkerchief, Russell, my damned lip's bleeding," he said, but he kept on laughing.

"Oh, Norman, don't *laugh!* What are you laughing about? Oh, God, I wish we were alone for a few minutes. I have to talk to you. You look so awful!"

"Jesus, knock it off," Norman said from behind the handkerchief. "You're going to make me bleed to death. Tell me, baby, why does your mind automatically run in one channel?"

"Oh, Norman, please, I only want to talk to you, I need to tell you that I'm sorry!"

"Lay off, Norman," Russell said.

"Shit, it's written all over her," Norman said, muffled. "You don't think she wants to talk, do you? She wants to make me feel better. She'll even get on top and do it that way if it makes me more comfy. Hey, Sharon, watch Inspector Hamedi. He likes you. Do you know what you are?" Norman said, taking the handkerchief away for a moment. "I just figured it out. You're the crazy mixed-up WASP version of a Jewish mother, that's what you are. Tell me, how many guys have you screwed while you were out here, just to make them feel better? You know, you pass that cunt around like it was kosher chicken soup!"

"O.K., Norman, your lip's opening up pretty bad," Russell said. He rose and pushed his chair away. "Just say good-by, will you?"

"Hey, Sharon," Norman went on. Behind the purple swellings his eyes burned. "How was it with the Arab Chief of Police? That is, as compared with Jewish pricks? I'm only asking."

"You're a bigot," she said in a loud, clear voice. "I always said you were a bigot, Norman. You've got a real hang-up."

"Norman," Russell interjected. "You know I wouldn't hit you

with your face all messed up. So why don't you knock it off?"

"George, you're a real Okie knight in shining armor; you give me a pain in the ass. You come off it, too. Just like this crazy bird."

"You're getting blood on your tie," Sharon Hoyt told him.

"Jews are always bleeding," Norman said. "It's a natural condition. I'll see you in New York, huh, Sharon? I get my mail at the Joint Distribution Committee."

"Listen, I want to get as far away from you as possible!" she shouted. She leaned across the table, her face almost in his. "Say, Norman," she said with sudden mock sweetness, "I heard you killed a lot of people. Murdered them in their sleep, actually. What's it like to kill somebody?"

"I don't know, ask Chaim. Or," he added, "you can get me at 313 West 114th Street."

"I know where you're going," Sharon shrilled. "You're going back to Tel Aviv and your damned war! You're probably a secret bomber pilot or some great thing that helps you to establish your Jewishness by killing innocent Arab children and civilians and things like that, right? Well, don't say I didn't wish you luck! You're going to need it, the way things are going now!"

"That's enough, both of you," Russell said. At Norman's elbow Inspector Hamedi was writing furiously.

"Get her out of here before I rape her," Norman told him. "Damn, now I've lost my scab," he said, looking into the handkerchief. "Jesus, but this is some crazy broad! Can you rent her out, like nerve gas?"

"I hate you, I hate you!" she was shouting.

"Good-by," Inspector Hamedi said, getting up. "Good-by Rosul," he said, and grinned.

"I'm going to slug him," Sharon yelled. "At least I can hit him, can't I?"

"Put your hat on," Russell said. "It's raining again."

17

The Bedouin herd
moves on, across
the interminable desert
without shelter. . . .

—*Virgil*

But she cried all the way down the hill from the
Tunis Hilton.

"He really hates me now," she wept. "Because you can see from
the way he acted that he thinks I'm a nothing slob who sleeps
around with half of North Africa. As well as making it once with
him. That's what's really getting to him, that I slept with him, too.
Big deal. Oh, Jews like Norman think they're so tough and broad-
minded but they're not. They're really very puritanically uptight. Just
like the original ones. You know, the Israelites in the bible who killed
off the Canaanites and took away their country just because they
thought they were God's chosen people. Real tough, and real uptight. And now," she said, in a fresh burst of tears, "he thinks I'm
some sort of spaced-out groupie giving it to everybody, while good
people like his friend had to get killed. You can tell by the way
Norman even looked at me that all the time he was thinking this
world would be a better place if people like me were dead and Chaim
was alive again."

"Don't be hard on yourself," Russell told her.

Frankly, he hadn't gotten the impression that Norman Ashkenazi
hated Miss Sharon Hoyt at all—quite the opposite. But Norman

345

certainly hadn't wanted to be pleasant company. Whatever his source for gossip up there in the Hilton (probably Hamedi, Russell decided), the stories had had their effect. And Norman had a lot of things bugging him at the moment. Nobody could speculate as to what the future held for him: possibly the one thing Norman would want the most, to be back in the field, was blown for good.

The main thing bothering him, though, had been pretty apparent. Norman was pretty well busted up and still feeling it, still loaded to the ears with Darvon and a shot of something stronger to make him sleep at night, unless Russell missed his guess. From what he had gathered from Cynthia Guffin, Norman had not only gotten it pretty good in the face but he also had two taped ribs, a little spleen trouble, where Khefacha's coup crowd had booted him around rather thoroughly, and a bad knee. If Khefacha hadn't wanted the General's papers so badly it would have been worse; they would have killed him on the spot. As it was, when Miss Guffin finally located Norman with the help of half the Jews in and around Metlaoui and Tozeur, in a jail in a flyspeck town near the Algerian border, Norman was in pretty desperate shape, swelled up like a basketball with bleeding and edema. But he wouldn't let them take him to the hospital. Wouldn't even let them take him to the local doctor.

Well, Russell allowed, Norman had probably been right, at that. Feeling was still running high, and the local people down there were still confused as to which side was running things. In the excitement the Arabs might not have understood the intricacies of how Norman was more or less an unofficial, sometime, marginal hero.

Still, Norman's noble sacrifice of his own hide in the matter had not been in vain. Miss Guffin had got that call through to the Hotel Miramar in time to warn the motorcade. And something else had been garnered from Norman's efforts: the General's papers were still where he had left them (and where they were found four days later), undisturbed in a nest of ants between the formica top and the leg of a dining room table in the Hotel Splendide in the oasis of Tozeur.

Good old Norman. He might be tough and morally uptight in the judgment of Sharon Hoyt, but he could think in a pinch.

"And you can see some bastard told him all about Ali ben Ennadji," Sharon Hoyt said. "I think that was what really burned him, too. Because Norman has a thing about Arabs, I wasn't kidding when I said that. It's just built into him, I guess, after fighting them so long." She paused and rummaged around in her pocketbook for a Kleenex. "Do you really think he can get his nose fixed?" she said anxiously.

"I wouldn't give it a second thought. New York doctors are used to working on Jewish noses. Norman'll check into Mount Sinai, and in no time at all he'll be the old model. You can meet him in New York and have a drink about it and laugh."

"Not me," she said bitterly. "I never want to see him again."

Russell swung the jeep into the Avenue de la Liberté. He was going to have Miss Sharon Hoyt's company until five o'clock, and then he was to take her back to the Tunisia Palace, where Cynthia Guffin would take over for the evening.

"Where are we going?" she asked, looking through the rain-streaked windshield of the jeep. "We're not going back to Carthage, are we?"

"Around and about," he said. "Just thought you'd like to ride for a while. But I want you to turn off the misery, do you hear? You're the one who wanted to go see Norman. I worked my ass off to set it up and finally had to pull strings to do it. So don't yell about what happened. Sit back and enjoy the ride. This is the country you came to see, isn't it? O.K., you're an American, and you're lucky —you're going back home in style. There's a lot to be thankful for. Tomorrow you'll be in the land of drive-in movies, credit cards, the whole American grab bag. I know," he said quickly, as she opened her mouth to say something, "but don't knock it. Just remember, you don't have to eat another bowlful of couscous in your life if you don't want to. As an American you've still got the biggest, best options in the world. Nobody's got their foot on your neck, your family's not in debt for the next three generations to some loan shark, you don't have to wait eight years until your boy friend can scrape up enough dowry money to marry you. You didn't have to leave school in the sixth grade to work in the fields. You won't have to see your children go hungry and maybe starve as a fact of life. You won't have to walk the roads with your husband, a baby strapped on your back and another baby in your belly dragging you down, looking for some kind of work, turning you into an old woman before you're thirty-five. And that's what we've got here. Dead, unrelenting lack of hope for about ninety per cent of the people."

"You don't have to yell at me," she said.

But she stopped crying. She didn't say a word until they got to Salammbo.

"What did we come up here for?" she wanted to know, surveying the gray sky, the sheer drop to the sea, and the dim leaden shadow of Cap Bon in the horizon. Nancy Butler's villa was somewhere below them and to the left. "I've been looking at all this for days."

"I know. I just thought you might want to take a look at the Old World again. Sort of put your troubles in perspective, you might say." Russell got out of the jeep and opened the door on her side. "I don't have time for it much any more, but I like to come out here every once in a while and look around. When I see these rocks and stones lying around and think of the people who actually used to live here—the ones who griped about their mothers-in-law, or went broke, or lost their sons to the army, or got blackballed by the local version of the Carthaginian country club—it reminds me that, as the world turns, people don't amount to a hell of a lot. When you come right down to it, nobody even remembers."

She gave him a curious look, "Is this supposed to be for my benefit?"

"I'm trying to cheer you up," he said, grimly.

Scudding dark rain squalls were passing over the sea, and he didn't expect that she would want to stay long. The ruins of Carthage were spread over the side of the hill, and the wind was up and blowing hard, and they were getting pretty wet. He suggested having lunch at the Reine Dido, below them and in sight, but she wasn't interested. She wandered around over the grass with a scarf pulled down over her face, her hands jammed into the raincoat, peering at the stones.

The Musée Lavigerie up the hill was more interesting if she really wanted to spend any time, but she wanted to hang around Baal-Hammon. It seemed to fit her mood. In the rain, she bent down to examine all the little votive steles to the Carthaginian children sacrificed to Baal-Hammon Saturn, the god in his war aspect.

"Nobody really believed they sacrificed them, until they found all this stuff," she observed gloomily. "And found all the little urns with ashes in them."

"Well, the Romans wrote about it, but history thought they were just prejudiced."

"I don't think I could take it," she said, squatting to look at the inscription on an oblong stone. "I couldn't go around for nine months, pregnant with my first baby, like they did, knowing that when it was born—and my God, you had to even go through having the baby and the pain and all that—that the priests would take it away and throw it into the fire to sacrifice to some crazy god that didn't even exist. Why didn't the women revolt—you know, just refuse to let them do it?"

"They didn't know he didn't exist. Baal-Hammon was real enough to them, I guess. They thought if they didn't keep feeding the god the first-born babies he would wipe them all out with plague and famines. Not to mention take away good luck. They cheated, sometimes, if that makes you feel any better. The rich Carthaginian families bought slave children and substituted them for their own. That's what Hamilcar Barca did. He was a Carthaginian general, and the son he held back turned out to be Hannibal. It had sort of got out of hand, anyway; I suppose the Carthaginians finally realized that. But later on, at the end of the Punic Wars when Hannibal got his ass beat in and the Carthaginians were losing, they figured the cheating was what had brought it all about. So they started throwing kids in by the bunches. They rolled them down the arms of a big brass statue of Baal-Hammon Saturn into a big fire. Even the rich aristocrats' babies. But it was too late. Baal-Hammon just wasn't convinced."

"It was awful, it was horrible," she said getting up. "You really don't know what the human mind is capable of, I guess, until you start getting older and realize all about these things. I mean, it's never real when you're young. The world had to get better," she said thoughtfully. "It just couldn't go on being horrible like that."

"I don't know that it got much better. Hitler did pretty good burning babies, too."

He saw her shudder. He hadn't said it deliberately, but once again the question rose in his mind.

"I think it's time," he said, "you told me what scared you off down in Ez-Zahra."

"You're out of your mind," she said, not looking up.

"Come off it, now. I want to know what you found that you managed to keep to yourself for a change. That made you have that little talk with Charlie Benedict and then clam up. And that made you give me all that shit about not being interested in old Nazis any more."

"I'm not interested in Nazis," she said, her head bent.

"Look Sharon, I know about the photograph, and I know that's what put Norman on the General's trail. According to Cyn—from what I've been told, that's pretty much a matter of record now, and you don't have to go into all that. But I want to hear the part that's missing."

"There's nothing missing. If she—Miss Guffin—told you all about it, then it's all there."

He waited, and finally she looked up at him. But her face was shut, resistant.

"I don't have to tell you," she said stubbornly. "I don't have to tell anybody anything if I don't want to."

"You'd damned well better tell me," he said. She looked up, eyebrows raised. "Yeah, I'm really serious. You can chalk it up to my peculiar brand of curiosity, if you want, but I don't think you'd better get on that plane without spilling it now. What you're holding back."

"I don't know anything," she told him. "I don't want to know anything. Charlie Benedict knows who they are; he told me all about people like that. Why don't you write him? Cripes, some of them are still alive! The old SS."

"Just tell it like it is, if you don't mind. Without the melodrama."

"Melodrama! Listen, this whole thing is so fantastic nobody would believe me. Especially *me*. I just fall on my back for a little quick balling with anybody, remember? I want to forget it."

"I'll believe you," he said.

"Yeah." She waited a moment and then she said, "There wasn't any gold, the gold the Afrika Korps was supposed to have left behind when they had to surrender. I saw all the trash they left behind," she muttered. "Listen, people are supposed to be looking all over the place for it, but actually the gold was really always in Sebastian's house. But it wasn't gold, it was just Vichy francs. They weren't worth anything, and most of the people in Ez-Zahra knew it. Even the French government knew it. But Sebastian had spent his time sucking up to the Germans when they were around—I guess he figured if the Nazis didn't win the war at least he could get some kind of grabs on their loot afterward. They used his house as some sort of head-quarters for the German Army. I mean the Afrika Korps. And it was all full of records and papers and payrolls and stuff. When the Allies moved in so quick it was still there because the Germans didn't have time to get it out. But the money was just Vichy francs, what they called paper occupation money; that's what I'm trying to tell you. Cripes, the little Arab kids in the village had some of it for a while, just playing around with it! Then the Free French or whatever they were called came and cleaned out the records, because they were looking for the names of people who had collaborated with the Germans—this was a big deal then, to catch collaborators—and they burned a lot of papers they couldn't use. But before anybody, even before the American and British troops captured the house, *he* came over and got the photographs and some of the important things. They said he came over with Ahmed, his butler, and cleaned out boxes and boxes of papers from the Afrika Korps HQ and took them home with him. It was just across the fence, the tabia, anyway."

"You're talking about Moreau now."

"No, I didn't say anything," she said quickly. "I'm not naming names. It's strange down there," she said, making a sudden convulsive movement that was almost a shudder. "It's almost as though that place is haunted, you know? Like nothing ever changes. Even the house doesn't look like it's been empty for years and years. I've heard that even the beys used to go down to that little town to do things they didn't want people to know about. Weird. Sometime," she said, so softly that he almost missed the words, "they're going to send another man down there like the General, and it'll start all over again. I mean it. Because he's the contact man or something. He does it for fun. I don't think he was ever in any concentration camp like they said."

"Who told you Moreau came over to Sebastian's place and cleaned it out?" he wanted to know.

"Nobody."

"Did Ali ben Ennadji tell you this?"

"Nobody told me. Besides, when I saw all the junk that was still there, Ali fixed it up. He didn't like dirt and mess."

"Sharon, how in the hell did you get a tough nut like Ali to spill all this to you? What did you use to pry it out of him?"

"Oh, fuck off! I didn't pry anything out of anybody. Besides, don't you understand? He didn't know the connection, none of them did. They couldn't have. They were getting their guns and being told what to do through the Arab coup people; they probably didn't even know where they were coming from. Jesus, and the other side didn't even know who *they* were, either!"

"Now look, Sharon," he said after a moment, "Moreau is just an old man. I know he's got a houseful of knickknacks, but that doesn't mean he goes around collecting German Army records. Don't let your imagination run away with you."

"Don't play dumb. You just think about it for a minute. Think about all those people who came to his house all the time. They didn't arrest the President's cousin, did they? All those freaky bourgeois Tunis officials, a lot of them worked for the old French government and they were bound to know about the gold being just paper money. But they never let on. The General was supposed to be looking for the gold, but nobody ever came right out and said there wasn't any Rommel's gold and to forget about it. But after what happened, all those same people got busy and went all over the country looking for the coup crowd, and the old hands say they shot a lot of people. But nobody ever shot *him*, and they didn't shoot the cousin of the President, and they certainly didn't start shooting themselves—"

"Sharon, stop saying the cousin of the President, because you don't know what you're talking about." He had to raise his voice a little to override her. "You should have stayed out of the damned house; you were trespassing on government property and doing a lot of things you were told not to do right here in Tunis, and whatever you got out of Ali ben Ennadji while he had the running hots to lay you is totally unreliab—"

"You started it!" she yelled at him. "You wanted me to tell you, didn't you? O.K., I made it up! What do you think I'm going to do—run over to the Sûreté office and tell them that I know who really ran the coup, and if they'd just go down to Ez-Zahra and start down there and forget about how many times I gave it to Ali ben Ennadji and Norman and Salem, they'd find out how it worked? No, that would really blow things, wouldn't it? Because you don't know the people that came down to Moreau's house—there were bunches and bunches of them, and they were all big shots!"

"Christ!" He almost put his hand over her mouth but caught himself in time. "Now listen, Sharon," he said persuasively, "take it easy."

"*Phlagh!* And you said you'd believe me."

"Maybe I do believe you," he said hurriedly. "Dammit, Sharon, if you've kept your mouth shut this far, I guess you can keep on doing it, can't you?"

"Screw you! It wasn't my idea! You think I'm a real dumb broad, you still do. But I'm not so dumb. I'm not so dumb and sexually freaked out that I've blown my mind, no matter what you think. I know a little social history. I know it's the little guys that always get caught while the big cats hide or get let off. I know if they ever catch Ali ben Ennadji they'll really work him over, they'll set him up as the brains of the whole thing even though he wasn't, and they'll pull his teeth out and put electrodes on his testicles and make a jelly of him until they get a confession that says he did it all and makes the rest of them safe. You didn't think I knew that, did you? Because he didn't know where the guns were coming from any more than the kids did, but they'll pretend he did. All he ever wanted to do was bring about a revolution because he knew it was the only way the real people were going to break away from the corrupt governments who had sold out to the West and have some sort of identity and self-respect! Hell, these people can't wait any longer. Ali was a *bedu*, he'd had a lousy life—he knew what it was all about!"

"Stop screaming," he shouted at her, "and try to listen to me. Let me take it logically, step by step, because you don't know what in the hell you're talking about. In the first place, old German Army records weren't all that important. What in the hell did you think an old dodderer like Moreau was going to find, anyway?"

"Well, for starters," she said promptly, "they'd have to let him in on the deal after he found the photograph of the General and figured out who he was, wouldn't they? He put it right in the book and compared it."

After that, in spite of his attempts to make her do so, she wouldn't listen at all. He couldn't argue with her, couldn't convince her that she had jumped to a lot of wild conclusions without any real evidence. And to make it worse, his own insides were jumping; he had to deliberately set aside any idea of going over what she had told him and matching it up with what was already known, for fear of being completely distracted.

She didn't, he was realizing, understand a hell of a lot about what she had been doing these past few weeks; realities got tangled up with her impressions of Ez-Zahra, that decayed expatriates' ghost town, as a place of invidious evil. And as she talked he was impressed once again with what a mixture Miss Sharon Hoyt was of pretty sharp adult and blundering headlong adolescent.

But crap, he reminded himself, she was twenty-three or twenty-four, wasn't she?

Was everybody like this at that age?

He couldn't remember. But he was genuinely surprised that she could make him feel so sad. He felt sad as hell, looking at her. It was a very peculiar feeling. "Come on, cheer up," he said, getting back into the jeep.

They started along the shore to Sidi Bou Said, past the hill of the Forum Romanum, and then up to the cisterns and the Phoenician graves.

"They had a different life, that's all," he said. "It was a real honor to die for the state and your tribe or family. Especially family. Then all your relatives were famous and honored for ages, and got a big statue in the public square. That was important. One time, as I remember the damned story, the Phoenicians got into a big fight with the Greeks, who had a big town going over at Cyrene, in Libya, and they kept arguing over where the Carthaginian territory ended and where the Greek took up. So finally the Greeks and Carthaginians decided to hold games, like the Olympiad, to settle the matter. Which was pretty civilized, you've got to admit—war games instead of war. They were going to have a foot race between two teams, one starting from Carthage and one from Cyrene, and where the two teams met, the border would be laid out. But the two cities got into an argument and accused each other of cheating, so the Philaeni brothers, who were running for Carthage, said that if they were allowed to choose the spot they had reached as the frontier, they would agree to be buried alive there. And the Greeks agreed, probably because they didn't think the Carthaginians would do it after all; it was only a fight over a piece of desert. So the Carthaginians buried the Philaeni kids alive and got a big chunk of Greek territory as a result. That was considered quite a thing."

She had started crying again. The story of the Philaeni had probably been a mistake, he realized, but actually the damned account was fascinating. There came a time, Russell supposed, when you made your choice. If you thought the sacrifice of your life was worth it.

As with Chaim Dayag.

But not as with that poor Arab kid down in Ez-Zahra who probably thought he was going to live forever and be covered with medals and glory.

Wrong, Russell thought suddenly. I may be wrong after all. "He just fell down and stayed there as if he knew what was going to happen to him" was the way she had put it.

And God help us if even the kids are getting tough enough for that.

Sharon Hoyt had got out the gold ring and was rolling it around in her hand, slipping it on and off her thumb but not actually looking at it. As though just the touch of it was all she needed.

"Not all the babies got roasted," he said abruptly. "Let's try a few live ones."

The road to the Convent of St. Monica was muddy and the jeep wallowed, but the driveway to the main building and the office had been recently graveled and they made it. Russell parked the jeep almost parallel to the door so they wouldn't have to make too much of a run for it.

The Mother Superior was in her office, boiling water on a hot plate for tea, the only source of heat in the room. A bucket just beyond her desk was catching a leak from the ceiling with a steady thunk.

"George, *mon vieux mauvais*," Mother Jean-Claire shouted. The Mother Superior was a Marseillaise with massive forearms and a pair of lungs inherited from a long line of Provençal fishmongers. She grabbed Russell's hair and gave it a hearty yank and tossed him around a little playfully before she kissed him on both cheeks. "Ah, George, you rogue, we have not seen you in a long time!"

Sharon Hoyt had put the ring out of sight and was standing listlessly. Russell told Mother Jean-Claire that he wanted to visit the children's rooms, and she promptly swept them on with a wave of her large red hand.

"And come back for tea, *hein?*" she yelled after them.

The old buildings were fast going into disrepair and there were leaks all over; they had to duck down a passageway that was like a shower room.

"Babies!" Sharon marveled at the door.

"Thick as cockroaches," he agreed.

The floor was damp from the constant rain, but the Arab nurses had put the infants down anyway. There were mostly crawlers, but a few of the babies were so small they just lay on the blankets and waved their arms and legs. And not enough people to take care of them, as usual, Russell observed.

"Just don't step on them," he told her.

"Thousands of little babies! What's the matter with them, are they sick?"

"It's an orphanage."

"An *orphanage?*" Her hands went out as though she was going to scrape them all together in a lump excitedly. One of the nurses looked up from a copy of *Jeune Afrique*, then went back to her reading. "An orphanage? No kidding! Wow! Can I pick one up?" she said, regarding one who was trying to mouth a piece of her sandal.

"You can do anything you want to, only just don't knock them around," he said. "The floor's concrete."

"Aren't you going to stay?" She already had a baby with a waterfall of glistening mucus from nose to lip in her arms.

"Enjoy yourself," he said hastily.

Sometimes, he congratulated himself, he really had some brilliant ideas. Maybe it would keep her happy for a while.

"George," Mother Jean-Claire said when he came into the office, "what are you up to, my old one?" She went to get a tea mug for him. "Ah, we have missed you, now that you do not come to see us so much any more. How we used to tease the little novices when they saw your jeep coming up the drive! They twittered like birds. Go down, we would tell them, and help Monsieur Russell with whatever it is this time, and they would race away. And how they talked of you afterward! Did your ears burn?"

"Mother Claire," he told her, stretching his legs out in the rickety wooden chair, "I haven't had that job in years. I don't work with the *bedu* any more, so I don't get stuck with anybody's leftover kids."

In those days, especially during the killing summer droughts, the *bedu* girls of the southern villages would bring out some half-dead thing wrapped in a piece of rag and follow him around, silently begging him with their eyes. Waiting for him to take it away. Especially if it was female. And if it wasn't too half dead and looked as though it would make the trip, and he was headed north anyway, he would throw it in the front seat of the jeep and bring it along. It wasn't the damned starving little twigs of flesh so much as the dumb-animal looks of pleading on the faces of the mothers which prodded him. No words. Just dogging his footsteps with it in their hands, waiting.

He never asked how many of them survived or where they were, and the Mother Superior never told him. Hell, he didn't want to know, just as long as they took it away when he finally got there.

"So now," Mother Jean-Claire said, giving him a hearty Provençal dig in the ribs which made his tea slosh, "it looks as though you progress to the larger *bébé*, hey, George? This is a very pretty little one, a nice big girl for you. With this one you could make many nice giant American *enfants* of the six feet, all with blue eyes!" She gave a raucous cackle as she settled back into her seat.

"Mother Claire," he said evenly, "you're a dirty old lady. You've been around here so much you've got babies on the brain. So tell me, how goes it?" he asked, eying the bucket with its steady drip.

"Ah, well, *ça va.*" She shrugged. "As you can see, we are not spending the money for an expansion. Gently, it comes to a stop. No more little novices, no more ready hands from France, even the White Fathers on the hill, they get down to the old ones. I have not seen a young good-looking brother over there in years."

"You don't mean you're going out of business, do you?"

"*Naturellement*, what else?" Mother Jean-Claire poured herself another cup of tea, warming her hands around the mug. "After the *colons* left, we were only allowed to stay because we had a job to do. We take the little ones and they stay here until they are three years of age and then they are ready to go on to the government's Children's Villages. But now as the government builds more infant nurseries, we will take less and less here. Once in a while we are asked to go to the south and advise the setting up of babies' wards there, but not so much." She made a small grimace. "It is hard to know what they require of us. Now they have their own staffs and their own doctors, and they are sensitive to criticism as new people in new jobs. And of course they are much aware of being Moslems. So we make a suggestion here, a suggestion there, and enjoy the trip.

Besides, I tell you the truth," she said with a massive Gallic shrug. "They do not need much advice any more. It is not like the old days. No, I give them credit, they have accomplished miracles, these people, that I once would not have believed. They said they would make a better country and that they would take care of their children, and the *colons* laughed at them and said they were pigs, that they could not manage it. But they got the beggars off the street and the children into the orphan villages, in all truth. This is the way of the old President and his talent with American money—he is *formidable*. But he made them proud, these backward people who had come down to less than nothing. Oh, yes—*mon Dieu!*—he is a bag of wind, he talks forever, that one. Those radio speeches of the Father to his Beloved People are interminable; they go on until I have a desire to throw the radio out the window! But it is amazing, he has talked them back into their self-respect again, you know? Now of course, George, I am not *stupide*, I do not say that all is perfect. I know myself that the *directeurs*, some of them, sell half the food in the Children's Villages for profiteering and there is the usual corruption. But when one travels and looks it over—thousands of children!—that is a miracle. In 1958 I went south and it was a desert, the true desolation of the Sahara country as it has always been. Now I go down and there are olive plantations and the eucalyptus, which they bring in especially with these aid programs, and even fields of wheat. No, I do not laugh at them. I do not see how they have done it!"

"Maybe it's not enough," Russell said, pouring himself some more tea. "You see what happened the first of September."

"No, of course, nothing is enough for this world, which still limps behind like a crippled one in spite of the oil which is flowing sudden riches into many places in it! They want a revolution, these people —they want their money and their rights to the good world which the West keeps telling them they can have! But I do not think they can do it this way, with these crazy conspiracies. *C'est fou!* These children trained like the Al Fatah, this is not the way to bring down governments!"

"You'd be surprised," Russell said mildly. "It wasn't only the kids. The Marxist students at the University were in on it, too. Not to mention a good solid core of professionals in the Army and the police."

"Yes, and a *ragoût* of Berber tribes who are always the conservatives," the Mother Superior pointed out. "What a mixture! They would not dare all to get into the same bed with each other; it would not work. Also, they make the big mistake to allow the Bastis and the other Palestinian families who have migrated here to have a large say."

"Well, the Palestinians are pushing it all over the Arab world," Russell said. "They're the damned catalyst wherever they go."

"No, no," Mother Jean-Claire said, shaking her head. "They will not get anywhere with Nasser; the war with Israel is not a Tunisian war. You cannot sell it to the Moroccans, either. What does the Maghreb need with pan-Arabism? Look at Algerie, how suddenly she holds back, now, and talks of being busy with building steel plants and highways and cannot commit troops to Egypt. Even Lebanon, which is next door to the fight, it is trying to be a moderate still! No, there are too many faint hearts in the Arab world. I believe this. They see now that Russia and the United States make threatening noises at each other and that it is not a matter of Israelis and Arabs, but maybe the prospect of a big war from which they will profit no more than the Vietnamese have profited from theirs. I do not think they like that much—to have their country turned into a battlefield.

"Well, *alors*," Mother Jean-Claire said abruptly, "thank the good God this is not our business, now! The Church is finished here, my dear one. We sit on the shelf with our feathers and our ribbons drooping, poor old hats, and we know we will never be wanted again. One by one we will go into the garbage—*poof!*—and then they will have this country all to themselves. But George." Here Mother Jean-Claire leaned her bulk back in the old chair and sighed. "Sometimes I lie in bed at night and I look to the ceiling above where *le bon Dieu* is floating up there above Carthage, and I say to Him, Yes, well, let us not be hasty, as no one knows how these things will turn out yet, do they? They call themselves Arabs, these wayward people, but once they made the Church from here, on these very shores. They were the life's blood of the Church, very good Christians indeed when Rome was wicked and not so Christian, then. St. Felix, St. Cyprian—the thousands of blessed martyrs— once they were crazy for martyrdom, these Arab people! They wanted to lie down in the roads of Carthage and be slaughtered for the glory of God. And St. Augustine! What a marvel of a saint! And a Tunisian," she added slyly.

"Mother Jean-Claire, you'll be here another twenty-five years. Don't let it get you down."

"Hah! I do not fool myself. In another two years there will be no Convent of Saint Monica in this place. But George, I also tell you that the love of God has not deserted His people. I am a very bad old woman, may God and Pope John the Blessed forgive me! But I am not an enemy of the Moslem. It is not a bad religion at all. They worship God, do they not? And look what they say of us —of Moslems, Christians, and Jews—that we are the 'People of the Book.' Yes, it is the same Book we all follow and the same God; why should there be any fighting over it? We are all the children of God!"

"Mother Jean-Claire, you're not going to convert me," Russell said and smiled. "I thought you gave that up."

"*Tchah*, I would not convert you, Rosul, on the orders of the Pope himself!" she roared. "A Protestant is only the Devil in a business suit!"

"I'm not a Protestant," he told her. "I'm a Mormon from Nebraska."

"One and the same, one and the same," she said with a violent wave of her hand, "whatever that is. Now, *voilà!* Here comes your nice *bébé* looking for you."

"I can't get over the way they feel," Sharon Hoyt said, as they turned into Mohammed Cinq. "It's the most groovy thing: you pick them up and you expect them to be all squashy and limp and they're not. They're really great; they've got these great, tough, smooth, fat bodies, and when you feel them it really turns you on. It's the most physical thing, it's really weird. And it's all physical, I mean physical love, because you're in touch, you're together. I kissed them and it was the most out-of-sight reaction, because they think kissing is great; they turn on and they start feeling for you and pulling your hair and they laugh. They know what kissing is even at this really very early age. It's amazing. The communication is total; it just pours out. It's a whole sight, smell, love, sensuous thing."

"They smell of piss," Russell said.

"Cripes, yes! And some of them had this big dump in their pants that really stank—they don't have half enough people to take care of them. And they barf up sour milk, too. But it's still great. They smell so turned on I can't believe it. You know," she said suddenly, "it was a big mistake for the Foundation to send Judy down to Sousse to do clinic work and me to that weird little resort town full of freaks. Because Judy has no aptitude for babies. Oh, I know, she's the type everybody picks because she looks the plastic image, you know? But I was really the one. Even I didn't know it. But I would have been great for clinic work!"

"Maybe you would have," he said.

"And God, after a while when you think about places like orphanages it drives you nuts, because you can't raise babies that way. I'm a psych major; I ought to know that much. I mean, every one of them has to have this physical love thing or they just don't develop. I mean, that's nothing new. Jeepers, there have been statistics to prove that children, I mean especially in the first year and a half, that have been raised in orphanages are really warped by a lack of physical contact. Of physical love. I had only one course in Child Psych, which was really a summary because it wasn't my field—"

Goddamned rain, Russell thought. The top of the jeep was beginning to give. It probably would have held through an ordinary September wet spell, even as old as it was, but this month looked as though it was trying to set some sort of record.

"—and music. You don't have to wait until preschool—that is, around three or four—to begin the music bit, because I suppose humanity has known from the very beginning the benefits of having mothers sing to babies. Babies can feel the vibrations right through the mothers' bodies, which replaces the aural sensations they get while they're in the womb. But I suppose you come right back to the whole bodily physical contact thing, because I think really little babies, that is for the first month, don't really have their hearing developed. Oh, crap, I've forgotten so much! I could probably go back and take a really extended Child Psych, even major in it; it's not so hard to do. But Child Psych degrees only get you stuck in crummy desk jobs counseling and writing evaluations and reports. I wonder—if you had a whole roomful of kids—if they would respond to taped music and a light show? It's not as crazy as it sounds. No, it has to be physical. If you had a whole bunch of people *holding* babies while—"

"I'd better go in with you," he said, parking the jeep in the Avenue de Carthage, "and see if Cynthia Guffin's got here yet. You ought to eat some dinner."

Nancy Butler was waiting for them in the lobby of the Tunisia Palace.

"I'm afraid Cynthia couldn't make it," she explained. "Your visiting fireman has her working until eight or nine, 'New York style', as he put it. But of course she'll be down to see you off at the airport tomorrow."

"I can't take you to the airport, Nancy," Russell said. "The damned top of the jeep's collapsing, and I've got to take it to the garage first thing tomorrow. But I can take you out in a taxi if you want."

"No, no, never mind, George, you definitely weren't supposed to do all that. We can manage perfectly well. I've got my car."

"Then I'll say good-by," Russell said. He turned to Sharon Hoyt and extended his hand. "Good-by, Sharon," he told her. "We'll miss you."

"Good-by, George," Sharon said. "Don't worry about me. I just want to get out of this fucking country. I never want to come back here any more; it's been a mess. I'm not going to say anything to anybody, ever; you don't have to worry. Nobody'd believe me, anyway. My mother didn't even believe me when I wrote her about the weird characters down there, and that freaky little town. Like a horror movie with oranges. All she ever worried about was that I wasn't doing any work. She kept asking me why I wasn't teaching school. She thinks it's all my fault, I know."

"It wasn't your fault," he said huskily. "They never should have sent you kids over here to evangelize some damned unrealized, unplanned gospel in the first place. This is a tough, complicated part of the world for anyone to deal with, and no place for a wild-eyed experiment. I knew it, and Cynthia Guffin knew it, and we were against it from the start, but there wasn't anything we could do about it. New York wouldn't listen."

She didn't seem to be particularly impressed with what he was saying and he added, "It wasn't your fault, I swear."

18

Where they make
a desert,
they call it peace.

—Tacitus

The following morning George Russell drove the
jeep out to Liebman's Garage off the Place de Pasteur in an increasingly heavy rain which was, as he told himself, about the volume if
not the force of a damned typhoon. The weather, even for that time
of year, was outdoing itself. And the jeep top had just about had it
—one large water-filled spot in the canvas above the driver's seat
bulged ominously, and he could hear the collected water sloshing
every time he turned a corner. Finally it began to leak through in
little pinprick tears. The effect was just as though he was carrying his
own private rainstorm along with him. In the Rue Habib Thameur
he got tired of the interior drizzle and pulled the jeep over for a
moment to have a look at it, but just as he got out the whole thing
gave way at once. About two bucketfuls of water broke through,
drenching the driver's seat and the interior of the jeep, and he
avoided getting doused by jumping back just in time.

Not that it made any difference, he thought wearily, getting back
in; the whole damned world was turning to water anyway. Miserable
climate—feast or famine. At least he could take some comfort that
he hadn't offered to make the trip out to the airport. That would
have really made a mess.

At Michel's, he had to bang on the outside doors to the workshop

363

for about five minutes before anyone came to see who it was. The place looked deserted.

"Where the hell's Michel?" he demanded, when a little Arab mechanic in coveralls finally appeared. All he got was an empty stare, so he changed from French to Arabic.

"In France," was the indifferent answer.

"Well, when is he coming back?"

Not much interest there, either; the mechanic shrugged.

"Who knows? I am working for the brothers Raouad; they are running this garage now."

I'll bet, Russell thought, looking beyond him to the gray, lightless cavern of the shop behind, the unlit glass-partitioned office.

"*Essma*," he said, "I wish you to regard my conveyance. As you can see, the top has collapsed. Can you fix this for me now?"

The mechanic looked it over with even less enthusiasm.

"I do not know if we do such work now," he told him. "Here, we are working mostly with engines and things like that. Why do you not take it to an upholsterer?"

"I am not," Russell said evenly and in impeccable upper-class city Arabic, "going to take it to an upholsterer." Might as well get the upper hand and get it over with. "Consider, is this a sofa or an armchair which you see before you? No, it is not; it is an automobile. Therefore it does not go to an upholsterer, it goes to a garage. I am going to leave it here, and you are going to have the brothers Raouad look at it when they return, and you are going to tell these brothers Raouad for me that in the past the Frenchman, Liebman, attended to such repairs superbly and I wish to know if they can do half as well as he did. It does not take genius, only a little hard work. You tell them that."

Not that I expect them to bust a gut trying, Russell told himself. But I might as well go on record from the outset.

He left the mechanic staring with smoldering eyes at the sad sight of the jeep leaking water like the shower room of the Medina hammam and walked away.

The rain was coming down in fantastic gouts, coursing across the plaza of the Place de Pasteur in solid curtains of water and turning the gutters of the Rue de la Liberté into raging dirty rivers. Naturally, no cabs in sight. There was nothing to do but churn along on foot, in spite of the fact that a certain chill was seeping under the rain slicker, and at intersections the water damned near came to the tops of his field boots.

The wet had worked its way down into the collar of the raincoat and was turning his shirt clammy by the time Russell got to the Boulevard of the President. He looked into the windows of a couple of small cafés but they were jammed to the doors with Arabs seeking shelter from the storm, and he didn't feel like stopping long enough to get a warming cup of coffee. At least not in the deafening racket of Arab voices and the steambath of his clothes.

At the corner of Sadikia, Russell paused long enough to light a cigarette, not really expecting it to stay going. The first few soggy puffs were sour and unpleasant anyway, and he tossed it into the gutter. By the leaden light of the *sieste* hour the aluminum façade of the British Bank of the Middle East was a wavering light show of silver on silver. The damage in the main part of town was still pretty apparent, although most of the broken glass had been reamed out of the store fronts and the frames decently boarded over. The Grand Marché, pretty well sacked during the fighting of the attempted coup and the rioting which had followed it, looked permanently out of business. Along the Boulevard busy hands had been at work on walls and any bare spaces which presented themselves, scrawling graffiti to the effect that violence would purge the sickness of bourgeois and imperialist oppression, and prophesying victory for a united Arab world. On the temporary fence protecting the United States Information Center there was a whole gallery of Al Fatah posters, including the one with the particularly unflattering picture of Golda Meir side by side with that of a beauteous combat-out-fitted Palestinian girl. On one side the text ran: "Golda Meir, born in Russia, emigrated to the United States, temporary citizen of Palestine." And under the girl: "Fatima Juhena, born in Palestine, raised in Palestine, temporary citizen of a refugee camp in the Gaza strip." As you walked down the boarding there were row after row of Golda and Fatima until after a while you began to feel sort of sorry for the bulbous-nosed, grandmotherly face of Mrs. Meir, warts and all, next to her nubile Arab counterpart. And in between and above and below the posters of Golda and Fatima, the shadowy head of a *kaffiyeh*-wearing guerrilla brandishing his AK-47. ARISE AND FIGHT!

The median park of the Boulevard was where the events of September first still showed the most. Gone was the pleasant neo-French ambiance. Some of the trees damaged by gunfire had been cut down. The flower beds were torn up, the benches broken up and carried off for barricades. The old international news kiosk was a burned-out hulk. Russell bought a Paris edition of the *Herald Tribune* from an Arab in a soaked burnoose squatted at curbside.

The Café de Paris was still in good shape, although the famous old green awning was gone. Russell thought lustfully of a hot shower and a cold can of beer. He had decided that he was damned if he was going to go back to the office.

Let Crompton, he thought, worry about all that.

Maybe, he told himself, as he slouched past the high iron gates of the French Embassy, this was the day, finally, when he would type out the letter of resignation in triplicate on the old Royal portable and just mail it in. Cynthia Guffin would never believe her eyes.

At the end of the Boulevard of the President the modern city ended at the French cathedral, which had been a particular target in the fighting. The insurgents had peppered the front of the gray stone building with rifle fire as a gesture of contempt for this remaining symbol of the *ancien régime,* and while the bullets hadn't done a hell of a lot of damage to the granite they had given the old church a definitely battered look. Beyond the cathedral, the untouched Medina opened up its maw of alleys.

Frankly, Russell told himself, he couldn't wait.

The rest of the damned day was going to be his, Russell promised himself, as he opened the door to his flat. There was enough beer to keep him until he felt like fixing lunch—and if he decided to work himself up to really hanging one on, he could go down to the Boulevard later on and get a bottle of Scotch. At fifteen dollars a bottle it was almost too much to think about, but maybe by then he would have made up his mind about everything and he'd have something to celebrate.

"Jesus Christ," he said, standing in the doorway dripping a puddle on the tiles and still holding the key and his copy of the *Herald Trib* in his hands. "Who gave you entrance to my house!" he said finally, in Arabic.

"I came to your office," she said pertly, "but you were not there."

She rolled dark, flashing eyes in an excruciatingly familiar way. "The concierge let me in. She still knows me."

"Put your hat and coat on and go right back out again," he told her. "Attend me, Jamila, I am sick. I am getting very sick, right now, with the influenza."

But she only laughed.

She looked very, very good, he had to admit. The little pink suit was right from Paris, unless he missed his guess, and she had had her hair cut short, very *gamine*, and she had taken off a few pounds. Although she would never be less than what you could accurately call voluptuous. She saw him looking, and put her hand over the breast of the pink suit and laughed a little self-consciously.

Something new in the laugh, too, he noted.

"Oh, George, *mon petit*, you are the same," she said in French. She waggled her hand against the pink cloth. "You are not *looking*. Observe. See? You do not have to be frightened, now."

"You're married," he said, eying the gold band.

"But of course! I do not bring my husband—that would be too much, you know? He is a very jealous person and he would sense it. Husbands know another man, especially one like you, George. They would hate you."

"Well, by all means don't bring him by," he said quickly. "Just extend my congratulations to Monsieur—?"

"Ben Kaddour."

For a moment he just stood watching her.

"Oh, yes, I know what you are thinking," she said with a little sniff. Her face was still sharp and delicate as a Bedouin woman's, just as he remembered, but now a little thinner, and the fine slash of her mouth was a little more set.

Good luck to him, George thought. She always was a heller. She'll get her nails into his back if he runs around. As he probably will, sooner or later.

"Among the new Arab people," she was saying loftily, "the men do not obsess themselves with the virginity. Yes, I slept with him for two months before I let him marry me. It is much better this way—like the French do. More civilized. Then you know whether you are agreeable to each other."

"Yeah, well, the Berbers still do it," he couldn't help commenting.

"*Pfah!* You are the same George—you are a very cruel man! But this is why I come to see you," she said, lifting her chin, "to show you now that you made the mistake. You should have wanted me, George."

"I did," he said, and put a little fervent emotion into his voice for good measure. "I really wanted you, Jamila, but it was kismet, you know? Now just look at you: you make a great Madame ben Kaddour. So it all worked out for the best. I have to keep my respect now, and not mess around, right?"

"Yessss," she said, giving him the wide feline grin he remembered. "But George, you are terrible, you were teasing me all the time, yes? How do you like my suit?" she said abruptly. She turned around swiftly and then, over her shoulder, in a repeat of the old smile and a flash of the real Jamila, a gutsy Arab chuckle, "He has money, ay?"

The sudden switch to Arabic—and Arabic all over—made him laugh.

"He has perfect taste," he said in the same language, "in both clothes and women. Madame, you are superb."

"Oh, yes, you are right," she said, and sighed. She started to sit down, but he pulled her up quickly.

"Don't take chances, madame," he told her. "Husbands can be very dangerous."

"Oh, George," she said, standing very close to him. She rolled her eyes appealingly. "He is really a very good man. He is young, he is handsome, we are going to Egypt. He works for the Egyptian government. He is a journalist. Would you like to see his picture?"

"Listen, Madame ben Kaddour, I kiss your hand with respect," Russell said. He actually lifted her hand and gave it a hearty smack. "But I speak good Arabic—I'm a very good Arab myself, sometimes, right? So respect is what you get from me now. I wish you every happiness," he said formally. "I cannot resist a little remembrance—that I could get killed for," he added dramatically, and kissed her on the forehead.

That should do it, he thought. Happy—and get her out.

"Oh, George, I love you," she cried. "He is very good in bed, I must tell you—but not so good as you." He took her hand and led her to the door. "You must come to see us in Cairo. I promise you, it will not be what you expect. We have a very *moderne* flat and we will have a soufflé and a rosé—we drink wine; we are not narrow-minded." She had switched back to French again. "He is *adorable*. You must let me show you his picture."

"Let me imagine what he is like," he said, opening the door. "That is much better. I can be jealous too, you know."

But she kept her elbow against the door and got out a wallet from the matching pink purse and showed him a color snap. A nice-looking guy with a heavy black mustache, standing very self-consciously against a building which looked like Cairo.

He kissed her hand again and told her that ben Kaddour was very intelligent-looking and very much a man.

She was a pain in the ass, he thought, but she was funny. He had no doubt about the soufflé and the rosé and the inflatable furniture and the hi-fi, either.

"Jamila," he said, and his voice was inexplicably husky, "you be a good wife. He is a man with wise eyes in his head, this husband, and he knows a beautiful woman when he sees one. He is very lucky."

She looked down and bit her lip, and then looked up at him with a soft flash of brilliant eyes. "George, he is different, because he is an Arab, you know?" She had switched to Arabic again, and no nonsense, now: her voice was lush and throaty and he listened with no small admiration. "I love him very much. It is not true what I said about the being good in bed a while ago; I said this just to annoy you. I do for him the most loving—more than for you, George, because he is my Arab husband and this is proper. And at night he reads to me what he has written for the newspapers and the magazines. It is very good writing, it is about our struggles for a new Arab world, and to force the Jews to live together with the Palestinian Arabs once more. My husband is a Palestinian working for the Egyptian government now. George, it is a most exciting thing—I will send you these articles he writes for the magazines," she said suddenly, happily. "You must read them and see what a dedicated man he is."

"That's a good girl, you do that," he said finally, and got her out the door. But she knocked on it, and he had to open it again.

"*Filamen,*" she said solemnly.

Good luck.

"And to you, too," he said quickly. "*Aleiku moussalem,*" he told her, and got it shut and locked.

Later, after his shower, he was lying in bed with a bottle of beer propped on his bare stomach, holding the Paris edition of the *Herald Trib* awkwardly overhead and reading it that way, just too damned lazy to shift to a more comfortable position. The rain was drumming all around; it was as though the house, the room in the Medina, was enclosed in a beating thread of liquid sound. Beyond the window, water spouts roared into the street, into a hundred gutters and alleyways and cisterns of the old city, and tore down the hill to the salt lakes and the sea. Water washing on the stone-hard earth, tearing at the palm fronds of the courtyards, gurgling in the crevasses of walls—a secret, strange noise of a foreign place, distant floods, different weathers, familiar only to people who were born to them. Lonesome-making.

He sighed and shifted the paper and took another gulp of beer.

The room was getting damp, now. The wet weather had set in for good and would go on for weeks, the whole flat getting damper and moldier in spite of the rugs he would have to put down and the little electric heater he would have to get out of the closet and leave on during the day, so as to try to bake out some of the wet. He felt suddenly very uncomfortable and very tired.

He tried to concentrate on the *Trib* editorial page where the editors were reviewing the Israeli deep air strikes into Egypt and speculating as to whether this could be a part of Israeli policy to bring down the Egyptian government of President Nasser.

Well, if this was the new Israeli policy, Russell thought, stifling a yawn, the damned Israelis didn't know how much of a blunder they would be making. Because the way things were shaping up in Libya, with its new hard-line junta of revolutionary army officers, Egypt would only stand to inherit the same sort of crowd—and one that would make Gamal Abdel Nasser look like a rampant Zionist by comparison. That is, if the Israeli air pressure didn't force Nasser to bring in the Russians first. That was always Nasser's trump.

It's coming, Russell thought wearily. Just like everybody's been saying.

He put the empty beer bottle on the floor beside the bed and halfheartedly considered opening another. He didn't really want to get even mildly bombed that particular day, but on the other hand he didn't want to read—or think—about the Arab-Israeli situation any more. Let genius minds like Willie Crompton handle it for once.

For the past year or more George had lived through his due share of cocktail party conversations and secondhand foreign embassy speculations of coming events casting their shadows. Not to mention the endless talk of Arab friends and the ceaseless voices of the press and radio. And they were all absolutely right. Every last one of them right, no matter what they said, blisteringly, thrillingly right and prophetically accurate—for all the good it did. Yes, Russia will finally find herself most reluctantly coming in on the side of Egypt with more missiles, more MIGs, more stepped-up military adviser aid. And the U.S. will even more reluctantly (after all, the thing in Southeast Asia still has us pretty well involved) find itself delivering to Israel those Phantom attack jets for what is generally referred to as the Israeli aggressive-defensive policy.

Yes, we have all been absolutely right; it is now coming down to a Big Power confrontation with the Russians on one side and the United States on the other, he thought morosely. And as we all have been saying, it's just too bad we haven't been able to get anybody to listen to us before all this.

On the other side of the *Trib* editorial page a columnist was trying to make the rather painful point that there really couldn't be any peaceful settlement in the Middle East while Israel still retained the occupied Arab territories of the 1967 war: that is, the west bank of the Jordan, the Golan Heights of Syria, and Egypt's Sinai.

It was nice to see everybody finally getting around to that too— and the realization that, after all this time, the Arab nations still wanted those slices of their countries back. Of course, with Israel also saying that where Israeli forces were—on the Suez Canal, on the Golan Heights and on the Jordan—were, under the circumstances, the only places where they could maintain "defensible boundaries."

Strangely enough, he noticed, down at the bottom of the column there was a quote from Moshe Dayan saying that if—in some unpleasant extremity—the Arabs just had to have their territory back, the "permanent" Israeli settlements on the west bank of the Jordan and the Golan Heights would have to stay right where they were. With permanent Israeli residents.

You hear that, Norman? Russell thought. That's really a honey, that one. You're going to laugh your head off when you read it, over there in New York. Because even if the Arabs agree to a settlement like that—the fat chance—how in the hell do you maintain those "permanent Israeli settlements" in formerly captured Arab territory? Like, with the *fedayeen* slipping up at night to pick off your tractor guards, and dropping hand grenades down the ventilators of your underground nursery-school dorms?

I have an idea that not even you, Norman, are going to spend too much time in New York.

Russell reached over the side of the bed and got a fresh bottle of beer and the opener, and held the newspaper down with his elbow as he opened it up.

It was nice to see the *Trib* struggling so manfully with the problem. Quoting a high official in Washington as saying that the U.S. will not risk war over the territory Israel captured in 1967. That sooner or later the Israelis are going to have to abandon those territories and settle—with U.S. support—for the best deal they can get.

Nice, clean, decisive opinion, that. But, Russell told himself, whoever we're got in Washington making these marvelous high-level statements obviously doesn't know our friends the Semitic peoples too well. Dayan and his "permanent" kibbutzes deep inside neighboring Arab nations. Israelis settling for "the best deal they can get." And yes, Virginia, there *is* a Santa Claus.

Because, Russell told himself somewhat savagely, in their time the Semites—both the Arab and the Hebrew branches—have moved what we optimistically call the civilized world by their fire and talent and their indomitable wills; no matter what Washington or Moscow may think, we're not exactly dealing with a bunch of dullards. And there's no goddamned reason to believe now that both the Jews and the Moslems are going to back away from their fraternal fight just because the rest of the world wants them to. At least they sure as hell aren't going to play Alphonse and Gaston over that little chunk of Palestine-Israel they both love and covet so much.

Worse, don't rely on the reluctance of Russia and the United States to get involved. Even if the Big Powers manage to get Israel and the Arabs to the negotiating table, that's not going to solve much. Because now we have the damned *fedayeen* guerrillas—and they've announced they're not going to play according to anybody's rules. What started out as a cross between a holy war and an armed Boy Scout band in refugee camps is now spreading like an epidemic, scraping in the rest of the Arab world—the real revolutionaries who always stand waiting in the wings, the ALNists and the Baathist proseletyzers, the nihilist bomb carriers, the restless young of the streets who've seen *The Battle of Algiers* four times in the Arab movie theaters, the university students with diplomas and no jobs, the underpaid young army officers who long to get their sisters married off and buy their mothers a television set. As well as the itchy-fingered police structure which is such an integral part of this area of the world, the trade unionists looking for both a trade *and* a union in the best Marxist sense, and finally—at long last—on the very bottom of everything, Fanon's *lumpenproletariat*. The barefoot man in the blanket which is both coat and nightgown and portable address, the murder-minded fellagha who's so damned hungry he's got nothing to lose.

It's enough to give anybody a damned headache, Russell thought. I can't read the *Trib*; I can't forget it any more. It's gotten so my brains ache. If I had any sense, he told himself suddenly, I'd go home.

But what would I do? Stand on some street corner in New York or Washington and grab people by the collar and say, "Look, do you know the goddamned Arabs? Do you know what's going on inside the heads of our friends the fighting Irsaelis? Because if you don't, let me tell you all about it. We're not going to get out of this mess with a little slick thinking this time. Or land another load of troops. It is, as we have been saying out here for a long time now, Armageddon."

I can't see myself on the lecture circuit, Russell told himself, and couldn't help a smile. No qualifications at all. Except that my grandpa, like every other male Mormon, used to be a preacher. I can't see the New York office of the Foundation buying that, at all.

Russell tossed the *Trib* down to the foot of the bed and lay back among the pillows.

But I'd like to say it, he thought suddenly. Wherever and whenever anybody'd listen to me. Because it isn't just the damned Arabs this time, nor the Israelis with their traditional obsession with survival. What's coming upon us all is that thing which cast its shadow a few years ago in that nice little war for liberation in Algeria. Our growing Arab revolutionary generation that's gulping down a lot of half-baked Che and Ho Chi Minh and Frantz Fanon, and is going on to the siren voice of hard Marxist George Habash and the PFLP right now. Because Red China, not Russia or the United States, is going to feed the Third World guns and bombs and scare the shit out of established governments, little or big, who don't want to really get that deep into it.

And when Nasser and Hussein and the combined efforts of the U.S. and Russia can't control the *fedayeen*—who are now talking in terms of any army recruited from the whole damned youth of the Arab world—the Israelis are going to remind everybody that they've had their own little nuclear device for some time now, only they've been too shy and circumspect to bring it up. Which means that those other friendly Semites the Arabs aren't going to get caught, either, in that kind of race. Not with the French willing to sell their fissionable material any time, anywhere. Cash on the barrel head.

Isn't there some way, the *Trib* columnist had ended up by pleading, that the Arabs and the Israelis could be persuaded to work out a peaceful coexistence?

Yeah.

Mother Jean-Claire, Russell thought, studying the half-empty brown shadow of the beer bottle, this is where you come in. Because we are standing in the need of prayer. Especially if we are going to depend on the Arabs and the Israelis to lead off with the world's first example of peaceful coexistence. Allah—Jehovah—God—or whatever you want to call Him—is needed pretty quickly by the People of the Book.

And He better get moving, fast.